A Matter of Manners

Shades of Sin Book One

by

Terry Graham

A Matter of Manners

Contact Information: info@thewildrosepress.com

Cover Art by *Diana Carlile*

The Wild Rose Press, Inc.
PO Box 708
Adams Basin, NY 14410-0708

Publishing History
First Scarlet Rose Edition, 2020
Print ISBN 978-1-5092-2964-2
Digital ISBN 978-1-5092-2965-9

Published in the United States of America

**A marriage of convenience...
or could it be more?**

"Bollocks!" The expletive burst out, unbidden. He had to stop using the word before it slipped out in the wrong setting.

At least it got her attention. Her moss-colored eyes widened, and her lips parted in surprise.

Another flicker of want paralyzed him.

"I should go." With a grace that took his breath away, she rose and turned toward the door. This time, though, her feet inched forward.

"Stop!" Try as he might, it came out as a command.

She dropped into the chair, her porcelain skin fading to the pasty white color it had taken on when she vomited.

He raked his fingers through his hair. What was happening? Besides him losing control?

"You've done nothing wrong," he explained. "It's George I wish to thrash."

To his surprise, she harrumphed in a very unladylike manner. "Might I watch?"

Her hand flew up and covered her mouth. Wide, emerald eyes with thick, long lashes stared at him, half horrified. Then she lifted her chin in defiance.

Damn, she was pretty. Dark cherries and clotted cream pretty.

Footsteps echoed from the hallway, drawing her attention, but Jeremy continued to stare. He didn't care who entered. He wanted to ogle her for a few minutes.

"Speak of the devil," her luscious lips muttered.

Chapter One

London 1798

Jeremy Wyles, eighth Duke of Lexham, glared at the announcement on his desk as if it were an asp. Gold embossed lettering adorned fine paper, declaring the birth of a son to his cousin, George.

Four sons. George had four sons and two daughters. And that didn't include the four or five bastards. It was obscene.

Jeremy's hand squeezed the crystal glass in his hand and lifted it to his lips. Thick, amber Scotch warmed his throat, burning away the bile that threatened to choke him.

His gaze wandered across the room.

Leather-bound books from all over Europe filled dark mahogany-lined walls. Velvet chairs huddled in the corners. Beeswax candles perched strategically nearby, ready to be lit at a moment's notice. A Morbier clock from France graced one corner, quietly ticking amidst the darkness. Everything in the room reflected both his status and his desire for the very finest in life.

Even the windows had been an extravagance. Larger than most, there was an extra one in each room.

Like everything, the effort amounted to nothing. The sun didn't shine today. Hadn't in days. Carbon gray sky loomed outside, broken only by the rain

1

streaming down the glass and the occasional burst of lightning.

"Bollocks!" His fist slammed on the desk. He took a deep breath and uncurled his fingers to rub a tiny dent. The result of another fit of rage, a corresponding scar marred his hand where a glass he'd smashed had cut into his flesh. He left the gouge as a reminder of what happened when he let his emotions rule.

He tossed the offending announcement into a drawer before pulling a thick ledger toward him.

A knock interrupted before he opened the book.

"Enter," he growled.

Alfred, his butler, pushed forward, bowing his bent frame. Jeremy scowled at the sight. The old man needed to retire.

Alfred's gaze paused on Jeremy's glass, then glanced toward the half-empty decanter behind him. "A bit early to be imbibing, is it not, Your Grace?"

Jeremy glared. He ought to reprimand him but couldn't. The old man was as close to a father as not.

He nudged the glass away.

Alfred's gaze fell toward the floor.

Jeremy cocked his head. Something was wrong. Alfred stood motionless, white-gloved hands hidden behind his back, but Jeremy could feel him squirming. "What is it? Have you had enough of me? Are you going to ask if you can retire?"

Alfred's attention snapped up, brown eyes wide with surprise. "Only if you wish it. Do you require someone with more vim and vigor, Your Grace?"

Jeremy scoffed but let it pass. Further discussion would only waste time.

Alfred's gaze slipped away, and a linen towel

appeared. He shuffled forward and began to wipe nonexistent marks from the small table between two leather chairs. His hands trembled. He nudged the chairs, then pushed them back.

Jeremy narrowed his eyes but waited as patiently as possible.

"You shouldn't allow it to bother you, my boy," Alfred finally said.

"Shouldn't let what bother me?"

"George's…good fortune."

Good fortune? Is that what it was? "How can I not? It's like he's intentionally goading me."

Alfred's bushy brows rose before he scowled. "Don't be ridiculous. George is just being George. You should be happy for him. And it's not too late for you to have children of your own."

Jeremy sighed. "I know." Therein lay the problem. As much as he hated it, George was his heir. It wasn't George's fault he bred like a rabbit while Jeremy seemed impotent, and he didn't mean to be a ne'er-do-well. George had no responsibilities. That job was Jeremy's. Too bad he couldn't do his other job as well as George and produce a more acceptable heir.

Truth was, after two wives and numerous mistresses, he didn't even want to try.

As if he understood, Alfred patted his shoulder and returned to his imaginary cleaning. Crystal clinked behind him, decanters thumping.

"You've a visitor, Your Grace," Alfred announced a moment later.

"I do?" Who? None of his friends ventured out this early.

"You do. A young woman."

Jeremy stiffened. He'd chased away every eligible woman in London and every reasonable distance beyond. The picture dominated the space, a constant reminder of why. The portrait of a stunning blonde with bright blue eyes laughing as he stood beside her served to discourage him whenever longings for a wife reared up. He'd thought she loved him. He'd thought he loved her.

He turned his gaze back to Alfred. "A woman?"

"Indeed."

Jeremy's stomach sank, an all too familiar sensation.

"Is it another one of George's doxies?" Pregnant, no doubt.

Alfred's eyes widened and centered back on Jeremy's face before lowering quickly. "No, I don't believe so. I believe…she's a lady."

"A lady?" Jeremy leaned back and studied Alfred carefully. His grandmother's butler for decades, Alfred knew Debrett's by heart, better even than Jeremy. If Alfred believed her a lady, she was a lady. A lady wouldn't be calling though. And Alfred would have named her. Unless he didn't know who she was. "Has someone died?"

"I don't believe so." Alfred's face contorted. "She's a young lady, Your Grace."

With an arched brow, Jeremy waited.

The old man's feet shuffled. His hands remained hidden behind his back, but Jeremy suspected his swollen knuckles were wringing furiously. If he waited long enough, Alfred would spill whatever he was holding back, but he didn't have the patience this morning. "All right, old man. Spit it out. Who is she?"

"I...I'm not sure."

Interesting. A lady that Alfred didn't know? "Any guesses?"

"I never guess." He never dissembled, either. Yet he was now.

"She didn't give a name?"

Alfred's mouth opened, then closed, then opened again. A rumble of thunder drowned out the ticking of the clock. When he finally spoke, his voice trembled. "I think you should see her, Lord Jeremy." Alfred bowed his head and stepped forward. His gnarled hand stretched out and dropped an item on the desk. Gold spun on the mahogany surface.

Jeremy didn't need to wait for the spinning to stop. He'd see an oak tree, acorn, and bee carved into the surface. His signet ring, the design was as familiar to him as the sick feeling in his throat. The last time he had seen the ring, George had worn it as proof he was acting in Jeremy's stead.

What had George done this time?

"She claims she's your duchess, Your Grace."

****

Kathleen Brennan Lexham shivered as a rush of anger roiled through her. After a week bouncing over badly maintained postal roads and another day wandering through London, tension was all that held her together. The weather matched her mood. The entire journey had been gloomy, interspersed with bouts of angry storms and frigid temperatures.

Now she stood, waiting, while fear warred with anger and disbelief. What if he refused to see her?

Her gaze scanned the foyer of Lexham House again. Cold white marble rose two stories. Gorgeous walnut staircases flew up either side, no support visible beneath them. Before her, a huge Oriental vase displayed a bouquet of roses and lilies as large as she, their scent wafting through the room.

Her stomach lurched. She hugged herself, holding her breath until the wave of nausea passed.

She'd known he was a duke. And she'd known he had no intention of staying with her. She'd had no idea he was as wealthy as Midas.

The shanker.

A shuffle from above distracted her.

"The duke will see you now." The butler—he'd introduced himself as Alfred—paused at the top of the stairs, his kindly face stretched with a welcoming smile.

"Oh, please, don't come down." Katy clutched her sodden skirt and hurried up the stairs. Halfway up, she slowed. An old gown of her mother's, the wool had soaked up an entire lake's worth of rain. It didn't help that the waist was too small and her chest felt as if an ox sat on it. She'd worn the dress for courage and warmth, but all it did was remind her she wasn't the lady her mother had been.

"Are you all right, my dear?" A knobby hand reached out to help her up the last steps.

Katy pasted a weak smile on her face. Truth was she wanted to throw up, but it wouldn't be ladylike to admit it.

"This way." He gestured at a hallway and shuffled forward.

Katy followed, her attention diverted by the portraits lining the walls. Men and women stared into space with faces that resembled George enough to make her frown. Beeswax candles blazed, the scent adding to the churning in her stomach.

She inhaled deeply and lifted her chin when the butler pulled the door open. Her eyes widened and her determination hardened.

A two-story library, books lined the entire room. The smell of leather mixed with beeswax from more candles than she'd ever seen lit at one time. Her teeth clenched. If George thought he could come to Ireland, wheedle his way into her family, then leave as if nothing had happened, he could rot in hell. But not before he paid for his sins.

Fists stuffed into her pockets, Katy stepped forward. Her shoes squelched, whining as George had done the night she sent him packing.

"Kathleen, the Duchess of Lexham, Your Grace." It sounded strange. In Ireland, she was just Katy.

"Thank you, Alfred. You may go."

The voice came from the lone dark corner behind a massive desk. Firelight winked off cut crystal, drawing her gaze, reminding her of home. Was it Waterford? Did her father cut it? She blinked back tears.

Focus. Da is done with you.

Her gaze darted back to the figure hiding in the shadows. He could at least have had the decency to face her.

His shoulders seemed wider, his stance firmer than she remembered, his haircut sharper.

She lifted her shoulders and chided herself. *You're just scared. It's George. He won't hurt you.*

When he turned, her stomach lurched.

"You're not George!"

A wry smile curled his lips as he stepped into the light. An inch or two taller, his shoulders were definitely wider and strained against a dark blue jacket rather than the powder blue George preferred. Dark umber hair waved above a jaw with none of George's softness. Instead of watery blue eyes, his glinted silver-gray. He exuded confidence and power.

Katy stared as realization crawled through her.

Alfred had seemed confused when she asked for George. He'd said the duke would see her. He'd called this man *Your Grace*.

The determination and courage that had held Katy together burst like a poorly blown glass bubble. She swayed and reached out. What now? If George wasn't the duke who was he? Would George even be able to help her?

"Forgive me." A firm, gentle grip latched onto her elbow and guided her to a nearby chair. "That was badly done."

He eased her into the chair, then lowered himself to perch across from her. Unlike at home, his chair didn't creak or wobble. A strong, tanned hand reached out and claimed hers. Stunned, she stared as he massaged her icy hands and frowned at her tattered gloves. Shame rushed up, but the heat felt good.

He had nice hands with strong fingers. Not soft and pale like George's.

Katy blinked and sat up straighter.

Just because George wasn't who he claimed to be didn't mean she was any less a lady.

"I asked to see George." Somehow, the words came out calm and confident with none of the disquiet thrumming through her.

"George is my cousin. I've sent for him. He'll be here soon."

"George isn't the duke?"

"No."

Kathleen squeezed her eyes shut. Things had become much more complicated. Still, George had gotten her into this. There was no reason he couldn't help.

"You're Irish, I assume?"

"Yes." Katy opened her eyes. The duke had moved to feed the fire. Muscular thighs flexed beneath smooth gray flannel. A flare of appreciation shivered through her. What a shame it hadn't been him in her bed.

Stop it! You wouldn't be in this position if you hadn't given in to your wicked desires.

"Bloody mess over there. Glad George didn't stay long enough to get caught up in it."

Katy's gaze flew toward him, and her breath caught. Did he know what George had done?

"Forgive me. That was insensitive," he said as he rose and brushed off his hands. "You have family there?"

"I…" Her mind whirled. How much should she say? There was no reason to lie. Yet. Hopefully never since she wouldn't be going back. "Yes. My Da and stepmother. A few siblings." A few? By Irish standards, maybe. By his, it was likely a brood.

"With luck, they'll remain safe."

Her attention lingered as he rounded the desk. He moved like a duke, proud and sure, right down to the way he lounged back in his chair and studied her.

With a lift of her chin, she returned his stare, but inside she squirmed. He was judging her, and she knew she came up lacking. Freckled from the sun, her skin was too dark. Her hair, even in the braid she'd curled atop her head, was too red and untamed. She was too tall and thin with none of the plump breasts or hips a man wanted. No one but the butcher had wanted to marry her. Even George had other reasons for marrying her.

When the duke's gaze halted on her chest, then flitted away, shame flared up, peppered with resentment.

"Perhaps, while we wait, you can tell me what brings you to London."

Irritated, Katy considered several sharp retorts, but a tap on the door saved her.

"That's likely tea," the duke said before calling out permission to enter.

Silence descended while a footman wheeled in an elegant teacart. Laden with an assortment of cakes, fruit, pastries, and any number of other foods, it would have easily fed her entire family, livestock included. Her mouth watered when he lifted gleaming silver covers to reveal fluffy scrambled eggs and a rasher of bacon.

Her stomach growled. A soft snort from the duke sent another wave of embarrassment over her face.

"Thank you, Gregory. The duchess can pour. You may leave."

Kathleen fought a moment of panic. George had never let her pour tea. Said the Irish didn't know how to entertain properly. Her mother had taught her as a girl, but would she remember? Did one serve scones or savories first? Sugar before lemon, in the tea? After two days without food, she couldn't concentrate. What if she dropped the teapot?

"Duchess?"

Her gaze snapped toward him. Jeremy, he'd said his name was.

"Is something wrong?"

"No." She picked up a cup and saucer. Her hand trembled. The china chattered. "What do you take?"

His hand captured the chittering saucer.

"I need nothing." He settled the cup, grabbed a plate, and began scooping eggs onto it. "You've made an impression on Alfred, it seems. He's sent up an entire meal." His gaze swept over her again, before returning to his task. A generous portion of bacon followed the eggs and a blueberry scone. He passed the plate to her, snagged a small bowl, and filled it with assorted berries. A huge spoonful of clotted cream plopped atop the berries, and he set that before her as well, then eased into the chair across from her.

"Eat," he demanded and passed her a fork.

She snatched the utensil and stared at the plate. The aroma of the bacon wafted up. Her stomach rebelled. She swallowed hard. Bile burned.

"Oh, God," she groaned, unthinking, and gulped. Her stomach heaved, and the fork dropped to the floor. One hand grabbed her stomach. The other shoved the plate onto the cart. Silver and china rattled.

"Buggar!" Jeremy's chair fell back. Her hand pressed against her lips. Acid burned, but she swallowed it.

Two more heaves, thankfully dry, ripped through her. She closed her eyes and prayed.

"It's all right." A hand settled on her back. Something plopped onto her lap. She opened her eyes long enough to see an empty wastebasket. She clutched the edges. Another wave of bile surged. Tears prickled behind her eyelids and sweat beaded around her forehead. Unable to hold it in, she vomited.

To her relief, little came up, but two, then three times, her stomach rebelled enough to splatter hot juices. As she retched, he mumbled reassurances, and a soothing hand brushed back her damp curls. By the time the nausea eased, she shook like the legs of a newborn thoroughbred.

"All done?" The comforting hand washed along her back. At her weak nod, the container disappeared. She leaned back and let her eyes close.

"I'm so sorry," she whispered. So much for being a lady.

"It's quite all right." A hint of humor laced the baritone. She lifted one eyelid. An annoying smirk greeted her. She closed the eye and inhaled slow, even breaths.

"I guess that answers one question. You're pregnant." It was a statement rather than a question. Silver clattered, and the bacon scent diminished. "Try this." He stuffed a piece of toast into her hand. "Small bites."

She did better than small bites. She nibbled until the sour taste in her mouth faded. Although starving, she had no desire to eat. She did it for the baby. Just as everything she'd done for the last month had been. Eventually, the toast disappeared, and she forced herself to accept a second plate of food. Just eggs and a scone, the plain fare managed to stay down.

All the while, Jeremy played the perfect host, chatting about the weather and a cricket match he'd seen a week ago.

When she let out a soft exhale of relief and set

down the plate and fork, the duke rose and returned to the chair behind his desk. His face went blank. Hands clasped, he leaned forward.

"So…care to tell me what transpired in Ireland between you and George? Beyond the obvious." His eyes bored into her belly, and his jaw clenched.

Ignoring a flush of shame, Kathleen clamped her lips shut and debated. The entire truth wasn't an option. She shrugged. "There's not much to tell. George asked me to marry him. I figured it was a better option than the butcher."

The duke waited, but it was enough. After a couple minutes of study, he nodded and leaned forward. With a quick flick of his fingers, a ring spun on the dark surface. Firelight spit off the gold curves like a fire sparks at a damp log.

Was it the ring George had given her?

"He apparently left you in Ireland," he finally said. "I imagine he made up some story or another to keep you there. So why are you here now?"

"I wrote to him," she explained, "after the money ran out. He didn't answer." She knew why now. George was more of a coward than she'd suspected. "When I discovered I was expecting, I had to do something." She dropped her gaze, afraid the real duke would see just how desperate she was. "I figured maybe he was dead," she lied. In truth, she wished her brother had killed him after he learned his real reason for marrying her.

Moments passed, marked by the steady ticking of a clock.

"You realize you're not the Duchess of Lexham?"

Said quietly, as if he regretted saying it, Katy

ignored a flash of annoyance and nodded. He probably didn't mean to imply she was stupid.

When he said nothing more, she raised her eyes.

"You realize it was all a sham?" he asked, his jaw tightening.

At first, she froze, afraid he knew everything, but his eyes had darkened to a gray as dark as the outside gloom. He picked up the ring and slid it onto his finger. As he did, Katy felt her stomach lurch again.

"Oh, God!" Her hand flew up and tried to stop the words. "I'm not even married, am I?"

His head shook, a pained look evident. "George married Emily years ago. They have six children. I'm sorry."

She stared, stunned, then looked away.

He was sorry. He pitied her. Just as the townspeople always had.

Her hands twisted. It didn't undo the knot in her stomach.

How could she have been so stupid? She'd known it was a sham, but at least she'd been married. Now she was just a whore. A stupid, gullible whore. Just like Da had warned her.

A small moan escaped. Somehow, she found herself on her feet and facing the door.

"I should go." The expanse of floor seemed endless, and her boots refused to move.

"Sit back down!"

She jumped, head snapping around.

The duke pointed at the chair. Instinctively, she dropped back into it.

"What will you do? Now that you know the truth?" he asked

"I don't know. Open a dress shop?" In Bath or Brighton. Places her momma had visited. "But I can't afford it." She couldn't afford a baby, either.

He dragged a book toward him, and the cover thudded against the desk.

"George has no money. He gets an allowance, but it's hardly enough to feed his legitimate brood." A pen appeared in his hand. "Your child is a Lexham, however; so, it will never go without. How much do you want?"

Kathleen gaped. The pen scribbled, scratching through the daze.

He wanted to give her money?

She blinked, calculating furiously in her head.

"One hundred pounds," she blurted out before courage failed her.

His hand froze. His head shot up, and she winced. His expression reminded her of Da before he went off on a tearing rage.

"One…Hundred…Pounds?" His brows rose higher with each word. She raised her chin.

"Very well." She sucked in a breath. "Fifty. I can't manage on less."

The pen clattered. An instant later, his chair crashed into the wall and he exploded to his feet. She scrambled up, only to have her legs buckle.

She fell back. Tears pricked her eyes. "Twenty, then," she whispered, afraid to look away.

"Stop!" He raised a hand, while the other formed a fist at his side. Tension radiated from him, his face contorted with anger. "Just…stop!" He dragged a hand through his hair, practically uprooting it. A vein pulsed in his temple, bulging like the fist that pumped at his side.

Kathleen closed her eyes. A tear escaped, burning a trail along her cheek. She had overreached. Again. Just as her father always warned.

Chapter Two

Egads! Jeremy stared at the young woman, conflicting emotions battling for supremacy.

One hundred pounds! She thought her virtue, and her child's well-being, worth so little? He paid his scullery maids half that much each year.

And now, he'd made her cry.

The lone tear caught the light, highlighting his inability to understand women and their fragile emotions.

This was why he avoided women. No matter how he tried, what he did, they ended up hating him. The only question was how long it took.

But, God's blood, she was gorgeous! Even in her sodden, twenty-year-old gown, with her copper curls plastered against her skin, coated in the London grime that the downpour outside hadn't been able to scrub away. As soon as she walked in, he'd understood George's motivation. It had been years since he'd felt his cock stir near a lady. But she stirred it. Not as much as he'd like, but even a twinge was a welcome change.

How had she made it from Ireland to London, without being raped or kidnapped? Did she have any idea how unscrupulous people were? She might have been locked in a whorehouse, forced to do things even he wouldn't inflict on a woman.

Where in Hades was her family? Why weren't they

taking care of her?

And George. George had to answer for this.

"Bollocks!" The expletive burst out, unbidden. He had to stop using the word before it slipped out in the wrong setting.

At least it got her attention. Her moss-colored eyes widened, and her lips parted in surprise.

Another flicker of want paralyzed him.

"I should go." With a grace that took his breath away, she rose and turned toward the door. This time, though, her feet inched forward.

"Stop!" Try as he might, it came out as a command.

She dropped into the chair, her porcelain skin fading to the pasty white color it had taken on when she vomited.

He raked his fingers through his hair. What was happening? Besides him losing control?

"You've done nothing wrong," he explained. "It's George I wish to thrash."

To his surprise, she harrumphed in a very unladylike manner. "Might I watch?"

Her hand flew up and covered her mouth. Wide, emerald eyes with thick, long lashes stared at him, half horrified. Then she lifted her chin in defiance.

Damn, she was pretty. Dark cherries and clotted cream pretty.

Footsteps echoed from the hallway, drawing her attention, but Jeremy continued to stare. He didn't care who entered. He wanted to ogle her for a few minutes.

"Speak of the devil," her luscious lips muttered.

"Please join us, George," he drawled without turning. Normally George dragged his feet, moving like the sloth he resembled. Now, when Jeremy preferred him gone, he arrived early?

Kathleen's reaction wasn't what he expected, either. Most women found George charming and amenable. She schooled her face, but not before Jeremy saw her eyes narrow and her jaw clench. George had buggered her, in more ways than one, and she had married him, but whatever had passed between them had left her angry.

Rightfully so.

"I believe you know the Duchess of Lexham."

George faltered, mid-step. His face froze, the customary smile fading along with his color. The effect made him look clownish, blotches of rouge highlighting the excessive powder he used on his face.

An idea niggled at him, an idea that filled Jeremy with the first twinge of hope he had felt since his second wife died. Would it work? *Could* it work?

She'd hate him.

She'd hate him either way. He might as well get something first.

"Will you take tea with us? Lady Kathleen and I have been getting to know one another."

Kathleen scowled, spine stiffening, but stayed silent. The movement afforded him even more of the creamy whiteness spilling over her neckline. His cock twitched. Annoyed, he retreated behind the desk.

George's eyes also fastened on her chest.

"Sit down, George!" Gentling his voice, he added, "Would you serve, please, Lady Kathleen?"

"She doesn't deserve that title." George puffed up his chest but plopped into the chair at Jeremy's glare.

In truth, George was correct. Only daughters of

nobility deserved to be titled as *lady*, but it was no more incorrect than calling her duchess or Lady Lexham. Due to George's actions, she deserved a modicum of respect and she'd get it, even if Jeremy had to demand it.

"Technically, that's true," she agreed with a fake smile. "But I do have a noble parentage." With aplomb, she reached out and served. After again asking what Jeremy wanted in his tea, she performed the ritual perfectly, as if to prove her claim. She then served George's exactly the way he liked, without being told. Jeremy's teeth ground, like unglazed china scraping against itself.

"My mother was a lady," she continued. A gloved hand held out George's cup and a slight frown marred her forehead. "Please excuse my gloves, George. I haven't had time to change them. They're rather wet and dirty, given I had to traipse through London this morning."

George glowered, lips tight, arms crossed over his chest like a petulant child.

Kathleen's hand quivered.

"Take your tea, George."

George hesitated.

"Now." Jeremy's cup rattled as he set it aside, prepared to rise and make George comply.

Once again, George's true nature emerged. He snatched the cup, tea spilling over the rim.

"My grandfather was an earl," Katy added, then faltered. She lifted her own cup and sipped. Shoulders slumped, her throat working more than a single sip required.

She didn't know what more to say.

"Who is he?" Jeremy asked and dredged through his memory. Brennan wasn't a noble name.

"I don't know. I…Da…" She searched for the proper words. "Momma…I mean my mother…was disowned. She told me his name once. But I was young. Da…" She stumbled again, before continuing, "My father got angry any time anyone mentioned him."

"You never told me that!"

"You never asked." Kathleen stiffened and glared until George dropped his eyes.

Jeremy settled back in his chair. Not only was the woman stunning, but she was more than capable of handling George.

"Is your mother still alive?" The question was rude, but curiosity and his burgeoning plan trumped civility.

"No. She passed when I was ten." Her gaze dropped, and her lip trembled. Jeremy's cock twitched.

"I thought Noreen was your mother."

"Noreen's my stepmother. If you cared enough to ask, you would know that."

George blinked, too dim-witted to realize he'd been chastised, then cocked his head and narrowed his eyes. "What about your brothers?"

Jeremy peered. Why did George care about her brothers?

"Thomas and Caitlin are full siblings. Alec, Brody, and Patrick are half brothers. Nora's my half sister."

"Ah, I see." George sipped at his tea, but Jeremy narrowed his eyes.

George's schemes had caused him more grief than he liked to remember. Sometimes, they revolved around making money or were just sick attempts at jokes. Often, they came out of nowhere, for no reason, like the time when he was eight and poured oil on the top of the stairs. He'd wanted to see the maid tumble down, too stupid to realize she might end up hurt or dead.

What scheme had convinced him to marry an Irish commoner? Or had he known she wasn't as common as she appeared?

When George glanced over and saw his interest, his throat bobbed. "I liked Thomas. He took me to the good alehouses."

George was lying. The vein in his neck pulsed, and he tugged at his carefully tied cravat. George never touched his neckcloth. Except when he lied.

"Good alehouses? There's only two in Scullabogue." Kathleen looked skeptical.

"He took me to others. In other towns."

Another quiet harrumph escaped. Kathleen scowled as if George were the cockroach he often was. They were hiding something.

Jeremy's gaze wandered to the picture above the fireplace. George couldn't be trusted. He'd seduced Anna, knowing Jeremy loved her. Now, he'd married an Irish nobody with noble ties?

Silence fell, highlighted by the ticking of the clock and the rain tapping at the window.

Jeremy's gaze wandered back to Kathleen. Dark circles lined her eyes, and her posture showed signs of fatigue, but she held herself regally. The bones in her cheeks stood out. He'd felt her ribs beneath the heavy wool of her gown when she retched. She was pregnant and altogether too thin. Yet she'd traveled from Ireland, alone. Why? Was it truly just for money? Or had she expected George to acknowledge her and her baby?

Whatever her motivations, she had determination

and courage. Her professed plan showed a willingness to work and a reluctance to return home.

George, on the other hand, never expended unnecessary energy.

Still, George was family.

"Why, George? Why do you continue to sully our name?"

As startled as Jeremy, George swiveled his head. An odd look appeared on his face. Jeremy would have called it shame had it not disappeared. George's throat worked, and he stole another glance at Kathleen.

With an imperceptible frown, George gazed at the ring on Jeremy's finger. The frown turned into a scowl. "What did you expect me to do while I was in Ireland? It's not as if there's anything to do there."

"I sent you to buy horses," Jeremy snapped, "and negotiate a supply contract, not to entertain yourself. I hoped you'd show some interest, demonstrate that you won't run our family name into the ground when I'm gone." His hands fisted. If he had his way, George would never wear the ring. "I should have known better."

"You're right. You should have." An ugly expression marred George's painted face. A sick smile exuded mockery. "You know I'm nothing but a disappointment, incapable of anything useful. You think you can change that overnight by just wishing it so?"

Resentment surged. Jeremy squeezed his eyes to shut out his biggest disappointment. His nails bit into his palms.

"You might as well ask her to keep her legs closed."

Jeremy's eyes snapped open.

George kept going. "You'd have more luck with that. She wasn't even a good tup."

Stunned, Jeremy leapt up, ready to pound George into the floor.

Kathleen saved him the effort. She rose to her feet, all traces of fatigue gone, eyes blazing. Taller than most women, she towered over George's seated form like a Greek goddess looking upon a mere mortal.

"You're a bastard," she spat. "A lying, despicable bastard. With a small pecker." She stepped around the edge of the teacart, teacup and saucer still in hand. With a grace at odds with her words, she narrowed her eyes.

George glared back like a toddler caught stealing but unwilling to admit it.

"I'm so glad I'm not your wife."

Tea showered over George's dove-colored pants. He howled, grabbed his privates, and scrambled away. The chair scraped, then toppled. Hot liquid darkened his crotch. Blue eyes flared as hot as the tips of a fire, then narrowed.

"Stop!" Jeremy roared and surged forward. George's fist slammed into Kathleen's stomach. Jeremy felt it in his gut.

As softly as a leaf falling to the ground, Kathleen crumpled, then lay still.

****

"Kathleen."

Kathleen moaned and burrowed back into the covers. She didn't want to move.

"Kathleen, wake up."

This time, a gentle nudge accompanied the voice. Again, she curled up, cuddling the edges of sleep. She didn't want to leave the dream. George had come back. He'd brought decadent pastries and soft, warm clothes. Except it wasn't George.

"Kathleen!"

She bolted up, eyes popping open, and stared at the man who'd shouted at her. Blessed Mary, he was gorgeous. Even the scowl marring his face made her weak. Why was he frowning? What had she done wrong this time?

In a rush, it flooded back. The horrible journey from Ireland, the helpless frustration of London, the mix of relief and worry when she'd found Lexham House, and the travesty of learning the truth.

Her stomach lurched. Had she actually poured tea in George's lap?

Her hands flew to her stomach. He'd punched her!

"The babe's fine. Or so Maggie tells me."

She continued to stare at the real duke while the mix of guilt and momentary panic receded. None of it made any sense.

"How…how did I get here?" She lay atop a bed of feathers with sheets so white they looked and felt like clouds. Gone was her mother's heavy wool dress, replaced by a white lawn nightgown trimmed with the finest lace she'd ever seen.

Her eyes widened in horror. The soot and grime had penetrated her shabby gloves, coating her skin. Against the stark white linen, she looked as black as ash.

"Maggie put you to bed." The duke turned on his heel and crossed to a huge marble fireplace. Bending down, he grabbed a scoop of coal and tossed it onto an already blazing fire. The way his shoulders strained the seams of his jacket was sinful. As sinful as the way she admired his ass.

Heat flooded her face. She looked away. To the right, two windows flanked a seating area with a yellow settee and matching corner chairs. Sun streamed in between cream-colored brocade drapes proving that the weather had improved. The entire room looked like a sunny day with sky blue walls and white trim.

It was the image of the room she'd always wanted and never believed existed. Her version had never been this large and opulent, though, and hadn't contained cherubs at every corner.

What a waste. She'd slept the whole time she was here.

She caressed the sheets one last time before slipping her legs out. Her feet landed on the carpet, and she rose from the bed. A surge of dizziness made her grab the bed post.

"Where are my clothes?" she asked, frowning. Her legs matched the ugly gray of her arms.

"I told Maggie to burn them."

Her gasp split the air. "What?" Her hands convulsed.

"You won't need them again."

Frantic, she shook her head. "You...you don't understand."

"Relax." The duke strode over and held his hand out. A familiar emerald and platinum pin winked at her. "Is this what you're worried about?" Kathleen clutched the bedpost tighter as relief sapped the last vestiges of her energy.

He lifted the ornament and examined it from all sides, one eyebrow rising. "Did you steal it?"

"No!" With a scowl, she snatched the precious heirloom. How dare he?

"It's worth a considerable amount. Where did you get it?"

"It's none of your business." Clutching the cool metal, she scrambled for somewhere to hide the last link she had to her mother. "I need my clothes."

"I'll send for the seamstress tomorrow." As if it were of no import, he wandered away. She watched him until it became clear he had no real purpose. Now and then, his gaze would flit back toward her, then skitter away as quickly as it landed.

Katy frowned. What did he mean? Why would he send for a seamstress? She couldn't afford a new dress. "I'd rather have my mother's dress back."

The duke paused in his rotation of the room to cast a studied look at her. She blushed as his gaze lingered on her bare ankles. It took all her control not to crawl back into bed and cover them.

"I'm afraid that won't be possible." He studied his nails for a second, then continued to amble about the room. His hand snaked along a small vanity with a mirror large enough to display his entire torso. A patch of skin showed above his cravat as if he'd tugged the linen loose. His hair betrayed a similar messiness. "I told you," he reminded her. "I had it burned."

"Why?" Katy demanded. Was he insane? Even if he had no use for it himself, the gown was perfectly serviceable.

"It was a rag."

"It was *my* rag. You had no right."

Once again, he stopped and spun to study her, then shrugged. "It's already done. I'm sorry if I've upset

27

you. It wasn't my intention."

"So, I'm just to wait here until tomorrow, with nothing but a nightgown to wear? So a seamstress can come and make me a dress I can't afford?"

"Of course not." His lips thinned. "You'll eat, and Maggie can draw you a bath. I sent for the physician as well. To check on the babe. And there are a few books in the library that might entertain you. You may explore the house. And you'll have plenty of other things to keep you occupied."

Katy shook her head. A few books? Entertained and occupied? Did he think she had time to worry about such things?

"I have to leave." Though a bath sounded lovely. And food.

As if to convince her, her stomach growled, followed by the sour taste of bile.

"There are crackers on the nightstand," he said.

Another wave of embarrassment washed over her.

She grabbed the package of crackers and stuffed one into her mouth. The plain dry wafer soaked up the acidic taste and gave her an excuse to remain silent.

He was being kind. He'd let her sleep and would feed her. And in truth, having a physician check on the baby would be a welcome boon. She couldn't afford one. She hadn't been able to in Ireland, and she likely wouldn't be able to anytime soon. First, she needed a job and a place to live. Any money she made would go toward housing and food.

"Thank you," she whispered. The enormity of her situation overwhelmed her. Her father had drummed it into her that she was an ungrateful chit, too proud to accept help. She should latch onto any help offered, not rebuke it. "I don't need a new dress though. I'll be infinitely grateful for one of the maids' cast-offs."

The quiet footsteps that had punctuated the duke's prowling around the room ceased. When she looked up, Katy found his silvery eyes fastened on her, an annoyed scowl etched on his forehead.

Did the man ever look happy?

"I don't think you understand." He crossed the room and opened a beautiful white and gold armoire. Lavender wafted toward her, followed by the rush of silk as he tossed a brilliant red garment at her. "Cover yourself," he barked.

The fabric fluttered down, brushing her forearms. Grasping it, she held it up and gasped. Gorgeous oriental embroidery adorned the crimson silk with vibrant multi-colored flowers and tiny people. Her fingers brushed over the perfect stitches of an expertly formed gull.

"I can't." She resisted the urge to smooth it over her cheek. "I'll ruin it."

"Good. It belonged to my second wife Sarah. It's about time it gets thrown out." He started to pace in earnest, his booted stride muffled by the carpet, then louder as he stepped toward the edges of the room. "You'll need an entire wardrobe, so there will be multiple fittings. And you'll need to hire a maid unless you prefer Maggie choose one for you. I've engaged a tutor for you. You'll have lessons twice a day, two hours in the morning, and two in the afternoon."

Lessons? For what?

Uneasiness crept through Katy. Her hands strangled the fragile fabric. "What do you mean?"

He paused, eyes flickering over her again. Katy let

the robe unfold, holding it before her as if it were a shield. He averted his gaze and lifted a perfume bottle off the vanity. A whiff of lilac sent another wave of nausea over her.

"I'm assuming you'll want to take your place in society," he explained. "And I'm willing to allow it, so long as you don't disgrace the Lexham name."

"Excuse me?" Katy snapped her mouth shut as soon as the words left it, but the duke didn't react.

"You'll receive all the advantages of being my wife." He dropped the perfume with a distinct thunk. "With none of the disadvantages."

Katy shook her head. "I'm sorry," she lied. She wasn't sorry at all. Her stomach was churning with fear. "Could you start over? Because I'm absolutely certain I don't understand. What exactly are you saying?"

Jeremy spun. His eyes sparked with icy determination. Tall and stiff, he bowed at the waist, then straightened, lips and face tight. "I'm going to honor George's commitment. You'll be my wife in all the ways that matter."

Stunned, she dropped to sit back on the bed. This time her head shook so hard her hair whipped around and stung her chin.

He wanted her to be his wife?

No, he didn't want her. No one ever wanted her. *None of the disadvantages.*

The robe slipped to the floor, forgotten, as realization crawled up from her center. Jeremy's gaze seemed to follow the sensation.

She snatched the robe. "You want the baby!"

"You'll be well compensated."

"Compensated?" She gasped, disbelief morphing

into anger. "I'm not an ever-lovin' whore, you bastard." Whirling her head around, she searched for something to throw. Finding nothing, she stomped toward the armoire. "You think you can just decide you'll honor George's indiscretions, and I'll meekly accept it?" She ripped open the doors. Stuffed with glorious colors, she pawed through velvets and brocades. Her gut cramped. So many beautiful gowns.

Frantic, she pulled the plainest looking gown from the armoire. She'd have to remove the bows and ribbons, but at least it was a plain gray color. It would do. Clutching it to her stomach, she slammed the door and rounded on Jeremy.

He lounged against the wall, arms crossed over his chest as if she were a painting he viewed out of politeness.

"Oh, wait! You probably expect me to thank you. Shall I fall down on my hands and knees and kiss your god-like feet?"

In an instant, his demeanor changed. Instead of silver, his eyes blazed white-hot, and a tic pounded on his left temple. His form stiffened, making him look even larger. His chest expanded, the tempo matching his clenching fists.

A flicker of fear licked at her. Had she gone too far? Again.

A clock ticked. Tick-tock. Tick-tock.

Katy swallowed. He looked like he might hit her. He wouldn't be the first to do so, even if she didn't count George. It would hurt, too. Like Colum O'Conner used to do until Thomas beat him into pig slop.

She stepped back and clutched the gown. The armoire smacked her in the back.

When he spoke, his tone frightened her more, measured and quiet. "You're right. You don't understand. I'm not asking. I'm telling." He didn't move, but his nostrils flared. A deep breath relieved enough tension that his shirt no longer threatened to rip its seams. "You're carrying George's child. From this day forward, it's mine. You can accept it and reap whatever benefits you wish, or you can fight me on it. But I'll still win."

Katy swallowed once more. A lump of anxiety choked her, lodged as tight as a half-chewed hunk of chicken.

"You can't make me." Her voice barely carried, but there wasn't enough air to do more than whisper.

His jaw clenched, and his eyes flickered, but his voice remained as hard as a diamond. "Maybe I can't force you to stay, but the child is mine. George has already agreed. He's been paid extremely well. And if you try to take the baby away, I'll send every bobby in London to find you. I'll take it from you. You can't win this. All you can do is decide if you want to be with your child."

He stared at her for a measured second as if to see her reaction. Then he turned on his heel and, with a ramrod straight back and controlled steps, headed toward the door. Try as she might, Katy couldn't find a single response.

"Oh, baby," she moaned, cradling the almost nonexistent bump. "Your momma is in a pickle."

****

"You look better than you have in a long time. Did George break his neck or something?"

Jeremy glanced up just in time to absorb the blow

on his shoulder. Miles Brant's chocolate brown eyes twinkled as he slid onto the sofa beside him. The Earl of Beccles, Miles was his closest confidant and one of the few who could get away with laughing at him.

After asking if he wanted a drink and gesturing to the footman nearby, Jeremy scanned the room. As usual, at ten in the morning, Boodles was largely empty. He'd chosen a secluded corner seating area.

"What did you want to see me about? A woman?" Miles teased. Jeremy wasn't on the market and hadn't been for years. Miles knew it. His friend lounged back, one leg crossed over the other. Like Jeremy's, his hair curled just enough to be fashionable and his attire set him apart from even the more well-heeled. Unlike Jeremy's, his light-hearted character attracted women the same way finely wrought jewelry did.

That light-hearted character hid an intelligence Jeremy needed.

"Actually, yes."

Miles sobered, brows arching in surprise, and glanced around the room before leaning closer. "George bugger another one?"

Jeremy scowled. That George's misconduct occurred often enough for Miles to go there was beyond the pale. He had no choice but to answer. "Worse. And better." He sipped at his bourbon, then continued. "Remember when I sent him to Ireland?"

Miles nodded, then pasted his jovial face back on while the footman served his drink. As soon as the liveried servant left, he asked, "A couple months ago? Yeah. You sent him to buy that fine black gelding I've been begging you to sell me and to set up those army contracts."

"Exactly." Jeremy proceeded to tell him about Kathleen's arrival, his meeting with her and George, and how he planned on dealing with it.

By the time he concluded, Miles regarded him with an expression best described as unreadable, then leaned back. "So, what do you need?"

Jeremy took a deep breath. It wouldn't be easy. The number of men who could help him was few; Miles was one of only three or four Jeremy knew with the proper connections. Even asking him was only an option because they'd known each other since prep school. They'd both been scrawny boys, too thin and smart to be popular. Together, though, they'd pummeled a rugby player or two.

Another quick scan confirmed that no one could hear them, but Jeremy lowered his voice all the same. "You have someone over there now?"

Miles' gaze darted around much as Jeremy's had while his smile remained light and cheery. "I might. Depends on what you need. But first, I have a few questions. And I promise nothing. I'll have to clear it with Wickham, first." He dropped his glass on a small table and adjusted his seat.

Jeremy nodded. Wickham ran the Alien Office. If Miles had to tell him, Wickham would keep it to himself. Unless it threatened the Empire, he'd save it as a bargaining chip at worst.

"So, you're planning to take an Irish chit, pass her and George's seed off as your own, and expect no one will discover it?"

"That's the plan."

"Why?"

"You damn well know why." When a couple of

men looked over, Jeremy lowered his voice. "I'm done dealing with George's messes, and this time he handed me the perfect solution."

"Oh, I agree with that. I'm just not sure that's a good reason. What's she like?"

Jeremy buried his annoyance, partly because Miles could refuse to help and partly because Miles asked as a friend.

"She's pretty." His groin rebelled at the description. "Seems intelligent enough to pull it off, with a little help."

A genuine teasing smile crawled over Miles' lips. "Pretty? How pretty? And how smart could she be if she let George near her?"

Jeremy stiffened. He disliked it every time he thought about George anywhere near Kathleen. He absolutely hated the idea she'd been willing. "Pretty enough for George," he said with a growl.

"I didn't ask if George thought she was pretty. George likes anything with long hair and bumps on their chest. I want to know if *you* like her."

"She's…lovely." Jeremy shifted. He'd spied on her while she slept. Even now the memory of her, hair flowing around her like liquid copper, chest rising and falling like waves on the ocean, lips parted, had his blood thrumming.

A slow, knowing smile spread over Miles' face. "Fair enough. One last question." His gaze locked on Jeremy. "What if she loses the babe?"

"She won't," Jeremy snapped.

"Humor me. What if she does?"

Jeremy looked away to consider the question. A few members had arrived and nodded at him. An earl, a viscount, and a couple barons—he wondered what they would think if they discovered the truth. A niggling of disquiet made him pause, but then his gaze fell on the window. Covered in heavy dark green velvet, the sun peeked between the panels.

What would he do? Pay her off as he had all the others and send her on her way? After forcing her to stay when she had no wish to do so? "I'll stand by my decision. If she wants."

"All right then," Miles pronounced, sitting forward and clasping his hands before him, arms on his knees. "Tell me what you need."

Chapter Three

Two days later, Katy paced about the bedroom, clad in one of the second duchess' altered gowns when a timid knock sounded. Halting mid-step, she whirled toward the door.

A white-capped girl slipped in, her back to Katy, dragging a wheeled contraption. No more than fifteen, the girl strained to move the huge metal bin, her thin arms distorting the black uniform all the maids wore.

"Let me help you."

With a shriek, the maid's grip failed. Her legs flew out, and her ass thudded on the polished wood floor. Katy hurried over.

"Oh, blimey." As Katy reached her, the maid scuttled back, eyes wide, hands flapping. "Please, Mum." Her gaze darted toward the hall, then back. "Don't fire me, Mum. I didn't know ye was in here."

"I'm not going to fire you." Annoyed, Katy scowled. All morning the servants had tiptoed around her as if she were a starving cat and they were mice. It wasn't her fault Alfred had fired the scullery maid who called her an Irish whore. "Give me your hand, and I'll help you up."

The girl's eyes widened further, and she scrambled backward. Her head shook, dark chestnut curls escaping her mob cap. "No, Mum. Ye'll get yer hands all black. I'll just come back later."

"Nonsense. It won't be the first time I've blackened my hands." Katy stepped forward and grasped a flailing hand. "Nor the last. And I could use the company."

A skeptical look crossed the girl's face, but she didn't pull away. A tug later, she stood before Katy, swiping a pair of grimy hands over the serviceable black skirt.

"I was just collecting the coal, Yer Grace," she explained. "It won't take me long. Mrs. Darby says it's time to clean out the fireplaces for the summer." Her gaze flew toward the door again. "Please don't tell her I barged in on ye. I didn't mean ta."

Without waiting for an answer, she circled around and bent to push the cart, a beautifully painted tin with wheels, through the door. Katy had never seen one as lovely. Nor one so overloaded with coal. Amazed, she watched as the bin moved forward with only a slight creak as the wheels began to turn.

"I won't tell." Katy had met all the servants, an endless stream of faces who'd gazed at her with various expressions of doubt and in some cases animosity. The housekeeper, Mrs. Darby, had appeared as stern as Alfred had been welcoming. Katy had little doubt the woman would fire someone for so minor a transgression. Already, she'd chastised Katy for wielding her own needle and thread rather than waiting for a seamstress. "Would you stay and talk with me a bit, Lucy?"

"Me?" Lucy's voice squeaked, and she straightened, a rush of red staining her cheeks. "You want to talk to me?"

"Well, I doubt Mrs. Darby will tell me much, and if

I'm to be the mistress here, I need to know what's going on below stairs, don't I?"

Lucy's mouth opened, then she scowled and turned away. "I'll not be telling tales. If ye wish to fire me, just do it." After stomping back into the hall to grab a shovel and broom, she crossed the room and began to clean.

Deflated and angry, Katy scowled at her back. How was she to make a life here? The duke barely spoke to her. Even the polite chitchat he'd utilized to put her at ease when they met was now stilted and distant. Although they ate together, the length of the dining table and the presence of an army of footmen prevented any real discussions. Mrs. Darby plainly didn't like her, and Lucy wasn't the first staff to rebuke her overtures. The footman who'd served her solitary midday meal the previous day practically had an apoplexy when she'd attempted to engage him in conversation.

"Lucy," she said, lifting her chin the way her mother had when teaching manners, "please stop that clanging and look at me."

Lucy stiffened, her spine poker straight. Slowly, she obeyed, the pink in her cheeks draining away.

"You don't truly wish to be fired." The slight tremble in the girl's lower lip proved that, as had every word she'd spoken. "Any more than I wish to fire you. So tell me why you're so skittish."

Lucy gazed at her feet, seemingly mesmerized by the fact they wouldn't stop moving. "I'm sorry, miss—" She turned beet red, "I mean, Your Grace." Her hands twisted in her apron, strangling the cloth. "I like it here. His Grace treats us nice. Even gives us extra vittles to take home. We *all* like it here. We're just afraid."

"Of what?"

She hadn't thought Lucy could get any redder, but even the roots of her hair turned crimson. "Of you."

"Me? But why? I'm a nobody."

The curls bobbed, nearly knocking the cap off her head, then the big brown eyes lifted and met hers. "We're afraid you'll be like the others."

"What others?"

Lucy dragged in a deep breath and glanced at the bed. Then her gaze flitted toward the door leading to the duke's chambers.

"The other wives?"

"They weren't very nice." Lucy bit her lip, then continued, as if she realized it no longer mattered what she said. "We all hated them. There was no pleasing the first one. She fired Mrs. Darby, even, and Mrs. Darby's the nicest housekeeper I've ever seen. Fired half of us, she did. For no reason. And she hurt the duke. Real bad. He hired us all back, after she died, but it was never the same. The light had gone out of him. And he'd get angry, over stuff he'd never cared about before. But the second one, she was worse. A real cold one, she was."

Cold. The second duchess had been cold. Like her?

When Lucy looked back at her, Katy's stomach sank while Lucy's chin rose. "He's a nice man, miss. And we'd all rather be fired than watch you hurt him."

"What do you mean by cold, Lucy?"

Lucy shrugged. "She was uppity. Didn't even notice us servants. Which was a blessing after the first duchess. But she didn't care about him. 'Twas one o' those arranged marriages, Alfred says. She came from good family."

"Isn't that normal?" It wasn't what she had ever wanted, but for an aristocrat, it was more usual than not.

"Well, I suppose. But she didn't even try to make him happy." Retrieving the shovel, Lucy resumed scooping coal, her motions practiced and smooth. "She hardly even spoke to him. They'd sit at dinner for hours and never say a word. 'Twasn't natural, if you ask me."

Hours of silence? Katy hugged herself. She'd die of loneliness.

"When they wed, we had hopes, 'cause 'twas said she loved her first husband. He died of the pox, though. Left her penniless. We all felt sorry for her at first, 'cause of it, 'til we saw His Grace getting sadder and sadder. We didn't understand why." Her gaze darted toward the open door, then she lowered her voice. "But then Beatrice overheard her one day. She told the duke it was her time, when it wasn't."

Katy blinked, but before she could say anything, Lucy continued. "She told him that a lot. If she'd been bleeding as much as she said she was, she'd have been dead after six months. I think she just didn't want him in her bed."

"Oh." Katy dropped to the sofa and gripped the arm as the picture came together. She'd gathered enough from the duke and Alfred to know the first wife had died in childbirth, hence the reason for a second arranged marriage and her current dilemma. As a duke, it was his duty to continue the line.

"How did she die?" she asked as Lucy switched to wield the broom.

"'Twas a sick stomach. Hurt her real bad." Lucy twisted her lips in a grimace and continued to sweep the ashes as she talked. "I could even hear her screams from the coal cellar. Much as I didn't like her, I felt bad. Fevered her from the inside out, the doc said. Took her a week to die."

With a final swipe, Lucy bent and gathered up the last of the gray dirt. "His Grace pretended to be sad, but if ye ask me, I think he was glad." Her eyes widened. "Not that she suffered. Just that she was gone." Setting aside the broom and shovel, Lucy gathered the fireplace tools and set them back into the opening, then the top of the coal bin thudded down. "I be done here now, Mum. Will ye be wanting the big bough pot in front of the fireboard?"

Compared with everything she'd learned, the choice of decoration held little interest, but Katy managed to respond enough to send Lucy on her way. The hole of uncertainty she'd exposed wasn't as easily banished.

As the door closed behind the maid, Katy rose and resumed her pacing.

Would the duke come to resent her the way he had his second wife? He'd vowed there would be no marital demands in the bedroom, but how could a man as virile and assertive as he not want more? She had no illusions of her own. Should he decide to seduce her, she'd capitulate. She'd caved to George's half-hearted attempts only to regret it almost as soon as she did.

Perhaps it would be different this time.

Her hand rose to her mouth. At the sharp sting of a hangnail, she snatched it away and stared at the accusatory redness. Try as she might, she couldn't break herself of the habit of chewing her fingers to the quick. What made her think she'd change any of her other bad habits? Even if she managed to hide the inevitable distaste during the act, she'd lash out later. She'd berate him or shun him, punish him for a fault that was not his.

Her gaze followed the hazy cloud of dust that trailed to the door. It wouldn't take long for the servants to hate her.

Disheartened, she marched to the window and gazed out. Situated on Park Lane, Lexham House overlooked Hyde Park's expanse of green. Yesterday, she'd seen London's peerage promenade for hours on end, the fancily dressed aristocrats nodding and smiling at each other, never touching. Right now, the park lay largely empty, the sight of trees and unspoiled grass beckoning. In the distance, a herd of cows ambled about, lowing and munching the blades while barefoot lads cavorted nearby.

Decided, she crossed the room and tugged on the bell pull.

Almost instantly, a footman appeared. Gregory, if she remembered correctly.

"Gregory?" she asked, clasping her hands before her as a proper lady should. "Does the duke have horses?"

He blinked at her. "Yes, Your Grace. He has a rather extensive stable."

Of course, he did. He'd sent George to Ireland specifically to add to it. Now that she thought about it, she remembered George bragging about how superior his horses were to the one he purchased.

"Would you have one saddled, please? I wish to ride in the park."

His eyes looked her up and down and his mouth

opened but no words came out.

Buggers. She'd forgotten. She glanced at the armoire. There was no riding habit, and nothing suitable as one. No matter. She'd ridden in breeches often enough.

She raised her chin and shot him a questioning look.

He lowered his gaze.

"I…I shall confer with Alfred, Your Grace."

"Why?"

"I…" His Adam's apple bobbed while he searched for the phrasing. "He'll be better able to answer your question."

Katy sighed as he backed out, bowing every other step. Before he reached the exit, she held up a hand.

"Is His Grace here, Gregory?"

"I believe he's in the library, Ma'am."

Galvanized, Katy swept past the young man and sprinted down the hallway. Without so much as a knock, she barged into the room.

The duke sat behind his desk, hair mussed, cravat hanging askew. At the sight of her, he leapt to his feet.

"Egads," he barked, grabbing a nearby jacket and shrugging his shoulders into it. Turning his back, he reached up, head bent, muttering beneath his breath. When he turned back, the neckpiece sported a less than perfect knot, and he had patted his umber hair back into place.

A sliver of disappointment shot through her and heat rushed to her face. He was an aristocrat, not one of the Scullabogue lads she ogled as they tossed bales of hay, half naked.

"Can I do something for you?" he asked, eyes

sweeping up and down in a manner that made her teeth clench.

"I wish to go riding."

His brows dipped. "No."

No *I'm sorry*. No *why*? Just a simple, adamant *no*.

"Why not?"

Any discomfort her invasion had caused no longer showed. He strode forward, his long shapely legs chewing up the distance. Her breath caught as he towered over her, staring into her eyes. A hint of coffee and honey drifted from him.

Good lord, he was a fine specimen.

"I won't risk it. You may ride all you want after the babe is born."

Unsure if it was his silvery eyes or the answer itself that mulled her brain, Katy had to repeat the words in her mind before his meaning penetrated. The baby? She couldn't ride because of the baby? "That's silly. Pregnant women ride all the time."

"*Expectant ladies*"—the emphasis made it plain that the two were different classes—"don't."

"I'm not a lady."

One dark eyebrow rose. A tic on his forehead fluttered. "Nevertheless, you are my wife, and the horses are mine. As such, it's my decision. And I say no."

He turned his back and headed toward his seat. To her horror, her foot stomped the floor, earning a glance over his shoulder and another arched brow. She tamped down the urge to pick up a nearby book. Hurling it at him wouldn't gain her anything.

Reining in her frustration, Katy inhaled then exhaled. She couldn't stand another minute in this house.

"Am I a prisoner?" she asked, more annoyed to find he had turned his attention back to whatever she'd interrupted.

His head jerked. "Of course not. You may go anywhere you like."

Anywhere, so long as she came back.

"And where would a *lady* go in London?"

He blinked once or twice, face wrinkling as if he'd never considered the question. "Well, you could pay calls…" At least he had the grace to blush as he realized she knew no one. "You could go shopping." His expression brightened, reminding her of the blood he shared with George. "Bond Street would occupy you for a time, I'm sure."

"Shopping," she drawled. "Me and my full purse?"

"You don't need money. They'll bill me. Gregory will accompany you."

Before she could exhale in disappointment, he pushed himself up and crossed to a small safe in the corner. The sound of tumblers rumbled. Katy's eyes widened. When he turned back, a small pouch nestled in his hand.

A thrill whispered through her. A horse would get her farther, but London could hide her just as well as distance. With money, she'd be able to bribe people to help her.

His gaze fastened on her face. She inched her chin up, hoping her thoughts didn't show.

Slowly, he dangled the soft leather pouch. "There's twenty pounds here. For baubles, ices, any little things you might want. When you need more, come see me and I'll refill it."

Twenty pounds! For baubles?

Schooling her face to hide the bubbling excitement, she lowered her gaze. Twenty pounds would hire a coach to take her almost anywhere and still leave enough to live on for a month or two.

"Thank you, Your Grace," she murmured, curtsying as deeply as possible.

She'd worry about the consequences later.

****

A knock reverberated through the library three hours later. *Finally.*

Jeremy pushed the account ledger away and, after carefully returning the pen to its holder, leaned back. He'd stared at the same column of figures for the last hour, calculating six different sums, just as he had the previous two pages. "Enter."

He stared at the offensive numbers as Gregory entered. Math wasn't his strong suit. He didn't even like it. He did the books himself as an exercise in discipline, just as he forced himself to attend Almack's once a week or attend the opera.

Just as he'd forced himself to wait for Gregory's return, knowing well that Kathleen wasn't shopping.

With a deep cleansing breath, he glared at the footman. "Let me guess. The duchess gave you the slip."

Young, the lean fellow swallowed hard. "I'm sorry, Your Grace. I don't know what happened. I thought she was buying ribbons."

An unfamiliar knot formed in Jeremy's stomach. He'd known she would run. He'd expected it, prepared for it, and would counter it, but waiting for it had left him unfocused and unsettled. He didn't like it.

Unable to remain still, Jeremy stood and rounded the corner of the desk. He grabbed his discarded jacket and slipped it on, tugging the sleeves into place before turning back to glower at Gregory.

"Fetch my cloak," he barked, "the old one, and have the carriage brought around. Once that's done, you're to station yourself at the entrance around back. A young boy will arrive with a note. You'll bring it to me immediately."

Jeremy's jaw felt like obsidian, hard and dark and unbreakable. Tempted to fire the man, he held back. He'd deliver that tidbit after he'd repaired the damage.

Once Gregory nodded and scurried out, Jeremy walked to the window and waited once more. The clear morning sky had evaporated. Clouds had rolled in, and the afternoon threatened rain once again. At the moment, the street was barren, even the crossing sweeper absent. The library overlooked the servant's entrance, where the rat-catcher boy, Tod, would arrive. It might be hours, but it didn't matter. He would wait.

Tod would come. Hired when Jeremy saw his dog run over by a carriage, the youngster's loyalty ran deep. He and Ned took care of Jeremy's less savory activities, the ones few knew about. Unlike Gregory, Ned wouldn't let Kathleen slip away any more than Kathleen would know he'd followed her.

A glimmer of guilt shot through Jeremy, quickly drowned out by the thrum of anticipation.

He'd warned her. He'd treated her like a lady, been the gentleman his grandmother would have demanded. She'd called his bluff, tested his resolve. Just as he'd feared, he couldn't trust her.

Now he'd reap the reward.

****

Katy shrank into a dark corner of the Lost Swan Tavern, nerves firing with excitement and guarded triumph. A tiny establishment tucked into an alley near Covent Garden, the Lost Swan's only recommendation was the proximity to the convergence of seven streets and a myriad number of similar pubs. Given the hour, a steady stream of patrons pushed through the door, some hoping to relax after a long day, others to partake of the tavern's fare like the watery stew on the table before her.

Her gaze darted over the patrons. Small groups formed, merchants in one, a couple chimney sweeps in another. Her focus paused on one man sitting alone, a battered cloak draped over his shoulders. Middle-aged, his head swiveled, scanning the room, while his fingers tapped on the table. When his gaze wandered over her, she tensed. An instant later, a prostitute walked up behind him, laying her hand on his shoulder and shoving her bosom into his face. He grinned, turning toward the woman. Katy relaxed.

It was all so ordinary. She might as well have been in the Scullabogue Inn, watching her brothers.

Except she wasn't. It didn't feel like home, and she'd never be welcome there.

Biting her lip, her hand settled over her stomach. She had to eat, but unappetizing blobs of grease floated in the reddish water that passed for stew. Dipping a spoon, she stirred the pools of fat into the liquid. They skittered away, reforming as quickly as she destroyed them.

A trickle of unease crawled over her. All afternoon, she'd felt eyes on her. She scanned the smoky room again. The middle-aged man was gone, as was his companion. No one else looked familiar, aside from the one chimney sweep who had come in after her. He still sat nearby, concentrating on the bowl before him, his younger apprentice chattering away beside him. A few new patrons milled about, all equally non-threatening— a dustman, a chandler, a group of coal porters.

After another quick look, Katy nudged herself farther into the corner. She was just being paranoid. Even if the duke realized she'd slipped away, it would take him time to track her. She'd only escaped Gregory's vigilant attendance two hours ago.

To calm herself, she fingered her mother's brooch. Dulled by the thin fabric she'd hastily sown it into, the familiar filigree shape soothed her until her hand knocked against the weight of the duke's money.

Guilt reared up, kicking her in the gut, burning in her throat.

It wasn't stealing. He'd given it to her. Even if he hadn't, he'd never miss it. She needed it, for the baby.

Unable to stomach the stew, Katy ripped off a mouthful of grainy bread and chewed. Dirt crunched with every bite, and when she swallowed, it stuck in her throat. She forced herself to take another bite, her jaw aching with the effort.

She washed it down with yeasty ale, but the choking sensation remained.

You're just tired. Her arms hugged her abdomen. *After a good night sleep, and a few hundred miles between yourself and London, you'll feel better. You can do this.*

Except she didn't want to. She didn't like running away. She didn't like stealing. She didn't want to bring a baby into the world with no family to love it. Mostly, though, she feared being alone.

The scrape of a chair drew her attention. A gaunt, pock-faced man slid into the rickety frame beside her.

"It be me lucky day," he drawled in a harsh Cockney accent, watery eyes locked on her. His gaze crawled over her chest, like a millipede army, sending shivers up her spine. A reptilian tongue slipped out through a gap between teeth the color of pus. When his gnarly hand reached out and clawed her skirt, she jerked away, eyes darting about for help.

There's no one else, Katy. You have to take care of yourself.

Gritting her teeth, she steeled her spine and did her best to glower. "It will be your *unlucky* day if you don't leave right now."

His cackle grated her frayed nerves. "Come on, luv. I'll pay ye well. I like a little fight. I'll e'en let ye bite me."

A dirty hand snaked up, reaching for the edge of her neckline. Katy smacked it away, shuddering.

"'Ow about I bite ye, instead?" His hand shot out and trapped her wrist.

Wrenching pain shot up her arm. He yanked, sending another hot jolt through her shoulder. Her feet slid forward. Panicking, she clutched the worn edge of the table, kicking wildly, but the flowing skirt prevented any real effect.

With a bang, another chair slammed on the floor. A black-clad figure swooped in, pinning the man by the neck. A yowl split the raucous crowd noise. Freed, her wrist smacked against the table.

"Get lost," growled a menacing voice. "She's

mine."

Tossed as effortlessly as a rag, the scrawny form hurtled through the air and landed with a dull thud. The crowd separated, then closed the gap as if nothing had happened.

Katy cradled her throbbing wrist and peeked at the man who'd saved her.

She froze with disbelief.

The duke's silver-gray eyes bored into her, cold and accusatory. A late day growth on his jaw added to the iron resolve on his face. He reminded her of a smuggler or highwayman.

"Ned?" His short booming voice carried with ease, making her jump.

A sliver of disquiet sliced through her. The chimney sweep from the bar, the one she'd dismissed as no one, sidled up behind the duke. Looking closer, she realized there was no ash visible on him. He was just dark and thin and dressed like a sweeper. A long scar ran the length of his face, from brow to chin.

"Aye, Govn'r?"

A purse, larger than the one he had given her, flew over the duke's shoulder. Ned snagged it in midair.

"Empty the tavern, please, and lock the doors. No one's allowed in until I leave."

Katy swallowed the dread in her throat. Not a trace of forgiveness showed on the duke's face.

In a surprising matter of minutes, the noise and chaos of a full tavern died away. Like ripples in a pond, the tavern cleared, the shuffling of feet growing farther away and quieter. The duke's fingers tapped quietly on the table, echoed by the rise and fall of his left thigh.

Before she knew it, the door thudded shut. The

lock tumbled, then went silent. Her stomach dropped, like the pebble that created the ripples. What was he going to do?

"Give me the purse."

Her hand slipped into her pocket, clutching the smooth leather. If she gave it to him, she'd have no chance to leave again.

There'd be no other chance, anyway.

Resigned, she withdrew the leather pouch. It thudded on the table, coins clinking like chains.

"And the brooch."

"But that's mine!" As soon as the words escaped, she snapped her mouth shut and peered at him. His eyes flashed, and the tic in the side of his forehead jumped.

Was she a total idiot? Nothing was hers if he decided it wasn't.

"I'll pretend I didn't hear that." His hand opened, and his thigh thumped once. His other hand flicked, and a penknife appeared. He held it out. "Don't even think about using it on me."

Her eyes widened. How had he known she'd sewn the brooch into the lining?

Of course, he knew. Just as he'd known she'd run. Even before she had. The pin had been sewn into her clothes when she arrived in London. Why wouldn't he expect her to do it again?

Katy fingered the small knife and reluctantly turned out her pocket. Razor sharp, the blade sliced through the serviceable gray fabric and the metal heirloom tumbled into her hand. With a final caress of the forest green gem, she placed it on the rough table surface.

Like a hawk, his hand dove and captured it. It

disappeared into a fold in his cape. His hand opened until she placed the knife back in his palm.

The knife disappeared, and the duke sat back. Uneasy, Katy shifted and stared at him.

He didn't speak. He merely stared back, unsmiling, as if waiting for an explanation.

What could she say? That she couldn't stay because she was a rebel? That she felt guilty living in the lap of luxury while her family starved? That she was uncomfortable and couldn't relax? Or that she didn't want a cold, stiff, strait-laced husband who never even looked at her?

He was looking now though. With a gaze that showed more heat and passion than she'd ever seen. Heavy-lidded, his eyes swept over her chest, lingering where she'd been unable to cover the swell of her breasts. There was none of the disgust she'd imagined, either. His chest rose and fell, slow and steady, nostrils widening with each breath.

He didn't look cold or strait-laced, either. His long body lounged in the chair, dwarfing it, one leg crossed over the other. His hand created small circles over his knee, fingers stroking the buckskin. Her nipples tightened, as if his fingers stroked there, instead.

Stop it! Think about something else. He's a gentleman, not a romantic scoundrel who takes what he wants. No matter how much you might want it.

She dragged her attention away, scrambling to find something to focus on, something other than the guilt and imagined desire.

"You said 'please.' "

"Excuse me?"

"Just now. When you told Ned to empty the

tavern."

His head cocked, brows lowering. "Of course, I did. It's a matter of manners."

"They matter a lot to you? Manners."

"Appearance is everything." He lowered the leg and shrugged off a long black cloak. Nondescript, with signs of wear, she realized it looked like every other black cloak she'd seen in the tavern. With infinite care, he peeled off a pair of ordinary working gloves as scuffed and worn as a working man's. The gloves slapped on the table. "One can be anything one wants, as long as one plays the part. And one can get away with a multitude of sins if one doesn't draw attention to it."

Katy sucked in a breath. Did he know her sin? Had that snake, George, told him?

"I didn't come here to discuss manners, however, so let's stop pretending, shall we?" The duke leaned forward, hands clasped before him on the worn oak table. He rubbed at an ink stain on his middle knuckle, frowning.

Katy waited, uncertain. Despite his words, he didn't look at her as he would if George had spilled her secret. Surely, he'd have brought the Runners with him or a contingent of lobsterbacks.

He didn't look angry, either, which is what she had expected once he discovered she'd fled. She tensed. Anger she could deal with; she was used to it. This calm control wasn't a reaction she'd ever encountered.

"I don't want to separate a mother and her child, Kathleen. When you showed up, I took you in. I treated you well. Anything you asked for, I gave you. I told you what would happen if you defied me, and you did it anyway."

Katy bit her lip. Nothing she could say would help. Either he was going to take her baby and send her away, or he wasn't. He didn't seem the type to give second chances though. And there was nothing she could do. What was worse was that she couldn't even argue it. The baby would have a better life with him.

A life with a mother and a father would be better. She had to convince him to let her stay. "I…I made a mistake. I'm sorry."

"I trusted you, Kathleen. Why should I believe you won't leave again the next chance you get?"

"I won't. I promise." She grabbed his hands, clutching them as if that would help. Pain shot up from where the old man had wrenched her wrist. She ignored it. "Give me another chance. Please. It's my baby."

His heavy sigh echoed, stirring the air. One of his hands turned over, palm up, and captured hers. They both stared down at her pale white hand. He could crush it if he wanted. A shiver ran up her arm when, instead, his thumb caressed the faint bruise that was forming.

"I have to punish you." With a resigned tone that reminded her of her da, his grip tightened, locking over her fingers.

Katy tried to pull away, but his hold clamped down harder. Her fingers felt as if they might shatter, much as her heart did, knowing what his punishment was. How many times had she heard her father use the same tone, saying, "This is going to hurt me more than you" before he spanked her for one disobedience or another? She'd never believed him. And no matter how she begged, he'd never relented.

Her da's spankings hadn't been bad, though. He'd loved her, and she'd learned that as soon as she started whimpering, he'd stop.

The duke wasn't her da though. He didn't love her, and he wasn't going to spank her. He was going to lock her away until her baby was born. And then he would banish her.

"No." Her voice cracked. She couldn't let him do it. Not without a fight.

Ignoring the twisting pain, she wrenched her hand from his steely grip. Her eyes darted. Why had she picked this seat? There was no escape route, no quick exit, nowhere to hide. She could run, but all he had to do was extend an arm to block her.

She couldn't fight him, either. Unlike George, his muscles were real, not padding in his jacket. He'd swept down on her would-be molester and trapped her hand before she'd even registered his presence. And even now, he watched her with a determination as cold and unyielding as ice.

But he wasn't her da, and ice could be melted.

She bounded to her feet, moving around the edge of the table, and fell to her knees. "Please," she begged, lowering her forehead to rest against the swell of his thigh. Her hands clutched at the buckskin on either side. "I'll do anything. Anything at all." Her voice broke, the words blocked by the knot of fear in her throat. "Please don't take my baby." Her sob dropped into the silence, like a candle's final guttering.

"Anything, Kathleen?"

With a vise-like grip on her chin, he forced her to look at him.

She swallowed hard. His eyes glinted in the

candlelight, brows arching, the silver reflecting as hot as the molten glass her father formed. His nostrils flared, reminding her of a bull ready to charge.

All she could do was nod, a slow, hesitant movement that reinforced the fact she was at his mercy.

His eyes never left hers as his thumb dragged across her lower lip. Firm and smooth, with none of the calluses most of the men she knew had, it sent a shiver of awareness through her. The leather gloves had left a pungent scent behind, but she could still taste the salt on his skin.

Sex? Could it be that easy?

She let her gaze drop. Surely enough, his breeches bulged, the darkly dyed buckskin tenting tautly mere inches away. As she watched, the lump twitched.

When she looked up, a sly smirk molded his lips. He tsked, a harsh sound that grated over her nerves.

She beat down the flicker of annoyance.

"What would you do, Kathleen? To make me willing to forgive your defiance?" His hand dropped away, leaving her on her knees, hands still splayed over his rock hard thighs. Without his hand holding it back, the smells of the tavern smothered her. Spilled ale, straw left too long, even the acrid odor of urine beat her senses.

"I told you," she whispered, shame dragging her eyelids closed. "Anything you want."

His chair scraped back, and he rose, pushing her hands off. She fell back, her ass trapping her skirt against her heels, too defeated to rise.

"Not good enough." His strides pounded her ears, the beat just as firm and controlled as ever. "I want to hear you say it. Tell me what you'll do."

"I'll…" Her da would kill her if he could hear her. "I'll let you tup me."

A harsh laugh opened her eyes. He stopped a few feet away, towering over her, a scornful twist on his lips. The candlelight flickered, giving his face a contorted look.

"You'll allow it? You're my wife. Carnal relations are my right."

She schooled her face to hide her scowl. Once again, he was right, much as she disliked it.

"I…I could take you in my mouth." She lifted her chin but couldn't look him in the eyes. Instead, she focused on a beam behind him. As black as night, scarred by knife cuts, it held the tavern up, likely as old as the sin she'd just proposed.

The duke took a single step forward, blocking her view. Arms crossed, he asked, "Why would I want that?"

Why, indeed?

"I don't know." Her face heated. She dropped her gaze and stared at the floor, knowing it wouldn't hide her. "It just seems like men like it."

Squatting, he lifted her chin again. His eyes roamed her face, slowing as they played over her lips.

"How would you know that, Kathleen?"

She swallowed and bit her lower lip before answering. "I used to watch Cliona, in the stables." The fire in her face raged, much as the heat in her loins had. The play of emotions on the men's faces had mesmerized her, the way their eyes would scrunch up, as if in pain, then widen with an ear-to-ear grin when finished. "She…earned her living that way."

A glint of amusement curved the corner of his lips,

gone as quickly as lightning. His eyes flashed and locked on her lips once more.

"And you'd be willing to do that? To me?"

She dragged in a breath, ignoring the trickle of heat between her legs. A hint of cloves and mint cleared away some of the tavern odors. "I told you. I'll do anything you want."

His eyes narrowed. Dropping his hand, he bounded to his feet and resumed pacing. "While the offer is tempting, I must pass. I can pay any whore to do that."

Katy hadn't thought she could burn any hotter with shame, but his words heated her to white-hot. Of course, he didn't want it. He hadn't wanted to tup her, or he would have by now, and he didn't want her mouth on him. He probably didn't want her at all. No one ever had. Even the butcher had only wanted her because no one else would have him.

Fighting back the self-pity, Katy clutched her skirt. Her knees ached from the bits of straw and bunched fabric biting into her skin, and her muscles were tight from the unaccustomed position. Reaching out for a nearby chair, she started to rise.

"Stay on your knees." The command brooked no defiance.

With a muffled sigh, Katy sank back down, shifting position in a vain effort to minimize the discomfort. If he wanted her on her knees, or on her back, or in any other position, she'd do it.

"Please, Sir." The words choked her. "Tell me what you want."

The pacing stopped. Firelight framed his form, red tongues licking the tall, confident posture. Clad in a homespun linen shirt and leather breeches, hands clasped behind his waist, wide shoulders back, his bearing still bespoke authority and purpose.

Desire trickled through her, like a warm breeze after bathing in a cold stream.

Her heart lurched as he strode toward her, steps swallowing the distance.

"Stand up," he snapped.

She scrambled up, hesitantly accepting his outstretched hand. When more desire sparked, she jerked away and stumbled backward. Her leg muscles tingled, knees screaming with relief. Her stomach felt as if it had remained on the floor.

She flinched back when his fingers trapped an errant curl near her neck. The slight brush sent a shiver of fire down her back.

"Take down your hair."

Obedient, she plucked one of her hairpins out, a silver butterfly she especially liked, and glanced about. There was nowhere to put it. Tables with ale tankards and half-eaten meals littered the room, but none were within reach. Nearby, a candle hissed and sputtered, then died.

"Just drop them," he commanded. "I'll buy you new." The low growl in his voice vowed she'd lose more than hairpins should she disobey. That he promised new ones sent a sliver of hope through her. Would he do that if he intended to send her away?

When she looked up, his eyes focused on her cleavage, lashes shuttering the silvery depths, as if he wanted to tup her. A gush of warmth in her loins made her blush.

Swallowing hard, she pushed the thought aside, plucking pins from her hair. The butterflies seemed to take up residence in her stomach, fluttering with each plink as they hit the floor. When the last one fell, she reached up one final time and unwound the braid at her nape.

"Undo it."

Before she could react, he strode across the room to the bar where Ned had sat. A worn bag squatted on the floor. He lifted it as if it weighed nothing and returned in two long steps.

The bag plunked onto a nearby table.

"Kathleen?" A lifted eyebrow reminded her of her task and the consequences.

What did he want? He still hadn't said.

She pulled her braid over one shoulder and worked on unraveling the thick rope of hair. Given the length, just short of her waist, it took a while. Her fingers trembled, shaking as she looped each strand over the other. Every inch she freed added another knot of worry to her stomach.

Was he going to cut it? The thought made her lip tremble. She'd spent her entire life growing it. She devoted hours to brushing and braiding it to ensure it didn't get caught during chores, massaging the rosemary oil she made into each strand.

Maybe he'd let her keep the locks. She could make a doll for her baby with them.

Reaching the top of her braid, she clutched the thick cord of copper and raised her eyes.

He stared at her, gaze sliding along the length of her hair. Her stomach clenched.

"Let it go."

"Please, Sir." She tightened her grip, unable to release the one thing she had that was beautiful. "What are you going to do?"

Something flickered in his eyes. His forehead wrinkled, and his eyes narrowed. Then he drew something through his hands. Something long and silky.

"I'll tell you what I'm going to do." He inched forward. His hands moved, one pulling the black object through the other fist. It swished, then fluttered down, like a molted snakeskin hanging from a branch.

He stopped before her, close enough she could smell the cloves from his soap and a hint of citrus, probably from the orange cookies Cook had sent up with lunch. Heat from his body covered her front. She resisted the urge to step back and stared up at him.

"I'm going to spank you," he said. The black fabric threaded through his hands again. "Then I'm going to do other things you aren't going to like."

His fingers fastened around her hands, prying hers open, still holding the black fabric. The silk should have felt cool to the touch, but the repeated journey through his hands had warmed it. As his words penetrated, her fingers relaxed. Hair slipped from their grips, showering over her front, some escaping to drape down her back.

Spank her. He was going to spank her. She inhaled, surprised. A gulp of cool air filled her lungs.

Glancing up, the rush of relief choked her. Her entire body froze.

Lust blazed in his eyes. His lips parted, breath hissing in and out.

He was going to spank her. Then do *other things*.

"What kind of other things?" The pounding in her veins muffled the words.

"Whatever kind I want."

Her eyes widened. Moisture gushed between her legs. "Is it going to hurt?"

That flicker of something she didn't recognize flashed in his eyes again before hc masked it. "It wouldn't be punishment if it didn't." He smiled, a cruel twist of his lips that tightened the knot in her stomach. A finger snaked down her collarbone. Shivers of awareness raced behind it, dipping down, following as he probed the space between her breasts. The finger stopped, but the trickle continued lower, feeding the wetness between her legs.

"You said you'd do anything I want," he continued as if her consent were necessary. "This is what I want. I want you to submit. Without complaint. Without question. Without hesitation. Do that, and I'll pretend you didn't defy me and try to run away. We'll pretend this never happened, and we'll go back to pretending you're my obedient wife, with all the benefits that come with it."

Why? The question battered at her. Why would he want this?

Why did the very idea make her soft and warm and ready to kneel again?

Her hand settled over the only reason that mattered. "What about the baby? You won't hurt the baby, will you?"

His head snapped back as if she'd slapped him. Red boiled up over a clenched jaw.

"Of course not!" A painful grip locked on her upper arm, snagging strands of hair. Pain pricked in her scalp. Fear paralyzed her.

"Last chance, Kathleen." His growl was raw and

demanding.

"Yes!" She grabbed his shirt, curling her fingers into the coarse linen. "I'll do it. Just tell me what you want. I'll do it." A sob escaped as much from the feel of his chest beneath her hands as from the fear he'd change his mind. She wanted to splay her hands over the heat radiating from him, climb onto his lap, and curl into him. Which made no sense.

He locked her hands in his, forcing her away. A sense of loss weighed her down, fusing her feet to the floor. She shivered at the sudden cold.

"Eight, Kathleen. When you can't take any more pain, you tell me eight."

She blinked, shaking her head. What did he mean?

"I'll ask you for numbers, one to ten. For how much pain you're in. If you get to eight, I'll stop."

"Oh." It made no sense to her. But it didn't matter. She'd almost ruined it with the last question. She wouldn't risk another one. She raised her chin and waited.

She could do this.

****

"Take off your clothes." It had been so long since Jeremy felt the rush of desire pounding through him that his voice sounded rough even to him.

He forced himself to look away from the stunning waves of copper-gold and focused instead on the bag Ned had left. Silk scarves, a wooden paddle, assorted nipple clamps, two whips—he recited the list in his mind. It was a technique he'd learned years ago to control the demon need that threatened to rule his entire life.

Why did he have this compulsion to hurt women?

Why couldn't he be normal? Why did it take another's pain to make him hard?

Kathleen made him hard though. His prick had a prophetic ability when it came to her. Maybe it was her scent wafting ahead of her or some other imperceptible clue that she was near, but it invariably started twitching moments before she entered a room. At times, he thought that maybe, just maybe, he could be normal with her someday. Maybe he could have a wife he could want without the need to hurt her. It was likely a dream, but it was a dream he'd embrace, a dream that would vanish if she left.

A whoosh drew his gaze back to her, and his chest tightened. Her ugly gray gown blended into the shadows at her feet, a pool of white linen atop it. Her skin glowed like an opal against the fiery glow of her curls. To his surprised satisfaction, she'd stripped completely. One hand shielded her generous breasts, and the other covered her privates, just as Botticelli's Venus had.

Venus paled in comparison.

His hands clenched the black silk scarf as he slid forward. "Give me your hands."

When she didn't instantly comply, his teeth ground down, but the fear spilling from her emerald eyes stopped him from barking a punishment. She wasn't Mari, his mistress. She didn't know the rules. She shouldn't even be here, forced to satisfy the demands of a monster.

Instead, he arched his brow.

Reluctantly, she exposed her breasts and extended one hand, then the other. A pretty pink blush spread over her, deepening to rose, while she lowered her lashes. Her bottom lip turned into a scarlet line he wanted to taste, gnawed raw by her snowy white teeth. He'd seen her do it before, usually when concentrating, like at breakfast when she read the paper. It drove him—and his prick—crazy.

With practiced speed, he wrapped the black silk around her wrists, deftly forming a French bowline, winding the loops between her wrists. He scowled at the bones. Too thin, she needed to eat more.

He tugged the silk, checked the snugness, then tied it off. A niggle of amusement tickled him when she held them out in front of her and tugged. The motion pushed her creamy breasts forward until she shrugged and let her hands drop.

That wouldn't do. Her restrained fists hung over the coppery curls between her legs. And her eyes studied him, large green orbs that shone with wariness.

"Turn around and close your eyes." He'd punish her, and he'd enjoy it, sick bastard that he was, but he'd not watch the hate build.

He lifted the scarf and placed it over her eyes. The scent of rosemary wrapped around him, tightening his loins. He loved the smell of her. It haunted the halls of Lexham House these days, causing his cock to perk up at inconvenient times. Rosemary and lemon. It made him hungry, in a way he hadn't been hungry for years.

Soft, riotous curls trapped his fingers, tangling and thwarting his efforts.

God's blood, he wanted to push her down on her hands and knees and sink himself in her until she felt him in every nerve in her perfect body.

But this was for her, not him. A lesson, nothing more. Just enough to make her think twice, or three or four or five times, before leaving again.

Finally, the blindfold cooperated, and Jeremy let his hands fall onto her shoulders. Silk skin rippled beneath his fingers as he pulled her back. A shiver rewarded him, but he still had to suck in a steadying breath as his cock rubbed against her ass, reaching for what it couldn't have.

"These are the rules," he whispered against her ear. "You do what I say, when I say it. If you hesitate, you'll get to feel my hand or whatever else I've chosen to spank you with again, harder. You'll count the spanks, and if I ask you a question, you answer, otherwise you don't speak." Unable to control the urge, he let his hands slip down her arms, savoring the trembles and shivers each word caused. "When you do speak, you address me as Master. Forget, and the count goes up. Do you understand?"

She nodded, no sound filling the smoky air. A peek around her head confirmed she still chewed at her lip.

This was going to hurt him as much as her, he realized, and a thrill swept over him. His cock pulsed angrily. "I don't hear an answer."

Her head dipped, and she inhaled, unaware of the way it pushed her breasts up, presenting their perfect, pert nipples to his hungry gaze. Crinkled, with a merlot tint, they responded to the wash of his breath. "Yes, I understand."

"That's an extra one."

She stiffened, and her forehead crinkled above the blindfold. He waited, easing away from the beckoning heat of her body. No matter what he did, his prick complained, but it would be easier to ignore if it didn't keep rubbing against her luscious ass.

"I think you meant 'Yes, I understand, *Master*.'"
He stepped around her, facing her, and lifted her chin.
The black silk stood out in stark contrast to the pearly
color of her skin. "Am I right?"

This time there was a slight hesitation before she
uttered the correct response. The hitch in her voice, the
tremble in her lower lip, red from the constant worrying
of her teeth, and the sudden release of the tension in her
body combined into a submissiveness that threatened to
strip his control.

If only it were real. Offered freely. The things he'd
give her would be beyond her imaginings.

Jeremy choked back a disappointed laugh. She
couldn't imagine what he was going to give her
anyway. The only difference was she might want the
things he'd give her if she came to him willingly.

But as Grandma used to say, "Wishing wouldn't
make it so."

"So, *ma petite*, how many spankings do you think
you deserve?" He chose the endearment purposely.
Anna had hated it. She'd called it demeaning and cruel.
Kathleen might not even understand French, but it
didn't matter. He had no way to know which
punishments would be most effective. He'd use the
ones that had made his first wife hate him so virulently.
She'd cheated on him with the one man she knew
would wound him the most, the cousin who had been as
much a brother as cousin. How fitting was it that he
now found himself punishing yet another woman who'd
chosen George?

While the question lashed at his esteem, he turned
back to the bag. His hand wrapped around the handle of
his favorite whip. Wrapped in the same soft leather as

the thong, use had worn it as smooth and comforting as sleep. A sliver of need shot to his cock, painful and yearning, but he pushed it aside. Instead, he pulled out a smooth wooden paddle of handcrafted rosewood with a similar leather-wrapped handle. A third padded leather instrument joined the first, larger but with a different feel, before he turned back.

Kathleen's chest rose and fell, and her fists clenched where they hung before her.

"That's another one, for not answering."

The sharp note made her flinch, but her chin rose and her lips tightened.

"None. I've done nothing wrong." She took a deep breath, her breasts taunting him as much as her words. Her lip caught in her teeth for a second, then she added, much more meekly, "I agreed to this, but I don't deserve it. And I never said I'd lie. Punish me if you must, but don't expect me to condone it."

Jeremy tamped down the guilt that snaked through him. She was right. But there was nothing right about the things he liked.

"Fair enough." He reached to grip her chin. She flinched, snapping her head back. He frowned, then leaned in to caress her abused lower lip. Raw and red, it still felt like the softest leather, smooth and supple. He ran his tongue along its length, tasting the lemony sweetness, breathing in the rosemary and fear.

Her breath paused, then rushed out, bathing him in warmth. Her posture melted, like candle wax beneath the flame.

Without warning, he grabbed the lip in his own teeth and bit down just enough to hurt. Clamping down on her upper arm, he dragged her forward until she stumbled and fell against him. His cock jumped, eager to sink into the heat radiating from her.

"Let's count, shall we? One for not addressing me as Master once again, plus the three already earned. Then…seven, I think, one for each remaining month you would have stolen from me until the baby's born. That's almost a dozen. I'd like to add another dozen for the years I'd miss if I never found you, but I'm feeling generous, so we'll just call it a dozen, plus one for my trouble."

She tensed, and Jeremy tightened his grip. She'd regained her balance, pulling away, so Jeremy jerked her back. He liked the feel of her, soft but strong, lean but supple; the excruciating scrape of her nipples against his chest, the squishy feel of her stomach molding around his cock, the quick rasping of her breath along his collarbone. He wanted to rip his own clothes off, experience the full joy of skin-to-skin contact.

Clenching his teeth, he eased her away, careful to grip her so she wouldn't fall, and turned her around. The sooner he finished, the better. At this rate, his cock would take over, and any chance he had at fulfilling the far-fetched dream of a willing family would explode as hard as his prick.

The *thwack-thwack* as he slapped the pair of paddles against his thigh made her jump. With a slight pressure, he guided her toward a nearby table. Another swing of his arm cleared the surface, sending half-empty tankards and plates clattering to the floor. Each clang caused her to flinch.

With a nudge, he urged her against the table. The perfect height, the edge lined up with her mound, and he pushed her down, lifting her arms above her head.

The sight of her round ass, white and unmarred, with the light dusting of red peeking out between her legs, made his mouth water. Unable to resist, he reached out and caressed the curve. Her muscles convulsed, rippling beneath the slow motion. His cock jerked. He placed the wooden paddle aside and wrapped his fingers around the handle of the leather paddle.

"Count them." The order came out raspy and low as the first blow smacked. *Thwack*. The leather against skin mimicked the sound he truly wanted to hear. Louder, and much slower, it sounded similar to the glorious smack of balls against bare skin. He closed his eyes for a moment, enjoying the thrill that ran through him, sad that it wouldn't end with the real thing. All he'd heard was a gasp and the thump of her body reacting.

"Do I need to add to the count, *ma petite*?"

"One." He didn't need to see her to know her teeth and hands were clenched. He began another count in his head. He made it to two before she added, "Master."

"Very good." He rewarded her with a soothing hand. Heat ran up his arm, coaxing him to caress the reddening skin more. He could reward her for every blow, but he wouldn't be able to finish if he did. Every touch made his body tighten.

He lifted his arm and let it fall, aiming for the other cheek. *Smack*. Her body jerked.

"Two, Master."

As a reward, the next blow fell. She counted, her voice losing a bit of the fight. Her ass cheeks bounced, growing brighter, a beautiful crimson that tightened the noose around his loins. Her fists relaxed, no longer clenched so hard her knuckles were white, and her breath eased, going from strangled gasps to a more rhythmic sucking of air. The shock was lessening.

Using the tension in his core, he raised his arm higher. The warm glow of exertion flowed through him, stoking the power as he launched the next blow. Harder and faster, it cracked with each slap. This time her gasp split the air, followed by a satisfying sob. The table jumped. The next followed just as quickly, not waiting for her count, spreading the shock to the second cheek.

"Five, Master!" Her knuckles were white again, her voice loud with a hint of shock. Air rasped from her lungs, but she remained tense, waiting.

Her surprised cry when his hand smoothed over the hot skin sent a surge of satisfaction straight to his groin. Her ass relaxed, the fear draining away with each caress, turning her soft and malleable. As he worked the sting out, her back started to bow. Her ass rose, welcoming his touch, fueling his contemptible urges.

God's blood, he wanted her. He wanted her on her hands and knees, her ass in the air, pussy exposed, wet and ready for him. He wanted to ease his finger into her ass, feel the muscles tighten around his knuckle, while his cock pounded her hot, tight quim. He wanted to hear her moan and beg and scream his name.

Instead, he groaned and leaned forward. His hand stilled, soaking up the heat and sting while he slanted down to place a gentle kiss on her shoulder. She tasted salty from the fear, salty and sweet. A faint musk and rosemary filled his lungs. Unable to resist, he let his fingers wander down the arc of her ass.

His breath caught.

She was as warm and wet as bath water. When his finger dipped, a quiet moan escaped her. Her muscles quivered, and he felt another trickle of moisture.

He lurched up, backing away, staring. Confusion slammed through him.

Kathleen lay on the table, all fight gone. Her breath slipped in and out, quick and ragged. The red glow had spread over her entire form, deeper red on her ass, but a definite blush colored her face and her pussy. As he watched, a shiver rippled over her.

She looked like a woman in the throes of passion.

He shook his head to drive out the demons. It was his imagination. She was a lady. She didn't want him. Anna had done the same thing, turned wet and soft and even begged, eventually. But she'd hated it. She'd hated him.

Jeremy snatched the wooden paddle and raised it.

No! Not like this. Not in anger. She might tolerate the punishment. Maybe even, in time, forgive him. But not if he went too far.

He sucked in two deep breaths and stared at the woman who had wound him so tight.

Her unusual height allowed her toes to touch the ground, but she lay limply, submitting in a way Anna never had. Another soft, choked moan escaped her lips. She raised her head, searching blindly for a sign of what was coming.

The vision of Kathleen dumping her tea in George's lap replayed in his mind. She wasn't Anna. Anna wouldn't have done that. Anna would have smiled, then spread some malicious rumor behind George's back. Anna wouldn't have worried about ruining a silk robe or refused a new dress in favor of an older one. She would have worn the robe and made a disparaging comment about how the stitching chafed her delicate skin.

Maggie had never complained about Anna making her own bed or hanging up her own clothes, leaving the staff with idle hands, as Kathleen had done the last two days. Not that Anna would have ever done those things. No, Maggie had bitten back different criticisms, afraid of being dismissed while Anna berated the servants and doubled their workload. If he hadn't demanded an explanation for the steady stream of resignations, Maggie never would have spoken up and the entire staff would have left long before Anna sacked them. Kathleen made them want to stay, smiling and thanking them with a frequency that embarrassed most.

This woman wasn't Anna. This was Kathleen. As much as he might want to hurt her, because of what he was, he didn't want to physically hurt her. Not like he'd ended up wanting to hurt Anna.

He sighed. *Discipline. Follow the plan. Don't give in to the need.*

He reached out to sooth her. And himself. "Almost halfway there. You're doing great."

Kathleen arched beneath his hand, her cheek falling back down against the wooden table with a sigh. Too bad his cock wouldn't obey as well as Kathleen did.

He raised the wooden paddle and let it fall with less force. She rewarded him with a groan and an immediate count, Master included. The next blow fell, a bit harder, with similar results. Reassured, the familiar focus returned, calm and controlled, more satisfying than anything else he'd ever encountered. He fell into it, landing blow after blow with experienced precision. By the time he reached ten, his balls ached, his arms had a pleasant strain, and the euphoria he lived for filled him from head to toe.

Unfortunately, he still wanted to bury himself in her.

"Three more, sweetheart." His voice strained to sound normal as his hand slid over mounds of red-hot skin. Kathleen moaned and pressed her face into the table, ass arching up, just as he liked. Whatever she felt, it made her gasp and groan and writhe to get away, or closer, and he wanted to give her whatever she needed.

"Please." So muffled and drowned out by the rush of blood in his ears he almost missed it, he leaned closer. His hand stilled, soaking in the heat. Her scent filled the air, and he inhaled. Why had he never realized how intoxicating rosemary was?

"Please, what?" His lips touched the side of her forehead. Salty and moist, it still tasted of lemon. Unable to resist, he stretched himself along her back.

She tensed, then melted. Her ass cheeks softened, and his cock nestled in the crack. "Please, *Master*." Her breath sobbed. "I forgot. Please don't punish me for it."

"I won't." His lips curled, and he brushed her hair away from her face. Silken red-gold curled around his knuckles. "But what was it you wanted?"

He had to close his eyes. She felt so wonderful. Just as he remembered from those first few times with Anna when she'd been willing and he'd thought she loved him. When he thought he'd loved her.

"I—" She swallowed and her ass rose. His balls tightened until he tensed. "Please. I—" She drew a deep breath, and her whole body spasmed. "Touch me…please."

It was a whisper, so soft it might have come from heaven. Or his imagination.

Half afraid he'd heard her wrong and half afraid she'd change her mind if he hadn't, Jeremy caressed her. His palms stroked down her spine, then along the curve of her waist and over her buttocks. Lean muscles shivered, and a quiver raced along the same path his fingers took. A shudder wracked her, and her back arched as he neared her anus. He slowed, rimming a single finger along the edge, then circled toward her core. Another muffled plea broke the silence.

His heart skipped a beat as he delved into her heat. Her pussy wept, wetter and thicker than water but thinner than honey. His cock hardened further, and his mouth watered. How would she taste?

She moaned, struggling. Tiny gasps shattered the air, shards that sliced his control.

He slipped his middle finger forward, a tentative whisper of a touch over her soft, swollen nub. She bucked and hissed.

"Do you like that?" Without waiting, he stroked it again, then pressed gently. Her heartbeat hammered there, her flesh hot and wet.

"Yes! Please! Master." Another buck collided with his cock, throbbing in unison with her clit. He pushed back and sucked in a hiss.

He could take her. Right here. Right now. She'd let him.

His head fell forward. He could. But he wouldn't. That wasn't the plan. It would be momentary bliss at best. It wasn't worth the risk.

Still, he savored her warm, wet need, massaging

the proof that, at this moment, she wanted him as much as he needed her. Teasing, he stroked her clit, easing around the slick opening his cock wanted while she moaned and writhed and strained.

When he thought she was close to coming, he stopped.

"No!" Her shriek hurt.

"I'm not done." He slapped a bare hand against her right ass cheek. "You owe me three more." Three more, and the *other*. He hadn't been sure about the other, but he was now. The spanking was punishment. The other was for him. And maybe for her. Only she'd know if it was punishment or reward.

Eager to get to it, he lifted the paddle and landed three more in rapid succession. Harder, with less time between slaps, the flesh turned crimson, the hue spreading in bright red circles. Kathleen did her best, but by the third one, she was sobbing too hard to finish the count.

"Deep breaths, sweetheart," he advised and dropped the paddle. It thudded and bounced on the floor.

Stepping closer, he lifted Katy's hands and urged her to stand. Her legs quivered while he turned her to face him. Her mouth trembled, bottom lip trapped in her teeth until he bent and stroked his tongue along the tender flesh. A shudder wracked her body. Her mouth opened, and he allowed himself one long taste of the velvety wetness.

When he dragged his mouth away, he saw a tear trickle beneath the blindfold. Had he hurt her too much?

"Is it over?"

He brushed the tear from her cheek. Why? Why

did he need this? "Are you going to run away again?"

Her head shook. "No, Master. Never again."

He almost believed her. Almost.

"Good." He lifted her by the waist, so slender his fingertips practically touched, reminding him again that she needed to eat more. "We're almost done. Lay back." He nudged her, steadying her as she drifted toward the table. Unable to resist, his hands slithered up her torso and palmed her breasts. Smaller than fashionable, they fit perfectly, the nipples nestling in the center of his palm.

God's blood, this was sweet torture. Her legs draped over the table; her pussy hovered on the edge, bright pink and glistening.

With a foot, he dragged a chair over and settled himself. Muffling a groan, he dragged his hands from her breasts and kneaded her thighs. As he pushed them wide, he steeled himself. Anna had hated this more than anything else. Kathleen probably would, too, but he couldn't help himself. He wouldn't fuck her, but he had to have something to ease the ache.

Her whimper scraped at his focus. He blocked the sound.

Mouth dry, he lowered his head and touched his tongue to her pussy. She jerked, then stilled.

Honey mead. She tasted like honey mead. Smelled just as heady. Felt like silk covered velvet.

Drunk with need, he sipped and savored every drip, every moan, every quake of her muscles. A musical moan and whimper urged him to greater effort. Hungry, he lapped at her core, licking the swollen folds, sucking the tip of her womanhood until she shuddered and bucked against him.

Still he couldn't stop. Like the lone treat he allowed himself each day, she was as delicious as lemon cheesecake, velvety against his tongue, tart and sweet at the same time. Unlike that daily indulgence, he'd only get to taste her once, so he teased and taunted, breathing in the need and desire, stoking the fire until they both threatened to incinerate. He held her still, fingers clamped over her thighs, and gloried in the desperate flex as her legs strained for release.

Release. He'd get none. But he could live with that. The thrill thrummed through him already. Life rushed through his veins as intoxicating as the finest brandy. He'd milk her until she surrendered. Just once, he'd demand her total submission.

Pausing, he lifted his head and inhaled the scent of her desire, earthy and tart. As his breath rushed out, her quim quivered, and she threw her head from one side to the other. The nest of reddish curls blended into the brilliant color of her skin.

He could eat her forever. But she'd never let him. Soon, she'd hate him.

He released one thigh. Too dazed, she didn't move, just lay before him panting with need, her nub pulsing and dripping.

"Come in my mouth, Kathleen." Hoarse, the command hovered over them. His head dropped between her thighs. He sucked the hot nub into his mouth. A scream echoed. Gently, he bit down and slipped his fingers in alongside his tongue. Stripped of control, her fingers tangled in his hair, pulling and pushing at the same time, her body jerking. Triumph raged through him as powerful as the hot wet pull of her pussy.

He could take her. She'd let him. She'd let him do anything right now. His own need pounded, his cock marble-hard, balls so tight a single touch would cause them to explode.

Tempted, he beat down the urge again. She might look like she wanted him. She might even want it enough to beg, but she wouldn't when the effects faded. Already, he could feel her withdrawing, her muscles slackening as the onslaught of sensation ceased. She no longer tore at his hair. Her fingers slowed, then released him, the need no longer forcing her surrender. Soon, her mind would rule her body again. And she'd detest him. He'd not make it worse by breaking his promise. No marital relations, he'd said.

Saddened, he laved one last taste and eased his fingers from her heat. He squeezed his eyes shut while he dragged in one final memory and planted a gentle kiss where he'd bitten.

Then he lifted himself from his knees and stripped off her blindfold. Dazed, she stared up at him, wide-eyed and panting. A final shudder rocked her body.

Then she burst into tears.

Chapter Four

"Good morning, Alfred."

Katy edged into the breakfast room as she greeted the butler. As usual, a sideboard sent delicious smells into the air, the silver covers unable to hold in the tempting scents. This morning, maple dominated the room, wafting from a large bowl of what she suspected was oatmeal.

She took her usual seat in front of the window where the sun warmed her back. Disappointment warred with relief that the duke's chair was empty.

"Has the duke eaten already?" As she lifted her napkin, she glanced at Alfred. Back toward her, he lifted each cover, checking the contents of the plates and bowls, while Stanley stood nearby, ready to serve.

"I don't believe so." The curt tone caught her attention. She cocked her head and studied the ramrod stiff form.

Alfred hadn't greeted her.

He set a plate before her. Scrambled eggs and buttered toast, just like every morning. The first morning, she'd been surprised. Butlers didn't serve. But she'd quickly realized Alfred wasn't a normal butler. Every morning, he personally served breakfast, just as he had when Jeremy was a boy and he a mere footman. She'd looked forward to the meal each morning since. It was as close to being home as she could hope to be.

Now, with practiced moves, he positioned a bowl of strawberries just above and to the right of the plate, then a spoonful of clotted cream plopped atop it. "Will you have oatmeal this morning, Duchess?"

Her stomach tightened at the cold formality, even more than it had when she woke and realized she'd have to face the duke after last night. Alfred never called her Duchess. She'd asked him to call her Katy that first day. He'd resisted but finally used her name in private after she'd begged him to do so.

"No, thank you, Alfred." Katy stared at the eggs. What little appetite she'd had was gone.

When she'd awoken, she felt wonderful. After days with little to no physical activity, the tension and *punishment* of the night before had drained her completely. The emotions, and the overwhelming sense of relief had drugged her, resulting in a sleep so deep she doubted she'd moved after the duke placed her in bed.

Her entire life, she had watched men and women sneak off into the shadows only to return with smiles and contented expressions. She'd listened during the night while her da and stepmother coupled, holding her thin pillow over her ears to shut out the noises of pleasure. When she looked for a similar connection and let most of the village boys kiss her, Da found out and called her a whore. She'd even made the mistake of letting Dean put his hand on her breast. That error had convinced him he wanted to marry her. Those few encounters left her mystified that anyone wanted more. When she'd married George, she'd asked him to tup her, more to prevent an annulment than because she'd wanted it. It had proven less distasteful than she'd feared, but she'd had no desire to repeat it.

What the duke had done to her erased any concerns she was frigid. She understood now why people searched it out. It had made her feel things she'd never felt.

The sound of tea sloshing into her cup called her attention back to Alfred. His face was inscrutable, the way she knew most butlers should be, his movements automatic and precise.

"Are you angry with me, Alfred?"

"That would be inappropriate, Duchess." He turned away, setting the teapot back on the sideboard, placing the tea cozy over it. When he turned back, he held a small plate with slices of lemon. "Lemon, I assume, Your Grace?"

Inappropriate. Not *no*, not *of course not*, no encouraging noises to tell her she was being silly.

A flicker of a frown marred his forehead, then disappeared. He squeezed the lemon into the tea, stopping without awaiting her indication it was enough. He always waited, either verbally asking or at least watching for a gesture. But not today. He squeezed then stopped. "You should eat, Your Grace. The duke will not be happy if you don't."

He turned away, returning to stand beside the sideboard, and stared at the wall behind her.

Katy's hands fisted in her lap, and she clenched her teeth. If the duke wanted her to eat, he could tell her himself.

Her gaze shot toward the empty chair at the end of the table. Alfred had said he hadn't eaten, but it was late. By now, he'd usually appeared and finished eating. The few times she'd slept late, he'd still been here, almost as if he waited until she came down before he left. On the increasingly infrequent mornings when she'd felt too nauseous to eat, he'd frowned at her and ordered her to eat anyway. Between him and Alfred, they'd pushed dishes at her until she relented and forced food past her lips.

But now, when she wanted him here, he wasn't.

She blinked away angry tears, surprised at the sudden prick of emotion. Why wasn't he here? "Have you seen the duke this morning?"

Alfred's gaze flitted toward her, then resumed studying the ruby brocade wallpaper. "Yes, about an hour ago."

"But he didn't eat?"

"No."

After waiting for more and realizing it wasn't coming, Katy lowered her gaze to the table and gnawed at her lips. The strawberries taunted her. She'd mentioned missing fresh berries one morning. The next day, there had been strawberries, blueberries, and gooseberries. She didn't know if it was Alfred or Jeremy who had arranged it.

Now, Alfred was angry with her and the duke was avoiding her. Because she'd run away? "Why are you angry with me, Alfred?"

"It wouldn't be my place to be angry with you, Duchess."

Her jaw tightened. She balled up her napkin and threw it on the table. "Bull-beef!" At least that got his attention. His eyes widened. "Your place or not, you're mad at me. Why?"

His form stiffened, adding a half-inch to his height. His eyes locked on the wall again, and his nostrils flared.

She narrowed her eyes. The only time she'd seen Alfred angry was when he talked about the first duchess and how she'd treated the staff. And how she'd hurt Jeremy. Guilt churned in her gut.

"Is it because I ran away?" Someone must have told him, but Jeremy hadn't seemed hurt by it. "Gregory told you, didn't he?" Jeremy hadn't. She didn't know how she knew; she just did.

"Gregory isn't here to tell me." Anger radiated from him, the words pushing through his teeth. "I dismissed him this morning."

"What?" Katy stared in shock. "Why?"

Alfred finally looked at her, his brown eyes condemning. "Because the duke ordered it. The duke ordered him to keep you safe. He failed. The duke doesn't abide failure."

"Oh my God." Katy slumped in her chair. Guilt twisted her gut, ripping away the anger.

As usual, she hadn't considered all the consequences. Her punishment had been easy. The duke had spanked her, but he'd also pleasured her, and when he wrapped her up in his cloak and carried her out of the tavern, nestled against his heat, she'd felt forgiven and cherished. He'd tucked her into her soft, warm bed, whispering it was over and she'd never have to think about it again, that he'd never hurt her again.

But Gregory wasn't forgiven. The duke had punished him. Because of her. Just as they would punish her brother if anyone learned what she'd done. She had to fix this. "Do you know where he is?"

****

Jeremy glowered at the empty expanse of the room

chosen for the nursery. Situated between his room and Kathleen's quarters, the location was ideal, but the room felt lonely and bereft of happiness. Painted a dandelion yellow with green trim, it should have felt cheerful and airy. On this side of the house, morning sunshine streamed through the windows, but all it did was highlight the dust stirred up by his entrance.

Stripped of furniture after Anna died in childbirth, the hole from his fist still marred one wall. Anna had told him the child was George's, but like now, he'd vowed to treat the child as his own. That the boy had died, too, hurt more than he'd thought possible.

Just like Katy's tears last night had stripped him of any false hope she might accept him and his vile needs.

His hands fisted at his side. The quiet sobbing had soaked his shirt until they arrived home. By the time he'd tucked her in, his heart had drowned.

His balls still ached though. Her tears had robbed him of the ability to deal with it. Withholding his release was a penance for selfishly taking her pussy in his mouth and making her cry. Not joining her for breakfast was another. He hadn't realized just how much he enjoyed seeing her every morning.

With a sigh, he pushed the thought aside. The room needed a new coat of paint. Maybe violet. Would Katy want to pick out the furniture? Anna hadn't. She'd insisted he do it, but maybe Katy would want to make the choices. Would she let him help?

"Your Grace?"

Jeremy shook his head and closed his eyes. Now he was conjuring her voice, a result of no sleep and his need to torture himself. His prick stirred, imagining a rosemary and lemon scent that wasn't there. How was he going to endure the next seven months? He never should have tasted her. Now, he was starved for more.

"Jeremy?"

His eyes snapped open, and he whirled toward the sound.

Clad in an orange day dress that had brightened Anna's blonde features, Katy stood in the doorway, draped in shadows. The color was hideous on her. Her expression crippled him though. Eyes downcast, hands wringing, she looked as if she wished she were anywhere but here.

What did he expect? Anna's voice echoed in his mind. He'd debased her, making her submit well beyond the point of forgiveness.

"Katy?" Afraid to make things worse, Jeremy remained where he was. "Do you need something?"

She stepped into the room, into the sunlight, and lifted her face, the way she did when she was afraid. The way she had last night when she offered to suck him.

Tensing, Jeremy's cock stiffened. Damn his urges.

Her throat rippled, pale alabaster reflecting the harsh sunlight, until her gaze brushed over him. Then a flush of pink flooded her face. He turned away, but not before her teeth bit her bottom lip, sending another bolt of desire straight to his groin.

The rustle of the ugly orange silk scraped his ears. Rosemary drifted over, strangling him with need. "Alfred tells me you dismissed Gregory."

"Yes." He gritted his teeth. He'd almost relented until he pictured Katy's hand in the claws of the man in the tavern.

He heard her move closer but still hissed when her

hand touched his shoulder. "Please reconsider."

"No." He pulled away, too hungry with the need to reach out and trap her hand, to drag her against his hard length. This was why he hadn't gone to breakfast. His control had evaporated. Even now, he wanted to throw her onto the cold, hard floor and fuck her until she screamed.

"Please." The breathless request hammered through the pounding of his blood.

Katy circled around, her hand burning through the thickness of his jacket and shirt, branding him. The whisper of her gown stole through the rasp of his breath, promising untold joys if he just ripped the fabric from her. Sunlight fell on her face, exposing the curve of her cheek, revealing the plea in her eyes, the raw redness where her teeth abraded her lip. "Don't punish him. It wasn't his fault."

Jeremy didn't dare move. Her heat swirled over his front, teasing his impatient cock. He could see the swell of her breasts above the neckline, smell the lemon and rosemary. If he dipped his head, he'd be able to taste her mouth, nip the tender flesh of her lower lip, devour her breath.

"He let you get away." It didn't sound as harsh as it should.

Her other hand fluttered along his ribcage. He inhaled. His prick jerked.

"It was my fault." Her touch hurt, slipping down slowly, following the line of his lapel, down toward his stomach. "He trusted me. I used it against him. I'm the one you should punish."

His whole body froze at the word, then in a flash, his blood sizzled. Her hand traced along his waistband.

89

The top button on one side of his fall released, her fingers brushing it loose.

When her hands grasped the sides of his waist and she slipped to her knees, his eyes widened. Another button disengaged.

"Katy." Hoarse, his voice formed her name, but nothing further followed. His hands clenched, nails biting into his palms, but he couldn't move. He didn't know what she was doing, didn't know how to stop it, knew he'd regret it if he did.

She gazed up at him, a question in her eyes.

He ought to make her stand. The floor had to be hard and icy.

Another button popped open, then another. Cold air rushed in, but he didn't care.

"I know you said you could hire a whore. And I know it isn't worth that much. But if I do this, would you give Gregory his job back?"

Jeremy swallowed. She knelt before him, his stiff cock inches from her lips. Her eyes implored, deep green with red-gold lashes that swept over crimson cheeks with each blink. Her tongue slipped out and moistened her glistening lips.

His cock jerked. Molten desire slammed through his veins.

This was wrong.

"Christ, Katy." Unable to resist, his fingers uncurled and slipped along her scalp, pulling the pins from her hair. Molten, the copper curls flowed over her shoulders, reaching out to lick his cock, shooting flames through his veins. His hands burrowed into the tresses, pulling, tugging, yanking her head back farther.

A strangled gasp echoed through the room, but her

eyes remained locked on his as submissive and entreating as in his dreams.

"Hold your hands behind you," he said, sure the words would choke him.

As ordered, she clasped her hands. Her breasts pushed out, nipples pebbling through the silk. His free hand slid along the neckline, dragging it over the creamy curves. Flesh spilled out, one mound after the other until both were exposed.

He pinched each nipple, twisting, mesmerized by the tiny ruby knobs and the accompanying hiss of pain.

"Gregory isn't worth this." His hand squeezed one breast. A perfect fit, round and soft, it molded to his touch. Despite being tight, the nipple hardened more. "Are you sure you want to do this?"

"Yes, Master." Her eyes sparkled, and her lips parted in promise. Warm, moist breath hit his cock in ever quickening beats, enveloping the hardness.

A surge of jealousy made his teeth grind. That she'd do this for Gregory was wrong. That he'd let her was worse. But he'd lost control the minute she dropped to her knees.

The hand wrapped in her hair tightened and twisted until her eyes widened.

"Lick me." He pulled her head closer. His own fell back at the first touch. With a strangled moan, he closed his eyes. Her tongue stole any remaining control, teasing pleasure with each swirl of the tip.

When her lips circled his engorged head, his grip loosened. His strength drained away, then surged back up to lock his legs. As soft as velvet, her mouth wrapped around his cock, sliding the entire length. Another groan leaked out as he hit the back of her throat. His hips rocked. Pleasure exploded. His fingers bit into her skull, dragging her back before she suffocated. No way he'd let that happen. Her mouth felt too good. His cock thought otherwise and surged forward, following the path of her head.

No! He forced his hips to obey and dragged his cock out. His grip slipped. Her mouth moved forward, swallowing him again, drowning him in pleasure.

"Oh, God, Katy." His voice shook as much as his body. His hips hammered into the softness, sliding into the moist heat as effortlessly as the sun pierced the sky.

She shouldn't be doing this. He shouldn't be letting her.

If only he didn't want it so badly. If only he wasn't already so close. His balls tightened, desperate to prolong the ecstasy, demanding to finish. With a final plunge, his cock exploded against the back of her throat, reveling in the slight gag before slipping deeper.

Wave after wave of glorious release hammered through him. His head fell back, fingers curling through her hair. Powerless, he groaned. An instant later, a shock of cold air rushed in to replace the heat of her mouth.

His legs buckled. Icy hardness slammed his kneecaps. One hand slapped on the floor to steady him. It felt even icier than he'd imagined.

When he opened his eyes, Katy gazed back, a concerned look in her mossy green eyes. Hands still clasped behind her, hair gloriously disheveled, her breasts heaved and a flushed sheen spread over her skin. As he watched, her lashes fluttered and her head dropped. The pink flush turned scarlet.

What was wrong with him? Had he really let her

suck him like a whore? In exchange for something he should have done merely because she asked?

"Get out." His voice rasped, unwilling to see the look she'd give him once she realized how despicable he was.

****

Three days later, overwhelmed and more confused than she liked to admit, Katy stood in the center of her sitting room while the dressmaker the duke hired tortured her with pastel gauze and sheer white laces. Clad in a shift so thin it hid nothing, Katy yearned to hug her arms tight to her chest, both to hide her lack of curves and to minimize the goosebumps lining her arms, but every time she did, Madame Batiste scolded her as if she were a three-year-old.

Batiste, my ass. More like Madame Bat.

The fat tyrant's ass reminded her of a hay bale draped in velvet as she leaned over to paw through a trunk of fabric. Madame Batiste was no more French than she. Her accent slipped every time she spoke to her assistant, Clara, a young frightened thing who scurried faster than a chipmunk.

"Over there," Madame Batiste snapped, pointing at a flimsy gauze. "The orange one." Under her breath, the old harridan muttered yet another disparaging remark about the poor girl.

Scattered around the room, bolts of exquisite fabric covered every surface in the room. Ribbons and fashion plates peeked out beneath folds of silk and brocade. A dream come true, Katy itched to fondle each scrap. So far, Madame Bat hadn't let her touch a thing. Her gaze lingered on a brilliant emerald silk deemed too vivid for her coloring. If given her choice, she'd fashion a ball gown with it, modify the pattern Madame Bat discarded as too old-fashioned. Instead, the supposedly renowned modiste insisted on pale colors, flimsy fabrics, and styles that made Katy blush.

Clara dragged the bolt over but tripped when Madame Bat threw a hatbox into her path. Cursing, Madame Bat's claw-like hand swooped out to strike the poor girl.

Katy snared her fat fingers and wrenched her arm back. "Touch her again, and I'll see you fired."

Too stupid to back off, Madame Bat narrowed her eyes and lifted her chin. It did nothing to hide the rolls of blubber. "The duke hired me. He gave me *carte blanche*." She pronounced it *cart-e blank*.

Katy drew a fortifying breath to point out that Madame Bat had described her own mind, but a niggling of doubt stopped her. She pushed both thoughts aside. The Bat wouldn't understand her, and the duke was either a coward or a beast. After an hour standing as still as a marble statue while Madame Bat picked the worst colors and ugliest fashions, she'd had enough.

"It's *carte blanche*," Katy enunciated. "And I'm his duchess." Her voice rose since the woman only responded to aggression. "Do you really think he's going to take your side over mine?"

"Is there a problem here?"

Both women's heads spun toward the door. Katy's breath hitched. Clad in a sapphire jacket over dove gray pantaloons that hugged his thighs, the duke stood in the doorway. A frown furrowed his brow, arms crossed over his chest. A shiver of awareness raced through her.

She'd not seen him since the day after the tavern.

Every meal had been a solitary one, and when she asked, she'd been told he left before she'd risen. At first, she'd been relieved, glad to avoid the embarrassment. The relief had quickly changed to doubt and confusion.

Had she imagined the entire night? Or had he been so disgusted by her actions the next morning that he couldn't bear to look at her?

Silvery eyes sliced into her, skimming over her near naked form.

Dread settled in her stomach, roiling and sour like rotten bread.

"The duchess…how do you say it…makes a doubt about the choices I make."

"Is that so?" The duke's expression cleared, and he turned into the genial gentleman she remembered from their first encounter. He sauntered forward and eased himself into the one chair not buried in dressmaking accouterments. Lounging back, he settled one Hessian clad ankle over his knee. With a wave, he added, "Please, let me see what you've chosen."

Mortified, Katy stiffened her spine while Madame Bat beamed and draped various fabrics over her. Handing corresponding plates to the duke, the woman prattled in pseudo French and crooned over the wonderful designs she planned.

Despite his periodic glances at the designs, every look he directed at Katy heated her skin. Her nipples pebbled, and a tingle settled in her loins. To her relief, the duke didn't seem to notice.

Most of the fabric Madame Bat hung over her did nothing to hide her near nakedness. The fashion plates depicted gowns stuck to curvy limbs, as if the women had just bathed, adding to her embarrassment. While no prude, the thought of appearing in public in the designs and fabrics Madame Bat had chosen horrified her as much as memories of how she'd reacted to the duke's punishments.

His smile and periodic nods stole any hope of reprieve. He fingered fabrics in a way that sent ripples through her and quietly asked questions about the trims and styles that further degraded her confidence.

When he handed the last fashion plate to Madame Batiste and stood, Katy's shoulders drooped.

"Clara, please pass a robe to the duchess." He circled the room, reaching out to stroke some of the bolts Katy desired while the young girl complied.

Katy snatched the robe, tossed it over her shoulders, and tugged the belt tight. Tears pricked her eyes.

Stop it. It doesn't matter what you wear. He doesn't want you. He was only punishing you.

When the duke ambled over and forced her chin up with a light touch, her breath caught once again. His eyes slid over her face as unreadable as ever.

"Madame Batiste," he said, eyes glancing at the fabrics she yearned for most. "Your services are no longer required. You'll be paid for your time, but I'm afraid you won't be clothing my wife."

Madame Bat gasped, and Katy's eyes widened. The duke's lips curved, then he spun and started pointing.

"Leave these bolts." He indicated the forest green, the deep rose, the purple, and others Katy had coveted. "Clara, I'd like to offer you a position in my household."

"What?" Madame Bat screeched with outrage. "How dare you!"

"How dare you?" the duke yelled, rounding on the fat woman. "I saw how you treated her and my wife." He stomped over and glared at the dressmaker. "My wife is a duchess. You dismissed every suggestion she made and chose gowns a strumpet would wear. Your assistant jumped to do your bidding and still managed to smile at my wife and treat her as she deserves. Clara isn't a slave, and no woman is mistreated in my house. If you hadn't already managed it because of the way you treated the duchess, you would have lost your sale the minute you raised your hand to Clara."

Katy gaped, as speechless as Madame Bat and Clara. The duke oozed power and control. Aside from raising his voice, the only sign of agitation he showed was a slight tic in his forehead. Katy shifted, discomfited by the thrill settling low in her abdomen.

"You won't need Clara, anyway." He bent and retrieved a bolt of white muslin and passed it to Clara. "By the time I'm done, you'll be lucky if you see another customer. You assuredly won't see anyone with noble blood. Now get out. Clara will package up your goods."

No one moved, aside from Madame Bat's mouth opening and closing like a dying fish, until, with an outraged huff, she heaved her girth toward the door. The duke followed, gone as quickly as he'd come.

****

You can't avoid her forever. Be a man and face her. The worst that can happen is she'll pretend you don't exist.

Was four days long enough? Or was it too long?

Was she stewing with hate and revulsion?

Stopping in the hall, Jeremy straightened his waistcoat and ran his hand through his hair. He hadn't been able to read Kathleen the previous day. Aside from the flash of anger at Madame Batiste, she'd resembled an ice queen, even more statuesque than usual. He hadn't intended to speak to her, afraid of how she'd react to him, but the witch's disrespect had overruled his sense.

A tinkle of silver and china drifted from the morning room where breakfast was served. It was a soothing sound, one he hadn't heard in a long time. He hadn't realized just how quiet and dead the house seemed since his second wife's death. Sarah hadn't enlivened the place as much as Kathleen. Sarah had been reserved, a match based purely on social status and family ties. When she died two years after the wedding, he'd been relieved. The few attempts he'd made to beget an heir on her had been half-hearted and unsuccessful.

A soft laugh lured him forward. His cock, as usual, stood up expectantly. Ignoring it, he strode through the door.

Her laugh halted. His prick cowered, then died.

"Good morning." He bowed, as deeply as if she had been born a duchess.

Somehow, she had modified one of his dead wife's dresses so it looked just as fashionable today as it had five years ago. A mint green, the gown had washed out Sarah's coloring. On Kathleen, it enhanced the little color her skin contained. She'd added a creamy lace chemisette that circled her neck. Red curls tumbled around her face, escaping the knot designed to restrain them. Lace tickled her hands where she'd added detail to the sleeves.

A deep blush spread over her face, and he recalled a similar blush spreading over her entire body when he punished her. Her eyes slid over him, teeth catching her bottom lip. Discomfited by the unexpected appraisal, Jeremy dropped into his chair and slapped his napkin over his lap. Never content to lie low, his prick stirred, ever hopeful.

"Good morning, Your Grace." Kathleen's color deepened, and her gaze flipped toward her plate.

Bloody hell, he was in trouble. Try as he might, he couldn't block the image of her submission.

Alfred saved him, setting The Morning Post at his right hand, as he did every morning.

"All things considered, I think it would be allowable for you to address me as Jeremy." He glanced at Alfred, requested coffee, then turned his attention back to her. With a deep breath, fully expecting a set down, he asked, "May I call you Kathleen? In private only, of course."

He should have asked before, instead of assuming.

She blinked. A rush of hope filled him when the blush darkened once more. His prick perked up a little more and lifted the napkin.

"I…" Her forehead wrinkled, and her lip disappeared behind her teeth. Then she lifted her chin and looked him straight in the eye. "Katy, please. If you don't mind. Kathleen is what my da calls me when I've done something wrong."

"I see." He didn't really. All he saw was the most beautiful woman in the world, looking at him with a challenge in her eyes. He didn't dare read into it. For all he knew, her father was a gentle vicar whose idea of discipline was a verbal dressing down.

"I'd also like to thank you. For yesterday."

Jeremy scowled while Alfred placed his usual fare before him—a poached egg, two sausages, and the one sweet Jeremy allowed himself each day. Today, it was an orange scone dripping with honey. Combined with the scent of lemon wafting from Katy's teacup, his balls tightened.

Stop thinking about it. It's never going to happen.

"There's no reason to thank me." He forced himself to focus. "I chose Madame Batiste for a reason." It had been a test, arranged before Katy ran away. One that might have been a miscalculation on his part.

"You're a duchess, now," he continued. "I suspected Madame Batiste might hone in on your lack of confidence. She's…not known for her deference. I wanted to see how you'd deal with it, and I also wanted it known it won't be tolerated. By this time tomorrow, the Ton will be abuzz with the story. Probably a nauseating number of times. And they'll know anyone who disrespects you will deal with me." He didn't mention he'd told Alfred to make sure the story made the rounds.

Katy stiffened, her posture as stiff as his cock had been three nights earlier.

"You needn't worry." As icy as her posture, the words stripped Jeremy's burgeoning hope. "In fact, you needn't bother with a new modiste. You can cancel the tutor as well. I won't be attending any functions where I might embarrass you."

Jeremy started to protest, then snapped his jaw

shut. When would he learn? For a man whose manners were emulated by most of the aristocracy, he had a knack for saying the wrong thing. For once, he'd shut up and not make it worse.

He stared at his breakfast, no longer hungry.

Alfred broke the heavy silence, clearing his throat. "I don't believe the duke meant to insult you, Your Grace."

Her gaze flitted back and forth. When her eyes settled, he offered an apologetic smile and reached for her hand. She snatched it away.

"Alfred's right. I wanted to protect you. The Ton is like a pack of wolves. If they think they can hurt you, they will."

"Perhaps it would be best if they don't get the chance then." With a toss of her head, she reached out to lift her teacup. The bone china chattered until she lifted the cup. Her hand and lip trembled before the cup met her lips.

Protectiveness surged up, hardening his resolve.

"No. It wouldn't be best." No one would hurt her. "You're just as much a lady as anyone and more than most. If anyone dares imply otherwise, they'll see their mistake soon enough. But you're right about the tutor. You don't need one. Emily can teach you any fine points you need to know."

"And what if I'd rather not? What if I don't want to lie and pretend I'm something I'm not?" The teacup clattered into place.

This time, she let him capture her hand. It fisted, but not in time to hide the flutter of fear. He stroked her thumb and took courage when the fingers relaxed.

"Give it a month." He squeezed her fingers. "If you

hate it, I'll not ask you to stay." Her eyes flew wide open and locked on his as surprised by the offer as he was. "I won't let you go, but if you like, I'll send you to one of my country estates. You and the child can live there in peace."

Where the idea had come from, he had no clue, but having uttered it, he realized it made sense. He'd get a month to win her. And he'd have a month to decide if he could control his urges.

She shook her head and pulled her hand away. It disappeared beneath the oak table. He resisted the urge to push. He'd given her no reason to trust him, and he'd just reversed himself for no apparent reason. She needed time to think about it.

Her eyes fluttered, and an uncomfortable silence descended on the table. For once, his manners deserted him. Afraid he'd unwittingly insult her again, he said nothing and picked up his fork.

Finally, Katy spoke. "Are you going to read that?" She nodded toward the paper.

Normally, he did, but he pushed it toward her. He'd rather watch her, and if he intended to make a go of this marriage, it wouldn't hurt to spoil her a bit.

She rewarded him with a shy smile and then leaned toward the inked page. Jeremy cut up his sausage and prepared to eat. From his vantage point, he could make out many of the headings; advertisements for the theater, a short article on diseases of the chest and lungs, an announcement of royal fireworks scheduled in four days. Katy scanned the first page, her lip gently tucked under her teeth, oblivious to his regard.

Or so he thought. Until he noticed that, every now and then, her light-colored lashes swept up, her head cocked slightly, and the color in her face deepened.

Cautious optimism curved his lips, and he began to eat, appetite restored. For whatever reason, she seemed ready to accept her situation. He'd not risk ruining it by staring like a lovelorn suitor.

The sounds he associated with home resumed. Silverware clinked against china. Alfred shuffled about refilling the tea and coffee cups. Katy's skirt swished as she shifted, and the paper crinkled as she turned the page. The tension in his shoulders drained away. Maybe he could have a family if he behaved.

Even his cock calmed, only throbbing when a whiff of lemon or rosemary stirred the air. His poached egg and sausage tasted better than he ever remembered, and the orange scone melted in his mouth, tart from the citrus and dripping with sweetness.

The honey taste made him glance at Katy. She was staring at an article, her face whiter than the paper.

"Katy?"

Her gaze snapped toward him.

"What's wrong?"

"Wrong? Nothing's wrong." She flipped the paper closed, and a wooden smile appeared. Jeremy eyed the paper, then examined her plate. She'd eaten nothing since he entered the room. A half triangle of toast and a quarter of a scrambled egg remained. The bowl of strawberries with clotted cream perched nearby, untouched.

"Eat your breakfast." It wasn't the first time he'd given the same order. He'd done it too many times the first few days. He'd ordered strawberries brought in every day, because she favored them. Usually, she scowled at the order to eat.

Today, she picked up her fork and stabbed at the eggs. A yellow blob disappeared into her mouth, followed by a bite of toast. His eyes narrowed and peered at the paper. The letters blurred as he tried to make them out.

"I was wondering," she said as she switched to a spoon and scooped berries. "Would it be all right if I made Clara my lady's maid?"

"You're the mistress of the house. You may do as you please with the servants." At the moment, all he cared about was getting his hands on that paper.

****

A week later, Jeremy led Miles toward the library, eager to hear what his friend had learned of Katy and her family. He had homed in on the article that caught Katy's attention that morning at breakfast readily enough but had decided to leave his questions for later.

A thousand Irish rebels had been put to death and the rebellion had spread to Wicklow and nearby counties. That Katy had family and friends involved and that she worried about them was understandable. In time, he hoped she'd trust him enough to share her concern and let him help, but for now, he'd leave that discussion until they were on better terms. It wasn't worth upsetting the tentative peace settling over them, especially when the information might be gathered from other impartial sources. Like Miles.

"I trust your time in Ireland was fruitful?" he asked as he reached for the handle on the door. His friend's tan had darkened marginally, and his hair curled more than normal. Instead of his usual attire, his jacket resembled a country baron's, threadbare in the elbows with shiny patches. Jeremy suspected he'd worn even less expensive garb while in Ireland, blending in with the lower class.

"In some ways."

Jeremy shot him an annoyed look, pushed the door inward, and stopped. Kathleen perched on a ladder, reaching for a book above her. As he watched, she stretched higher, fingertips brushing against the thick leather spine.

"Kathleen!"

Her head swiveled, one foot sliding on the rung near his face. Heart pounding, he reached up to steady her, but all he could grasp was an ankle.

"Jeremy?" Wide-eyed, she held onto the ladder with one hand and pushed her skirt so she could see him.

"Get down this instant." He didn't even try to temper his tone. How dare she endanger herself and the child?

She blinked, and her gaze wandered toward Miles, but she turned back toward the ladder and obeyed.

"Have I done something wrong?" Feet firmly on the ground, she rotated to face him. She tucked her hands behind her, and after a second of meeting his eyes, her lashes softly fell until he could no longer see the green of her irises. Her bottom lip disappeared beneath her teeth.

"What were you doing up there?"

Her gaze flew back up, incredulous. "I needed that book." She pointed at the offending tome, two inches thick, one shelf above where even he could have reached from that rung.

"And you felt the need to fetch it yourself?"

She glanced around him. "Who else would do it?

There's no one else here."

"Stanley!" She flinched as he bellowed the name of the footman he'd seen in the hall.

Stanley appeared in less than two seconds, bowing.

"Which book is it?" Jeremy ground out, half-sorry when she shrank back.

"Debrett's." She pointed again, a slight frown on her face.

Debrett's? Jeremy stared at her, speechless, while Stanley clambered up and retrieved it.

As if she could read his mind, Katy added, "Emily said I should memorize it. So I don't make any *faux pas*. At the ball."

Now that the danger was past, and Jeremy's mind had processed the fact, he allowed himself to take a deep breath or two. Scaring her wasn't helpful.

"We pay servants a goodly sum of money." She listened intently, her gaze darting at Miles, then firmly back to him. "It's their job to climb ladders and fetch things. As the lady of the house, it's your job to let them."

"But—"

He held up his hand. "No buts. From now on, I don't want to see you climbing ladders, riding horses, lifting boxes, or anything else that might endanger you or our child. Am I clear?"

Her eyes had widened to huge green saucers as he spoke, and she bit her lip, turning the pink flesh to white. Her eyes closed and her head dropped.

"Am I clear?" His voice rose, and her head snapped to meet his gaze.

"Yes, Sir." He could barely hear her. Her hands were wringing as if she'd strangled the words out of them. A sheen glistened when her gaze rose to meet his. "I wasn't thinking. I'm sorry."

With a sigh, the anxiety drained out of him. He palmed her cheek, then let his thumb brush over her abused lip. "And stop biting your lip."

The rosy hue he loved to see washed over her face. "I'll try, Your Grace." Her gaze slipped back behind him, back toward Miles, and the blush grew deeper.

"Don't try," he snapped, irritated that she'd reverted to Your Grace. "Do it."

"Yes, Sir." She dipped into a quick curtsy. Silk rustled and rosemary wafted up, calming him.

Taking the book from Stanley, he passed it to her.

"You don't have to memorize it." She remembered every servant she'd met, along with every one of their family members after she asked about them. "I'll be at the ball with you and will explain who everyone is. And if I'm not there, Emily will tell you."

A wide smile blazed across her face, and she curtseyed. "Thank you, Sir. I feared it was a hopeless task." Her eyes twinkled, and she curtseyed toward Miles. "I'll leave you to your business now."

"This is Miles Brant, the Earl of Beccles. He's my dearest friend."

Miles stepped forward and, with his usual charm, captivated Katy's attention. After a couple minutes exchanging inane conversation, she excused herself and left.

As Stanley and Katy exited, Jeremy sidled over to the cellarette and poured a pair of bourbons. When he turned back, Miles had tossed himself into a chair, a grin stretching across his face.

"What are you smirking about?"

The grin evaporated, transformed into a guileless, wide-eyed look of innocence as he accepted the crystal glass. "Me? What could I have to grin about?"

Miles wasn't innocent or guileless. Frowning, Jeremy's gaze flew toward the door. He hadn't sported the usual hard-on her presence created, but Miles had an uncanny sixth sense for reading people.

It didn't matter. Miles knew his secrets and had similar ones of his own. But it had nothing to do with why they were here.

"So, what did you find in Ireland?"

Miles ignored the question, running a finger around the lip of his glass. "She's quite beautiful."

Jeremy peered at Miles, glass halfway to his own lips. "Obviously, Ireland didn't blind you. What of it?"

"You still planning on a marriage of convenience?"

The question sent a sliver of jealousy snaking through him. "That's none of your business."

"It might be. If you are."

"She's a lady," he snapped, fingers curling around his glass until the crystal bit into him. Miles' tastes tended toward bondage and more acceptable forms of sex play than his. Acceptable enough that women flocked to him. "And she's my wife."

The smirk reappeared. Miles lifted his glass. "Just as well, I suppose. She's not really my type. I like a bit more fight. No need to tie them up if they're willing." He took another sip from his glass, then plunked it on a side table and leaned forward. "I couldn't find out much. Have you talked to George at all?"

"No. If I never talk to him again, I'll consider it a blessing."

Miles shot him a disgusted look. "You might want

to. He may be able to tell you more since he was there longer. The Irish are a close-knit group. They closed ranks on me. Even the butcher, a fellow by the name of Dean Evans, who's as simple as a straight stick, refused to talk. All I could get out of him was that she was supposed to marry him. Said George forced her, but I think it was just his way of convincing himself she didn't want George."

"Will he be a problem?" Jeremy choked back the surge of jealousy. Katy was a desirable woman. Of course, other men wanted her. He'd learn to deal with it, the same way he dealt with the idea she'd slept with George. By ignoring it. That George might have forced her was ludicrous. George didn't have the backbone to force a frog to jump.

"I don't think so. He's not intelligent enough to cause problems, and George did everything right, aside from the fact he wasn't who he said he was. I talked to the priest who married them. Nice man, one of the few who would talk to me. Said her father was insistent that she be married by him and not a Protestant, and he was happy to do it. Seems Kathleen was a lonely child and her father resented her. Looks just like her mother, aside from the red hair. The priest remembered the mother, too. Didn't know anything about her family, but said she was always a lady."

So far, Miles hadn't told him anything useful. "Will the marriage hold up?"

"As I said, George did it right. Father Bannon showed me the license. Fowler, the Archbishop, issued it, and George had a Protestant minister stand in with Father Bannon, so it's as legal as if you had stood in front of both yourself. I paid the Archbishop a visit, too.

Made a donation for you. As thanks for allowing George to act as your proxy. Only way the marriage can be dissolved now is if you declare it a fraud." Miles' forehead wrinkled. "George couldn't have locked it up tighter if he'd tried."

Jeremy hadn't realized how worried he'd been until he exhaled. The tension drained out of him, and he leaned back in his chair.

"I really appreciate you dealing with this for me." He drained his glass, gaze wandering toward the portrait of his first wife. Everything had seemed perfect then, too. Like nothing could destroy what they had. Nothing except his unnatural needs. The last week had lulled him into believing he could make this marriage work though. He focused on work and making sure Kathleen wanted for nothing. She seemed to settle in, working with the housekeeper and engaging with the new dressmaker while soaking up the inane social niceties Emily was teaching her.

Every morning, she poured through the papers, though. She'd asked for a subscription to the *Observer* in addition to the *Post* and *Gazetteer*, and Maggie had found copies of the *Oracle*, *Chronicle*, and various other papers in her room.

"Find out anything about her mother?" Katy rarely talked about family, but the topic of her mother came up often. Aside from her name and the fact that she'd been disowned, Katy knew nothing that helped identify her origins.

"Nothing you didn't already know. She just appeared one day, married to the father. No one knows who she was or how he met her."

"What about the rest of the family?" he asked.

"There any issues there?"

"That's a murkier situation. With all the unrest, no one's talking to strangers. I think her family may be involved in the rebel activities but couldn't confirm it."

Jeremy's lips tightened. He didn't agree with everything the Crown did, especially in Ireland, but he couldn't condone rebellion either. It explained her obsession with the news though. "They were all alive and unharmed when you left?"

"Yeah. I checked on them before I left. You going to tell Kathleen?"

Jeremy shook his head. "No, and I'd appreciate it if you didn't mention it. Somehow, I don't think she'd take kindly to the idea I sent you to spy on her family."

Chapter Five

"Oh, Mum, this gown is perfect." Clara clapped her hands with glee before tucking the last pearl pin into Katy's hair.

Katy stared at the complete stranger in the mirror, afraid to breathe for fear her bosom would pop out. Clara had applied a light dusting of powder to lighten her freckles, adding alkanna root to the powder over her cheeks. The hairpins held her hair away from her face, piling much of it atop her head, with a cascade of curls falling down the back. The net effect softened her features and accentuated her long neck. A deep sapphire blue silk overdress covered with dainty white lace and stray pearls called attention to her long legs. The ivory underdress had a high waist and a low neckline that made her small breasts appear larger than they were.

She looked like a little girl playing dress-up, a fake, a fraud, a colorful counterfeit version of her mother. "I think I'm going to be sick."

She clutched at her stomach, whirling away from the vision in the mirror. During the week, the dread had grown. Emily, who she liked much more than she'd expected, had drilled her on every aspect of polite society. Despite the duke's instructions, she had memorized much of Debrett's, focusing on the families Emily indicated. They had called on Emily's closest friends, practicing the skills needed by a duchess, and attended a few dinners with a carefully chosen subset of the duke's acquaintances. Through it all, she'd felt like an outsider, watching a play in which she wished to participate.

As a result, word of her existence had spread like cholera, resulting in a constant stream of invitations. Aside from the select dinners, the duke had declined them all until Emily declared her ready, then pondered the handful he considered acceptable. Tonight's ball was her official coming out, hosted by the Marchioness of Thetford, a friend of his dead grandmother, and would likely include the Prince of Wales. Nausea had simmered all day. Now it boiled up, burning her throat.

How had she thought herself capable of this charade?

She sank onto the edge of the bed, a keening sound echoing through the blue and white room.

"Shall I send for someone?"

A wash of guilt mixed with the bile. Clara's face furrowed with worry as she pushed a bowl at her mistress. Clara's experience with Madame Batiste had given her the basic skills needed in a lady's maid, but she had no confidence in her abilities or knowledge of how a noble house functioned. She reminded Katy of herself. That and her knowledge of London's underside were why Katy had offered her the position.

"No." Katy forced herself to sit up straight. Emily had worked too hard, and the duke had made repeated comments about how much he was looking forward to the evening. No matter how she felt, she couldn't disappoint them. Besides, Clara's attempts to find information about the Wexford rebels had come to naught, and it was a perfect chance to talk to George. "I'll be fine." She pasted on a smile. "It's just nerves."

She stood and rescued her gloves. Smoothing the white kid leather, she forced herself not to strangle them and turned back toward the mirror. "You've done a wonderful job, Clara. You've made me quite beautiful."

"I fully concur."

Katy whirled toward the voice. The gloves slipped from her grip. Her mouth went dry, liquid pooling between her legs. Clad in a black velvet tailcoat and tan breeches that hugged his thighs, the duke stared at her with the same hungry look she remembered from the tavern.

Clara's deep curtsy sent a rush of heat to Katy's face, sending her into one of her own.

If she couldn't remember her manners here, what chance did she have in a room full of nobility?

He moved into the room. "If you're finished, would you leave us, please, Clara?"

Katy accepted the duke's outstretched hand, surprised to find her own as cold as ice, and rose.

Warm, strong fingers lifted hers to his lips. A featherlight kiss sent a shiver down her spine. "You look…exquisite."

"Thank you, Your Grace." The overwhelming panic receded. The way he looked at her, his eyes lingering on her face before sweeping over her form, almost made her believe him.

"I'm not sure about the neckline, though." His frown stole her confidence.

She'd known the gown was a mistake. The revealing fashions of the day didn't suit her slim frame.

Her neck was too long and her chest too flat. She should have added a lace bib or raised the neckline.

"Perhaps this will help." A black velvet bag appeared, dangling before her eyes. When she didn't reach out, he took her hand, sandwiching the bag between her hand and his. "It's a gift, Katy. Not part of the family collection. They're yours. You may even sell them if you like. Later. For tonight, I'd like you to wear them."

"Why would I want to sell them?" Although he no longer gave her money, she had everything she needed. If she didn't, she asked and it appeared.

He shrugged. "I hope you won't. But one never knows."

It was a strange comment, but he smiled at her with the expectant look of a little boy.

Curiosity spurred her to open the bag. Peering in, she saw a pile of small white balls and the glint of glass. With a gasp, she reached in and wrapped her fingers around them. Dozens of perfectly matched pearls cascaded out. Tiny diamonds winked, strung between the seed pearls on a wire as delicate as a thread. As she pulled it out, it became apparent there was more than one string. A silver bar tied three strings of varying lengths together.

"Oh, Jeremy!" Hushed, the words hovered in the air. Unable to help herself, she bit her bottom lip as tears filled her eyes. No one had ever given her a gift as beautiful.

"Do you like them?"

"Like them? I love them. They're…wonderful." She let her fingers slide along the fragile chains, caressing the tiny balls, then handed the two ends to him. Her fingers trembled as much from surprise as from the rush of desire that shot through her at the touch of his hands. "I… Would you fasten it for me?"

"With pleasure."

She turned back to the mirror as he lifted the chain around her neck. The sight of the two of them stole her breath. His dark umber hair and the strong lines of his face contrasted with her soft curls and the paleness of her skin. His silver eyes glinted and slanted over her cleavage as the iridescent globes slid against her chest. It reminded her of the portrait in the library, with her peering up at him instead of the gorgeous blonde.

Her smile faded. A shudder shook her body as his hands brushed her collarbone.

He'd loved Anna. When she'd asked him about his wives, he'd brushed the questions off, but the mood that settled over him each time Anna's name came up had quickly convinced her to avoid the topic. His smile, rare enough as it was, evaporated, and he went quiet, or he would bark at the staff or vanish for the rest of the day. Mention of Sarah had a much less severe effect, and occasionally he'd even bring her up himself, but Anna's memory punished him.

He'd never love her the same way.

She closed her eyes as another sliver of longing cut through her core. He'd fastened the necklace, but his fingers continued to wander along the bare skin of her neck and shoulders. The ripples of pleasure crowded out the chill of anxiety, warming her from the center out.

He'd never love her, but he wanted her. She'd seen him harden when she entered a room. She'd seen him watching her when he didn't think she noticed. She'd felt it when he punished her.

He never acted on it. Hadn't then or since. But he would, if she had any say in it.

But not now.

"Your Grace?" she prompted as his knuckles brushed her spine. Her knees felt weak, and her focus was fading.

"Ummhmm?" His gaze locked on her chest, his eyes hooded. Warm breath battered her ear, washing in waves over the pearls and her skin. She inhaled, savoring the scent of soap and sandalwood.

"We should go." Her breath shuddered as she exhaled and inched away. She wanted to sink back against him, enjoy the rock-hard evidence of his desire, but the time wasn't right.

First, she had to prove she could be a lady. If she could, she'd worry about the rest later.

The distance, as slight as it was, served its purpose. The duke blinked as if she'd slapped him, and the usual mask settled over his features.

"Yes, we should." He glanced around, eyes sweeping over her once more with an assessing look. A quick nod bolstered her confidence before he dipped to retrieve her gloves. "Do you have a wrap?"

She twisted toward the armoire. Pain lanced her. Her eyes widened, and a strangled gasp exploded.

"Katy!" He grabbed her. "Are you all right?"

She swatted his hands away, burying the pain. "I'm fine. It's just a backache." Gritting her teeth, she straightened. Her hand reached back, rubbing at the spot.

"I'm sending for the doctor." Jeremy locked a hand around her elbow. She frowned and jerked her arm away.

"I'm fine. I just moved too fast." As proof, she knelt and picked up the dropped gloves. The ache in her back twisted again, but she ignored it, plastering a smile on her face. She couldn't miss the ball. Having to suffer through another week of dread would be unbearable.

"I think we should send for the doctor."

"No!" She lifted her chin, the way her momma had when da tried to lord it over her. "I'm going to the ball. You can come with me or you can stay here, but I'm going. If you want to send for the doctor tomorrow, I'll be happy to indulge you, but tonight I have plans."

"The baby's more important."

Katy turned away, screwing her eyes shut as she reached for a pale blue lace shawl. Thankfully, the pain eased, fading away before she turned back.

"Do you honestly think I'd endanger the baby?" she asked, staring at him, careful not to swallow or show any other signs of the fear churning in her gut. She'd been spotting the last two days, but Noreen had spotted through her entire pregnancy with Nora, her youngest. It meant nothing. This was just a backache. She'd rest tomorrow.

She wouldn't lose the baby. She couldn't. Not when she'd decided to stay.

****

"Congratulations on your lovely wife, Your Grace."

Jeremy turned toward the elderly gentleman who had spoken. One of the few men with enough height to tower over him, the Earl of Margate was well into his eighties. He'd been a good-looking man in his day, and Jeremy remembered his grandmother remarking on his

118

impeccable bearing and station, but there was a definite stoop to his frame now. His skin looked pasty and his milky blue eyes had a haunted look.

"Thank you, My Lord. I fear I'm quite taken with her."

"As are most of the men here." The earl's eyes bored into the group surrounding Katy. "Might I inquire where you found her?"

An impertinent question, Jeremy considered whether to answer but found no reason to avoid the truth. The story was already making the rounds, and Margate looked as if he might not have enough time to wait until the gossip mill reached him.

"Ireland. I was buying horseflesh in Wexford County." He'd been in Scotland, which was why he'd sent George in his stead. Anyone who wanted to uncover the lie might manage it, but Jeremy couldn't imagine any reason anyone would care, and it didn't matter.

"Ah, I see." The papery skin in the earl's neck rippled like dry leaves. "Forgive me for asking, but what do you know of her family?"

Jeremy peered at the old man. He'd never spoken with him at any length and, upon reflection, realized the earl's presence tonight was a rather rare occurrence. Rumors said his daughter had died years ago, lost at sea. His only son died a decade later in a hunting accident. Since then, the man characterized as mean and miserly had become a recluse.

But he was here tonight, staring at Katy and asking about her.

"Why do you ask?"

"Just curious. She reminds me of my wife.

Probably just an old man seeing things he wants to see."

Maybe. Or maybe the resemblance was real.

"Her mother was nobility." No sense getting his hopes up too high without some evidence. "Her name was…" With a cock of his head, Jeremy joined the earl in staring at his wife, recalling the conversations they'd had, then turned to watch the earl as he recounted what he knew. "Mary, I think. Her father disowned her. Katy doesn't talk about it much."

"Mary? Are you sure?"

"Let's go find out." Jeremy set his glass on a tray the footmen always had available and patted the earl's shoulder. Bone met his hand and even the gentle pat made him stumble and lean on the cane he carried. The old man was alone and probably lonely. Whether or not Katy was his granddaughter, he deserved a smile and kindness, and Katy never stinted on either.

"No, no." Margate shook his head. "Let her enjoy herself. She doesn't need an old geezer like me spoiling her night."

"Nonsense. I insist. If for no reason than that I'm getting annoyed by all the virile young men showering her with attention."

A laugh bubbled in the earl's voice. "Get used to it, my boy. My Violet was the same way. Couldn't have kept them away if I'd showered her in garlic." He sighed, his eyes devouring Katy as if he were starving. "Violet was blonde, though, with hair as straight as this cane." He thumped the floor. "Margaret, my daughter, was the same. I always hoped they were wrong." He turned to Jeremy, frowning. "Her ship went down, you know. Off the coast of Cornwall."

"I heard that. And I'm sorry for your loss. Come. I'm sure Katy would love to meet you." Not taking no for an answer, Jeremy clamped his hand on the earl's free arm and steered him through the crowd.

Halfway there, Margate stopped to catch his breath. Jeremy waited, scanning the knot of people surrounding Katy, searching for the easiest path.

"Actually, Lexham, I'm feeling a bit tired." The earl began to wheeze and cough, a horrible raspy cough that shook his skeletal frame. "Would it be all right…if I call…on your wife? Tomorrow, perhaps?"

"Of course." Jeremy glanced around, switching direction. "Let me help you to your carriage."

A claw-like grip fastened on Jeremy's arm, surprisingly strong, and halted him. He waited while another coughing bout assaulted the older man. When it passed, Margate straightened and his eyes wandered back toward Kathleen. A sheen brightened his eyes. "May I give you some advice, my boy?"

"Of course."

"Don't squander your time." Jeremy followed his gaze. Katy glanced over and a bright smile slipped over her lips. "She loves you. Don't waste it."

Did she? Jeremy stared at her. She flushed, and her lashes fluttered. Pride and some other emotion unfurled in his core. Hope, maybe. There was no doubt she was the loveliest woman in the room, and he'd seen her win over many of the Ton tonight. Both the Marchioness of Salisbury and the Countess of Essex had commanded him to bring her to Almack's, an order even he didn't dare ignore.

The earl's grip released, and he patted Jeremy's shoulder. "Go dance with your lady. I'm not so old I can't get myself to my carriage."

"Nonsense. The next set doesn't start for another five minutes. I can see you out and be back in plenty of time."

"Your grandmother would be pleased, Your Grace. She always wanted the best for you." Relenting, the earl allowed Jeremy to help him navigate the crush of people, alternating between short comments about Jeremy's grandmother, his own family, now long gone, and cutting barbs aimed at people they passed. Progress was slow, but Jeremy enjoyed the time. Despite his reputation as a hard-nosed curmudgeon, the earl's wit and astuteness appealed to Jeremy. That he regretted some things he'd done was clear, but Jeremy expected he'd experience that trait himself when he reached Margate's age.

After handing the earl off to his footmen and seeing him off, Jeremy turned back toward the ballroom, his step lightened. When they'd arrived, he hovered over Katy, worried that she'd lied about the pain he'd seen on her face before they left. Whatever it had been had passed, overridden by nerves and excitement, but Jeremy hadn't been willing to leave her side until Emily barked at him, banishing him to the other side of the room. He understood why now. Katy had blossomed after he left, relaxing and charming everyone she met. For some reason, he made her nervous.

While ludicrous, the earl's pronouncement that she loved him gave Jeremy the dash of hope he'd lost after he used her mouth like any two-bit whore. He still wanted her, in all the ways that would push her away, but he'd managed to control his desire. He released the need every night, just remembering how she'd dropped to her knees and serviced him.

He'd woo her. If she'd done that, willingly, and didn't despise him, there was hope. Maybe he could temper his needs, take it slow, back off at the first sign of distaste. He could take her as his real wife, in the normal way, by just remembering the pleasure she'd given him.

He wended his way through the crowd, back into the chattering masses. The orchestra had resumed, the soft lilt of violins drifting over the murmurs. The throng parted before him, nodding and dipping as he passed, heading toward the conclave that surrounded Emily and Katy.

His stride halted as he drew closer. The smile stretching over his lips froze.

Where had she gone?

Emily continued to laugh and flirt with the never-ending parade of gentlemen. Ever-popular, she epitomized the ideal lady. Tall enough that men could look her in the eyes but short enough they felt taller, her lush figure appealed to most men. She dressed in the height of fashion, an expense Jeremy considered worth every penny since she put up with George. Tonight, she wore a pure white gown that revealed just enough to lure the men without giving false hope.

Jeremy scanned the group, then his gaze ventured out. The deep blue of Katy's gown was nowhere to be seen. His gaze washed over the line of women lining up for the *contredanse*.

"Looking for your wife, Lexham?"

Jeremy exhaled in relief. "I am." He grinned, until he saw Miles frown. The tightness in Miles' lips transferred to Jeremy's chest. She couldn't have collapsed. Emily would have gone with her if she had. Emily would have accompanied her to the retiring room as well. "Have you seen her?"

Miles nodded, his eyes shuttering as hc handed a glass of bourbon to Jeremy. "You won't be happy." Miles pasted a fake smile on his face as a shy young debutante tripped against him. Petite and pretty, her eyes widened in horror. He steadied her with a soft apology, as if he'd been the one to collide with her, before turning his attention back.

"Tell me."

"She slipped out. To the garden."

"The garden?" Jeremy's gaze flitted toward the glass doors lining the wall. Due to the heat, the doors gaped open, beckoning partygoers to venture out. His jaw clenched. He knew what went on in the gardens. He'd taken advantage of the shadowy corners himself, not to enjoy the company of women, but to escape the attentions of the occasional determined suitor. "Was she alone?"

Miles avoided his eyes, lifting his glass to his lips before answering. "No."

All sorts of emotions bubbled in his chest. Jealousy, anger, hurt. That Miles wasn't offering more scared him, stealing his breath. The rakes had swarmed over her, like bees that scented an endless supply of honey, ready to sting anyone in their way.

"Who?"

"Promise you won't do anything stupid."

"I never do anything stupid."

"You might this time."

"Just tell me." Jeremy's teeth hurt; he ground them

so hard. There were a few he'd kill but not many.

"It might not be what you think."

"No? And how would you know what I'm thinking?" Even Miles couldn't guess he envisioned Katy being raped by an overzealous rake or, worse, repeating what she'd done to him for whatever reason she might consider worthwhile.

"I don't. But the look on your face worries me. And I know there are reasons other than the ones that will come to your mind when I tell you."

"Dammit, just tell me."

Miles sighed. "George. She's out there with George."

****

He would kill George, stomp him into the ground like the snake he was.

Jeremy's blood pounded with as much force as his boots as they hit the stair steps. The air was as stifling as it was inside, laden with the nauseating scent of lilacs. He hated lilacs. They'd been in bloom when his grandmother came out and told him his parents were dead. He could still hear the strident command demanding he not cry and George's reaction when he had. George had pitied him.

George wouldn't pity him now.

Stopping at the bottom step, Jeremy scanned the grounds. Renowned for its gardens, he had played here as a child while Grandma took tea with the marchioness. To the right was the maze he had been lost in for hours, another memory he stomped down. To the left lay the rose garden, where he'd ripped his jacket, earning a different sort of dressing down from dear old Grandma.

God, he hated it here.

He headed straight ahead toward the smoky lights sprinkled over the grounds. Copses of trees littered the area, designed to offer seating for ladies to rest during leisurely walks or for couples seeking a moment or two alone.

Gravel crunched, reminding him to relax his jaw before his teeth shattered. He forced his steps to slow and nodded at the strolling partygoers, a wooden smile plastered on his lips. He'd have to listen for them. It wouldn't do to simply pop his head into the cloistered shadows. He had no desire to embarrass anyone. What others did in private wasn't his concern.

Why had she come out here with George?

Behind him, the sound of The Patriot's Waltz taunted him. He'd looked forward to dancing with her, flaunting the rule forbidding gentlemen to dance with their wives. That they played The Patriot's Waltz now was ironic. Her family was likely anything but patriotic. It amazed him still that he didn't care.

A giggle off to his right captured his attention. A stand of pale white birch trees nestled nearby. In the darkness, the limbs danced, like skeletons waving him forward. Glancing around and seeing no one nearby, he sidled closer.

A male voice filtered out, too deep to be George's.

The crushing tightness in his chest eased. Exhaling, he moved away, following the path, gravel disappearing until his feet encountered pure dirt.

A looming collection of the dreaded lilacs threatened to suffocate him again. He knew a carved stone bench hid in its depths. He'd admired it occasionally after the flowers died, because it curved nicely with ends the perfect height for spanking a woman.

Not hearing anything, he shimmied around the first trunk and peeked through the blooms.

Empty. Except for the mental image of Katy bent over it.

His jaw tensed. There were a few other, similar benches out here.

Thankfully, George didn't enjoy the same abnormal urges he did.

No, George wooed women with soft words and lies, sentiments ladies appreciated.

Jeremy turned his back on the lilac bushes and hurried along the path. He'd told George what would happen if he came near Katy. He'd thought threatening to cut off his funds would be sufficient. He'd thought, despite George's actions, that he loved Emily and his children enough not to jeopardize their welfare. That he was wrong made him sick to his stomach. That George was forcing him to follow through made him want to vomit.

Another burst of quiet laughter assailed his ears. He veered toward it, stepping silently, until another male voice rustled through the fragrant juniper trees. His eyes widened at the whispered suggestion until the woman responded. The voice belonged to a widow even more depraved than he was. With a shudder, he fled, remembering his short liaison with her. She'd wanted to be his puppy, so she could defecate in a locked crate. He didn't enjoy beating puppies.

With a shake of his head, he continued his search, methodically circling the garden one bush at a time. Each hidden copse seemed to hold another couple.

Most merely chatted, a few engaged in activities frowned upon but tolerated. None revealed the people for whom he searched.

The journey allowed his anger to cool, the white-hot ire burning out until it felt more like an ember boring through his center. He still found it hard to breathe, the sticky air filling his lungs with lilac. It wasn't the lilacs that made his chest tight though. It was fear. Fear of what he'd find.

Just as he debated going back inside, deciding that some things were better left alone, he heard her. Off to the side, near a pocket of darkness, nestled an arbor covered with wisteria. Most of the copious purple blooms were dead, their glory spent, but the greenery formed a wall of privacy as impenetrable as stone.

It wasn't enough to block the sound of her pleas. Those shot through the darkness as swift and cutting as a crossbow.

"Please, George. I'll do anything."

Jeremy froze, closing his eyes as if it might help, and slumped against a nearby oak tree.

"I can't, Katy." George's voice held an edge of regret. "And I know what that means. I also know Jeremy will have my head if I do. I can't risk it. If it was just me, I'd do it in an instant, but it isn't. He'll cut me off. Emily and the children will starve."

"Please, George." Jeremy could hear her dress rustle. George's muffled curse sounded like his own oath when she'd offered *anything* in exchange for forgiving Gregory. He opened his eyes, sucking in air, but it didn't stop the image from forming. He might not see them, but he knew what was happening.

"Stop, Katy," George sounded hoarse, but Jeremy

didn't wait to hear more. He'd heard enough.

With heavy footsteps, he turned away and traced his way back to the house. Miles would see her home. He wasn't sure he could look at her again.

****

Katy slipped into the ballroom and glanced around, patting her eyes with the handkerchief George had given her. Hopefully, her eyes weren't too red. She didn't normally cry, but his refusal to help her and his insistence she tell Jeremy everything had been too disappointing. He didn't understand how much it might cost her.

The heat was still stifling, laden with too much perfume, and the sickly scent of sweat assaulted her as she eased past the dancers. Emily hadn't moved, surrounded still by a bevy of young men who vied for her attentions. She couldn't blame them, or George for his refusal. Emily was the sweetest woman she'd ever met, and her looks matched her personality.

As her gaze swept the room, she flipped her fan open and fanned herself. While the entire night had gone better than she hoped, the effort of smiling and greeting hundreds of strangers had taken its toll. Her back ached, her feet hurt, and George had known nothing to ease her worries about her family. She wanted to go home and curl up in a ball.

And now that she wanted to leave, Jeremy was nowhere to be seen.

"Duchess Lexham."

It took a moment to recognize the gorgeous man standing before her. The chestnut hair and chocolate brown eyes seemed familiar, but she couldn't imagine why she couldn't place him. He was too stunning to forget. Almost as tall as Jeremy, he looked her in the eye, and his body was just as sinfully built. An ebony waistcoat topped a pair of forest green pantaloons tucked into glistening black Hessians.

"Lord Beccles? I almost didn't recognize you." She offered her hand at his nod, surprised to find the light kiss he bestowed had none of the effect she felt when Jeremy touched her. It was neither disturbing nor comforting.

"Ah, well, I was hardly prepared to meet a lovely lady the first time we met. It's been years since Lexham House had a mistress. Had I known you were there, I would have made myself presentable before barging in."

His sweeping assessment and piercing gaze left her disturbed. He looked as if he wished to devour her like a marzipan candy.

She snatched her hand away and peered around behind him. "Have you seen Jeremy?"

He stepped back. She inhaled in relief. The lascivious gleam in his eye evaporated, replaced by a faint bored look. "He's gone. He charged me with seeing you home safely."

Gone? He'd left her? Her eyes pricked again. What was with this sudden urge to cry at every turn?

"I see. It's unnecessary, however. Gregory can get me home." She turned her back, horrified that a trickle slipped over her cheek. She wiped it away and lifted her head.

A firm grip snagged her elbow. Whether or not she wished it, she found herself headed toward the marchioness. "On the contrary. The duke was adamant. I'm to see you home and hand you over to Alfred. You should thank your hostess before we leave."

"I need to let Emily know."

"I have already informed Lady Emily."

Instead of her usual annoyance at being ordered about, a sense of the inevitable settled over her. Glad that the ordeal was nearly over, she allowed the earl to guide her. Within moments, they had thanked the marchioness and Katy found herself helped into the carriage. The earl climbed in behind her and stretched out on the opposite seat, and the carriage lurched into motion.

With a sigh, she sank back into the velvet-padded seat. "Where did Jeremy go, do you know?"

The wheels sang over the cobblestones, marking the moment of hesitation. "I believe he's off to see his mistress."

"His mistress?" The words stuck, and her stomach lurched.

The earl didn't reply, but his shoulders shrugged. Hurt, she made no attempt to fill the silence. She hugged herself, squeezing her eyes to stem the tears. The answer rolled around in her head, cycling through with every turn of the wheels.

The earl shifted, cutting through the endless litany, then said, "Read nothing into it. Obviously, I don't know what he's doing, but it's possible he's ending it. I know he's been contemplating it for a while."

"Really? Do you think so?" She doubted it. Jeremy obviously had no interest in her. He'd rejected her few, hesitant overtures.

Miles shrugged again. "It's not really any of my business, but I rarely let that stop me, so I'm going to say my piece. Take it or leave it as you wish."

He turned and looked out the window. The carriage light lit one side of his face, creating a mask-like effect that sent a shiver through her.

"I've known Jeremy since we were boys. We met when his grandmother sent him to boarding school after his parents died. He...had a tough time. Got into a lot of trouble. But we became friends. He'd spend an occasional holiday with me. Him and George. They were very close, but there was always a rivalry between them."

His face shifted as if he recalled memories he didn't share. She waited, starved for the information she hadn't been able to get from anyone else.

Beccles sighed. "Jeremy's happy, or at least happier, since you arrived. I haven't seen that in a long time, so I'm giving you the benefit of the doubt tonight." His gaze turned toward her, hidden in the shadows. "I don't know what you were doing with George in the garden. I can make an educated guess because I know why George married you. I shouldn't tell you, but Jeremy sent me to Ireland after you arrived. I don't really care if you like it or not. All I care about is Jeremy."

Katy stared, her heart skipping a beat. If he knew why George married her, why wasn't she being dragged away in chains? Oh, Mother Mary, was that why Jeremy left? Was the mistress just an excuse because he couldn't bear to look at her? Were the troops waiting at Lexham House?

"Does— Why—" There were too many questions. She didn't know which to ask or how to ask them.

"I haven't told Jeremy, if that's what you're trying to ask. And I won't. As long as this conversation remains between us. Of course, should your family's activities become known, I won't be able to keep silent."

"Why?" Katy pulled out her fan and waved it. The carriage had become much too warm. How much did he know? He'd probably learned that Alex and Brody were up to their eyeballs in rebellion, but did he know what she'd done? "Why even tell me then?"

The earl leaned forward, arms on his knees, hands clasped before him. She shrank back, the scent of brandy and cloves turning her stomach.

"Because I saw something in you the other day. And I saw Jeremy react to it. Because I watched you tonight, and even though I could see you were nervous, maybe even terrified, you never once chewed your bottom lip."

Katy's head shook. "I don't understand. What does that have to do with anything?" She'd tried very hard not to gnaw her lips, because Jeremy had ordered it. But why would this man care?

"Jeremy and I are…different from most men. For me, it's not a problem. But Jeremy's always struggled with it." The earl's leg began to tap, up and down. After a long pause and a deep breath, he continued, "He won't tell you, and I shouldn't, but I'm going to come right out and say it. He likes control. He likes to inflict pain. He likes his sexual partners to beg."

Katy's fan slowed, then stopped. While not ordinary, she'd heard rumors of similar men, and it fit what had happened at the tavern.

"Suffice to say, Jeremy's tortured by it. He's convinced, wrongly, I think, that no woman will tolerate it. But I think you might."

"And you want me to let him hurt me?"

"I don't want you to do anything you don't want. But I don't want you to hurt him, either. Do what you want with the information and consider it when he does things that might not make sense. But stay away from George. There's history there, and nothing good can come of it."

The carriage rolled to a stop, the rhythmic noise of horse hooves and iron wheels grinding to a halt. Katy snapped her fan shut and tucked it into her reticule while the earl leapt out of the carriage. As she descended the step, his grip on her hand tightened.

"We never had this talk, Duchess. Stay away from George. Make Jeremy happy in whatever manner suits you, and your secret stays with me. Hurt him or tell anyone what I've said, and your family's lives become much more complicated and much more uncertain. Do you understand?"

Now that they stood outside the carriage, she turned to look at the earl. In the dim carriage light, shadows darkened his jaw, but his eyes glinted. She recognized the look in his eyes. It resembled what she'd seen in her brothers' eyes when they decided to join the United Irishmen. Determined.

"Yes. I think I do." With a shiver, she turned away. "Thank you, My Lord." Whether she was thanking him for the information or for bringing her home was uncertain, but she rushed up the stairs without waiting.

Was it home? Or was it another place she didn't belong, filled with people who wanted her to conform to their idea of whom she should be and what she should do?

Chapter Six

Katy had a restless night. When she'd arrived home, Jeremy wasn't there. After regaling Clara with as few details as she was able, she had fallen into bed, exhausted and thankful the evening had ended.

The nightmare had plagued her sleep, though, amidst the unrelenting worry about her family and the newer concerns the Earl of Beccles had expressed.

With a concerted effort, she dragged herself out of bed for breakfast.

"Good morning, Your Grace." Katy waited while the footman pulled out her seat, then sank onto the plush upholstery. "I'll have coffee this morning, please, Stanley. With three sugars." She smiled, despite the regret that it was Alfred's morning off.

When Jeremy's customary inquiry about her night didn't materialize, she glanced at him. Impeccably groomed, his snowy white cravat was starched and tied to the point he could hardly turn his head. His glossy hair licked his nape at the perfect length, and a gold watch fob dangled from his pocket. He too looked tired, smudges of gray beneath his eyes, mouth turned down at the corners. Still, her breath caught, sending quivers of anticipation to her core.

"I thought the evening went well," she commented as she spread her napkin over her lap. "Did you enjoy yourself? I was sorry you didn't see me home." It was one of many things that had disrupted her sleep. Each time the nightmare woke her, she wondered where he had gone and why. It bothered her much more than she liked.

"I had other things to attend to." He never looked at her. His eyes scanned the paper in his hand, a frown darkening his expression.

"Yes, so Lord Beccles informed me." Katy smiled and thanked Stanley as he set her coffee and a plate of fluffy blueberry pancakes before her. Visible waves of heat rose from the pile, sending wafts of maple to mate with the coffee smell.

Jeremy flipped the page of the Morning Post, still glowering at the black ink. His plate lay before him, a single triangle cut out of the pancakes, the syrup soaked into the doughy surface. Stanley's murmured offer of a coffee refill betrayed the fact he'd been at the table a while. The other papers, ones he'd normally offer to her as soon as she sat, lay near his elbow, neatly folded.

Katy frowned, a niggling of disquiet adding to the discontent from the restless night. "Is there bad news in the paper?"

"No. Just the usual." He closed the paper, lining up the folds with precision, smoothing the creases as he folded them, then he set it atop the other three. Still not raising his gaze, he lifted his fork and cut into the pancakes. "Stanley, could you ask Alfred to let me know about that shipment of bad wine? And thank Cook for the jam tart. It's especially good this morning."

As he lifted the fork to his lips, Katy realized her usual bowl of berries was missing.

"Are we out of berries?" She'd been insinuating

herself into the workings of the household, looking over the menus and learning the habits of the kitchen staff. Cook often complained about the expense and scarcity of certain items but had said nothing about a strawberry shortage.

Stanley shot a glance at the duke and stammered, "The duke sent them back to the kitchen. Shall I fetch them, Your Grace?"

"It's not necessary, Stanley. The duchess can eat the pancakes."

Gaping, Katy stared at Jeremy. The telltale tic on the side of his temple wasn't pulsing, but the set of his jaw was tight. He hadn't looked at her once, hadn't greeted her or made small talk of any type. Something was wrong.

Slowly, she picked up her fork and poked at the pancakes. Soft and laden with blueberries, all she could find the effort to do was push the fork around on the plate. The pool of syrup turned reddish, like blood drops in water.

Had he seen her with George? Or had she made a horrible *faux pas* last night of which she wasn't aware.

She replaced the fork. The clatter as it hit the table jarred the silence. "Are you angry with me, Your Grace?"

The jam tart hovered before his lips. His brows lowered. "Have you done something wrong?"

"Not that I'm aware of." Her hands twisted in her lap as she reviewed the previous evening. The last time she'd seen him, he'd been helping that old man. They'd disappeared toward the front of the house. That was when she'd cornered George. Sometime between then and the time she returned, he'd left. "If I've done something wrong, please tell me."

Dread twisted her stomach. Her da had punished her this way, pretending she didn't exist because she'd forgotten to churn the butter at the right time or gone off to read a book when he wanted her to take care of some task he'd never mentioned. At times, the silence would last for days.

The duke's chair scraped across the floor, and his frame towered over the table. "Eat your breakfast, Kathleen. Don't make me tell you again." He spun about to leave. Just as he reached the door, he turned back. With a disdainful look, he added, "When you're done, go change. The Earl of Margate will be calling."

"Who's the Earl of Margate?"

His lips twisted. "I believe he's your grandfather. Bring your mother's brooch."

Shock snapped her head toward him. He wanted her to greet the man who'd disowned her mother? Thrown her out because she'd wed a man beneath her? Ignored the letters she sent every year for a decade, begging for forgiveness?

"No. I'll not receive him." Her curls stung her cheek as she shook her head. Jeremy didn't know. She'd never told him. "I hate him."

His feet slammed across the marble floor. She jumped as his hands slapped the table. "I don't care. You'll receive him, and you'll make him feel welcome."

"I won't." It was too much. Nothing could make her do that. "I can't."

"You will. As my duchess, you'll treat him with respect and kindness. As my wife, you'll do as I tell you. Or you can go back to Ireland and find another bastard to take to your bed. I'm sure there's another lonely duke or earl who wants a diversion."

Her head snapped back in shock. She didn't deserve this.

She pushed herself to her feet and threw her napkin on top of the syrupy red mess.

"I'm not a *leanbh*," she said with a glare, reverting to her early Irish tongue. "And I'll not be treated like one. You can't order me about. I'll see who I want. I'll refuse who I want. And I'll eat if and when I want. I'm tired of trying to please you. You're cold and unfeeling. You can lock me up, punish me, do whatever you like, but you'll not make me do anything I don't want to do."

"No." His laugh was harsh. "No, you'll not do anything unless you want it." The tic was pounding in his forehead, his teeth clenched so tight his lips were white. "But you'll do anything for George, won't you? Tell me, Kathleen, did you like it as much as you did with me? Or more? What did you get for your *anything*?"

His hand smashed the table. His plate jumped. Coffee sloshed, a dark stain spreading across the pristine white linen.

Katy froze, her stomach sinking to the floor. He'd seen her. Or heard them. And he thought she'd bargained with George the way she'd convinced him to forgive Gregory?

"No." Strangled, the word died in her throat, and she sank back into her chair. She opened her mouth to explain, but when she looked up, it was too late. He'd stormed out, his tailcoat flying after him like the devils that controlled him.

He wasn't angry. He was jealous. Just as the Earl

of Beccles had tried to tell her in his own twisted way. But his warning had come too late. The damage had already been done.

At least, she knew what she'd done wrong.

It was time to plan her rebellion.

****

It was afternoon before Alfred knocked on her sitting-room door to tell her the Earl of Margate had arrived. Late enough that the duke had returned from whatever business had occupied him the whole morning and late enough that Katy had reined in the simmering emotions that had ruled her all night and all day.

"Show him to the music room, please, Alfred."

Katy turned to survey herself in the mirror one last time. She'd chosen a simple day dress of soft blue muslin and long sleeves with a white gauze fichu to fill in the neckline. Elegant and flowing, it gave her a modicum of confidence, but not enough. Already her hair was escaping the bun and twisted length of muslin designed to keep the rebellious tendrils in check. Despite the outfit, she felt like the forlorn child she'd been when she realized she was the reason her mother had been disowned.

Clutching her mother's brooch, she trudged toward the stairs. As she approached the library door, she slowed and debated her decision. The duke had hidden himself in the room when he returned, telling Alfred he didn't want to be disturbed. By anyone.

Steeling herself for rejection, she fisted her hand and tapped on the door, pushing it open with the other.

He stood at the window, a hand wrapped around a crystal glass. A shaft of sun broke through the clouds behind him, hitting the cuts in the crystal, spiraling off in different directions.

"Your Grace," she began, then changed her mind.

The annoyed frown on his face nearly killed her courage. She needed the man, not the duke.

"Jeremy…" Closing her eyes, she paused. This was harder than she thought. "I have many things I need to say to you," she finally began. "And I will. If you'll listen. But the earl is here now."

When she opened her eyes, he hadn't moved, but the furrows on his face had changed. Relief made her legs weak. He hadn't thrown her out yet. He was listening. "I…I don't think I can do this alone."

With a swallow that felt as dry as eating flour, Katy waited, hoping her eyes showed her plea better than her words. His gaze, still shuttered, circled her face, sending a rush of heat to her cheeks. It deepened when she felt a trickle between her legs. Why did she feel wet every time he looked at her?

The glass thudded as he dropped it on a nearby table, and she exhaled as his first step echoed.

"Are you asking me for help, Katy?"

"Yes." She sucked in a lungful of the reassuring sandalwood she associated with him. "Please. I'm scared."

A sad smile erased any remaining hardness from his face, and he reached for her hand. His lips barely touched her, the effect shielded by her gloves, but she felt it through her entire body.

"You've no need to be afraid. He's going to love you. How could he not?"

Katy's fear fell away. She didn't care if her grandfather loved her. All she cared about was that Jeremy didn't hate her.

****

Jeremy lent what little support she needed, soaking up the pleasure that had swelled through him when she asked, and wished it could be more.

She didn't need him though. After his quick squeeze of her hand for encouragement, she swept into the music room with the same grace she'd exhibited the previous night. Her curtsy, minimal as befit a duchess greeting an earl, was executed to perfection, and her smile revealed none of the hate she'd claimed at breakfast. Like everything she did, it swelled his chest with pride. She'd ordered tea and taken over the conversation as if she'd been born to the role. Satisfied that she had it under control, he'd eased out of the discussion, content to watch her claim her place and act as his duchess.

Too bad his own reactions weren't as appropriate as her demeanor. His cock was as hard as the piano keys. As soon as she'd entered the library, it had swelled to a crippling extent. When she'd pleaded, it sent shards of pain through his balls. Every step from the library to the music room had been a punishment. The pain had traveled up, crushing his heart as tightly as his balls. It was less than he deserved, however.

As George had pointed out as soon as confronted, he was a total ass. Katy hadn't acted the whore. She'd broken down into a puddle of tears that paralyzed his cousin. Luckily, George didn't know what he'd thought. As it was, he had received a berating from his cousin that exhibited a maturity and perceptiveness that astonished him.

Which prompted the question—what had occurred between George and Katy in Ireland? George hadn't strayed in years. All his indiscretions had been early in his marriage when Emily was far into her confinements. The last had been almost five years ago. Why risk losing his family for a sham marriage?

George had offered no excuse. He needed to ask Katy, he'd said.

His eyes settled on Katy. Her smile had lost the wooden edge he'd seen when she first entered the room. Her hands, originally fisted so tightly he suspected she had nail marks in her palms, had relaxed. They lay in her lap now. With her filmy blue gown and a gauze cap over her hair, she looked more like a fiery angel than a mere mortal.

Across from her, the earl reminisced about his dead wife, son, and daughter. His eyes glinted with tears, his wrinkled face stretched smooth with a smile.

Jeremy shifted in his chair, trying to ease the ache in his groin. He wanted to smile like that. He wanted to face death knowing he'd loved as deeply as the earl.

When he glanced back toward Katy, their eyes met. She bit back a smile, gaze sliding over his lap. Like an actual caress, his body felt it, and his prick throbbed like a plucked harp string. When her golden lashes fell and that beautiful rosy blush he loved flowed up between the folds of her fichu to color her cheeks, it hit him with the impact of a runaway carriage.

He could love her like that.

She wasn't Anna. She hadn't betrayed him with George. Her smiles were genuine. Her kindnesses were heartfelt, not motivated by selfishness. She'd sucked him off to save Gregory his position, a sacrifice out of proportion to her perceived sin. When she'd stood up to Madame Batiste, it wasn't for herself, but for Clara. She treated Alfred and the staff as if they were family, and she'd never once belittled him, scorned him, or rebuked him. Not until this morning. *Cold and unfeeling.* That's what she'd called him.

He'd demanded her baby, and aside from one attempt to escape, she'd shown no signs of resentment. She'd asked George for help, a man she'd called a lying despicable bastard not that long ago. And she'd looked to him for emotional support, after he'd called her a whore mere hours ago.

He didn't deserve her. She was too good for him. But he wanted her. Even if it meant he'd never again have the release that hurting a woman gave him.

Decided, he rose to his feet, sidled over and placed a chaste kiss on her forehead as she craned her head to look at him. "If you'll excuse me, my dear, I think you have things under control here. I expect you and the earl have a lot to discuss, and I have an errand to run."

The flicker of disappointment that crossed her face gave him the last bit of incentive he needed. With a bow, and a nod at the earl, he turned toward the door.

He'd visited his mistress last night, little good that it had done. Like much of the last year, he'd failed to find the satisfaction he needed.

The time had come to end it. It was time to earn his good fortune.

Chapter Seven

That night, Jeremy navigated his way through an unexpected crush of people, annoyed at the effort required, but buoyed by the successful completion of his afternoon's task and by Alfred's pronouncement that Kathleen had allowed the earl to escort her to the evening's entertainment.

Mari, his now ex-mistress, had hardly batted an eye when he informed her he'd no longer visit. He gifted her with the house he'd maintained for the last ten years and handed her a banknote sufficient to ease the transition. In effect, it meant she'd never again have to entertain a man other than by choice. Strangely, he'd felt nothing but sadness that he'd never wondered if she loved him.

"Braxton." He nodded at his host, then greeted the man's newly acquired wife. He'd accepted their invite, mainly because the new bride had fretted that the turnout would be humiliatingly low and partly in hopes that Kathleen would find it enjoyable and more relaxing than the previous night's ordeal.

The bride's anxiety had been sorely off the mark. Glancing about, Jeremy saw many of the Ton's most highly sought out personages. Beau Brummel held court in one corner, a bevy of well-dressed young men hanging on his every word. In another direction, William Blake's voice filtered through the crowd.

"Is that the prince I see?" he asked the petite hostess, Caroline, nodding toward the far side of the dance floor, perfectly aware that it was.

"Indeed, Your Grace, though I fear he's been upstaged by your lady wife. She's a bright star, stealing the light of all the other guests."

Her gaze apprised him of the path he needed, and after another minute, he excused himself and wove his way toward his goal.

Caroline hadn't exaggerated. If Katy had been regal and polished last night, tonight she dazzled. With her curves draped in a ruby red satin and a square neckline emphasized by white satin ribbons, her fiery hair framed her shining face in a riot of curls. The necklace he'd given her graced her long neck, the diamonds dulled by the twinkle in her eyes and the smile on her face.

It took a concerted effort to move his feet. What if her smile faded when she saw him?

He circled around, slowly wending his way forward until he stood behind her. It didn't surprise him in the least that no one even noticed him.

"May I request a dance with the loveliest woman in the room?" he whispered. Lemon wafted over him, tightening his groin and sending a shiver of contentment through him.

She gasped, spinning around so fast, she stumbled. Without waiting for permission, he slid an arm about her waist and captured her hand, leading her toward the dance floor.

"Have I been such a beast," he asked as he swept her amidst the fluctuating couples, "that you're shocked by a compliment from me?" The idea burrowed into his soul, making him slow. Years ago, he'd been considered a rake, as beguiling and sought after as George or Miles. Somewhere, he'd lost his charm.

No, he hadn't lost the ability, just the motivation. Galvanized, he beamed a smile, determined to make her smile back.

Instead, her gaze fell, and color crept up her neck. "I did wonder for a moment if George had inhabited your body."

He missed a step, shocked she'd bring up George's name after his accusation at breakfast. Then he registered a slight hitch in her breathing and a twinkle in her eyes.

Was she teasing him?

Afraid to believe it, he arched a brow and lifted her chin. "Where do you think George learned his skills, if not from me?"

"From Alfred?" She cocked her head and tittered.

"Minx." He chuckled, pulling her closer than socially acceptable. Her sigh sent a surge of satisfaction through him.

"You'll bring down the wrath of the Matrons if you hold me any closer, Your Grace."

"Umm, I'll risk it." Was it wishful thinking or had she just pressed herself against his erection? Either way, he intended to enjoy it. Whispering, he nuzzled her throat, just below her ear, "In fact, I may even dare to steal you for a second dance. Test their resolve."

Her giggle rumbled through him, resonating like the violin strains surrounding them. His cheeks felt strained, his grin so wide the muscles struggled to hold it. He likely looked a lovesick idiot.

They moved together, circling the dance floor

silently. Jeremy savored the feel of her in his arms, dreading the imminent end of the music.

"Thank you for this afternoon," Katy said, breaking the connection between their bodies all too soon.

"How did the visit go? Did you show him the brooch?"

"Yes. He said it was his wife's." She hesitated. "I never expected him to be so old. And lonely." Her face twisted in pain, and her head shook in denial. "Momma wrote him every year. She begged him to forgive her. But he said he never got her letters." She lifted her gaze, her eyes filled with entreaty. "Do you think that's possible?"

"Anything's possible. What's more important is whether it matters. He's obviously forgiven her. Will you hold it against him that it came too late?"

"No." The word sighed from her lips. Any other answer would have surprised him.

"Katy, I need to apologize." Her head shook, but he forged ahead. "I was a beast this morning."

"There's no need. I upset you."

"All the same, I'm sorry for what I said. It was unforgivable." Whether it was to comfort her or himself, he didn't know, but he let his hand slide up her back.

"No, it was my fault." Her head shook, and her teeth grabbed her bottom lip. Red flooded her face. "I never should have…you know. But I would never do *that* with George. Or anyone else." Her eyes closed as if to block the memory. "I was curious. I'd seen women do it and wanted to see what it was like. It's no wonder you think me a whore."

His heart skipped a beat. His feet refused to move.

Couples whirled around him. Katy stumbled, then halted, staring in puzzlement.

"I never want to hear that, Kathleen." His voice carried, despite his attempt to temper it. Katy's eyes widened. Around them, a murmur started. Grabbing her hand, he dragged her off the floor and out into the garden.

A cool breeze wrapped around them. Slowing, he pulled her toward a corner of the marble balcony.

"You're right," he told her, gripping her chin to force her to look at him. "You shouldn't have done it. And I shouldn't have let you. But it doesn't make you a whore." Locking eyes with her, he waited, willing her to believe him. When the guilt didn't drain away, he gentled his voice. "You're one of the most giving, sweetest women I've ever known. You did it to save Gregory's job. And I love that—" Hell, he'd loved every second of it, but he wasn't about to tell her that. She'd be on her knees sucking him off every time she felt guilty. While it sounded like a wonderful problem to have, there was no way he'd be able to control himself. The very idea nearly undid him. "But you'll never do it again. Do you understand?"

"Yes." The words were so meek and quiet, Jeremy had to close his eyes against a surge of desire. A second later, he heard an even quieter, "Sir." It wasn't *Master* and he knew it wasn't intentional, but it had the same effect. Lust poured through his body, hard and demanding.

He beat it back. He'd been a gentleman most of the night. It couldn't be that hard to rein in his lust for the rest of his life.

****

Restless energy bubbled through Katy the next day, sending her down the hallway with the feeling of flying. Jeremy's attention and apology the night before had driven away most of her nightmares, and he'd been equally solicitous at breakfast. For the first time since arriving in London, she thought she could be happy with Jeremy if only she could find out about her family.

Her knock on the library door reverberated, the door swinging open as if blown by a gale. Her excitement fizzled.

At the desk, Jeremy's head bent over the surface. His hand clutched the side of his temples. Slowly, he looked up, but not before she saw the pain twisting his features.

"Jeremy?" Should she go away? Before her mind processed the question, her feet rushed forward. "What's wrong?"

A thud sounded. Jeremy straightened in his chair, his head rotating. His jacket draped over the chair in front of the desk. His cravat was nowhere in sight, but Katy saw him glance at the floor before his lips curled with resignation.

"I'm fine." His expression brightened with a welcoming smile that almost chased away her concern. This was Jeremy, though. If she'd discovered nothing else since she arrived, she'd learned he hid his deepest feelings beneath a veneer of politeness.

Gliding around the desk, she brushed a hand over his shoulder and peered. A cloud of paper dust swirled in the daylight, obscuring the leather-bound book titled Accounts. Beside it, a black blotch of ink marred the blotter. Beside the blotch, a broken feather pen lay discarded. Another pen poised ready in his hand, ink seeping into the blotter, clutched in a grip so tight it too looked ready to snap.

Glancing at him, she found his gaze riveted on her chest. Warmth slithered through her stomach, teasing the corners of her mouth.

With a twist of her wrist, she flipped the book back open. His forehead furrowed, but he didn't stop her.

Columns of numbers lined the first page, neat and orderly, the same as the next few. As she turned them, she noticed the writing transformed and every other page or so had been removed. On the ones that remained, scratched out figures and blobs of dried ink scarred the columns. Turning to the latest page, scribbled sums at the bottom of the column marred the page, three different values, all crossed out, and a fourth totally obliterated. On the facing page, a similar mess was displayed with a final value circled by a heavy line.

Jeremy's deep sigh sent a wave of frustrated heat over her arm. "I'm not very good with numbers." His fingers curled around the hand still on his shoulder, and he rubbed his cheek over it. "I actually hate them."

Peeking out the corner of her eye, she saw his shoulders slump. Shamefaced, his face redder than she'd ever seen, he looked totally defeated and utterly humiliated. She might have said emasculated if not for the tingle of awareness racing through her at the sight of his bare, tanned chest at the V of his shirt.

She searched for something to say, something that would bring his smile back without further unmanning him. "Not everyone's good with them. My da has the same problem. He swears they switch places when he's not looking."

His head snapped up, eyes wide. "They do. How

can anyone add them up when they do that?"

Careful to hide her amusement, she nodded at the pen. "May I?"

"No." The mask fell back into place. "I can do it. You have better things to do."

"I do? Like what?"

She stood and crossed her arms in front of her. Seeing it placed her too far up for a good view of her chest, she turned around to perch on the edge of the desk. As she hoped, his gaze dropped from her face to her cleavage.

"Well?" she prompted. "Should I check the menus? Count the sheets? Annoy Alfred with questions about the staff?" They were all tasks she'd attempted, usually resulting in the staff's thinly disguised resentment.

When he didn't answer, his lips tightening stubbornly, she decided she needed to give him more incentive. She slipped down, caressing the hard muscles in his arms as she went. Clutching the arm of his chair, she raised her face, intentionally snagging her bottom lip in her teeth. "Please? I feel so useless. Let me do this for you."

As she'd expected, his face contorted, and he shifted uncomfortably. As much as she wanted to, she resisted looking at his lap. She knew what she'd see. She could see it in the way his breathing stopped, then quickened when it resumed. She could see it in his eyes, brightening to quicksilver before her gaze.

She let her hand slide onto his knee.

He trapped it beneath his. "Don't, Katy." His voice rasped, and his tongue flicked out to moisten his lips. "Please get up."

"As you wish." She emphasized her sigh, making

sure he got a good view of her breasts as she rose, her hand pressing down, slipping up his thigh just enough to make him hiss.

It wasn't a very good plan, she realized as she stood before him. He looked tortured, his gaze turned away, focused first on the floor, then flitting toward the window, then the door. Anywhere but on her. His eyes had darkened, and he sat stiffly, as if afraid of what would happen if he shifted. Only his hand moved, his fingers squeezing hers while his thumb stroked her palm. Quivers raced with each pass, shooting through her, robbing her legs of strength.

What was worse, her own lungs couldn't pull in air fast enough and touching him had sent a surge of yearning straight to her quim. Her plan was backfiring, making her as hungry for him as she wanted him to be. But she couldn't follow through if her plan was to work.

She needed the real Jeremy, the one who barked commands in a voice she couldn't help but obey, the one who ordered her to eat because he cared. She needed—and wanted—the Jeremy he hid away. And for that, he had to trust her. Which meant she had to trust him.

She sank back against the edge of the desk. "I came in to ask you something." She curled her fingers, forcing his thumb to stop playing with her nerves. It was hard enough without the thrum of desire. "I hoped George would help me. But he said I should ask you."

He finally looked at her, a shuttered look slamming over his face as soon as she uttered George's name. He yanked his hand from hers.

"I'm worried about my family," she rushed to get

out her request, as afraid he'd withdraw completely as she was that she'd lose her courage. "They…they might be involved in…things…that they shouldn't."

"And you think George could help with that?" Skepticism dripped from his voice.

Of course it did. He didn't know that George was just as involved as her brothers.

"Well, I thought he might be able to write to someone. Find out if they're all right. Those newspaper articles don't tell anyone anything." Every morning, her stomach tied itself into knots. She poured over the articles each day, relieved she didn't find the names of anyone she knew and just as frustrated that there were so few names.

"Why don't you just post a letter yourself?"

Shame flushed her skin, making her wish she had a fan. She stared at her wringing hands, wishing Jeremy still held them. "I…I didn't tell them where I was going. I don't want them to know."

Jeremy's brows arched in surprise. "Why?"

It was horrible. She had so many reasons, and none of them alone seemed adequate. He wouldn't understand them. There was the suffocating protectiveness of her brother that made her want to scream. The never-ending disappointment and resentment that lined her da's face every time he looked at her and saw her resemblance to Momma. The scorn her half-siblings held for her, with her *highfalutin'* ways, ways she didn't want to change because they were the only thing that let her hang onto her mother's memory. And the shame.

He might understand that.

"They all said I would be sorry when I wed

George. They said he'd leave me, that I was just a whore he didn't want enough to pay. When it happened, it was bad enough. But when I discovered I was pregnant, I wanted to die." Tears leaked from her eyes. She swiped them away. "The babe…wasn't supposed to happen. Not when it was just once. George didn't even want to do it. I made him."

The memory made her cry harder. He'd wanted to marry her, so he could spy on her family, but he hadn't wanted to touch her. The wooing had been as false as everything else.

"Wait!" Jeremy stared at her in disbelief, his words laced with the confidence that made her feel so secure. "What do you mean he didn't want to? Why the hell would he marry you if he didn't want you?"

Katy swallowed hard. She'd promised George she wouldn't tell Jeremy about the spying. And she couldn't tell him George had blackmailed her into it. Not without telling him how. So she lied. A half-lie really.

"It was my idea. I didn't want to marry the butcher. Da wanted me to. Said he couldn't support all of us any longer. That it was high time I put aside my unreasonable expectations." Unreasonable. That was what he'd said when she told him she wanted a husband she could love, instead of a smelly, bloody butcher whose touch made her want to vomit. "George…I liked George. And he flirted with me. Made me feel pretty. So, I asked him."

"But he didn't want you?" Jeremy choked out a laugh. "And I suppose you're going to tell me you didn't want him, either. But somehow, here you are, his brat in your belly."

The bitterness in his words sent another burning tear down her cheek. She ignored the splash as it hit her hand, burning her soul.

Why did nothing ever work out the way she intended? This talk was supposed to be easier. She hadn't meant to tell him this, bare her soul. Baring her breasts, taking him in her mouth had been easy. This was hard. Hearing the hurt and disbelief in his voice was nigh unbearable.

"I had to do it. Da would have had it annulled if I didn't." He wouldn't understand that. Only a Catholic would. With a deep breath for courage, she took a leap of faith. "And I was curious. I never understood why people couple. I wanted to see if I would like it. Because I liked George."

"And did you?"

She shook her head. "No. It was…strange. I just kept waiting. I waited to feel something. It wasn't horrible, the way it was when Dean kissed me, but I kept thinking. Why don't I feel anything? When will it be over? Then it was. It didn't even hurt. It just pinched. Even George didn't enjoy it."

A heavy silence descended, aside from Katy's sniffling. She continued to stare at her hands, too afraid to look at him, afraid he wouldn't believe her. Every now and then, she swiped at her cheeks or nose. When he pushed a handkerchief at her, she snatched it.

"And now you're afraid," he finally said, voice laden with understanding. "Because you'd have to explain why I'm your husband and not George."

A fresh flood of tears shuddered through her entire body. She hadn't realized how much she needed him to understand. It felt as if someone had unlocked a hundred-pound chain wrapped around her chest.

"Come here." He grabbed a hand and tugged. She fell onto his lap, crying even harder as his arms wrapped around her. With a sob, she burrowed into his neck, breathing in soap and sandalwood. Heat emanated from his body, making her realize just how cold she'd been.

He let her cry, dropping little kisses on the top of her head, stroking his hands along her arms and back, chasing away the chill. When the storm finally eased, he said, "Your family is fine. As soon as I saw that article, I made arrangements to make sure they were all right. If anything happens to them, I'll know within days."

She drew in shuddering breaths. "Why didn't you tell me?"

"Because you never asked." With a single finger, he tipped her face until their eyes met. "They're your family, which makes them my family. And I take care of family."

"Even if they're—"

"Even if they're traitors." He sighed, chest expanding beneath her cheek. "I won't say I like it. And even I can't do much if they're caught. But I'll do what I can, and at least you'll know." His fingers slid into her hand, knitting with hers, and he lifted them to his lips. "God knows I've put up with George's follies all these years. A rebel or two ought to be easy in comparison."

****

"Are you sure you want to do this?" Katy asked, clutching the side of the barouche as it bounced over a particularly bad hole in the road. Like the pair of matched grays pulling it, the fancy carriage was a delight. Springs and straps absorbed the majority of bumps, but the driver seemed determined to fly, and even he couldn't avoid them all. The soft leather hood had been lowered, contributing to the feeling she might soar from its confines.

Jeremy's heavy arm about her shoulders and the grip he had on the hand in her lap allowed her to enjoy the journey without fear, but still, she felt the need to ground herself. The day was too perfect, with wispy clouds that protected them from the heat of the sun. Even the breeze blew warm and gentle.

"It's a bit late for me to change my mind, don't you think?" He chuckled, amused no doubt that she had waited so long to ask. In truth, she had been afraid since he'd suggested the outing. The idea of an afternoon in the country and dinner with George's family had seemed too good to be true. That he'd accepted Emily's invitation astounded her still, given the bouts of jealousy George's name created. "Besides," he continued, "it's been too long since I spoiled my nieces and nephews."

"Do you think they'll like the gifts I picked out?" In addition to the joy of the actual outing, Jeremy had sent her shopping. In the boot of the carriage were toys and sweets. She'd discovered so many wonderful items that she worried Jeremy would think she'd absconded again. After nearly an entire afternoon, she'd finally chosen a kaleidoscope, Jacob's ladder, and *bilboquet* for the boys, a dollhouse and dolls for the two girls, and a toy theater and new rocking horse just because they were irresistible.

"I'm sure they will." He squeezed her hand. "You should start setting up the nursery soon. The painting's done."

They'd agreed on a light mint green. Katy had wanted something cool and airy since her cheeks burned every time she entered the room, thinking about what she'd done there.

Luckily, the house came into view before the silence grew noteworthy. A small manor house, ivy covered the lower brick exterior. Greenery surrounded the structure; a hedge on one side and what looked like an herb garden on the other. Lawn flanked the narrow drive, wildflowers cropping up in spots, then gave way to forests of oak and willow. As the barouche approached, it turned, leaning into the modest circular drive.

Emily waved from the top of the stairs, a tiny child hiding in her skirt. George's head popped up amongst the greenery in the garden, a basket on his arm. Katy exhaled with relief. Her own dress, a simple linen affair, matched their casual attire.

Springing from the seat, Katy had all she could do to wait while Jeremy dismounted and turned to help her disembark. As her feet landed, she stepped forward and a raucous sounded. Like a herd of sheep escaping a wolf, the ground shook and four impish figures hurtled toward them.

Joy threatened to burst her chest open until the lead imp tripped. A foot away, his tiny body hurtled forward, straight at the bottom step of the carriage.

"Hey, there!" With lightening reflexes, Jeremy snagged the flying body and lifted it. Squealing, the boy grabbed Jeremy's hair, feet flailing as Jeremy sent him into a somersault in the air. Catching him as he fell, Jeremy set the tyke on the ground. "Slow it down, John.

Before you decorate the ground." He laughed, but Katy heard an edge of fear in it.

"That's silly, Uncle Jay. Why would anyone decorate the ground?" a little girl who slid to a stop asked. About five or six years old, Katy guessed she was Alice, the oldest. Covered in smudges of dirt, her white-blonde hair circled her head in a halo of curls. A long rip in one stocking showed a line of pink along the edges. Blood, no doubt, from climbing a tree or crawling through the bushes, proof that her angelic looks were only skin deep. Behind her, hovered an older boy.

"Say your hellos to Uncle Jay and Aunt Katy, please, children," Emily told them with a resigned amusement. "Then, take Alice inside and help her clean up, Eddie."

The older boy, a miniature version of George, bowed and reached for her hand. "I'm Edward, and it's very nice to meet you, Aunt Katy." Only the hesitant shuffle of his back foot and the sidelong glance at Jeremy betrayed any nervousness. At Jeremy's smile and wink, he dipped and kissed her hand.

An instant later, a broad smile crossed his face and his eyes began to twinkle. With a light skip, he raced up the stairs and waited at the top while Alice made her greeting. Not to be outdone by his older brother, John pushed his way in front of Alice and grabbed Katy's hand. At three, his technique left a bit to be desired, but Katy resisted the urge to wipe her hand on her skirt and crouched to look him in the eye.

"You must be John." His eyes widened. Silver like Jeremy's, they filled his face. "Would it be all right if I gave you a hug, too? I miss my little brother very much, and it would make me feel a lot less lonely."

Instead of the nod she expected, he launched himself at her, his chubby little arms wrapping around her neck. They squeezed each other, Katy feeling as if she might start blubbering. While the brother she meant was nearly twelve now and only a stepbrother, she'd found herself missing him dreadfully lately.

"Hey, brat. That's my wife. You better let her go, or I'll have to tickle you." Just as she thought he'd choke her to death, Jeremy lofted him into the air again.

Alice glowered at her, hanging back, then proclaimed, "I shan't greet her. I don't like her."

Emily gasped. Jeremy stilled, John tucked under his arm.

"Uncle Jay was supposed to marry me. Not her." A tiny foot slammed the ground.

With a chuckle, Jeremy placed John on his feet. "Don't worry, Alice. She's so old, I'm sure she'll be dead by the time you're ready to marry me."

Alice chewed her cheek, lips pinching. "Maybe. But I still won't like her."

"It's all right, Alice," Katy said. "You needn't like me. I often do things I shouldn't. But I shall like you anyway."

"Alice, please go clean up. Uncle Jeremy is probably hungry, and we can't eat with you looking like that."

"Don't mind my brats, Kathleen," George said as he smacked Alice lightly on her behind, sending her up the stairs. "I told them to misbehave so you wouldn't want to take any of them home."

"Oh, but I do want to take them home." Her eyes connected with Jeremy's. His own face mirrored hers, joy and longing evident in his grin and the way his eyes shone. Any doubt she harbored vanished. She wanted to give this man as many children as he wanted.

He held out his hand. She took it and stepped up the stair.

"Fire." The tiny voice drew all their attention. The youngest girl, the one who had burrowed into Emily's skirt, pointed at Katy's head.

Katy sank down again as she reached the top stair. "You must be Julia. Would you like to touch the fire?"

Hesitant, clutching Emily's hand, she reached out with the other and patted the top of Katy's head. A giggle rippled up, then she turned back into Emily's thick brown skirt.

"Let's go inside," Emily said with a laugh. "You must be starving."

They all chuckled when Katy's stomach let out a long low growl.

****

"Would you please promise me something, Katy?" Emily asked later that afternoon.

They sat in the garden under a huge oak tree. Katy held Giles, the newest addition to the family, gently rocking the baby while she hummed beneath her breath. Julia slept on a blanket a few feet away, and the rest of the children laughed and played, their voices carrying from nearby. George and Jeremy stood in a corner, examining a walnut tree whose bark showed a reddish tinge. Too far away to make out words, it was obvious the two cousins had enjoyed the day. Both wore the expressions of men who had eaten well and were content with life.

"That would depend on the promise."

"Promise that no matter what happens, you won't let him shut himself away again."

Katy let her gaze settle on the two men. The entire day, she'd felt a yearning she'd never experienced. While she'd enjoyed the attention Jeremy had showered over her recently, she'd never seen the man she saw today. She'd felt glimmers of desire, and moments of affection for that other Jeremy, but the one she'd seen today was a Jeremy she could love.

"I assume you mean Jeremy?"

"Yes. George missed him. As did I. It's nice to have him back."

"What do you mean?"

"Jeremy's been very unhappy for a very long time. He and George used to be incredibly close. Then something happened. Something Jeremy won't talk about. And he started to hate George."

"Why? Do you have any idea? I assumed he'd always disliked George until the Earl of Beccles told me the same thing. That they used to be close."

"We don't truly know. I suspect it was that witch he married. Anna Carlton. She must have said something or done something to set him against George. That's when it started, about a year after they wed." Emily refilled Katy's glass of lemonade, then beamed at her sleeping son before continuing. "I never liked her. She was one of those people who would cut others just because she could. Her father was only a viscount, so she wasn't even that special. But that never stopped her. She thought because she was beautiful, she was better than anyone else."

Emily shook her head, mouth twisted in distaste. "I never understood why he married her. He could have had the pick of the Ton." A smile crept across her face, and her eyes wandered toward the two men. "You should have seen the three of them. George, Jeremy, and Miles. The Three Dandies, they called them. They could slay a woman just by smiling at them."

Emily's own smile faded. "But for some reason, Jeremy picked Anna. As if he couldn't see past the pretty face. Of course, she never showed him the ugly side." She shook herself, like a duck coming out of the water. "But all that's in the past," she said. "And George was right. He's madly in love with you."

"I doubt that." Katy shifted, switching the baby from one arm to the other. The conversation was becoming much too personal for her comfort.

It must have shown on her face because Emily patted her forearm. "Don't worry. George told me everything. I know what happened in Ireland, and I don't mind. As long as you love the baby as much as it looks like you will, I'm happy."

"What?" Katy gaped at her, guilt seeping up to choke her. George had *told* her?

"Oh, don't look so horrified. It was just sex. It used to bother me, but I know he loves me to distraction. And it's made Jeremy so happy. He has this silly idea that he can't have babies of his own. Which is ludicrous. Even if Anna got pregnant by someone else, which is unlikely, he's hardly tried enough to be sure."

Mind reeling and unable to keep up with Emily's rapid pace, Katy locked onto the one thought that concerned her. "Did he love her?"

Emily's eyes flickered toward the two men, face contorting. "I don't know. I know he was infatuated with her. I think he thought he loved her. But he changed while they were married. He stopped laughing. Stopped smiling. He was angry all the time."

To Katy's surprise, a tear trickled down Emily's cheek. She pulled a handkerchief from her sleeve and dabbed at her eyes. "I'm sorry." She sniffled, then forced a smile. "It's just so nice to see him happy. They grew up together, you know. Their grandmother raised them."

Giles began to stir, his tiny mouth forming little o's. Katy cooed at him until he settled.

"Jeremy doesn't talk about it much. Alfred mentions it now and then, but he doesn't go into details."

"Well, she loved them both, but she was old-fashioned. And much too old to raise a three and five-year-old. The duke had died years before, and I think she thought they'd fill the hole he left, so she didn't hire a nanny. She had rules that you wouldn't believe." Emily's eyes rolled. "Jeremy bore the brunt of them, being the eldest, but it took George years to relax his guard. Sometimes, I think that's why he was such a rake. He never felt loved, so he looked for it in other ways."

"What kind of rules?"

"Oh, the usual things. Sit up straight, mind your elders, don't speak unless spoken to. Nothing all that horrible. But she insisted on perfection. George told me about one time when he slouched at the breakfast table. He was maybe eight. She told him to sit there, properly, for an hour. But every time he relaxed, she added an hour. In the end, he sat there the entire day."

"That's horrible."

"That's why my children are little rascals. He lets

me discipline them to an extent, but not as much as I should."

Katy felt a bubble of pity well up, and her gaze settled on Jeremy. Even now, his posture was perfect. He'd told her to dress casually, but his own attire didn't qualify. Aside from his cravat, tied with as simple a knot as she'd ever seen him wear, he was in full dress, just an older waistcoat that showed a sheen in the elbows and an older, worn pair of hessians. In fact, the only times she'd seen him in anything less than full dress was when she barged in on him in the library, a place he likely considered safe from interruptions. Since she'd started stalking him there, he'd taken to leaving his jacket on, cravat tied.

And then there was that other time, at the tavern.

Her eyes widened.

Emily's voice droned in her ear, but Katy no longer heard. As if he felt it, Jeremy turned, stiffening. As soon as their eyes connected, his posture relaxed, so little most wouldn't notice, and his lips curved in a subtle smile. A rush of heat flooded her, wrapping her heart and squeezing.

She remembered his words that night, about manners and appearance. He'd said, "One can be anything one wants as long as one plays the part. And one can get away with a multitude of sins if one doesn't draw attention to it."

He'd been a different man that night. A dark, demanding man, who'd made her feel things she'd never before felt. Things that frightened but excited her at the same time. Things that made her cry because she felt safe and free.

Was that the real Jeremy?

Giles began to squirm once again, drawing her back, demanding attention as all babies and young children did.

"I think he's hungry," she said, watching his pursed lips rooting in the air. After a quick hug, she forced herself to pass him to Emily. "Thank you for telling me about Jeremy. Things make much more sense now."

"I figured it might." Taking Giles, she opened her dress and popped her breast into his mouth. "And please remember, I want you to think of me as a sister. That's why I told you I know about Ireland. I want you to tell me anything, ask me anything. It's hard loving them. I almost gave up on George, and he rebelled against his upbringing. Jeremy will use his to keep you out. But it's worth it if you can break through."

As Emily's gaze locked on George, her face transformed. Already beautiful, her complexion took on a glow and her eyes sparkled as bright as the sun.

A shout from the corner of the garden drew Emily's gaze, but the glow brightened and an adoring smile settled on her lips as the youngsters came barreling toward them.

It was unadulterated contentment. The type of contentment Katy wanted. The kind she wanted Jeremy to find.

Her hand settled on her abdomen. A flutter, like that of a butterfly kiss, answered.

Chapter Eight

Jeremy stared in awe at a neatly tallied column of numbers and wondered why he'd struggled for so long. Katy had nagged him the entire week until he'd given in and handed over the offending task. In a matter of hours, she had copied over the entries going back to January into a new journal. As she went, she'd added up each page. The result was a crisp clean journal of sums he had no doubt were correct. She'd spotted errors in his math and questioned areas where the values made no sense. Turned out, the man he'd left in charge at Lexham Estate had been skimming money, enough to cover the new roofs he wanted for the families living there.

Now, he had more time than he expected, enough that he wished she'd not gone off with Caroline Braxton. He wanted to take her walking in the park or shopping so he could watch her face brighten at the sight of ribbons and feathers that, to him, looked like nothing more than strips of cloth.

Unsure what to do with the free time, his gaze slowly wandered over the library. He didn't allow staff to clean the room, aside from the desk, so a scattering of items lay in various spots. A book by Blake perched on a table near the window. In another corner, Katy had left her sewing, a tiny lace edged christening gown. His child was going to be the best-dressed infant in

England, no doubt. Every day, she exhibited another garment, and he praised her efforts. In truth, the tiny items frightened him. They were so minute and fragile. Was he ready to take care of a child?

His gaze lifted to the portrait above the fireplace. It was time to remove it. Time to replace it with Katy and him. Romney, the painter who had memorialized Anna, was too old now. Maybe John Hoppner could find time.

A breeze from the door opening interrupted his thought.

"We have a problem." Miles strode in, pulling off his gloves and handing them to Alfred, along with his cane.

Jeremy's stomach tightened. Miles wasn't prone to exaggeration, and the look on his face didn't bode well. His eyes were drawn, lips tight.

With a nod at Alfred, Jeremy gestured at a chair. Miles threw himself into it, long legs stretched before him. Reaching into his waistcoat pocket, he pulled out a missive and tossed it on the desk. "According to my man, your brother-in-law has disappeared. Hasn't been seen in more than two weeks."

"Which one?" Thomas was the only full brother, but Alex and Brody were likely involved, too, and Katy didn't seem to differentiate.

"Thomas."

Jeremy picked up the tattered paper, ignoring the urge to curse. A quick scan only frustrated him. Poor penmanship, along with the same issue that made math so infuriating, made it difficult to make out what it said.

Miles summed it up for him. "Billings lost track of him just before the battle on the twenty-first. Hasn't seen him since."

Jeremy exhaled a slow heavy breath. How the hell was he supposed to tell Katy? She'd finally relaxed, trusting his word that her family was safe. They'd both read about the battle in Enniscorthy that had defeated the rebel forces. Hundreds died at first, with a count that rose with each tally. She understood that any specifics would take time to reach him and never asked if he'd heard anything.

He had hoped he'd never have to tell her anything but good news. "Any chance he's still alive?"

"Impossible to say. He disappeared well before the battle." Miles gestured toward the letter with his head. "Could be he was smart enough to hightail it out, but I doubt it. I think he'd have surfaced by now if that were the case."

"Yeah." Another resigned sigh blew out, lifting the corners of the letter. It wasn't just Katy he'd have to tell. The Earl of Margate would need to know, too. This might well kill him. Why was joy always so fleeting? "Thanks for letting me know."

"You shouldn't tell her just yet. Billings is still looking. He'll find out one way or the other. But he needs money. This isn't government sanctioned, so I can't ask Wickham for it."

Miles colored, as if asking was an embarrassment, but Jeremy waved his hand, frowning. "Whatever you need. Just find him."

****

Katy stepped from Caroline Braxton's phaeton, exhilarated by the brilliant sunshine and the wonder of Caroline's mastery handling the horses. She'd had to beg Jeremy to let Caroline drive her, and he'd demanded Caroline's promise she'd keep the pace sedate and leisurely, an oath obviously given tongue-in-cheek. The ride had been wonderful—safe, yes, but anything but sedate—and she'd finally found a friend besides Emily. Instead of the catty gossip that dominated the rest of the female Ton's attention, Caroline had chattered with excitement about the high step of the matched roans and the springs and suspension involved in keeping the carriage upright.

While Caroline continued to chat, Katy surveyed the brick townhouse before them. Although situated in a fashionable Piccadilly neighborhood, the house lacked the sparkle and grandeur of Lexham House. The brick looked dingy, and a chip was visible in the top step. The huge oak door squeaked as a footman opened it, stepping aside in a plain gray livery.

A shiver ran up Katy's back, and she glanced around nervously. Down the street, someone was exiting another residence, but otherwise no one was in sight. It had to be her imagination, or perhaps Ned. Though she never saw him and thought Jeremy trusted her, it was altogether possible he still had the man following her. The last few days especially, she'd felt as if someone watched her.

Handing over her cloak, Katy and Caroline followed the stiff, impassive-looking man into the music room.

"Lady Jane, thank you for inviting us." With a slight dip, she greeted their hostess with a fake smile. She'd only agreed to attend because Caroline had begged. She didn't really like Jane. Like too many of the *haute ton*, she treated her inferiors as if they didn't exist.

"Thank you for coming, Duchess." A skinny,

hawk-faced woman, their hostess eyed Caroline, her smile straining as she looked her up and down, then turned away. "Please, help yourself to some tea cakes. The music will start as soon as everyone's here."

Annoyed, Katy exhaled, but bit her tongue. Were Emily here, she would have put Jane in her place, but Caroline merely winked with an amused smirk and headed toward the refreshments. As Caroline had said when she suggested attending, Lady Jane deserved a certain amount of forbearance. After two seasons, she'd still attracted no suitors, despite an extensive fortune and a decent family name.

"She's a witch," Katy whispered as they loaded their plates with heart-shaped sandwiches and marzipan.

"Yes, but her momma always hires the best musicians. I hear this quartet is wonderful."

An hour later, Katy had to admit Caroline was correct. The selections had been lovely and extremely well played. A number had been familiar Irish tunes, along with a handful of Scottish ballads, haunting and heart-wrenching, and the harpist had hands that called down heaven.

After the musicians packed up and left, the assembly quickly lost its appeal, but good manners prohibited their exit. Instead, they found their ears and sensibilities assaulted by Jane and the other ladies who clustered around her at every function. Bawdy songs, accompanied by atrocious pianoforte playing, added to the ugliness of the company. Unlike conversation, popular music seemed to have none of the circumspection expected of young ladies.

Embarrassed at the lewdness, Katy withdrew,

taking a seat as far from the bevy of young girls as possible, and sipped at the wine passed around by the small army of footmen. Caroline wandered off with another lady to view the paintings lining the walls.

The frisson of unease she'd felt when they arrived began to grow, along with an ache that had plagued her back the last few days. Shifting in what amounted to a wasted effort to ease the pressure, Katy glanced at the partygoers. Small groups were forming, heads clumped together, while giggles surrounded them. She heard the names of various eligible young men mentioned. The Earl of Beccles name registered at least three times.

Perhaps she could leave soon. Others were exiting, seeping out the door to thank the elder hostess.

"Duchess, perhaps you could enlighten us." Jane's strident voice cut through the murmurs. A gleam in her eye made Katy shift uncomfortably. Like a backward ripple, the noise faded.

"About what, Lady Jane?"

"I understand your husband is close friends with the Earl of Beccles. Is it true he engages in unsavory acts?"

Katy stiffened, careful to keep her smile. "I'm afraid I don't understand."

"Oh, please, don't be coy. We've heard the stories about the Three Dandies. The earl's said to like tying up women and forcing himself on them. And everyone knows the duke used to beat his wife."

Katy hardly heard the gasps through the pounding in her ears. Like the opening of a ball, women began to slide toward one side of the room or the other, a macabre dance lining up one side against another.

"You can tell us," Jane continued, her words

feeding fuel to the fire burning in Katy's chest. "Has he left bruises? Anna was friends with my sister. I remember seeing hers. Big ugly blotches where he'd spanked her."

Katy rose to her feet, head held high, despite a newer, wrenching pain that spread through her back.

"I can't speak to the first duchess' bruises. But in my experience, spankings are an acceptable form of punishment doled out to recalcitrant, spoiled children or wives who disgrace their husbands. Perhaps, if she had, in fact, been spanked, it was because she deserved it." She hoped her eyes flashed as hot as the anger that boiled through her. "And I can assure you, although it's none of your business, that my ass is as white and unmarred as freshly fallen snow."

****

Jeremy heard the commotion at the front door from the library, but it wasn't until he reached the top of the stairs that he realized what was happening. Caroline's petite frame supported a flagging Katy through the marble-lined foyer. Behind them, Ned elbowed his way through the door while Gregory and Stanley pushed him back. Bangs and thuds filled the air. A vase crashed to the floor and shattered with a pistol-like explosion.

One look at Katy's face sent Jeremy bounding down the stairs. Ghostly white, with lines of strain pulling at her mouth and eyes, she clutched her stomach and back, stopping every few steps. Gasps echoed, interspersed with the sounds of grunts and curses.

Through it all, Ned yelled, "I just be helpin'. The duchess needs me."

Rushing to her, Jeremy slipped Katy's arm from Caroline and heaved her into his arms.

"I'm sorry," she said between hisses of pain. Droplets of sweat beaded along her hairline. "Don't hate me."

Contorting in his arms, she curled up against him, panting. Her face burrowed into his neck, muffling moans and choked words.

Commanding his heart to keep beating, he raced up the stairs. When Alfred stumbled into view, they nearly collided, but the old man stepped aside just in time.

A kick at the bedroom door sent it crashing into the wall.

"Send for the doctor." To his surprise, the words came out calm and clear.

Laying her on the bed, Jeremy surveyed Katy. Scarlet blood soaked her knees and stained his arm. His neck was wet, too. A quick glance in the mirror revealed his cravat was wet, not bloody.

He knelt beside her and brushed her hair back. Tears streaked her cheeks. Words tumbled out, most making little sense. Why would he hate her? And who the hell was this Jane she kept mumbling about?

"I'm right here, Katy." He didn't know what to say. He knew what was happening. Knew the baby was gone. But helplessness paralyzed him. All he could do was touch her, reassure himself that she was alive.

Around him, he could still hear loud voices, strident and accusing, and a softer woman's voice hushing them, but he ignored it all.

"It hurts," Katy moaned, her body twisting into a ball. Her free hand clutched at her back. The other bit into his grip, squeezing harder than he believed possible.

A set of large hands tried to push him away.

Maggie's low voice urged him to leave, but he snarled and gripped Katy's hand tighter. Maggie patted his shoulder, then turned toward the door and began barking orders. A moment later, she lifted a spoon to Katy's mouth and urged her to swallow.

A few minutes later, the tension subsided, allowing Katy to suck in a long deep breath. His own chest heaved. Dragging in a breath of relief, he leaned close. Her lips moved, but he couldn't hear her over the din in the doorway.

"Everybody out," he bellowed. "Except Maggie."

The chaos quieted to faint murmurs heard through the door, and he leaned closer.

"So sorry," she whispered. "I tried."

"Hush. Don't talk. We'll talk later. Just rest. The doctor will be here soon." He shifted to relieve the pressure on his knees.

She clutched his hand, her face taking on a frantic look. "Don't. Don't leave me. Please."

"Never." He settled back. To hell with himself. If she wanted him on his knees beside her, that's where he'd be. He leaned forward and kissed her forehead.

She sighed, a shuddering sigh that ripped through her whole body. "I always wanted a real kiss…"

His heart skipped a beat until he saw her chest rise and fall. Her lashes closed, and her mouth relaxed. Slow shallow bursts of air battered her curls, fluttering them in rhythm with his heart. The words went around and around in his head.

He'd never kissed her. He'd spanked her and made love to her with his mouth, but he'd never kissed her. Not a real kiss.

All he could do now was hope it wasn't too late.

****

Katy pried her eyes open, the lids so heavy they felt like sandbags. Something pounded in her head as constant and annoying as water dripping. Her tongue scraped her mouth, so dry it hurt to swallow.

Not heaven. No cherubs. No Wedgewood blue walls. Only swathes of deep green interlaced with dark walnut.

"Katy?" It took most of her strength to turn. Words were too much effort, so she just looked.

Jeremy. He looked sad. And tired. Smudges of blackish green shadowed shiny red eyes. Had he been crying?

Her hand moved, but she was too tired. She'd just close her eyes for a minute…

****

When she woke the fifth day without the groggy look in her eyes, Jeremy felt the dread in his chest loosen. The doctor had said she'd recover, but he hadn't believed it. She looked too pale and lifeless. For two days, she'd burned with fever, so hot the wet cloths had dried practically before they cooled. During that time, she'd tossed and turned, tangling herself in the bedclothes, muttering and gasping as if chased by demons.

After the fever broke, the nightmares took over, robbing her of large chunks of sleep. He'd known she had them. He'd heard her through the walls when he wandered the halls at night, but he'd had no idea how bad they were.

Whatever haunted her nights involved Thomas and her sister, Caitlin. And George. Somehow, George inhabited her dreams. Another name slipped from her lips, too. A Henry. Who was Henry?

It didn't matter. Whoever he was or whatever had happened to Katy, he couldn't protect her. It had happened before he knew her. Even now, he had failed.

Anger swelled. Caroline had told him what happened. How Anna's vitriol continued to eat at his life, hurting Katy, who'd had nothing to do with any of it.

It didn't matter. All that mattered lay before him, staring at him with sleepy eyes.

"How are you feeling, sweetheart?"

"Confused." Her eyes wandered, head never moving. "Where am I?"

"My bed."

The corners of her mouth quirked. "Took you long enough."

He blinked, surprised, then pushed the thought aside when lines of pain etched her forehead.

"I lost it, didn't I?" Her hand settled on her stomach, and a whistling sound of agony raked the air.

"Afraid so."

"Was it a boy or a girl?"

"It was too early to tell for sure. The doctor thought it a girl." A girl. He'd thought he wanted a boy, but it felt worse, knowing he'd lost a little girl who might have looked like Katy, with blonde or red curls around a cherubic face.

"I'm sorry. I know how much you wanted it."

"Hush. It's not important." He brushed her hair back, hungry to touch her. "All that matters is you."

"Did the doctor—" Her gaze stroked his face in a way that made his rebellious cock stir. "Can I still have babies?"

Conflicting emotions tied his tongue in knots. Gratitude that no lasting harm had been done. Guilt, because she would never have babies if he had his choice. He looked away. "Yes."

Her fingers stroked over his hand, like a kitten kneading its mother. "Good. I want to give you babies."

Anguish ripped through him. He pushed it away. "I can't have children, Katy." Even saying it aloud hurt.

"Well, I suppose I could suffer George's attentions again. If you want."

His head snapped around, ire flaring. Then he saw the laughter in her eyes. Her fingers wrapped around his hand, strong and sure.

"We can try, Jeremy. It never hurts to try."

"No." He pulled his hand away. Hurt dimmed her eyes. He turned away. "No, and it's not open for debate."

He could live without children. He couldn't live without Katy.

Chapter Nine

The next month felt like a nightmare.

Katy slept most of the first week. The first few nights, Jeremy slept with her. She'd wake in the night, heart pounding from the nightmare of what she'd done in Ireland or weeping with emptiness because of the baby, and he'd wrap her in his arms. He even kissed her, long gentle kisses that left her moaning. But when she reached for evidence he still wanted her, he withdrew and pushed her away.

The second week he told her about Thomas. There'd been no sign of him anywhere. He never came out and said it, but Jeremy believed him dead. When George and Emily came to call, George had looked at her with the same guarded expression Jeremy wore. She didn't ask George. He would tell her if he knew anything.

The days started to run together, each day the same. They breakfasted together, both avoiding the topic of the baby, both pretending it didn't affect them. After breakfast, Jeremy retreated to the library and she wandered the house, too heartsick to bother with her usual activities. Often, she'd hear him yelling at the shady-looking characters that slipped in to see him. When she asked, the answer was always the same. They were searching for Thomas.

She studiously avoided the nursery. To her, it was

doubly damning. Not only was it a reminder she'd failed him in the one thing he wanted most, but he'd rejected her there the first time when she tried to make amends for her sins.

One day, an army of servants entered the room. Curious, she peeked in hours later. The entire room was empty. The crib, the changing table, the rocking horse had all vanished. Instead of mint green, the walls were hung with flocked beige paper-hangings. Tables lined the walls, bolts of fabric piled four layers high in every color imaginable. A chest stood before the window, filled with ribbons and lace. She should have been thrilled. Instead, she ached, sad that the baby she'd lost would be nothing but a memory in her mind.

She looked for the tiny baby clothes she'd crafted, wanting a small reminder of the hope that had filled her, but those too were gone. The drawer she'd filled in her room had been emptied, the half-finished christening gown she'd been working on gone from the library, the lace and silk she'd used nowhere to be found.

She cried that day. She cried for the baby she'd lost, for the brother she missed, but mostly for the man who seemed as hollow and lost as she.

Evenings and nights were the worst. They dined in the long dark dining room, too far apart to make conversation, too deep in the abyss of their own thoughts to want to try. Then Jeremy would excuse himself. Some nights, she would hear him leave the house and come back hours later, shuffling his feet down the hall outside her door. Other nights, he would lock himself in his room until well past midnight. In the small hours of the morning, she'd hear him wandering the house as she had done most of the day.

Once, he'd come into her room, well past the time she'd normally be asleep. She'd held her breath, praying he'd speak or touch her, but he hadn't. He'd just watched, his breathing rasping through the darkness for the longest time. Then he'd turned away, slipping back out as silently as he'd entered.

She had no idea how to stop the pain. It hurt from her head to her toes, an ache so deep she wanted to die.

****

"Your Grace, I'm sorry to disturb you."

Katy looked up from the cup of tea she'd been staring into, annoyed at the commiserating tone. She was tired of being treated like a sickly child who might die if taken out into the fresh air.

"What is it, Alfred?"

"The Earl of Margate is requesting an audience. Shall I say you aren't at home?"

The bone deep weariness almost made her agree. She'd wanted to go to him when Jeremy told her about Thomas, but like everything, Jeremy had dealt with it for her. Since then, her grandfather had sent her notes, condolences on the loss of the baby, little scribbles of encouragement, promises that Jeremy wasn't the only one searching for Thomas. She'd wallowed in her own pain, too afraid to add to his by showing it to another.

But the doctor had seen her the day before and pronounced her healed. She should resume her life. It would banish the melancholy and restore the color to her cheeks.

"No, Alfred. Have Gregory show him up." She placed her teacup on the small table beside her. "And from now on, make sure the footmen do their jobs themselves. You've your own duties."

"Very good, Ma'am." He bowed and started to turn toward the door but stopped. "If you don't mind, I'd like to say it wasn't because they were shirking their duties. They hate seeing you so sad, and I'm happy to do it. It helps, getting to see you periodically. Somehow, telling you a knife has been misplaced doesn't seem like a good reason."

"Thank you, Alfred." A bit of heat filled the empty space in her heart. At least someone wanted her. "Perhaps you could bring a fresh pot of tea for the earl."

Katy rose and wandered the room while she waited. Like her bedroom, it dripped with feminine sentimentality. Gold trim ran through the room, and lacy scallops topped the powder blue drapes. She still hated the blue and white. Every time she sat on the white brocade couch, she feared she'd spill something or just get it grimy. She knew all it would take was a word and Jeremy would redecorate. But the time never seemed right, and now she wasn't sure about anything. Would she want lavender or something more like Jeremy's woodsy green and brown? Did she even want to stay if Jeremy refused to make her his real wife?

After being announced, the earl stood in the doorway, hesitant.

"Please come in, My Lo—" The hopeful look in his eyes altered her words. "Grandpa." She'd never called him that. It hadn't felt right. But it did now. "May I call you that?"

"Of course." The low timbre of his voice shook, and he rushed over and enfolded her hands in his. "I'm so sorry for your loss and so glad to see you up and about."

"Thank you." Her voice trembled, and her eyes stung. His gloved hands looked like Jeremy's, large and long fingered, and they held hers with the same sure, comforting grip. It wasn't enough. "Would it be all right, if I hugged you, Grandpa?" Her mother had hugged her. Perhaps his hugs would feel the same.

"Oh, my dear!" His arms opened and pulled her against him. Despite the frail appearance, he hugged her with a strength that squeezed the tears from her. Like a lemon spitting out its seeds, they burst forth with gasping sobs, stopping and starting in spurts.

As he leaned his cheek atop her head and ran soothing hands up and down her back, she let the sorrow and loneliness out. It felt just like when her mother had held her as a child, a thought that made the torrent gain strength, until she heard the low whisper of "Baa Baa Black Sheep." Just as it had as a child, the ditty grabbed her attention, wrapping her heart with its familiarity.

When the ditty ended, she sniffled and pulled away. "I'm sorry. I know it's silly to cry. It isn't as if the baby was born."

"Nonsense. Never apologize for loving." With a flourish, he extended a handkerchief and waved her toward the chairs. "May we sit down? I'm afraid my bones don't enjoy holding me up as much as they used to."

He waited while Katy sat, then gingerly lowered himself beside her and engulfed her hand again. "It will get easier. But it's never easy. I remember when Violet, that was your grandmother, told me she was expecting your momma. I loved the baby that very instant. I don't imagine it's any easier or any harder no matter how old they are."

A rattle announced tea arriving, so Katy took the chance to compose herself further while Alfred wheeled in the refreshments. The ritual of pouring restored her equilibrium, allowing her to smile as she passed the saucer.

"Has there been any word about Thomas?" Somehow, she was able to ask him. The question always stuck in her throat when she tried to ask Jeremy. She knew Jeremy reported to him every day, and with her grandfather, there wouldn't be other questions she didn't want to answer.

He hesitated long enough she felt her throat close. "Possibly," he admitted. "A fellow in Cork thinks he remembers him. But you shouldn't get your hopes up."

"Cork? Why would he be in Cork?" Had he said Dublin, she could understand it. Thomas often ventured there to speak with other rebels or to gain information, but he never went to Cork.

"He might have boarded a ship if our informant is correct."

"And what about you, Grandpa? Are you keeping your hopes down?"

"No. If I learned nothing from your mother, it was that you never give up on your loved ones, no matter how slim the hope. Had I looked for her, I would have had many years with you and your brother and sister. Years I'll never get back now. Your young man understands about hope."

Did he? He continued to look, but the stream of men entering his study had dwindled and his efforts to keep her spirits up faded, apace with their arrival.

"I don't think so." Why would he? He'd never met

Thomas, had no reason to hope he survived. And if he believed in illogical optimism, he'd try to give her a baby.

"Is there something wrong, my dear?"

She pasted a smile back on her face, but when she looked at him, his face was stormy, and she needed to tell someone. Someone who would be on her side. "I'm thinking of leaving him. I don't think he wants me anymore."

His whole body jerked back. His eyes widened, and his lips hardened. Then, just as quickly, he shook his head in disbelief. "I won't tell you what you should do, but I think you'd be making a mistake. That boy would cut his heart out for you."

Her head shook. "I don't think so. He barely speaks to me since—" The loss was still too raw to say aloud.

His hand reached out and again clasped hers. "Let me tell you what I see in your duke. I see myself when I met your grandmother. I was so in love with my Violet that I couldn't tell her. As if telling her would ruin it somehow. So, I tried to control it, same way I did when your momma came home and told me she was in love. I told Violet she was going to marry me. Her father told her she was going to marry me. And I told your momma that she was going to marry…" His brow furrowed. "I don't remember who. Some viscount who had enough money that he seemed like a good choice. Anyway, Violet wasn't having any of it. She told me if I wanted her, I'd have to prove it. I had no idea what that meant. I had a good name, a fortune that would support her, a house as grand as this one here." His hands gestured at the opulent surroundings. "But still she refused me."

"What did you do?"

He snorted, a sound as ungentlemanly as any her brothers made. "Same thing I did with your mother. I dug my heels in and tried to break her like a horse." He winked at her. "Your grandmother was a smart woman though. She ended up leading me around by the bit, not the other way around." His grin died, his eyes turning inward. "Had she lived longer, she never would have let me lose your momma. See, Violet knew that beneath my domineering, stubborn exterior, I needed to be loved. She also said, many times, that men are like children. Some of them need to be told what to do for their own good."

"I don't understand. What did she do?"

He chuckled. "She let me lead her around, just enough that I'd know how good it felt. She let me dance with her and take her out riding and shopping. Her father never knew about those trips, because I'd buy her things I shouldn't have, like that brooch your momma gave you. Then when I was well and thoroughly hooked, she stopped seeing me. Took up with Viscount Hammerly."

"But you got her back."

He scowled. "Not by anything I did. I pummeled the poor man. Was quite the scandal. One that nearly cost me. But when she demanded to know why I'd done it, I told her. I did it because I loved her. Turned out that was all she wanted. Was for me to tell her. I told her every day after that until the day she died."

"So, you're saying I should tell Jeremy I love him?"

"No, my dear. I'm saying look at the man beneath the exterior. Figure out what he needs." He narrowed his eyes and stared at her, tight lipped. "I won't lie. I don't like the rumors I've heard about the man and his...needs. But I learned not to judge when your momma left, and I can see he loves you. It's up to you to decide. Figure out what he needs and decide if it's something you can give him."

He lifted his teacup to his lips, all the while watching her. Katy pondered his words, an idea forming, then nodded. His lips curved, and he placed the cup back on the tray.

"I'll leave you now, my dear. I hope my wisdom," he snorted at the word, "helps. Not that you need it. I expect you take after your momma and grandma, smart as Socrates and as beautiful as Athena." He dragged himself to his feet and turned toward the door. As he reached it, he turned back. "One last thing. If you ever need anything, anything at all, everything I own is at your disposal."

****

Something had changed.

Katy was humming, a gentle hum that nevertheless filled the library. Jeremy let his gaze rest on her as she leaned over the desk, her pen scratching numbers. In his hands, a treatise on farming methods dropped into his lap. He wasn't reading it. It was an excuse to be in the room with her. Because of the dank, dark day, a fire crackled beside him, casting a warm glow over her features.

He'd wondered if she would ever smile again. The leaden weight that had lodged in his throat when the doctor told him she lost the baby slipped an iota. While not a smile, her lips no longer curled downward. Her luminous green eyes had cleared. The hum sounded like

188

the greatest violin concerto, despite the slightly off-key higher notes.

He inhaled deeply, savoring the moment of respite, then let it out. Whether it was the visit from her grandfather or another reason didn't matter. She no longer looked tortured.

The book slipped from his fingers, landing with a thud. She jumped. Her eyes darted around before fastening on him. A hesitant, fake smile settled over her face. When she looked away, her hands curled into a fist and a frown furrowed her brow.

Had she finally decided to leave him? He'd been waiting for it, dreading it. It was inevitable. She wanted children, and he couldn't give them to her. He couldn't even try. The best he could do was let her go when she asked.

At least the constant throb in his balls would go away. It was the only advantage he could find in the idea. He suspected the ache in his heart would grow, though, eventually crushing his chest with its weight.

In the absence of her hum, the rustle of her skirt seemed overly loud. He watched, soaking in the view of her long limbs and fiery hair as she glided toward him. As always, his cock vaulted to attention as she neared. When she knelt down and lifted the book from the floor, his balls tightened.

Shame filled him. All it took was one whiff of her scent and his manhood reacted like a badly trained puppy, leaping and begging for a treat.

"Jeremy." His name fell from her lips, hesitant and hushed. "I've been thinking about something."

His entire body tightened, a combination of dread and a pitiful effort at control. Instead of rising, she sank back onto her heels. Her hand felt like a flaming arrow, burning his knee. He ought to remove it, but like ripping the arrow out, it would hurt more than the pain of leaving it.

Make it easy for her. She deserves a man who can love her.

His hand reached up and cupped her cheek. "What is it, sweetheart?" His thumb caressed the soft skin, knowing it might be the last chance he'd get.

Her gaze slipped down, and she started to bite her bottom lip, then stopped. "I know you said it wasn't up for discussion, but I want to talk about being your wife."

Confused, he frowned, his hand stilling.

Maybe she didn't know how to broach it.

"I've been expecting it. I won't stop you." God, it was harder to form the words than he'd thought. He inhaled, forcing the air past the lump. "I don't know about a divorce, though. I'll have to see if I can arrange it."

"What!" She jerked back. The cold where her hand had lain burned more than the heat.

She stared at him, paling, eyes as wide as the forest behind Lexham Estate. "You want me to leave?" Hurt reverberated in the words.

An instant later, she leapt to her feet, eyes blazing. "You bastard! You're worse than George." The book slammed into his chest. "I thought you wanted me." Whirling, her head jerked around, hands flexing. Another book flew through the air, heading toward his head.

He ducked, then grabbed her by the waist, just as she tried to launch herself at the door. Air whooshed from his chest. Her body slammed into him, legs kicking, elbows jamming his breastbone. Pain exploded as her other elbow smashed into his forehead.

"Let me go! You're a frigging cocksucking Maggot pie." Her feet, luckily bare, nailed his shin. He tightened his grip, hauling her closer. "I'm not a god damned brood mare." Her arms kept escaping. Nails dug into his forearm, ripping through the linen. "You can't just discard me."

"Whoa." Finally locking one of her arms, he dragged her onto his lap. Her ass landed hard on his cock. Pain shot through his balls. He gasped but tightened his hold. "Stop!" His voice boomed, cracking like the sound of wood on wood.

Instantly, she froze.

"God's blood, Katy." He leaned his forehead against the back of her head. "That isn't what I meant."

The claw on his forearm retracted. "It isn't?" Her body relaxed, slumping in his arms.

"No." He choked it out. "I never want you to go." He buried his face in the lemon-scented hair that had tumbled from her carefully crafted bun. "I thought that's what you wanted to tell me. I just—I wanted to make it easier for you."

"I don't want to leave." Sniffling, she dragged her arm out and swiped at her cheek and nose.

Jeremy took the chance to lift her, rearranging her on his lap. Blood pounded through his crotch. Hissing, he ignored it and tucked her into the crook of his arm.

He'd messed up again.

She didn't want to leave.

She wanted to talk. About being his wife.

He swallowed, the ember of hope dying. Outside, a

rumble of thunder rolled.

"What did you want?" Maybe it wasn't what he feared.

"I want to be your wife. I want to lie with you." Her hand soothed over his arm, caressing the raw area where she'd ripped the skin. "I don't care about babies. I just want you."

"I can't, Katy." He squeezed his eyes shut, cheek sliding along the top of her head.

"Why? Tell me why."

"I can't."

She drew a deep breath and pushed away from him. Her gaze locked on his face, her lips hard with determination. "You can't tell me, or you can't lie with me?" A note of anger crept into her voice. Another crack of thunder rocked the house.

He wasn't prepared for this. He should have been but wasn't. "I won't. I won't tell you, and I won't lie with you." His jaw set. It wasn't up for discussion.

He was certain her eyes flashed with lightning as she slipped from his lap. She stomped toward the door, turning as the heavy slab swung open.

"You're a coward, Jeremy Wyles. I told you I'd do anything you wanted." Her eyes fastened on his crotch, brows dropping, lips pinched. "I told you my secrets, trusted you with the fate of my family. But you can't even tell me why you won't love me. So, it doesn't matter if I leave or not. You'll always be alone. And so will I."

Chapter Ten

"I hope Jeremy doesn't kill me. It not too late to change your mind, you know?"

Katy huddled into her hooded cloak and peered out at the looming darkness. Situated on the edge of Covent Garden in Bloomsbury Square, the house before her was huge, with Italianate details. Music leaked from the windows, the lights inside barely penetrating the heavy drapes. It didn't look at all like a whore house. Emily had called it Madame O's. A brothel that catered to the unconventional.

"Jeremy's more likely to kill me than you." With another doubtful survey, Katy descended from the hackney carriage after Emily and slipped a half crown to the driver. Following Emily's lead, she slipped a black satin half-mask over her eyes and adjusted it.

Screwing up her courage, Katy followed Emily, clad in a nondescript cloak and mask. Emily moved with her usual grace and confidence, gliding up the stairs as if entering a Ton ball. When she reached the top step, a footman stepped out and Emily dropped her hood.

"Domme E. It's good to see you again." The footman bowed, gesturing for Emily to enter, and cast a dismissive glance at Katy.

Katy sighed with relief. She hadn't believed Emily when she'd said she could help. All she'd asked her for was the name of Jeremy's mistress. But when she confessed why she needed to know, Emily had confessed a few secrets of her own. Secrets that still had Katy reeling.

"This is my friend, K," Emily explained as they stepped over the threshold. "She's here as my guest. She won't be participating. Just watching."

"E, I've missed you." A woman appeared, sweeping forward. Of average height, she nevertheless dominated the space. Honey gold curls towered above a round face with stunning brown eyes and a ripe mouth. As well gowned as any society lady, her attire revealed enough of her curvy body to tempt without revealing too much. "We've a number of subs that have been asking for you," she continued, reaching out and clasping Emily's hands then circling her, with a keen hawk-like gaze. "You must stop letting G knock you up. You're getting soft."

"I like getting knocked up." With a shrug, Emily transformed before Katy's eyes. Instead of the gentle, maternal woman she knew, Emily slid off her cloak and held it out to the side, shoulder high. Her fingers released and the rich brown cloak fluttered toward the ground. A man leapt from the shadows, catching it before it hit the green and white marble floor.

Emily, who normally wore the popular white and cream colors of the day, revealed a low cut bright blue gown that hugged her form. Head held high, she cast a disdainful look at the man who had caught the cloak. In her hand, a crop slapped out, hitting the man's shoulder with a crack. Katy gasped. Bare skin gleamed in the meager light. Rotund, with breasts that sagged like an old woman, the man wore nothing but a pair of tight-fitting pantaloons.

"You let the hem hit the floor, M. That will earn you two more next time." With a snap of her fingers, she turned her face toward Katy. "Come along, K."

Swallowing, Katy edged forward. M, whose gaze never rose from his scrutiny of the floor, whispered an apology and stripped Katy's cloak from her shoulders. Bowing repeatedly, he practically crawled backward until the shadows swallowed him.

Emily glided forward through an inner door. As instructed, Katy followed.

A huge ballroom-sized room opened before her. Three chandeliers blazed, but the room looked as much like a conservatory as a ballroom. Potted plants broke the space into dozens of little alcoves, some more exposed than others. Like the balls she'd attended, people milled, laughing and talking. Unlike those balls, the attire was different. Both women and men wore garments that showed breasts and bums. Many wore masks, some covering more of their faces than their clothes hid. Cosmetics and jewelry enhanced many attributes, including nipples, aureoles, and cocks.

"As I explained in my note," Emily said to the hostess, recapturing Katy's attention, "there have been rumors about K's husband, that he had a mistress here. It's all speculation, of course, and we understand you can't reveal any knowledge you might have, but K wished to see firsthand what types of…what was the word they used, K?" Emily's lips tightened. She hadn't been happy to hear the details of Jane's accusations. "Unsavory activities, I think it was, that her husband might enjoy."

The woman stepped toward Katy and waved a

hand. "May I?"

"Of course." Emily's voice gentled much as it had when she'd confessed her secrets. "I told her if we came, she'd have to follow orders." Her voice regained its crispness. "I suspect she might have the exact nature her husband needs. If the rumors about him are true, of course."

The woman circled Katy, just as she had Emily, but at a much slower pace. Murmurs and tsks were punctuated by an occasional touch or tug. As she returned to the front, she lifted Katy's chin with her finger. A shiver ran up Katy's spine, and she stared at the woman's décolletage.

Was that what Jeremy liked? Round, white globes that spilled over a neckline? No matter how she might try, she'd never have those.

"Look at me." Katy's head jerked toward the voice. Assessing black eyes stared at her. "Tell me, K, do you pleasure yourself?"

A quick glance at Emily showed a matching rise of her eyebrows. Heat flooded her face. She considered not answering, but Emily had admitted she liked to dominate George and others. That confession had to be as hard as this. And Emily had no need to admit any of it. She'd done it to help her.

"Yes, Ma'am." The heat felt like a fire now. Looking away helped, but not much. Suddenly, the lack of clothing in the room made sense.

"To you, in here, it's Mistress. Mistress O."

Katy's heart leapt. Memories of Jeremy's punishment flickered through her mind. "Thank you, Mistress." It came out unbidden, and she raised her gaze.

Mistress O smiled, then winked. "And I know your husband well." She glanced at Emily and Katy. "Of course, I never said that, you understand."

"But—" The word slipped out as Katy's stomach plummeted. If Mistress O knew Jeremy, that meant…what? That Jeremy was like George? Emily said George liked to be ordered about, and Emily liked to do it.

She couldn't be like Mistress O or Emily.

"Don't worry." A chuckle accompanied the change in tone. "I'm what's called a switch. But my submissive talents are much more sought after and much more lucrative in cases such as your husband, where discretion is highly prized." With a gesture, she indicated a direction, then paused. "Are you certain you wish to continue? If you say no, I'll understand. It's not to everyone's taste."

"Yes. I'm sure." Even if she weren't trying to lure her husband to her bed, her curiosity would have been enough. Ever since the idea had popped into her head, she'd been determined.

"Very well." Mistress O waved her arm at the room before them. "As you can see, we have the common room. Most people like to play there. We also have private rooms for those who prefer discretion. You may recognize individuals. It goes without saying that anyone you see here expects you to keep it to yourself. There's a certain safety in the fact that everyone here shares each other's secret, but now and then we have to ban someone for breaking that unwritten rule."

They ambled over to a corner. A nubile young woman stood naked before a small crowd of onlookers while a middle-aged gentleman in a dark gray tailcoat wrapped strands of rope around her breasts and crotch in elaborate patterns. Blindfolded and gagged, a pinkish glow seemed to emanate from the woman. The tangy scent of arousal hung in the air. Hushed whispers from the onlookers created a strange counterpoint to the violin music threading through the room.

"Master P is demonstrating a technique he learned in the Orient. It's rather pretty, don't you think?"

Fascinated, Katy nodded. The two seemed separate from the crowd, moving together in a dance that only they understood.

"You'll see many different interactions tonight," Mistress O said. A light touch on Katy's elbow sent another tingle up her spine, leading her away. "There are many couples engaged in Dominant/submissive relationships, like E and G enjoy. I don't know how much she's shared with you." She glanced at Emily, then continued. "Theirs is mostly mental control with a bit of bondage. Others involve a more physical control. You'll see that later."

Mistress O guided them around a wall of bamboo and fronds. Four couples lounged about in various positions. A bench held a man and a woman on either end. At their feet, another person crouched, a man lapping at the woman's stocking clad foot, another male curled up like a puppy near the man. A cage hid in one corner, a naked young woman cowering inside, whining and whimpering while a man stood over her poking her with a stick. The last pair circled the room, an older woman leading a bare young man on a leash. He sported a rock-hard cock, and swollen balls hung beneath his thighs. Snapping commands while he pranced around her heels, the woman rubbed his head, offering bits of meat when her commands were obeyed.

"This is another mental domination. Rather more popular than you would expect." Mistress O's gaze swept over the group, then settled on Katy. When Katy shuddered, Mistress O's mouth quirked up in the corners. "There's also a corner for patrons who enjoy what's called horse play. Not the type parents accuse their children of. It's a bit more physical than puppy play. Crops are often in use. We'll skip that unless you wish to see it. It's a form of submission I tend to lack."

They resumed the tour, Mistress O explaining each area, dropping similar hints that rather clearly implied whether they might appeal to Jeremy or not. There were couples who pretended to be furniture, men and women who enjoyed humiliation, people wearing diapers, a number of couples fully engaged in copulation cheered on by an audience; all what Mistress O deemed *mental* power exchanges.

Katy soon learned that, while Jeremy often wandered about watching, he rarely participated in any of these public displays. She also determined that although the sex act itself lent a warm glow to her, the mental forms of play did little to excite her.

As they ventured farther into the room, nearing the darker, more cloistered areas, the moans and breathy gasps grew more extreme. A dread settled in Katy's chest. The groans sounded familiar, like forgotten memories.

"This is where things begin to get more physical." Mistress O led them through a screen wall draped in ivy. A musky scent filtered out, sending a quiver of anticipation along Katy's spine.

Less partitioned, the room nonetheless seemed

more private, despite a goodly number of masked duos and threesomes. Shadows rippled, and a rhythmic thwack echoed in the air. Mistress O paused, and Katy felt her and Emily's eyes on her, sending another shiver of awareness straight to her belly.

This was what Jeremy liked. She didn't know how she knew it. She just did.

Katy stepped forward, lungs shuddering, and let her gaze survey the room. As her eyes adjusted, the blobs of darkness took on shapes. Stools and benches, mostly unused, littered the area near the entrance. Other oddly shaped benches, with lower, thinner panels on either side came into view. One of them held a woman bent over it, her ass in the air, while another woman's hand smacked her.

Slap. Katy's breath caught at the familiar sound. Wetness pooled between her legs.

Swallowing, she followed the other sound through the darkness. Slipping around a large potted bush, she encountered the form of a man. Tall and lean, his chest glimmered in the low light, slick with sweat. As she watched, his arm rose, then snapped forward. *Thwack.* In his hand, an instrument made of flaps of leather flashed. As it came down, the strips slapped a woman. Just as slender and bare from the waist up, her back glowed.

"That's Master L," whispered Mistress O, "and C. He's flogging her." A soft moan rasped over Katy's ears. The wetness between her legs increased. "Notice she's not tied down. She could be, but Master L, like most of the best Masters, insists on willing participation. She hangs onto the straps to hold herself up and spreads her legs by choice. They're what some people call a sadistic masochistic couple. A few sadists enjoy forced pain. We don't allow them here."

Katy licked her suddenly dry lips. "What does it feel like?"

Mistress O chuckled, easing Katy back. "It's different for everyone. Some find it extremely pleasurable. I do. Others do it because it pleases their master. It depends also on the instruments used. We offer a full array of tools here. Paddles, floggers, canes, whips."

With a light touch, Mistress O gestured toward the far wall. Unable to help herself, Katy wandered toward them. Wooden paddles, wide and narrow, hung from the wall. The handles sported a wide assortment of sizes and shapes—ebony handles that looked like phalluses, wood with depressions to fit the fingers, even an entire paddle shaped from stone. Floggers hung in another area, whips covered an entire corner, and a large box contained canes.

"Would you like to know more?" Madame O picked up the ebony handled paddle and offered it to Katy. Hesitantly, Katy took it in her hands. The ebony was hard and cool, and the wooden paddle covered in supple leather that warmed in her hands. Madame O explained the uses of each instrument, what areas of the body they were used on, and more importantly the areas to be avoided. Fascinated, Katy listened, touching and filing the details into her mind, until Madame O turned away and led her into another room.

A huge wooden X came into view. A tall regal woman was smacking the muscular thighs of a slightly overweight man with a long thin switch. Between his legs, a fully erect penis quivered with each strike.

"This is Mistress W and her sub—or submissive, D. They like a bit of bondage, because D isn't as masochistic, but it's still a sadistic and masochistic relationship."

Long, thin, red marks lined the man's thighs, crisscrossing in a definite pattern. Every so often, the woman would run the tip of the switch along the length of his legs, slowing as it neared his erection. Soft low murmurs of approval whispered along with the switch, drawing moans and pleas from the man. Katy's breathing began to match the rapid sound of the switch.

"Why does he do it? If he doesn't like it?"

"Because he loves her. And because he knows she won't hurt him any more than she needs to and never more than he can take."

As if she heard Mistress O, the woman stopped and rushed forward. The man slumped, lungs sucking in sobs, while she fondled his cock. Katy shut out the words. Too intimate, too demanding, the questions made her yearn to feel the same connection. The ache between her legs grew, urging her away.

"Any domination and submission requires a certain trust to work," Mistress O explained. "A sadistic-masochistic relationship is even more intense. While on the surface, the Dominant is in control, in reality, it's often the submissive who holds the true power. A Dominant needs a submissive. If they can find one who meets their needs, they will do anything to make them happy. The same is true for the submissive. Both want to be needed and loved, taken care of in the way they need. For a sadist, the need to hurt isn't something they can control, so finding a submissive who will allow the level of pain necessary to fulfill the urge is precious and rare."

The words made sense. More importantly, Katy felt the truth in them. "Thank you," she said, the understanding clear in her hushed tone. "I think I've seen enough."

"I think you should see one more couple."

Turning away, Mistress O started toward a small arbor on the left. Ducking under a spray of lilacs, the heady scent filled Katy's lungs. Mistress O held out her hand, stopping Katy just inside the alcove.

Another X dominated the wall. Another form hung from wrist restraints, this one an older woman, completely naked. A well-built man lifted his arm and threw it forward. A whistling sheared the air, followed by the harsh snap of leather hitting skin.

Katy cringed as a hiss of pain split the quiet. Another snap and a shriek made her shrink back.

Why had Mistress O shown her this? Was this what Jeremy liked?

Katy stiffened. There was a familiar smell in the air. Fear. And blood. She recognized it.

Another strike hit the woman. Her body jerked. Too far away, Katy couldn't see it, but in her mind, she could. Caitlin had smelled like that. She had scars on her back now. From a whipping.

Another whistle. Another sharp crack. Katy jumped. The woman writhed with a keening sob. Paralyzed, all Katy could do was stare.

Another scream of the whip. Another scream of pain. Over and over, just like in her dream, the cruel leather bit the woman.

"Ten!" The woman shrieked. Another whistle whined, then another, even faster. The woman's body jerked, her ragged screams choking from her throat.

"Enough!" Mistress O's voice rang out, anger evident. A pair of burly men stepped out of the shadows, hovering behind them. "Take her down."

The muscled arm lifted again and shot forward. One of the men stepped in front of it, wrenching the whip from his hand. Both men stared at each other, faces hard with fury.

Then the man dropped his whip. The tension drained away, and he turned toward Mistress O.

Katy froze.

Even with his face hidden, she knew him.

"Forgive me, Mistress O," spoke a familiar voice, one that had haunted her dreams longer than she liked. His gaze shifted, landing on Katy. A slow wicked smile split the lips beneath his mask, steely gray eyes glittering in the holes. "I'm afraid I may need a new sub. Care to stand in?"

Chapter Eleven

It couldn't be him. He was dead. She'd killed him herself. Seen him on the ground, the bayonet stuck in his heart.

"She's not for you, Master A," Mistress O snapped. Even in the dark, Katy could see the fury in her eyes. Her gaze scraped over the man, scorn tightening her lips. Without turning her head, she said, "Mistress E, please take her out of here."

Still frozen, Katy recoiled, but the light touch broke the spell. Never taking her eyes from him, she backed out of the room. Emily guided her, hands on her shoulder.

"I'm so sorry, Katy. You shouldn't have seen that. It's not supposed to be like that." Emily's shudder radiated down through her hands, but Katy already felt tiny convulsions of fear.

"I just want to go home."

Hustling her out, Emily soon had her ensconced in a closed carriage, a heavy wool blanket over her lap. Katy shrank into the corner, glad of the blackness. Even Emily, who normally kept up a running commentary on any subject, sat in silence. Slowly, the carriage began to move, the click clack of the horses' hooves against the cobblestones soon picking up speed.

A shuddering exhale shook Katy. She forced her fingers to open, release the fists that had formed, the pain of her nails cutting into her palms easing.

"Do you know who he is?" she asked, afraid of the answer. More afraid of not knowing.

After a short hesitation, Emily said, "I think it's Viscount Alysham." Leaning forward, she took Katy's hand. "Please, Katy, don't think it's like that. It isn't. He should have stopped. Long before she used her word." Another shiver passed between them. "He's new. And he won't be back. I promise. Mistress O will strip him of his privileges."

Katy didn't care. She was never going back there.

She turned her head, pulling her hand from Emily's and staring into the darkness. Viscount Alysham. She ran through the litany of names she'd learned from Debrett's. Robert Edward Thomas Gaines, fourth Viscount. Heir presumptive, Bradley Lawrence Gaines. Not Henry Sharpe.

She squeezed her eyes shut. Her heart was still pounding. The vision of Caitlin, chained to a post, back dripping with blood, rose before her eyes. Her body jerked, remembering the feel of the pike as it hit bone, then rushed forward. The sight of the blood pooling around him. Her sick satisfaction that he was dead.

It was never going to go away. She'd be haunted by it forever. She'd thought the dreams were going away, the nightmare that had plagued her since it happened. But it hadn't. It had invaded her life.

She was going insane. The feel of eyes on her all week had been paranoia. And now she was seeing him, in people and places he couldn't possibly be.

"I knew this was a mistake. I should never have taken you there." Emily's foot tapped furiously in counterpoint to the clacking of the horses. "Jeremy isn't like that. Please don't be afraid of him."

Katy's eyes snapped open, and she stared at Emily. Unable to see her well enough in the dark, all she could go on was Emily's voice. She sounded panicky and angry with herself.

But this had been her idea, not Emily's. She'd known Jeremy liked to hurt women. The Earl of Beccles had told her. She hadn't known the particulars. She'd wanted to see it, to see if she could tolerate it. Whether she meant to or not, Emily had just confirmed that Jeremy liked whips.

"I'm not afraid." Her panic drained away at the words. "Jeremy would never hurt me. I know that." She knew it as much as she'd known that killing Henry Sharpe wasn't a sin. All she feared now was that someone would find out.

Which would feel worse? The look on Jeremy's face when he found out she'd killed a Coronet in the Dragoons or the feel of the noose around her neck?

She had to pull herself together. Aside from George and Thomas, no one else knew. And they wouldn't tell. They'd both hang with her if anyone found out.

****

"We should tell her."

"No." Emily arched her back and splayed her hands over George's bare chest, admiring the faint red marks crossing his chest. She'd hit him harder than usual, but three months without him was almost too much to bear. Madame O was right. She needed to stop getting knocked up.

"But she could be in danger. At least if she knows he's not dead, she'll be on her guard."

"I said no, George. And need I remind you, we wouldn't be in this position if you and Thomas had done your jobs correctly."

Slowly, she eased herself up on George's cock, throwing her head back. She was already getting hot again. She'd tied George's hands above his head, and his hips lifted just the way she liked, but he wasn't paying attention. It had been a mistake to let him come. Now, he was just going through the motions for her.

"How were we supposed to know he wasn't dead? Bloody mother, Em, the man lost more blood than a horse."

"Then you should have buried him, not thrown him on a battlefield." Her voice was harder than she intended, but she was getting annoyed. She didn't want to top him right now, and she didn't want to be Agent X, either. She wanted her husband to fuck her until she fell asleep. Because he wanted to, not because she demanded it.

"Yes, I suppose so." George sounded so defeated that Emily lifted her hips from his and threw herself onto the bed, an arm over her eyes. "But we don't have any evidence he's the mole. He might just be a sadistic bastard. And Jeremy loves her."

"I know, hun. But I'm ninety-five percent sure it's him." Her mind swirled, putting the pieces together.

It had seemed like divine intervention. Wickham had hired her to unearth the mole when his agents in rebel camps had started turning up dead. George had come home whining that Jeremy wanted him to go to Ireland, saving her the trouble of sending someone else who might not be as trustworthy. She'd sent George with explicit instructions to work with Thomas

Brennan, her own man, and bring back the name of the mole.

Instead, George had walked in on Katy and Thomas dragging a dead body out of a stable. Everything had fallen apart after that. Thomas only had the name of the mole. Brad. He'd never met him. Those who described him had said he was nondescript and dull. Some said black eyes, others gray. Plain brown hair, average height and weight. No scars. Katy and her sister Caitlin had called the dead man Henry. The leaks had stopped though, as suddenly as they'd started, at the same time.

She'd gone so far as to tell Wickham the mole was dead.

Then Thomas disappeared, with no word, and the leaks had started again. Wickham had given her a month to fix it. Now she worried about Thomas.

"We should tell Jeremy then. He'll put his man on watching her."

"He's already watching her," she snapped, rubbing the bridge of her nose. "And we aren't telling him. In fact, if you ever want to touch my pussy again, you'll keep your mouth shut about all of it." She'd told George too much. He was too susceptible to orders, and Jeremy had as much of an emotional hold over him as she did.

"If Jeremy asks about what happened in Ireland, you tell him he has to ask Katy." As far as Emily could tell, Katy didn't know her brother was working for the Crown. With luck, the fact she'd killed an English soldier would distract Jeremy and leave Emily her one chance to prove that Henry and Brad and Viscount Alysham were all one and the same.

She'd feel so much better if George would just fuck her silly or if her one chance didn't mean using Katy as bait.

****

"I know they say Bourbon doesn't go bad, but once it's poured, it's a sin to not drink it."

Jeremy glanced up as Miles dropped onto the sofa beside him later that day and scowled. The weather hadn't improved, but Miles showed no ill effects from being out in it. Because of the inclement weather, Boodles was half-empty, and most of the patrons were playing cards in the adjoining room. A fire blazed nearby, adding a pleasant warmth to the room. "Shouldn't you be out prying secrets out of someone or spreading false rumors to sidetrack the enemy?"

"Who says I'm not?" Miles chuckled but gestured at the glass of caramel-colored liquid. "I've been watching you for a good ten minutes, and you haven't even touched that. If you aren't going to drink it, can I?"

Jeremy nudged it away. "Go ahead. It isn't helping, anyway."

"It rarely does. Anything I can help with?"

"No. I have to figure it out myself."

Miles sipped at the bourbon, twisting the glass in his hands, watching the liquid. It climbed the sides, then fell back down, over and over again. "You always do. It's one of the things I like best about you. It's also one of the most annoying." His brows arched to emphasize it, and he raised the glass as if toasting Jeremy.

"How so?" First Katy accused him of…whatever she'd meant when she called him a coward, and now Miles seemed to be hinting at another personality flaw.

"You're very logical and thorough. It's a good trait when you need to solve a complex problem. But it takes longer. A deuced long time at times. And it can make your friends feel superfluous."

"I—" Jeremy stopped, unsure if he wanted to argue or apologize. Was he doing the same thing to Miles that Katy had complained about? "I don't know what to do," he finally admitted. "I've done everything I can think of to make her happy, but nothing works. Just when I think I'm doing the right thing, something happens, and it's the wrong thing. I thought she'd want to leave since the baby…" He couldn't even say it. "But she got upset. I think I hurt her." He paused, reaching back to knead the muscle in his neck. "It's illogical."

Miles leaned back and studied Jeremy long enough that he began to despair. Even Miles had no answers. Miles always knew how to fix things. "Do you want her to leave?"

Jeremy looked at him as if he'd lost his mind. "Of course not."

Miles drained the glass, then glanced around the room. When he spotted a footman, he pointed at the glass and held up two fingers. The glass thudded on the table, and a coin replaced it in his hands. A spark of hope lit in Jeremy as Miles began to manipulate it between his fingers.

"I'm not sure I can help much. After all, I'm the man who can't keep a woman for more than six months at a time. But here's what I see." The coin stopped between his first two fingers. "Logic cannot solve every problem. Sometimes, you have to trust your instincts. Most people call it following your heart."

The coin progressed to the next two fingers while

Miles locked his eyes on Jeremy. "You have a hard time trusting your heart. But you need to. Which is why I'm going to say something I've wanted to say for longer than I want to admit. Something you weren't ready to hear until now."

The coin traveled over the ring finger, deftly caught between it and the pinkie. The drinks arrived, and Miles waited until the footman bowed and left before he continued. "Anna was a bitch. A selfish, manipulative bitch. You need to stop letting her rule your life."

Jeremy swallowed. He'd never admitted it to anyone. Not even Miles. "I know. It was a mistake marrying her, but I'm not sure that has any bearing on Katy."

"No? I think it does." Miles swallowed a mouthful of bourbon, and the coin began to fly through his fingers. "I never told you, but I had an encounter with Anna before you knew her. I won't go into particulars. Suffice to say, I tied her up. Within minutes, I had her figured out. There wasn't a smidgen of passion in that woman, and submissiveness was as foreign to her as speaking Chinese."

"But—"

The coin stopped. "She was a Domme, Jeremy. One of the worst types. Her method of domination was mental, and she used your insecurities against you. She pretended to be a soft, scared submissive so you'd want her. Mainly because she wanted your fortune, and she wanted to be a duchess. Then she tore you down, shamed you for being what you are."

Jeremy's eyes widened at the tone of Miles' voice. Crystal sharp anger laced his words, anger that he'd never heard from Miles.

"I never asked him, because it wasn't my business, but I doubt George ever fucked her. It was part of her plan. Rip your confidence away, make you doubt your manhood, make sure you had no desire to touch her. Take away everything you loved."

Jeremy took a gulp of bourbon as the truth seeped into his brain. The burning didn't stop the twisting pain of loss. He'd pushed George away, never once questioning it, never once giving him a chance to defend himself.

"Why—" Why hadn't Miles stopped him? "You never said anything."

"Would you have listened?"

Jeremy's lips tightened. He wouldn't have. He'd always been stubborn. His mind churned, regret piling up as he thought of the times George had tried to reach out, tried in his own way to get Jeremy to talk to him. He winced, remembering George's confusion the first few times he'd rebuffed his overtures.

If George hadn't fucked her—

His eyes locked on Miles, who raised one eyebrow, and his stomach clenched. If the baby wasn't George's...

"What about Sarah? And all those others?"

As always, Miles knew exactly what he was asking. "Sarah was married to Harvey Kent for three years before he died and never once quickened. And how many times did you actually lie with her before you gave up? And the rest were all paid mistresses. You can't make a living if you get knocked up."

"Bloody hell, Miles." Jeremy drained his glass and motioned for another. All those years, lost. All those opportunities. All the women he'd rejected. "Why didn't you say something sooner?"

"You weren't ready to hear it. And I never saw any reason to force it."

Jeremy stared at the empty glass, clutching it tightly, then opening his hand. The scar from the glass he'd broken stared back, accusing him. He'd been a fool to believe Anna. "But you do now?"

Miles face brightened into a grin. "You asked me what you should do. Don't let Katy leave. She's what you thought you were getting with Anna."

A scoff burst from Jeremy. "Katy's not submissive. She dumped hot tea over George." He smiled, then frowned. "And upbraided that witch Jane." A jolt of guilt hit him in the chest. She'd defended him, and all the while, her baby had been dying. "She's the strongest, most self-assured woman I've ever met."

"And you're one of the smartest men I know. But when it comes to women, you're as blind as a brick wall."

Jeremy scowled but couldn't argue. Not when he'd just had his blindness pointed out to him. His new drink arrived, saving him the effort of replying, and he exchanged his empty glass for the full one.

"I've watched her," Miles told him. "She hides it. Might not even realize it herself. But I saw it the first time I met her. Do you remember that day?"

"Yes." With a doubtful lift of his brows, Jeremy replayed the scene in the library, then shook his head. He saw nothing submissive about what had happened that day.

"You told her to stop biting her lip. Have you seen her bite it since? Because I haven't."

Jeremy sucked in a lungful of air. She hadn't, for the most part. Just the time he'd given her the necklace. He'd thought she was going to cry. And today, when she'd risked disobeying him, to offer the one thing he most wanted and most feared to accept.

"Excuse me, Your Grace." Jeremy blinked at the interruption and scowled at the footman bowing at him. "This came for you. I…I don't know if it's important." The man's lips sneered as he held out a grimy note between two fingers. "An urchin delivered it. Didn't even ask to be paid."

Without hesitation, Jeremy snatched it, dread filling him. The paper was good quality, despite the scuffs of dirt and ash. A black wax sealed the paper, but no signet or markings revealed its origin. Smooth and shiny, a glass or the blade of a knife had pressed the seal.

Slipping his finger into the fold, he tugged. The seal shattered, spraying shards of the cheap black wax all over his tan pantaloons.

Your Grace,

Salutations. I had the immense pleasure of meeting your new wife at Madame O's the other night.

Jeremy's heart lurched, lodging somewhere that made it difficult to breathe.

The encounter exceeded my expectations. I've searched long and hard to find the sublimely satisfying red pussy I enjoyed in Ireland. She didn't even need to speak. The fear in her eyes and the memory of her mouth on my cock made the search well worth the effort. I was happy to hear she had found such a deserving Master as yourself and hope you will enjoy it as much as I did. Unfortunately, it cannot last. She deserves to be punished for her sins, and I doubt you have the ability to do it properly.

Frozen, the paper slipped from his fingers when Miles grabbed it. Fury burned through the iciness while Miles scanned the contents.

"Fuck!" Miles flipped the paper back over, as if it held clues Jeremy hadn't seen.

It didn't. Jeremy knew that as surely as he knew the letter lied. Katy had never submitted to anyone but him. Her mouth had been virgin, too.

"It's not true," Miles said. "No one touched her."

Jeremy's head snapped up, and he turned an accusing gaze on Miles. "But she was there? You saw her there and didn't tell me?"

"That's why I'm here," Miles snapped back. "You don't think I came here just to chat, do you? I hate it here." His hand waved at the room, reminding Jeremy that he'd only joined because Jeremy liked it. Stodgy and dull, he'd called it, joking that he had to join to prevent Jeremy from becoming just as judgmental. "She was there with Emily. I didn't see any harm in it." His jaw tensed. "No one came near her. Mari gave her a tour, nothing more."

Jeremy groaned. How the hell was he supposed to protect the woman? He had no doubt she'd gone on a whim, a result of Jane's comment and his own actions. The woman's generosity and impetuousness had no bounds. And his friends, even his ex-mistress, seemed bent on aiding and abetting her in her hair-brained schemes.

He tossed back the remainder of his bourbon and dropped the glass on a table. Pushing himself up, he pointed at the note. "Find out who wrote that. And find out what George was really doing in Ireland."

He'd ignored his gut long enough.

"Where are you going?"

"Home. It's time I gave my wife what she's been begging for."

****

Katy felt the thunder of his steps well before she heard him. Her hands slowed, the scissors snipping to a close as the sound grew nearer.

When the door slammed against the wall, the scissors clattered to the table. She looked up, her gaze locking on the man before her.

Power oozed from his frame, head held high, filling the bulk of the doorway. He hadn't stopped to shed his great coat, the cape adding to the width of his shoulders. Droplets of rain glittered off the black wool, dulled beside the hard sheen of his eyes. Despite the cold from the window, her body heated, flooding with the shameful wetness that plagued her every time he looked at her.

"Did you go to Madame O's?"

She blinked, confused. How had he found out so fast? Why did he look so…forbidding?

"Kathleen." Her name sounded as if it had been forced through his teeth. "I'm waiting for an answer."

She swallowed. "Yes." When the word came out too quiet to hear, she lifted her chin and repeated it.

"Why?" Like the snap of Master A's whip, the word made her jump. Unlike that time, her body reacted with another gush of desire.

"I…I wanted to see what it was like."

His eyes narrowed, scouring her face until heat filled her cheeks. It took all her will not to chomp her lip.

"And you thought there was nothing wrong with that idea?" He advanced on her, the umbrella in his hand striking the floor sharply.

She considered lying, but one look at his face convinced her against it. As hard and sharp as fresh cut glass, he looked as if he could explode if jarred.

"I wasn't sure. I see now I was wrong." She lowered her eyes, letting them squeeze shut for just an instant. Her lungs pulled at the air. She'd pushed him, tried to get him to let go and reveal himself. Had she managed it without realizing it?

Was she ready for it?

A shiver of anticipation lifted her gaze. He towered in front of her, eyeing her with the white-hot stare that made her knees weak. Her hands clutched the bottom of her chair, glad she wasn't standing.

"You have ten minutes to get yourself undressed and present yourself in my bedroom."

Her wetness soaked her skirt, and she moistened her lips. "And if I don't?"

His eyes flared. She saw his cock jump even though her eyes remained fastened on his.

His hands lowered to the table, one flat, the other wrapped around the umbrella handle. Smooth ivory attached to wooden ribs, the implement jutted straight out, canopy flaring in an attempt to escape.

"Don't tempt me, sweetheart." His breath swept over her, laden with bourbon. "You wanted to see what it was like. I'm going to indulge you." His gaze caressed her bottom lip, stealing what little air remained in her lungs. "Should you disobey, I'll have to indulge myself. And it will hurt considerably more."

Chapter Twelve

Katy had never stripped so quickly in her life. Even without Clara's help, she found herself standing outside his doorway five minutes later, shivering with fear and excitement, nothing but a thin silk robe covering her.

Her father was right. She was a sinful, self-serving Jezebel who should burn in hell, unrepentant in her search for pleasure. But, Mother of Mary, she wanted this man.

Wiping her hands on the smooth fabric, she examined herself. Already her nipples stood erect, standing out against the thin sapphire silk. The throbbing between her legs had grown steadily since the duke stalked out of the sewing room, and her hands trembled.

Should she leave the robe? Would he consider it a rule violation if she wore it into the room? Was he in the room already? She'd seen him tramp down the stairs, bellowing for a footman in that voice that melted her, commanding and confident.

She reached out a tight fist and rapped on the door. When no answer came, she glanced up and down the hall. Seeing no one, she slipped the robe from her shoulders. It pooled at her feet, the silk kissing her thighs as it fell, creating a resonant quiver in her stomach.

Dipping, she snatched up the robe, stood, and

turned the knob. The massive oak door swayed as lightly as a butterfly wing, and she slipped inside.

The room was empty. Her eyes swept over the dimly lit room, taking in the familiar green and brown furnishings, remembering her few nights here. A calm settled over her, and she tossed the robe on the chair Jeremy had used to watch over her after losing the baby. Her hand dragged over the brown coverlet on the bed. He'd tucked her in, like a cherished child, and held her beneath its warmth when she woke from the nightmares.

He'd taken care of her.

Footsteps and the sudden wash of air over her skin fanned the desire he'd sparked. She turned toward the door and instinct took over. She dropped to her knees, mimicking the pose she'd seen at Madame O's, and lowered her gaze, which was hard. She wanted to look at him, drink in the certainty and strength of his form.

The scratch of metal filled the silence, and the bolt dropped into place. A shiver ran up her spine. The house seemed shrouded in quiet, the sound of the rain outside muffled. Her blood rushed through her ears, the tempo of her breathing quickening.

She peeked through her eyelashes at the rustle of fabric and steady thudding of his boots. His fingers caressed the silk of her robe. Her pussy tightened. When his gaze slid toward her, she averted hers.

"Now that you've had time to think about it," he began, his tone calm and sure, "have you figured out why I'm unhappy about your unsanctioned visit to Madame O's?"

She hadn't reflected on it at all, so she scowled at the rug. The dark, leafy pattern offered no clues.

"Because she was your mistress?"

The pacing halted. She could feel his eyes boring into her. Heat flared at the realization he could see her taut nipples.

"Was? What makes you think she isn't still?"

She winced, and a surge of jealousy licked her. Anguish laced her voice. "I…I just assumed."

Stupid. The Earl of Beccles had surmised it, but she couldn't tell him that. And she'd wanted it to be true, so she'd believed it.

"And does it bother you? The thought I have a mistress?" He resumed pacing, his footsteps circling toward the window where the whisper of the drapes and receding shadows told her he'd pulled them open.

She didn't even think about lying. The thought of him with another woman sent darts of pain through her heart. "Yes, Sir."

"It's Master!" Two rapid-fire steps, and he grabbed her hair. Her head fell back, and she looked into his eyes. They flashed with anger.

She quailed. "I'm sorry. Master! I heard them use *sir* at Madame O's. I thought—"

"You don't think! That's your problem. And you're wrong. Sir is for temporary relationships." His hand twisted in her hair, and his gaze raked her neck. Her nipples tightened further, and she wiggled as moisture trickled along her thigh. "And I don't care that you met my former mistress. I care that you put yourself in a dangerous situation. Do you have any idea what could have happened if you'd gone there alone?"

She swallowed hard. She did, but she didn't think he wanted that answer any more than he'd consider Emily adequate protection.

"No, Master. I'm sorry." She'd scared him. Guilt lowered her gaze, spiraling through her like the lashes of a whip. It was the last thing she'd intended.

The pain in her scalp eased, but his hands remained entangled in her hair. Tiny slivers of pleasure ran along the lines of pain.

"I'm going to show you, Katy. I'm going to show you exactly what you want to know. When I'm done, you'll know what I am and what you'll get as my wife, since you seem so sure you want that. And I won't stop until I've taken everything I want. You'll endure it, and I promise you're going to scream because I'm going to take it just as far as you can handle. And when I'm done, I'll give you one chance to reconsider. So, think about that as I'm using you."

Her body reflected the lust in his eyes, tightening and pushing out her juices. Her chest rose and fell, and she licked her lips again. Was this part of the punishment? Him standing over her, not moving, making her wonder if she should do something, or worse, that he had changed his mind?

"You can start," his voice had lowered to a raspy hushed sound, "by apologizing. Take out my cock. I want your mouth on it." He stepped around, stopping in front of her.

She stared, feeling herself go softer, wetter. Even through the doe-colored cloth, he jutted forward, larger than she remembered. "I thought—"

"I told you to stop thinking. I don't care what I said before. Just do it."

Her heart stilled, then raced to catch up once it resumed beating. Dragging her gaze downward, she reached out. Her hands trembled, fumbling with the buttons while he stood stiff and unmoving. Glancing up, she blushed. His gaze burned with lust as clear as winter air.

Finally, the buttons cooperated, and his prick sprang forward. Her mouth watered. Smooth and thick, the shaft bobbed before her, pulsing with the same urgent rhythm she felt in her pussy. She'd enjoyed the feel of him in her mouth the last time, the taste of his seed. Already, a drop of cum glittered like liquid sugar. With a lick of her lips, she cupped his balls, caressing the fleshy orbs. Each touch sent a shiver of pleasure straight to her womb.

Much as she wanted to savor the sight, hunger urged her forward. She dipped her head, flicking her tongue to lap up the salty treat. The head leapt forward, pushing against her lips. A groan split the quiet, raw and guttural. His or hers, she wasn't sure and didn't care.

Nothing else mattered. With a determination that welled up from the depth of her pussy, she ran her tongue along the length, circling the ridge that throbbed near the head. It was hot and hard like a spoon left in soup. She laved the girth, curling her tongue, letting her lips slide over the tiny ripples leading to the root. Pulsing with a mind of its own, it nudged back greedily, following each time she pulled back. She teased it, enjoying the yearning and ripples of pleasure between her legs. She'd taste him, take her time. If he didn't like it, he'd have to take control.

She sighed happily. The tangy scent of desire aroused her, and she gave in to the urge. Wrapping her hand around the base, she slid her mouth along the entire length. His cock jerked, and his hips lunged forward. She pulled her head back, then relented and took him in, all the way. She felt him shudder, and this time she knew it was his groan rumbling through her. Low and hungry, she pressed her thighs together. She liked hearing his need, tasting the way he wept with the same desire that swamped her.

With renewed incentive, she repeated the dance. Swirling her tongue, desperate to taste every centimeter, she moved her head back, then drove down again, urging his hips forward. Swallowing each gag, her breath whistled through her nose, faster and faster. Taking her cue from his rasping gasps and the force of his lunges, she slowed and sped up until the need for air became almost unbearable.

"Oh, Christ, Katy." The cry tore from him, seconds before his hands grabbed her head.

Trapped, she swallowed as his cock slammed into the back of her throat. His body shook, and her own arched in response. Need tore through her, but there was no release. Gasping, her muscles tightened, but the need just built. He pushed her head back enough to let her take a breath, then buried himself again, his ass tightening with another painful grunt. Cum filled her throat, and she swallowed greedily.

Then his grip released, and she tumbled forward. Her hands scraped the carpet, stinging as she caught herself. Gulping in huge mouthfuls of air, she slumped on her hands and knees.

Jeremy's footsteps reverberated through the floor, adding to the pulsing need between her legs. Small circles of light began to appear, along with the smell of beeswax and the acrid scent of the tapers he used to light the candles. The sound of his breathing quickly normalized.

She opened her eyes and followed his progress. After lighting the candles, he sat down, removed his boots, then rose and crossed to a door on the far side. Pulling a key from his waistcoat, he unlocked a large padlock. The latch clanked, and he pushed the door inward, disappearing into the yawning darkness. Her forehead tightened with annoyance.

How did he do it? He'd stood there while she milked his cock, and now he wandered around as if nothing had happened. Tears pricked her eyes, and a moan rippled up her throat. Her hand slid between her legs, and she pressed against the throbbing nub. Lungs still sucking in air, she closed her eyes and stroked the swollen flesh.

Just a few touches. It was wrong. She'd go to hell, but she didn't care.

The muffled footsteps stopped. She opened her eyes, fingers pausing. He stood in the doorway, staring at her.

Shame flooded her. She groaned and pulled her hand away.

"Do you like to pleasure yourself, Katy?" He strode forward and extended his hand. She looked at it for a moment, then accepted the help.

His was the same question Mistress O had asked. Except he'd asked if she liked it, not just if she did it.

"Not really." Finding her feet beneath her, she pulled her hand out of his and clasped it behind her. "It's a sin. But I can't help it sometimes."

He began to unbutton his shirt. "Like now? You want release, don't you?"

She shuddered and whispered, "Yes."

He tugged his shirt over his head, exposing the most sinful torso she'd ever seen. Tanned, with a light chestnut dusting of hair, the muscles rippled. Sculpted, not bulging, like Thomas'. He made no move to remove his breeches, fall flapping. As she stared, his prick stirred, still erect but no longer purple. She swallowed, her mouth watering again.

"Lie down on the bed." He took two steps and moved to place a second candle before the mirror. The glow bounced back, better revealing the bed surface. "I want to watch."

Mortified at the thought, all she could do was stare.

"Apparently, I need to remind you of the rules."

Choking back a cry, she rushed toward the bed.

"I'm sorry, Master." The words tumbled out. "I remember them. I just forgot."

She blushed, feeling it to the roots of her hair. It was the most stupid thing she'd ever said. But he seemed to understand because his lips quirked.

"Good." He pushed her back until she hit the bed. A finger snaked down the center of her chest, grazing between her breasts, then dragging a line along her stomach. Need pulled behind the touch, making her hips squirm. "I've a few more."

Suddenly, his fingers curled and raked through the nest between her legs. She gasped, writhing. The throbbing pounded, and her hips rose. A finger slipped in, and his hand clamped down, preventing any further motion.

"This is mine. No one, including you, touches it without permission." Just as suddenly, he released her, leaving behind a yearning emptiness.

She panted and clenched her teeth. A hissing

226

escaped.

"Here's another." He stepped back. With the light behind him, he looked faceless. "You don't come until I give you permission." Another noise escaped her, more of a whimper than anything. "You'll get your release. But not until I say so."

He backed away. Katy tracked his movement, her fingers flexing with the need to touch him. He stopped in front of a small writing desk in front of the window and then turned. Directly across from the side of the bed, the mirrored light hit his face, casting shadows over one side and sharpening the planes on the other.

"Your apology was very nice, though," he said. "And I'd like to see what you like. So, go ahead and touch yourself."

She hesitated, shame warming her to the point she thought she'd incinerate, but when he reached down and pulled at his cock, all will evaporated. One hand snaked up to brush over her nipple. Hard as a raisin, the touch spiked through her. She moaned and locked her eyes on the sight of his cock, so far away but close enough to smell his arousal. That was what she really wanted, to feel him inside her.

"Your pussy, Katy," he urged, his voice a combination of demand and suggestion. "Touch your pussy."

She slid one finger between her legs and closed her eyes for an instant. It felt like velvet, slick with moisture, as smooth as silk. Slowly, she circled the folds, spreading the delicious wetness everywhere.

"Put your legs up. Bend your knees so I can see."

She did as she was told. She couldn't disobey. Had no desire to resist.

One finger wasn't enough now. She added another, slipping them around the nub, dipping farther into the heat, and watched his cock grow larger. Her other hand latched on to her nipple, rolling it until the pain shot through her. She felt as if each touch pulled at her from within. The surrounding air thickened. She turned her head, searching for cooler air but found none. She threw her head back. His chest rose and fell just as quickly as hers, his hand slipping up and down his shaft in the same rhythm.

She moaned and dragged a fingertip over her clit. Her hips jerked. She rubbed harder and groaned.

"That's enough." The slap of flesh against flesh ceased, and her hand froze. Rapid steps approached, and she forced her hand away.

So close. She'd been so close it hurt. Her legs shook, but she didn't dare lower them. Not until he said.

"You're so pretty." His gaze burned, making her clit pulse harder. He stared at her pussy, as if it were one of the pastries he allowed himself at breakfast. He licked his lips, sucking in his bottom lip and grabbing it with his teeth. A gush of desire shocked her. "Did you like it, Katy? When I put my mouth on you that night at the inn."

"Yes." Her voice shuddered at the memory. "Yes, Master."

A slap landed on her thigh, sharp and stinging. "Don't lie to me."

She gasped. "I'm not." Why didn't he believe her? "Please, Master. I wouldn't lie about it. I would never lie to you about that."

"You cried." Rough with accusation, the rebuttal

scraped at her guilt. "I heard it."

Hearing his confusion and self-reproach, she forced down her own. "I…I wasn't crying because I didn't like it. I cried because I did. I cried because I'm going to hell." She sobbed, no longer ashamed, only afraid, afraid he'd agree. "I'm a whore, just like Da said."

His hand lashed out and grabbed her wrist. "I never want to hear that. I told you before. Next time you call yourself a whore, you'll feel my hand on your bare ass. And I don't care who sees it when I do. Do you understand?"

She gaped, mouth open in surprise. She hadn't believed him when he told her the first time. "Yes, Master." She believed him now. The warm glow of desire rekindled, spreading out from where his fingers trapped her wrist.

"Good." A sharp crack split the air. Stinging pain jerked her body forward. He'd slapped her thigh. Her pussy cried out, sending a trickle down her leg. "Now you'll see what happens when you disobey me. Since you seem to have forgotten." He jerked her to her feet and pointed at the gaping door. Candlelight poured out, but her feet didn't dare move.

"I—" She snapped her mouth shut. His hand snagged her hair and pulled her back. It hardly hurt anymore, especially when it meant she could feel the length of his body against her.

"Don't even try to tell me you didn't disobey," he whispered, and an intoxicating wash of bourbon and sandalwood washed over her senses. "You knew I wouldn't like it, and you did it anyway. That counts."

His finger traced along the line of her nape, over her shoulder and down the length of her arm. She shivered, her body convulsing with need. How did he make her feel like this, hot and cold at the same time?

His arm circled her waist, pulling her back. His cock surged against her, so close to her pussy her knees weakened. "I'm going to fuck you this time, Katy. After I'm done. Would you like that?"

Too overcome by the sensations pouring through her, all she could do was nod. He nudged her forward, and she forced her legs to obey.

As she stepped over the threshold, her feet planted themselves. Before her lay a mini version of Madam O's, replete with the strange benches and the large X on the wall. Candlelight flickered over an array of tools lined up along a sideboard. Paddles like he'd used before, but other things, too. A huge four-poster bed loomed in one corner. Iron rings dangled from the posts.

"You remember what I told you before? About the numbers?"

"Yes." Her eyes halted on a leather object with a number of tails. A flogger. What would it feel like? Next to it was a similar object with nine leather strips.

"Yes, what?"

Her head snapped around. "Yes, Master." Against her will, her eyes slipped back, and dread settled in her stomach. "Is— Will— Are you going to whip me?" Her eyes flew to the X on the wall. Fear swamped her.

"It scares you?"

"Yes." More like terrified her.

He stepped closer, layering her back in a wall of heat. His arms enveloped her and pulled her close. His chest expanded, and a long slow exhale washed along the slope of her chest.

"This is who I am, sweetheart. I wish it wasn't. But it is. Just as you have to pleasure yourself, I have to do this. I could probably fuck you once or twice without it. But eventually I'd need this. It's a sickness with no cure." The resignation in his voice tore at her heart. It spoke to her. He needed this. Paid whores to do it because no one else would.

"We can try it without the whips. But I won't lie. That's my favorite." He nuzzled her neck.

Katy swallowed, desire flowing from where his breath heated her skin.

"Don't be scared. It doesn't hurt as much as you think. I'm told it can be pleasant even. And I'll watch you. Make sure it's not too much. Nothing that breaks the skin or leaves a mark. Nothing that makes you scream. Just enough to tame my beast." His hips rocked forward, pressing his cock into the soft flesh of her behind. "Just thinking about it makes me hard, Katy. It makes me want to watch you come. Over and over. It makes me want to give you anything you want."

Anything she wanted. Just as she'd promised him.

She wanted to be loved. Her heart skipped a beat. He wanted that, too. Was begging for it. How could she deny him?

When he spoke again, his voice was hoarse, as if the words tore him apart. "I want to take you in the ass, too. Would you let me do that, Katy? Just once."

Her eyes widened. Her stomach tightened, pulling at her pussy, and another surge of lust shook her. But it was a sin. Sodomy would damn her to hell.

But not if he ordered her. Wasn't that what the Bible said? Obey your husband.

"Jeremy." She twisted, escaping the hold he had on

her, and stepped away. "Master," she corrected and waited until his shuttered gaze lifted and met hers. Purposefully, she licked her lips and caught her bottom lip. His eyes flared, sending another thrill through her. "You should stop talking and start doing. I only want two things. A kiss and a blindfold. It's less scary if I don't see what you're using."

The air around them went still, and she realized there were no windows in the room. She could no longer hear the rain or the noises from the street, nothing but the pull of their lungs. Her breathing battered her ears.

His eyes narrowed, and his gaze probed her face, as if he didn't believe her. She held her breath, willing him to see what she'd left unspoken. Before her eyes, his qualms dropped away. Her Master returned, his stance hardening, shoulders lifting, seeming to add to his large form. His eyes flashed, then darkened.

Her body felt as if it were melting, blood rushing toward her sex. She could no longer feel trickles or gushes, just a pool of hungry wetness.

With one giant step, he closed the distance. A cruel grip locked over her jaw, and his mouth slammed against hers. There was no mercy in the kiss. His lips ground and assaulted her with the force of a hailstorm. His fingers pinched, forcing her jaw to release, and his tongue plunged into the depths. With a muffled whimper, her knees buckled, fingers clawing at his shoulders.

Demanding and thorough, he plundered her mouth. The pressure eased off her lips, transferred to the thrust of his tongue. She felt it in every nook of her mouth, stroking along her cheek, stabbing her cleft, driving so deep she feared she'd suffocate. It felt so good, she wanted to die. She was helpless against the onslaught. Her own tongue couldn't match it. It tangled around his, compelled to move where his directed. Air whistled through her nose, trying and failing to satisfy the need to fill her lungs.

Somehow, he backed her up against a wall. She hadn't moved, couldn't have if she'd wanted to, but velvet covered stone slammed into her back. His thigh lifted her, rock hard muscle covered by soft leather pressing against her swollen nub. She arched her back to relieve the torture, but it didn't help. She was pinned too tightly, feet off the ground, head bent back against the cushioned stone.

"Breathe," he commanded as his lips deserted her, hovering millimeters away. Her neck strained, but the grip along her jaw prevented any movement. Close enough she could taste his breath, he remained out of reach. A ragged moan scraped over her nerves, but she obeyed and sucked in air. Her chest heaved, her sensitive nipples sending shocks of need to where his thigh imprisoned her. Her hands, the only part of her body free to move, splayed over his chest. Instead of relieving the need, the dusting of hair teased her. Like everything about him, they weren't soft. They were wiry snips, abrasive and tense.

His thigh moved, just enough to send up an arrow of pleasure. She gasped, body jerking, and closed her eyes.

"No blindfold." His thumb scraped her bottom lip, softening the disappointment. When she opened her eyes, he stared back, his gaze as probing as his kiss had been. "I want to see you." His thigh rubbed again. An involuntary groan shook her. His lips curled ever so slightly, then his forehead furrowed.

"You want this, don't you?" Shame flooded her, making her even hotter. He didn't wait for an answer. He moved again, bouncing her on his thigh. Her head fell back. Waves of pleasurable pain rocked her.

Once more. Please. Her mind begged, but all she heard was her ragged breaths. Her mouth wouldn't form the words.

Her feet hit the floor, jarring her. Cold air smacked her where his thigh had been. The only thing holding her up was the fingers circling her jawbone. Slowly, he lowered his arm, never releasing her, until she sank to her knees.

"New rule. You'll ask me when you want to come. And remember, you don't until I give you permission. And another. Even if you forget every other rule, I want you to remember this one."

He dropped to one knee, muscle bulging against the constraints of his pants. She avoided looking at the jutting erection, focusing on his face instead, but couldn't resist the need to lick her dry lips.

"You'll allow yourself to enjoy anything you want, unless I tell you otherwise." His fingers tightened and he paused, preventing the instinctive lowering of her head. Her gaze escaped, though, landing smack on the thing she wanted most. Another hot wave of shame burned through her.

He nudged her jaw, prompting her to look at him. "You're mine now, Kathleen. There's no guilt or shame. You have no choices here. If we sin, it's on my soul, not yours. No one knows what happens in here. Not your father, not your priest or confessor, not the society bitches like Jane. You don't worry about what they might think. All you care about in here is me."

The understanding in his eyes did what the orders themselves never could have. It made her believe, set her free, like a hummingbird finally able to land. She could give in to the urges that should have disgusted her but somehow never did. She could embrace the desires that shook her to the core every time she looked at him. He knew what it felt like, the heavy weight of the shame, and he wanted to carry it for her.

"Is that clear, Katy?"

An edge of dismay crept into his face when she didn't answer.

"Yes," she whispered before it could take hold. His evident relief prompted her further. "Thank you, Master."

The most beautiful, wicked smile spread over his face.

"Good." He dropped his hand and fastened it on her elbow, dragging her. "Now get that glorious ass of yours over on that bench." A sharp slap on her buttocks sent her in the indicated direction.

Dark leather padded an angled slab similar to the contraptions at Madame O's. A thrill of excitement shot through her as she mounted it, spurred on by Jeremy's heavy-lidded look of approval. She lowered herself, the leather warming as her skin molded to it, her ass tilting up.

Her pussy clenched as cold air hit it, and she licked her lips, suddenly afraid until she saw Jeremy padding toward her, his cock lengthening before her eyes.

"Are you ready?" His eyes held hers for a moment, then he slid around until she could no longer see him.

Smack!

Katy jerked, body slapping the bench. Pain exploded and raced outward.

"That's for going to Madame O's without permission."

She gasped. The burn stung. Worse than the night at the tavern. Not a paddle, it felt more like a belt. Knowing there'd be more, she tensed, waiting. Just as she relaxed, thinking she was wrong, another landed, just as hard.

"That's for recruiting Emily for your scheme."

This time the shock rocketed through her nerves. A tear trickled out, and a sob escaped. He'd never before hit her so hard. She hadn't expected him to this time either. Not truly.

"Do I need to tell you why that was wrong, Katy?"

She sucked in a lungful of air. "No, Master."

"Then tell me, so I can be sure you understand."

"Because Emily could have been hurt." She hesitated before adding, "Master." Emily would have scoffed at the idea, but Emily was family, and Jeremy's protectiveness wasn't logical. It came from his heart. Just as what he was doing to her now did. She knew that. She just wished it didn't hurt so much.

"That's right." A soothing hand washed over the curves he'd hit. Katy shuddered, inhaling at the tenderness, her body softening, absorbing the slivers of heat that radiated from his touch. "Give me a number, sweetheart."

Katy gulped back tears. "Seven." It hurt. More than she expected, but less than she deserved.

His lips brushed her temple, a tender kiss that made her heart ache. "Don't move. I'll be right back."

She tried to compose herself as his feet padded across the floor. Wood scraped against wood, then thudded. Muffled rattles preceded more footsteps, then another clank and plunk.

What was he doing? Was he going to hurt her more?

"I counted eight transgressions, Katy. Mostly failures to address me properly." His palm stroked over her buttocks, easing the residual sting. "Would you agree with that number?"

Katy bit her lip. "Yes, Master." She hadn't counted, had no idea. Could she bear that many?

"Make that nine. One more for biting your lip." His hand slipped down and cupped her clit. Pleasure flooded her pussy. For that, she could bear more. For that, she could bear anything. She pushed forward. He let her, wiggling his middle finger, coaxing the need. Then he stopped, sliding the tip along the crack in her ass before a gentle slap landed. A frustrated groan made her frown.

She prepared herself, tensing for the next blow. Instead of the belt, he used his hand and took his time. It still hurt, but not nearly as much, and he followed it each time with a caress and praise. A single blow, then a *reward*—a stroke over her ass to distribute the burn, followed by a leisurely exploration of the wet need building between her legs. As much torture as reward, he teased the nub and the opening, caressing her until she began to pant and strain again, then he eased off, only to resume after the next slap.

"Please, Master," she ground out after the eighth. His hand slipped down into the wetness. Another convulsion rippled along her stomach muscles. "Please, may I come?"

His finger stroked and another wave of need clamped down. Her teeth clenched, waiting, sure he'd say yes.

"No."

She hissed, writhing away from the incessant play of his fingers. It was punishment, expecting her to resist as he slipped his magic fingers in, curling his knuckle, pressing the heel of his hand against the nub. She panted, sure she couldn't obey any longer, when he eased out.

"One more, Katy." His breathing was ragged, too. Not as harsh as hers, but she took what comfort she could from knowing he wasn't as unaffected as he appeared.

The impact burned, harsh on top of the other three or four that seemed to have landed on the same spot. No longer resisting, her body slipped along the padding, scraping her nipples. She hurt, more from the burning need that felt like an inferno than from the abuse of her skin.

"Do you have any idea," he asked as once more he palmed her, "how hard I am right now? How much I love the feel of you dripping?"

Hearing his blatant need almost made her come, and she pushed back, but he lifted his hand, leaving her yearning. Another convulsion shook her when he leaned over and placed a chaste kiss on her shoulder. Gently, he helped her up, one hand clasping hers, the other holding her by the upper arm. Her legs trembled as the weight shifted onto them, ready to buckle, but he steadied her and guided her toward the bed.

"Look what you do to me, Katy." He groaned and

tugged on his cock. A steady stream of cum dripped from the tip. "I've never been so hard." His gaze flowed over her, reigniting the smoldering heat the air had cooled. Her nipples ached and her pussy pulsed. The pure unadulterated lust in his eyes set her pulse to a hammering need. "Do you want me to fuck you?"

Her gaze shot up. His eyes mirrored the question, dark and worried, and she realized it wasn't her master asking. "Yes." The word tore from her. "Please."

His lips slammed down first, sucking the life from her. Then his hands followed, pushing her onto the cool silk sheets on the bed. The length of his body melded over hers, hard and hot, and his cock probed at the emptiness he'd teased from her.

"Now, Jeremy. Please."

"I'm sorry." His face screwed up, and he tensed. "I can't wait."

His hips lunged forward. With one smooth stroke, the emptiness vanished.

"Oh, God!" Pleasure rocked through her, and she clutched his shoulders, sure she'd die. This was why everyone wanted to couple. To feel complete.

She sucked in air, gasping to find words. She needed to come, to find that moment of oneness. But he'd stopped, buried so deep he touched her heart.

"You're so damned tight." The vein in his forehead looked ready to burst. His words sounded as choked as the ones lodged in her throat. His hips rocked. More explosions burst, rippling in her abdomen. "I don't want to hurt you." His chest heaved. "But I have to move." Every muscle in his body tightened. "I'm sorry."

A low keening filled her ears as he slowly pulled out. Her hips rose, desperate to drag him back. He thrust in, face contorting in pain, slow and steady. Then again and again, each thrust making it harder to not let go. Over and over, he stroked, and she held back, too breathless to ask permission, too determined not to fail him. Every plunge resounded through her, squeezing her heart and pussy, in ever-quicker bursts until it felt like her blood was thundering.

"Please, Katy," he choked out, through gritted teeth. "I need—you—to come."

The words shattered her. Pleasure spiraled through every nerve, an inferno of pain wrapped in ecstasy. An inhuman groan erupted, and Jeremy's hips slammed against hers, fingers clamping, locking their bodies together as if he'd never let go. Her hips arched in response, muscles squeezing, her mind going blank. Then they both collapsed, too spent to move.

****

When Katy finally came to her senses, it was later. How much later, she couldn't tell, but she knew it was. Instead of the windowless dark, she lay in the softness of Jeremy's bed, gentle raindrops reflecting back the candlelight. Slow gentle strokes calmed her, easing the ache of arm muscles held tense too long. She vaguely remembered him carrying her in his arms, but it was hazy and dim. She felt drunk, her limbs still too heavy to move.

"Master?" Her tongue stuck to her mouth, too dry to speak clearly.

"Just Jeremy, sweetheart. We're done for tonight." His lips brushed her forehead in an achingly sweet kiss.

She swallowed, finding a bit of lubrication. "But you didn't whip me." For some reason it made her sad. She frowned.

"No. You had enough tonight." He pushed her hair back and shifted her. To her amazement, his cock probed at her ass again already. Wasn't it supposed to take time? It couldn't have been that long.

"I'm sorry." She snuggled back against him. As hot as she'd been before, she couldn't seem to get warm now. He dragged another cover up, tucking it around her.

"For what?"

"I don't know what happened. It was only nine spankings." The first time had been twelve, and she hadn't felt like this, like a bowl of bread pudding made with too much milk. At least, not quite as bad as this.

He chuckled, a sound that made her heart leap. "But you wanted it this time. And I kept pushing you to the edge, then stopping. Because it makes it better. But it drains you more, too."

She nodded and rubbed her cheek along his arm. It made sense. As much as any of it did. "Is the whipping like that? And the…" She didn't know what else to call it. "…the sodomy?"

An ache built in her chest as she felt him retreat. She didn't need to see his face to know his smile died.

"We don't have to do those things, Katy. I—" He sighed. "What we did tonight was enough. More than I ever hoped. I don't need any more than that."

Shimmying, she flipped onto her back so she could look at him. He looked sad but content, too.

Her hand stroked over the shadowy beard that darkened his jaw. Tiny shivers warmed her as her fingers scraped the hairs. "That's a shame. I was warming to the idea."

A warm glow of happiness took root as his eyes

widened. "Truly? You'd do that for me?"

"Well, I do love you. And you are my Master. It might require an extra kiss though." She let her smile spread. It never completed though because his lips slammed back down and stole her breath away.

"I love you too, sweetheart," he murmured, between kisses; more kisses than she'd ever need. "More than I can say." He squeezed her so tightly, she couldn't breathe, but she ignored it until it passed. "Don't think I won't punish you, though. You ever put yourself in danger again, you won't be able to sit down for a month. And there won't be any release, either. So think about that before you decide to test me."

Chapter Thirteen

"Sit down, George." Jeremy used his most commanding voice, the one he'd used when berating George for the most egregious sins he'd committed. It worked. George blanched and dropped to the seat, his eyes darting about like a cornered rabbit.

Miles stepped into view, his fingers doing the coin trick that both men knew. It signified the Miles who analyzed complex problems with the speed of an eye blink. Jeremy had first seen him do it at age eight, staring down the group of six bullies ready to welcome Jeremy to school. They'd ended up running that day, but it had been the correct choice. Miles had led them straight to the garden where the headmaster had been trimming rosebushes. The four schoolboys stupid enough to follow ended up on kitchen duty for three weeks.

"It's time for a talk. I trust you'll be honest, because I'd hate to interrupt Emily's visit with Katy. I will, though, if I think you're holding back."

Jeremy leaned back in his seat, giving George time to process the threat. Instead of shrinking back or loosening his cravat nervously, George just eyed Miles warily and lifted his chin.

George wasn't afraid of Emily's reaction. She'd either already punished him for anything he might have done, or she knew about it. This might be harder than he anticipated. A quick glance at Miles confirmed his fears. Miles' brows lowered, and the coin paused, caught between his third and fourth fingers.

"I can't tell you anything." George stared at his hands, examining perfectly manicured fingers, but his jaw tensed.

"How do you know? I haven't even told you what this is about yet."

"I'm not stupid, Jeremy." George looked him straight in the eyes. Jeremy's spine stiffened. George had grown a backbone somewhere along the way. "You're going to ask about Ireland. And Katy. But I can't talk about it." His arms crossed over his chest.

Jeremy's teeth clenched. When George did that, there was no moving him. He'd dig his heels in for days.

"Wickham recruited you, didn't he?" Both men looked at Miles. The coin was flipping through his fingers faster than the thoroughbred George had bought. Unlike his words, the tone implied it was less a question than a statement.

"You know how this works." George stared at Miles, then turned back toward Jeremy. "If you have questions, you need to ask Katy. I can't help you."

Stunned, Jeremy watched as George stood up, brushed an imaginary crumb off his waistcoat, and headed for the door.

As the door thudded closed, Jeremy lifted his brows quizzically at Miles. The coin had slowed but still journeyed through the long fingers. He turned away from Jeremy's gaze and circled the room slowly. As his face came into view, his eyes darted from side to side, his feet tracing a familiar route that didn't need his attention.

Finally, he dropped into the chair George had vacated. The coin stopped and began to tap the arm of the chair. "Wickham almost never cuts me out of things. I'm going to have to call in a few favors."

Jeremy's stomach tightened. What had George done? And what did Katy have to do with it?

"Should I ask Katy?" The thought made his stomach hurt more. It was too soon. If he pushed, she might balk. Just as he needed to build her trust in the bedroom before he could whip her, he needed to let her decide what to trust him with and when.

The grimace that twisted Miles' face scared him. He didn't ask. Miles wouldn't tell him any more than George until he knew the details.

"Let's wait. There's only two reasons I can think of that Wickham would go around me. We have a mole in the Office, or there's a double agent working for us in Ireland." His gaze peered at the door, disbelief curling his mouth. "Why he'd choose George for whatever he needed is beyond me, but—" He shrugged. "Makes the second more likely, I suppose."

It wasn't just a physical reaction going on in his stomach. Jeremy spoke the fear that was churning in his gut. "Katy's brother's still missing."

"Yeah." Miles stopped tapping the coin. "We really need to find him."

****

It felt like forever since she'd been on a horse. She'd never ridden one as wonderful as this one.

Katy reached down and smoothed her hand over the glorious chestnut mount and beamed at Jeremy. A surprise he'd presented this morning, the animal was less of a gift than his offer to ride with her. With a softly clouded sky and a warm breeze, it was a perfect day, but the idea of riding alone didn't have the appeal it would have a month ago.

"What will you name her?"

"Ruby, I think, because she's so precious." Ruby turned, as if she knew Katy was discussing her and whickered, then threw her head back. High-stepping, the horse pranced in place while Katy waited for Jeremy to mount his own dapple gray named Ash. "Must we promenade first? Even Ruby wants to run."

"Patience, sweetheart," he responded with a touch of mirth. "You'll get your ride, but I want to show off my lovely wife first. Most ladies would be thrilled."

Katy rolled her eyes but stayed silent. Jeremy's step seemed as light as Ruby's before he bounded up from the ground and mounted Ash. As with everything he did, his posture was exemplary—spine straight, head high. The obvious joy on his face was new, though, causing Katy to melt. His eyes sparkled. His smile stretched clear across his freshly shaven jaw.

Lord, she loved him. In his tight fitting black jacket and light gray pantaloons, he oozed confidence. The horse seemed a mere extension of his body, moving without visible direction. An inexpressible urge to reach out and touch him squeezed her heart.

Ash ambled over, and Jeremy grabbed Ruby's reins and leaned toward Katy. A light touch of his lips made her shiver and stretch toward him.

"Will you use a whip on her?" he asked as the kiss ended. His hand cupped her chin, preventing her from looking away.

"What?" Katy blinked, totally confused.

"Ruby. Will you use a crop or whip on her?"

"I—" She felt a flush cover her face as she realized what he was asking. "I don't know. It will depend on her nature." She liked to ride fast and jump fences and brooks. Some horses needed encouragement, others didn't.

"If you do, will you take care not to hurt her?"

"Of course." Katy shifted uncomfortably as a new wash of moisture seeped between her legs.

His eyes darkened. His smile turned wicked, and his finger trailed along her neck. He knew. One look and she melted. One touch and she was wet. Two could play this game though.

Slowly, she licked her lips and whispered, "Will you ride me after you whip me?"

His eyes widened, and his eyes flashed, then he threw his head back and roared with laughter. After a disappointingly chaste kiss, he responded. "With infinite pleasure."

A warm glow settled over her as he handed back her reins, then wheeled Ash around and headed toward Hyde Park. He might be showing her off to the Ton, but beside him, she felt like a wildflower in the shadows of an exotic orchid.

Trotting after him, she admired the fine view of his form reacting to the animal, thighs bulging and ass lifting slightly with each step. His shoulders rippled as his hands directed the horse with swift efficient motions. As they neared the growing crowd, she became aware of just how lucky she was. Other riders passed them, nodding or calling out greetings. Most suffered in comparison, with paunches or sloppy technique. The women all devoured Jeremy with their eyes, adding to her resentment. Adorned in their finest, in carriages that gleamed or on mounts as fine or finer than Ruby, all she could think about was how he could have wed any of them.

But he was her husband. Thanks to George.

Her joy dimmed. Would he have even looked at her himself?

Jeremy halted, glancing back at her before his attention was claimed by a passerby. The woman stopped her horse beside him, chattering away, in an incredible gold riding habit that mirrored the golden ringlets atop her head. Gold epaulets and ribbons sent blinding glints of sun swirling while he leaned toward her. Head bobbing, it was obvious he hung on every word.

Katy scanned the other faces in the endless parade of well-dressed men and women. When she'd dressed, her confidence had been high. Now, she looked at the gauzy gowns and feathered hats and felt underdressed in her simple spencer-like jacket and full riding skirt.

Coming alongside, she hung back, hesitant to insert herself.

"Your Ladyship, it's wonderful to meet you." The woman laid a hand on Jeremy's forearm as she turned a pair of the deepest blue eyes Katy had ever seen toward her. Lush pink lips curved up between cheeks that showed a dimple. A flash of jealousy stabbed Katy, lancing deeper as the woman called him by name. "Jeremy tells me he met you in Ireland. How are you enjoying London?"

"This is Elizabeth Knight, Katy. She's my first wife's cousin."

Instantly, Katy stiffened and sat up straighter. "It's

rather crowded, if you ask me. I much prefer the rolling hills of home."

"Do you?" Elizabeth's hand dropped away. A touch of amusement lined her eyes, making Katy's jaw tighten in dislike. "That's good to hear. Jeremy never said so, of course, but it was obvious to me that Anna's insistence on spending every possible moment in London wearied him. She was a silly girl. Had he married me, I would have encouraged him to whisk me away to Lexham Estate every chance I had. Have you seen it yet? If you enjoy rolling green hills, you'll love it."

"No, I haven't. Jeremy's kept me prisoner here." The sudden rush of insecurity loosened Katy's tongue, and her manners deserted her. Pointedly ignoring Elizabeth, in hopes she'd move along, Katy directed her attention back to the passing crowd.

Was it her imagination, or were they all watching her? Even Jeremy stared when she looked back, his brows lowered and his smile wooden. Elizabeth's smirk twitched.

"I should be going," the beauty announced. Her gloved hand reached out and grasped Katy's wrist, squeezing gently. "My husband is waiting at Gunther's with the three hellions we call children. He gifts me with lovely horses like this and lets me run off and enjoy them while all I give him are little monsters and headaches." She released Katy and wheeled her mount, showing off the fine lines of a pure white stallion. "I hope you'll call on me while we're in London. Without your captor." She winked. "I'll tell you all the things Anna complained about. In case you need the ammunition."

Katy's stomach plummeted at the love in Elizabeth's voice when she mentioned her husband and guilt overwhelmed her. She'd been a bitch, assuming the woman wanted to poach Jeremy.

"I…I'd be honored—" She searched for the proper title but couldn't find it.

"Elizabeth, please, Your Grace. Anna may not have enjoyed being Jeremy's wife, but we all loved him."

"Thank you." Taking a deep breath, Katy screwed up her courage. "Elizabeth." Amends were in order. "Perhaps we could have you for dinner, one night." She glanced at Jeremy. He nodded in approval. "Your whole family, hellions and all."

With a smile and a promise, Elizabeth cantered away. Katy watched her go, but the sense of disquiet continued. She glanced about the park. She still felt as if she were being watched, despite evidence to the contrary. Most of the Ton were smiling and talking. If any were watching them, their attention was firmly focused on Jeremy, not her.

"Is something wrong, Katy?"

Jeremy stared at her, concern darkening his eyes. Another wave of guilt rolled over her. "No, of course not."

She plastered a smile on her face and tamped down the urge to turn tail and run. It wasn't the first time she'd seen him fawned over and ogled. Every time she stepped out with him, she felt inferior and wondered why he hadn't wed a more suitable woman.

Why did she feel as if it were all a lie? He'd told her he loved her. She felt it when they were alone. She needed to trust that.

With a gentle kick, she set Ruby in motion, easing into the stream of carriages and riders. She felt Jeremy's eyes on her as he fell in beside her. She focused on the beauty of the day, the splendid creature she rode, and the welcoming smiles and nods directed at her. If anyone had told her that she would be a grand lady, riding in Hyde Park with a loving husband beside her, she wouldn't have believed it. Still didn't.

Slowly, the gentle rhythm lulled her back into a smile. Caroline and her husband paused to exchange greetings with them, as did the Countess of Essex. As the agreed upon hour approached, Katy's spirits lifted. She reached down to give Ruby another pat of encouragement. Ruby whickered and increased her pace.

When Jeremy sidled up, she turned another beaming smile at him.

"I see Miles in the distance." He gestured with his head farther up the line of people. "I need to speak with him for a minute or two. I'll rejoin you as you approach."

"I can come with you." Katy pulled the reins to the left. Ruby instantly veered away from the main entourage.

Jeremy grabbed the tack from the other side, redirecting Ruby. The mare tossed her head in annoyance but obeyed.

"No, please. I need a minute alone. It won't be long."

"Very well." A surge of dismay totally out of proportion squeezed her stomach as she watched Jeremy ride off without her. Then she turned back, renewing a fake smile, and continued to exchange greetings with people she'd met.

A blast of cold sent her gaze toward the sky. The clouds had thickened, and the tree leaves whispered. In the distance, a smoky black cloud hovered above the tree line. If they didn't leave soon, the opportunity for a jaunt across the park might disappear.

A glance at Jeremy offered no reassurance. The two men lingered beneath an oak, heads together, hands gesturing as they spoke.

"Duchess?" The shrill call jerked Katy around.

A shiver ran down her spine. Scanning the mass of people, her eyes paused on a number of men who eyed her, but no one spoke and no one she knew gazed back.

Ruby balked, demanding her attention, and Katy patted her reassuringly. Ruby sidestepped, whipping her head in the air. A nearby gentleman scowled and eased his mount away. Katy frowned and tightened her grip, whispering soothing nonsense at the horse.

Finally regaining control, she drew a deep breath and pulled Ruby out of the stream of riders. As she did, a gold and black barouche approached, drawn by a pair of ebony stallions. A young, unknown gentleman drove the vehicle, hands held high. Beside him, a woman shielded herself from the sun with a gaily adorned parasol. A garish mustard yellow gown decorated with green-twilled sarsenet leaves hugged a stick-like figure.

"Oh, Duchess Lexham." The voice sent a shiver of revulsion through Katy. The parasol swung away to reveal Lady Jane Pearson's bird-like face. The barouche skidded to a halt, stallions prancing impatiently. "I'm so glad to see you."

Katy glued her smile in place and stiffened her back. What could Jane possibly want? Try as she might,

Jane would always be associated with her miscarriage, and she hadn't liked the woman even before that. Nevertheless, good breeding required a response. She'd done nothing that deserved a direct cut.

Katy nodded. "Lady Jane. Your stallions are fabulous."

Jane blinked, then looked at the horses. With a wave of her green-gloved hands, she dismissed them. "Oh, they're Lord Tod's. He's always going on and on about them. They're just horses."

Just horses. Katy admired the clean lines and beautiful coats. The pair matched perfectly and had to have cost a considerable sum. She cast a glance at the young man. She'd never met him, and he smiled back, eyes scraping over her, then lingering on Ruby.

"I've so wanted to call on you since you left my musical so early. I was so worried. I trust whatever ailed you has passed?"

Katy suppressed a shudder. "Yes, thank you. I'm fully recovered. It was just a passing stomach ailment." Few knew she'd been expecting, and she certainly wasn't telling Jane the truth.

"I'm so glad." Annoyance shot through Katy. Jane always seemed glad about something. "Momma is hosting another get together in a week. A ball this time. I'm sure she's sent you an invitation. I do hope you'll come."

Katy forced her lips to move back into a smile. "I'm afraid that would be up to the duke," she lied. In truth, he'd given her total control over their social calendar. Not that it mattered. He'd be even less inclined to attend than she was.

"Well, I'm sure you can convince him if you wish.

Please consider it. I was speaking to a friend of yours the other day, who asked me to encourage you." An elaborate lace fan opened before Jane's face. It matched her gown and hid her talon-like nose. "The Viscount is such a charming man." The fan dipped, exposing a pout on her thin lips. "It's so unfair he's taken with you. I'd love to be wooed by him, but he's obviously not interested."

Lord Tod snapped his head toward Jane, brows arched in disbelief. "Now, see here—"

"Hush," Jane smacked his knuckles with the fan. "I'm speaking with the duchess."

Katy's eyes widened.

Lord Tod shrank back, an ugly frown marring his face.

"Viscount Alysham says he followed you all the way from Ireland. It's so romantic."

Katy's head swiveled back and stared with horror. "Viscount Alysham?"

"Yes." Jane beamed at her and continued speaking, totally unaware that Katy had frozen. "He just inherited. His uncle and cousin both perished in a fire a month ago. Henry—" She stopped, blushing a sickly red color. "He said I should call him that, even though it isn't proper—was in the Guards. He almost died. Took a bayonet in the chest. It barely missed his heart. From what he said, the surgeons found him just in time, else he would have died for sure."

Jane locked eyes with Katy. "He said he was very disappointed to hear you'd wed, but he's very happy for you. He hopes you'll come and speak with him, since it wouldn't be proper for him to call on you without permission. He asked me to let you know he's here."

Jane opened a matching green reticule and pulled out a card. "In case you'd like to call." Her eyes flickered to Lord Tod, brows lowering, then turned back toward Katy.

She held out the folded card between two fingers as if afraid it would soil her gloves. When Katy made no move to take it, she leaned out of the barouche and tucked it into Katy's neckline. Katy jerked back, but the card had already wedged itself between her skin and the velvet of her riding clothes.

"Don't worry," Jane assured her with a knowing smirk. "Lord Tod and I would never tell the duke. And Henry said I should make sure you understand. Your secret is safe with him, but he needs to speak with you." Her brows lowered, and she turned a quizzical look on Katy. "He said he has your brother staying with him, and he would much rather turn him over to you than the authorities."

Katy's stomach lurched. Her tension must have radiated down because Ruby began to shift beneath her. She pulled back the reins. Thankfully, she didn't need to do anything else. Jane continued to babble a bit longer, then smacked Lord Tod back into motion after bidding farewell.

Katy stared into the roiling chain of promenading strangers, too stunned to move. The card scratched her skin, like the sting of a wasp, but she couldn't muster the strength to take it out. Henry's threat couldn't have been plainer. Meet him, or Thomas would pay the price.

What should she do? Unbidden, her gaze wandered toward Jeremy. Instead of comforting her, it added to the turmoil, tying her innards into knots. She couldn't tell him. Henry wasn't dead, so she didn't need to worry about Jeremy turning away because of that, but how could she tell him what she'd done when she wasn't even sure what had happened?

Caitlin had never spoken of the incident. She'd stared at Katy blankly as she undid the restraints on her hands and ankles. And she'd stared in horror at the blood surrounding Henry. She'd lain unmoving and mute while Katy cleaned and dressed the stripes on her back. Katy had heard her crying into her pillow late at night, when the others were asleep, but they'd never talked about it. She had assumed Caitlin was too broken and upset. She'd thought Henry intended to rape Caitlin based on what she'd heard, but Jeremy talked to her the same way, telling her what he intended to do before he turned her into a quivering mass of orgasms.

What if the horror she'd seen in Caitlin's eyes had been a result of seeing her lover murdered by her sister? What if the tears were tears of loss, not tears of remembered torture? Henry had been wooing Caitlin for weeks, maybe even a month. Da hadn't been happy, so Caitlin had sneaked out at night to meet her English beau. And knowing what she'd seen at Madame O's, Katy could no longer pretend. What if it had all been consensual? How could she tell her husband she'd almost killed a man for something Jeremy wanted to do to her? Something she was becoming more and more willing to consider?

She couldn't, any more than she could let Thomas suffer for her actions.

"Is something wrong, Katy?" Jeremy pulled back his reins and wheeled Ash alongside Ruby. "Who were you speaking with?" His head rotated to examine the barouche, just long enough for Katy to compose herself.

"It was Lady Jane. Asking how I was." She pushed the edge of the card deeper into her cleavage. It dug at the skin along her breast, boring into the swell like a dull knife. "She asked me if we'd received the invitation to her mother's ball next week."

Jeremy snorted, then frowned at the heavy black cloud looming in the distance. "We should go for our ride now. Before it's too late. It looks like rain coming in."

Katy sighed deeply and peered at the cloud. "Yes. We should." She kicked Ruby in the side and turned her toward the open expanse of green farther in the park. With a quick glance at Jeremy to make sure he followed, she lowered her torso and urged the eager horse to accelerate.

Ruby leapt forward, chewing up the distance, but it didn't matter. No matter how far and how fast she ran, it wouldn't be fast enough. She always paid for her impulsiveness. And she'd pay this time, too.

****

For the first time, Jeremy found no satisfaction as the flogger landed on Katy's bare back. The thud echoed in the dim room, followed by a low moan, just as he liked, but he was still frustrated. She was holding back.

He raised his arms and flung the leather strands through the air again. *Thwonk.* Another breathy catch of need. And still she held on, her long slender arms stretching for the loops on the St. Andrews Cross, legs spread. He let the flogger drop to his side and stepped forward.

His cock throbbed, jumping as he neared, and he inhaled deeply. Her spicy rosemary and lemon rushed into his lungs, but the musky scent of her arousal drowned it out. With his free hand, he stroked her bare skin. Heat radiated up in waves, and her body reacted, arching into his hand with a low groan. If he slipped his hand lower, over the tempting ass and into the space between her invitingly spread legs, he'd find her wet and slippery. She'd moan more, maybe even beg as she pressed against him, but he resisted the urge. That would be a reward, and she hadn't earned one.

She'd asked him to flog her. She liked it. The first time he'd done it, she'd surrendered almost immediately, melting beneath the strokes. He'd started with gentle blows, then increased them until even he was surprised by what she could take. A massage, she'd said. It had felt better than the massages her brother had given her. When he'd led her to the bed and fucked her, she flowed around him like water. She had let go, given in to the sensations robbing her of will.

But not now. Even as his hand smoothed along her waist, he felt the tension. Her chest rose and fell, deep, rapid breaths of need, but she didn't fall against the length he melded against her back. He kissed her nape, aware of the tiny start that ran through her.

"Whatever's bothering you," he whispered in her ear, "you need to let it go." He nuzzled her, inhaling her desire, willing her to trust him. "It's just you and I in here. Nothing else."

He let the flogger slip from his hand. She jumped as it hit the floor with a thud. As punishment, he slid his hands to the front of her torso and cupped her firm breasts. Smooth and round, they fit his hand perfectly, with tiny sandy nubs puckering at the center. Clenching his jaw to hold back the surge of lust rushing to his cock, he grabbed one of her nipples and twisted.

"Aaahhh!" Her head fell back, body convulsing at the shock. Her ragged breaths throbbed through him, tightening his balls. Still, she resisted. Her arm muscles flexed, and she shifted, her legs holding her up with ease. "Please," she begged. "Touch me." Her hips rocked forward, her body folding to maintain the contact between her breasts and his hands.

"No." He stepped back, hands fisting. He needed her to let go, think about nothing but him, feel nothing but his touch. Whatever worried her, whatever had passed between her and Jane, she could keep to herself if she wanted. He wouldn't push her to tell him even though he wanted it as badly as his cock wanted her pussy. But he'd not let her wall herself away.

Determined, he crossed the room and fondled a cane. The thin rod quivered in his hands. A sliver of anticipation raced along his nerves, but he replaced it. It would hurt too much. Like the whip, he'd work up to it, after she trusted him to know how much she could handle. While his gaze scanned the options, he heard her feet shuffling against the floor, her breathing moderating. Other floggers offered themselves. One with shorter, wider ribbons that he'd used before, another made of rope, one with tiny knots on the ends. The one on the floor had longer thinner strands. None would hurt too much unless he decided she needed it.

His eyes flickered toward a horsehair flogger, then slipped away. They could cut, and he didn't really like it. A swivel handed favorite caught his eye, but he discarded that as well. He wanted maximum control, and it required more technique.

When his eyes landed on one of his other favorites,

he hesitated. With nine leather falls, the cat-o'-nine-tails would sting more than the others, approaching that of a whip. He'd intended to wait a considerable time before pulling it out.

Peering over his shoulder decided him. Katy stood, arms and legs still spread, but her chest no longer rose and fell in desperation. Head back, eyes closed as if waiting, her long neck exposed, she looked the picture of surrender, but the tension in her body told him she was far from relaxed.

His fingers wrapped around the smooth ebony handle. His cock stiffened further. He grabbed that, too, giving it a reassuring tug, and murmured, "Down, boy. It may be a while."

His long legs chewed up the distance in one stride. She shifted, her feet sliding together to steady herself.

"Give me your hands." Pulling a strip of silk from his waist, he waited. Her eyes met his, and he saw a flicker of hesitation before she extended her hands. He wound the fabric around wrists, looping between her hands, then tugged just enough to form a cuff with a long tail. Lifting himself on his toes, he slipped the tail through a ring and pulled. When he deemed the stretch of Katy's arms taut enough, he tied it in place, tugging to test the knot, then stepped back.

She stared up at him, green eyes wide with trust. His stomach clenched. Why didn't she trust him enough to tell him what was bothering her? She trusted him with her body, but not her mind. And he wanted it all.

With more brusqueness than he intended, he pushed the handle of the cat against the inside of her thigh and nudged her legs apart. She obeyed, breath catching, until her arms held no slack and he feared her legs wouldn't hold her.

"Take a half step closer together," he commanded, touching the outside of her thigh.

A tendril of satisfaction wrapped around his balls. Her chest rose and fell in need again, and she licked her lips, nearly gnawing her bottom lip. Still using the cold rounded end of the handle, he dragged it across her nipples. A ragged sigh rippled up, and the rosy peaks hardened again.

His other hand squeezed one fleshy mound, rubbing his thumb over the pert nob. Leaning in, he stared at her lips and licked his own. Just as she began to lean in and open her mouth, he pulled back. His fingers clamped on the nipple. "Are you sure there's nothing bothering you?"

The tension around her eyes, the tightness he'd noticed when he returned from his conversation with Miles, increased, and her gaze slid away. "I told you. I'm just upset because it reminded me about the baby."

He could hear the grinding of his teeth. His fingers tightened, slowly twisting her nipple until she gasped and her body began to flex straining to get away.

"I told you, *Master*," he reminded her. He'd dispensed with the term for the most part, much preferring to hear his name on her lips but the protocol might help break through the wall she'd created.

Sure enough, her eyes softened as she spoke, mimicking the correction. The tension in her spine eased, pulling her arms tauter. The flush in her face seeped down, slowly spreading over her chest to the point he could feel it warming him.

"Are you wet for me, Katy?" He leaned in again, teasing her, loving the way her eyes darkened. Just out of reach, he stopped.

Her nostrils flared prettily, and she swallowed, eyes glued on his lips. "Yes, Master."

"Do you want me to touch you there?" While gratifying in its immediacy, her nod annoyed him. It was another sign of her unconscious resistance. He snaked the ebony handle along the center of her stomach, slowing as it reached the apex of her womanhood. The pace of her breath increased, and her muscles rippled.

He stopped before he reached the magic spot and leaned close enough to whisper in her ear. "I want you to think about that. About how good it's going to feel. And I want you to focus on the pain that comes first." He flipped the handle in his hand and let the falls tickle her thighs. "It's going to hurt more than anything I've used before, so remember your numbers. And think about how much it's turning me on every time you moan, about how hard I'm getting each time you twitch, and how good it's going to feel when I'm inside you."

A low groan brought a smile to his lips. Her hands tightened around the binding above her head, telling him her knees were getting weak. He let his hand slip, grazing over her clit, and her whole body shuddered. When he stepped away, the groan turned to a quiet moan.

He bit back his own groan. His blood hammered at the sight of her. Long and elegant, she clutched at the binding as if it were a lifeline, her legs spread at an angle perfect for whatever access he desired. There was just enough light in the room to cast a glow over the golden-red nest of curls, moisture reflecting off the wetness glistening between her legs.

Egads, she was going to kill him if she didn't submit soon.

With a deep breath, he extended his arm and slung the falls at her back, careful to go as slowly and gently as possible. At the last moment, he lifted his wrist, insuring a sharp slap as it hit the left side of her back.

Katy gasped, arching away from the sting. At her exhale, her leg muscles relaxed. As Jeremy watched, the fear drained from her face, replaced by a look of surprise.

He let his arm circle and swing again. This time, he followed the swing with his hand, pushing the flogger forward. A thud echoed.

She stiffened momentarily but stayed silent and relaxed more quickly. The play of emotions over her face calmed him. Whatever had furrowed her forehead all afternoon was evaporating in the wash of sensations. Eyes closed, the muscles in her face twisted in contemplation. The first blow had been meant to be sharp and attention getting. The second hit deeper, with a delayed heat that blossomed later. Neither were meant to induce severe pain or fear.

"Give me a number, sweetheart."

As expected, she hesitated, not believing. "Two." A second later, "Master" followed.

With a smug smile, Jeremy repeated the cycle, a sting then a thud, with a bit more strength and a similar effect. After a second round, her expression grew less intense, more pensive and calmer, while her body absorbed the battery of eroticism. Jeremy's satisfaction grew with each round. By the time she called out a response of six, he was convinced she'd forgotten whatever plagued her. Her breathing battered at him, her panting laced with the need for release.

He paused, as needy as she appeared, and came up behind her to bestow a soothing brush of his palm over the reddened skin. The burn seeped through his hand, charging his blood. A ragged moan as he caressed her ass added to the sense of satisfaction. Her leg muscles tensed, trying to maintain contact with his hand. He slowed and watched her body arch until forced to fall back.

Following the curve of her waist, Jeremy circled his hand over her hip and around her waist, urging her to nestle along the length of his body. His surging cock probed at her ass, drawing a needy sob from her. Splaying his hand, he pressed her stomach and rocked his hips.

"Please, Master," her head rolled against his shoulder, sending hot puffs of air along his chin.

"Please what?"

"Please whip me, Master."

A jolt of shock cooled him, but he didn't pull away. "No." Why would she ask for that? Had he misread her? He thought she'd turned off her mind and let go. She should be begging for release or be unable to ask for anything. She was still thinking.

Gritting his teeth against his lust, he swiped at her pussy with the falls of the cat. Her ass bucked, body convulsing. His balls clenched.

"What do you think I want right now, Katy?" He moved away, to minimize the contact rapidly stealing his control.

"To...to whip me?" Disappointment swamped him. "To fuck me?"

His forehead dropped, and he inhaled. Perhaps another round with the cat. Something told him it wouldn't matter. He wanted both those things. He always wanted those things. But he wanted something else, too, and he wanted her to understand it, to feel it in her heart. But she wouldn't tonight. She didn't trust him enough.

Gently, he released her hands from the binding and steadied her by wrapping her in his arms. "No, Katy," he murmured as he led her to the bed. "Right now, I just want to take care of you. Give you what you need. Nothing else." He kissed her and laid her on the bed. The look of confusion on her face stabbed at his heart.

He proceeded to do just that, making her come until she screamed, but it was just sex. There was no real satisfaction in it. It was just a physical release. Until she trusted him, it would never be anything else.

****

Jeremy lay in bed the next morning, elbow tucked under his head, and watched Katy sleep. A quick glance at the clock showed what he expected. Not even five yet. Too early to wake her. She'd had another nightmare in the early hours, moaning names—Henry, Thomas, Caitlin, and even George—thrashing about until he'd wrapped her in his arms so tightly she couldn't move. His heart ached for her. But he couldn't fix it. Not if she didn't tell him what haunted her.

And Thomas was still nowhere to be found. Miles had tracked the ship he'd boarded in Cork. He'd disembarked in London four days ago and vanished. With nothing but a description to go on, even Miles couldn't follow the trail. No one remembered a red-haired man leaving the ship. Unless he'd jumped ship, he'd disembarked as a brunette.

Why was he in London? Was he searching for his sister?

Jeremy sighed and reached out, careful not to wake Katy, and wrapped one of the red-gold curls around his finger. The tendril coiled around the digit, clinging to his flesh, tiny wires of fire that snaked up and wound around his heart. Right now, her sleep was restful, her face soft and content in the dreamless slumber of early morning. He matched his breathing to hers, slow, deep breaths that filled his lungs with hope.

She brought him peace. Blessed, soul-satisfying acceptance he'd never expected to find. He wanted to do the same for her.

Her breathing changed, so he smiled when her lashes fluttered open to reveal green eyes. She smiled back, sleepily.

"Good morning, sweetheart." He leaned over and placed a chaste kiss on her lips. For once, his cock was sated, barely stirring. Taking care of her had drained him. She'd never let go completely, but he'd made sure she had no energy left to feed the monster driving her.

She sighed and stretched, one arm slipping above her head, her body arching beneath the covers. Her hand cupped his cheek, brushing over the thick morning beard. Her gaze caressed him, her lips curving happily.

For the moment, at least, she seemed to have forgotten her troubles.

Maybe it really had been the thought of the baby.

God, he hated not knowing, not being in control.

"Is that all I get?" Her thumb scraped over his bottom lip. The covers rustled, just before her foot ran up his leg. Desire flared, hardening him before she reached the curve of his calve.

"What more would you like?" He didn't move, despite the urge to tweak her nipples and slip his hand into her juices. He might not have control over her nightmares, but he had control here, and right now, he wanted her to ask him.

She pouted, her luscious bottom lip sticking out in mock disappointment, and she shifted onto her side. The covers slipped off her breast, exposing a single white mound. He arched his brow as she cupped it, using her thumb to play with the pebbled nipple. It took all his control not to move. Thankfully, the covers bunched over his cock, because it wasn't playing the same game as the rest of his body. It leapt eagerly, like a toddler waiting for a treat.

"You're hateful."

His chuckle hurt, pulling from his groin. "Why?"

"Because." She fell back and scowled. The sheet slipped down to her waist, revealing the other breast.

"Is it truly so hard to ask?" Relenting, he bent over and tasted her lips, a slow leisurely exploration designed to make her hungry for more. With a supreme effort, he lifted his head and gazed at her. "Just tell me. Tell me what you want."

She stared up at him, eyes dark with need, lips wet from his kisses, and a ragged sigh shuddered through her. "Please, Jeremy. Please, love me."

His body moved faster than his mind. Before he knew it, his cock was inside her, his tongue in her mouth, and they were both groaning with desire. She'd asked for something he'd never been able to give before, and his body obeyed. In what seemed like minutes, they both came, then fell back, panting but replete. As his head hit the pillow, the clock told him the truth. Almost nine, they'd killed the dawn as completely as she'd sucked the life out of him.

He'd stay in bed with her all day if she let him.

He slipped his arm around her waist and pulled her against him. Her curls tickled his chest, and her lips dropped a quick kiss near his collarbone.

"Is that all I get?" he asked, chest rippling with laughter. Her hand smacked him, surprisingly hard. He grabbed it, trapping the fingers into a fist and lifted it to his lips. "Careful, darling. I have a whole room full of paddles, you know. It's never too early to punish you."

As soon as he saw her expression, he regretted it. The glow turned to a sick pasty gray, and her lashes fluttered. Her head fell back against his chest, and she hugged him. A shiver shook her, too faint for her to hide it.

He scrunched his eyes and cursed. He'd reminded her. Stolen the few moments of peace.

His fingers stroked along her spine, a silent apology. In the background, the sounds of the household taunted him, normal sounds of an ordinary home. Closer, the quiet ticking of the bedroom clock hammered away.

"What's wrong, Katy? You aren't afraid of me, are you?" He didn't think so, but he hadn't thought Anna was either. Until it was too late.

"No, of course not." Her cheek smoothed over his bare chest. "There's nothing wrong. Please stop asking."

His mouth curled in a frown. With a light touch, he lifted her face until he could see it. She wouldn't hold his gaze.

"I know there's something wrong. You don't have to tell me what it is. But I'm not going to stop asking. And I'm not going to stop trying to find out. It would be easier if you told me, but I won't force you to do anything. Just know, I'm not going to stop until I find out."

Instead of reassuring her, it made it worse. The pain in her face bit deep, etching lines in her forehead and burning away the light in her eyes. He let her go, let her burrow her face against his heart.

"What if you don't like what you find?"

"Whatever it is, we'll deal with it." His mind ran through the possibilities, including a few so outrageous they didn't even seem possible. "And nothing will change how I feel about you. Nothing could. Not even if you told me you'd purposely killed the baby."

With a strangled gasp, her fingers dug into his waist, and she stared up at him in shock. "I didn't! I wouldn't! Ever."

"I know. But it's the worst thing I could think of, and I'd still love you."

Her gaze flew over his face, assessing, her features twisting with thought until she nodded, and settled back down against him, fingers wandering over his body as if memorizing it. He let his own hands map out her body, soaking up the warmth and softness while she pondered it.

"Would you tell me something?"

"Anything."

"Why wouldn't you whip me last night?"

Jeremy's hand stopped on the curve of her hip. He knew the whip scared her. It wasn't an unusual fear. And he knew she wanted to please him. Why the sudden fascination though? "You aren't ready."

Her head shook, curls sliding over his stomach. "How do you know?"

"It's my job as your Master to know." Perplexed, he answered more completely than he might have. It couldn't hurt. "It's complicated, being a sadist. Some sadists like to hurt people just because they can, but not me. I want you to want it, too. And I think you will. But if I rush it, it's just pain. I want the connection that comes from it and that takes time. When you're ready, I'll know. And you will, too."

"How long does it take?"

Jeremy shrugged. "Everyone's different. For some, it's quick, but it takes more time if you're new to it."

"How quick is quick?"

"A month? Depends on the master, too. Even if the sub's experienced, it takes a while to learn how far you can go. Going too far, too fast, can scar the sub. Not just physically, but mentally, too." He'd seen it happen once. He never wanted to see it again.

His fingers began to move again, stroking tiny circles in her skin. Slowly, he felt her melt and nod in understanding.

"Thank you," she whispered. "That helps."

He could feel it. The tension he'd felt yesterday, the tension she couldn't release, had evaporated.

If only he knew why.

Chapter Fourteen

Katy examined herself in the mirror the next evening. The woman who looked back at her was a stranger. Her unruly curls behaved, wound into glorious ringlets that cascaded down her back, a single strand kissing her left shoulder. Gone were the coarse wool garments that had made her itch, replaced by the fine silks and satin she'd fondled at the dressmakers the few times she ventured into New Ross. Even the linen of her undergarments seemed alien, nearly as smooth and soft as the silk. Her tan had faded away, leaving her skin as white as porcelain, and Clara's trick of using lemon on the freckles had diminished them to an acceptable dusting.

She was the woman she'd always dreamt of being, a duchess wed to a duke, with an army of servants and enough money to do anything she wished. Her husband loved her to distraction, and amazingly, she returned the sentiment in spades.

And she was about to throw it all away.

Turning away, her gaze took in the room. She'd miss the newly decorated haven. A light mint green, the cherubs no longer serenaded her with their fat stomachs. Instead, a light tan trim broke the expanses of green. Cream-colored drapes allowed the sunlight to brighten the room even when drawn. All she'd done was mention in passing that she hated the decor and a decorator had appeared the next day, samples of colors and trims in boxes. Just like the nursery, the fake heaven had vanished during a weekend with George and Emily.

"Clara, could I ask a favor?"

The once scrawny young girl looked over her shoulder in surprise. Bent at the waist rummaging through a drawer, she'd filled out into a plump, round-faced girl who grinned with delight. "Ye needn't ask, Yer Grace. Ye know I'll do anything ye need."

"You, Clara. You're saying ye again." A sliver of guilt shot through Katy. She'd been schooling Clara to aid in her dream of becoming a governess or nanny. What would happen to the girl after she was gone? Would Jeremy fire her for her part? Or would his sense of justice prevail?

It didn't matter. There was no other choice. All day, yesterday and today, Katy had scoured her brain for an alternative. She couldn't go herself. Jeremy's protectiveness hampered her own movements. She had no doubt that Ned or someone similar watched her every time she went out. She had one chance to slip away unnoticed, and that one opportunity would be needed later.

"I need you to deliver a note for me." She crossed to the bed and lifted the corner to withdraw the carefully worded missive. Her fingers traced the smooth red seal. She hadn't used a signet to seal it. The woman sending it was Kathleen Brennan, not the Duchess of Lexham. Whatever Henry wanted of her, the duchess wouldn't be involved. Jeremy's name wouldn't be besmirched by it.

What did he want? Would he kill her? Or have her

arrested? She shivered. Or did he want to finish what she'd interrupted in Ireland?

Clara skipped toward her, then skidded to a halt, eyes fastened on the note. "Oy, Your Grace. Is it a love letter?" Her head cocked, hands on her waist. Her brows lowered, and she backed away. "Nay, I'll not do it. His Grace will fire me for sure."

"It's not a love letter." Katy slipped the card Jane had given her from her sleeve and scrambled for a lie that would work. "It's…a friend of my brother's. He has information as to where he is. But he doesn't trust Englishmen. He'll only speak to me. And His Grace won't allow it." It was close enough to the truth and would appeal to Clara's independent streak. "Besides, it's near to where your beau lives."

Clara eyed it with distrust, lips pursed. Katy held her breath. "Where is it?"

"St. Giles Circus."

Clara chuckled. "That ain't near Ludgate." Her fingers snatched it from Katy. "But it's on the way. I think I could maybe get it there for you." She peered at Katy. "You sure it ain't a love note? 'Cause I won't do that to His Grace."

"I'm sure." To hide her relief, Katy spun about and flew across to the jewel box on her dressing table. She withdrew a crown and held it out. "So you won't have to walk. That should get you there and back."

"Aye. And then some." Clara grinned, then her face fell. "But I can't get there and back before bed. Who'll help you undress?"

"I think I can manage." Katy laughed. "And His Grace is content to let me sleep late, too, so enjoy yourself."

****

"We're missing something."

Jeremy paced around Miles' sitting room, a scowl on his face. Across the room, Miles stared at the list of facts they'd accumulated, fingers tapping annoyingly on the oak desk. An antique roll top, the scarred desk had seen better days. The entire room had seen better days, highlighting a fact Jeremy had ignored for too long. Miles was in trouble financially. He'd known it for a while but hadn't realized just how bad it was. The fireplace had bricks missing, the rug showed spots worn through, and the windows rattled with every breeze. He'd missed the signs. Just as he was missing something now.

"I'd press Wickham for more information, but I'm not sure he knows much. Aside from the name of his outside specialist, I think he told me everything he knows, and he adamantly refused to give me that."

Jeremy clawed at his hair, stepping around the worn spot in the carpet. "Let's go over it again. What do we know for sure?"

Miles groaned, head thudding against the desk. They'd been at it for hours already, but he lifted his head, sighed heavily, and began. "Katy's family is involved in the mess over in Ireland. We don't know how much or in what way. My sources over there give conflicting stories. Katy herself doesn't seem to have been involved, just her family."

"Conflicting how? Anything that concerns Katy?"

Miles stopped tapping his finger on the list and a gold guinea began to dance through his fingers, flashing sunlight through the air. "Katy has four brothers, all of them tied to the rebels. That's one of the problems. The three half-brothers are hot heads. There are numerous stories that make me think they're knee-deep in trouble. Most of it's just the usual drunken brawling young men engage in, but they target loyalists. Hard to say how much is just coincidental and how much is calculated. Brody and Patrick took part in the battle at New Ross and are rumored to have been part of the deserters involved in the barn massacre at Scullabogue, but no one can confirm that."

Jeremy winced. As ugly as rebellion was, that particular incident had turned his stomach. Men, women, and children had died, all merely because they were loyal to the Crown. Katy had followed the news about it closely but no closer than any of the other news coming out of that area.

"What about Thomas?" Jeremy's gut told him Thomas was at the root of whatever motivated Katy. He just didn't know how.

"That's trickier. Thomas is quieter. One of my sources says he's one of the brains of the rebellion but can't point to anything specific. Another says he's just a peripheral player. Wickham agreed to let me use more agents to track him down but doesn't know his role any better than I do."

"And we're sure he's in London?"

"As sure as we can be. It still leaves us with the original question, the one that sent Wickham outside the Office. Who's the mole and what does any of it have to do with Katy?"

Jeremy circled the room, fingers slipping along the wood frame of a ragged sofa, skirting an equally ugly puce chair. The answer was on the edges of his mind, hiding in the shadows.

"You think Thomas is the mole?" It made sense, in a way, though the possibility sickened him. Having a rebel brother-in-law was distasteful enough. What Wickham had accused the mole of went beyond espionage. It was out-and-out sadism of the worst sort. Agents had been found flayed, skin turned inside out, their families tied up and forced to watch, then executed. Female agents had been whipped to death—

"Oh, fuck." Jeremy's feet froze. He clutched the edge of the chair, fingers gripping the wood so hard it crumbled.

"What?" Miles bound to his feet.

Slowly, Jeremy dropped to the chair, mind processing so quickly he couldn't keep pace. Miles would though.

"Katy's been obsessed with the idea of being whipped. And she's hiding something. Thomas is in London, and no one can find him."

"And George is at the center of it all."

Jeremy looked up at Miles, puzzled.

Miles' gaze darted about, the coin flying through his fingers, then the coin slowed and a smile crept over his face. "Wickham tried to hide it, but he hesitated when I asked him if he'd recruited George." He paused, brows raised as he stared at Jeremy, waiting for him to follow his reasoning. When Jeremy shook his head, Miles' lips curled. "George knows who the specialist is. That's who hired him."

Eyes widening, Jeremy fit the piece into the puzzle. The knot in his stomach tightened. "George was hunting the mole."

Miles nodded. "George and maybe Thomas."

"And Katy? How does she fit in?"

"That's the part I can't figure out." Miles shook his head, and the coin began to travel again. "Maybe she knows something?"

"If she knows something, why don't they just ask her?" What could she know? The identity of the mole? It didn't seem likely. And why hide it? Unless it was Thomas.

Jeremy rose to resume pacing. It didn't feel right. If Thomas was the mole, Wickham's specialist would have figured it out by now and dealt with it. It would have been done even before George left Ireland. Thomas hadn't gone missing until recently.

He didn't get an entire step in before it hit him. "The mole's gone to ground. Thomas knows who it is but doesn't know where he is." Sheer terror gripped him as the last piece fell in place. "He's expecting him to come after Katy. That's why Thomas is in London."

****

Katy wiped her sweaty palms on her skirt and followed the Earl of Margate's footman into the most wonderful room she'd ever seen. Sunny padded furniture and buttercup-colored drapes offset off-white panels. Light oak trim on the furniture and a cream rug adorned with multi-colored flowers added soft color, but the highlight of the room was the life-sized paintings on the wall.

One instantly caught her eye. A group portrait, with a stately blonde seated in a chair, a handsome man gazing down adoringly from behind her. At one knee, a serious-looking tow-headed young girl clutched her skirt. Seated near the other knee was an equally blond toddler in blue.

A tear pricked her eye. Looking at the woman

dressed in a mint green gown was like looking at a memory that had been revised. Her mother had died at about the same age as the woman in the picture after giving birth to Caitlin. Katy had been eight and Thomas six, but she remembered her father looking at her mother like that, as if the world revolved around her.

The thump of the earl's cane heralded his entrance, but Katy couldn't take her eyes off the picture. She'd always wished she had a picture of her mother. To see one, even one of her as a child, was too precious to waste.

"Do you see the brooch?" the earl asked as he stepped up behind her and joined her in her contemplation.

She dragged her gaze from the subjects' faces and scanned the woman's torso. Sure enough, the filigree emerald and platinum brooch winked at her.

"I miss her." The words slipped out, and Katy realized she'd never uttered them aloud. She hadn't believed the earl was her grandfather either. She'd been too afraid. It meant she'd have to let go of the resentment. But she did now.

"I've missed her every day since she left. But what I regret most is that she died thinking I'd never forgiven her. At least I was able to tell my wife I loved her when she passed. I never had that blessing with your mother."

Guilt slammed through her, releasing a single tear. Jeremy might not get that blessing either. Not if Henry, or the Viscount, or whoever he really was, decided to kill her. She wasn't sure she'd be strong enough to prevent it. But she had to try. The earl deserved to meet his grandson.

She took a deep breath to ease the fluttering in her

stomach and turned to face him. "Grandpa, I have a favor to ask."

"Anything, my dear. I told you that. Come sit down though."

"I can't. Another time, though." God willing, she'd keep that promise, if only to make up for the lies. She forced her hands to unclench and lay an entreating touch on his arm. "I need to sneak out your back door if it's all right."

The frail old man stiffened, a fierce scowl turning his face into a storm, remnants of the proud young man in the portrait evident in his posture.

Before he could speak, she stroked his arm. "Please, Grandpa. Jeremy has me watched like I'm a common criminal, and I just want to go and buy him a birthday surprise."

His jaw remained stony. "Your husband was born in March."

She felt her skin heat with shame. She hated lying to him. She dropped her eyes and stared at the floor. She had to appeal to his sentimentality. "I know," she whispered. "But I want to get him a surprise. He gives me so much. I want to give him something back." In order to make herself blush, she thought back to what she best liked to give him, then added, "I was hoping you'd give me some money to buy it, too." It never hurt to let a man think a woman needed him.

The earl's lips slackened, though he still peered at her with suspicion. "What did you have in mind?"

She hadn't thought that far, so she scrambled through her mind. "I thought perhaps I could go to Tattersall's. Get him some new tack." If she was truly buying him a present, it would probably be a whip, but

Grandpa wouldn't want to know that. "He's very fond of his horses."

He didn't look convinced. Although his stance had weakened, she feared it was due to disuse. His brows still reached across his nose bone, forming an unbroken line.

"You'd have to take one of my footmen with you. I'll have to see who's available." He moved toward the bell pull.

Katy stopped him, tightening her grip on his arm. "Oh, I don't want you to go to any trouble. Perhaps a watch would be better. His pocket watch is losing time. We nearly missed the ball last night because of it." Her skin heated again. They had arrived late, a fact Grandpa knew since he'd seen them, but it wasn't because of the pocket watch.

Without warning, he relented and patted her hand. "Very well, my dear." He slipped from her grip and headed toward a writing desk in the corner. "Just let me draft a note for you, telling the jeweler to bill it to me."

With a slow deep breath, she watched him limp toward the desk, unsure whether he really believed her or not. She hadn't expected him to, but it seemed he did. At any rate, she only needed enough time to slip away from Gregory's constant scrutiny. In an hour or two, Grandpa would figure it out. In fact, she was counting on it.

****

"Welcome home, Your Grace."

Jeremy shrugged out of his greatcoat and glowered as Alfred opened the door. "Where's Stanley?"

"I asked him to polish the silver." Alfred's hands flexed, the knobby fingers creaking. "In exchange, I'm manning the door. I hope that's all right."

"Where's Her Grace?" Jeremy tamped down an unexpected surge of fear. He didn't care an iota who manned the door, but Katy sometimes did. If she saw Alfred here, she'd berate Stanley for not polishing the silver in the foyer, as if there was no reason he couldn't.

"Gregory escorted her to the Earl of Margate's." Alfred took the coat and hat and handed a pile of mail to Jeremy.

Reassured, Jeremy flipped through the pile. Two were from people he knew were holding balls in the next couple weeks. One was from his bank, and the rest were calling cards. He handed them all back except the one from his bank. Katy would deal with them.

A shiver shuddered up from the floor, reminding him of his lesser worry. Miles' house had been cold, and the chill had settled in his bones. It was time to come up with a plan to alleviate the problem of Miles' insufficient fortune. Perhaps a rich wife. If nothing else, the idea might push him to swallow his pride and accept a loan and some investment advice.

"I'll be in the library. Please ask Her Grace to come see me when she returns. Beccles and George will be arriving as well. Hopefully, there will be a third man with them. Send them up when they get here."

The thud of his feet as he headed up the marble stairs pounded at his nerves, but it did nothing to pierce the quiet that descended when Katy was out. The silence fell over him like a shroud as cold and hard as the stone beneath his feet. Even the lingering scent of lemon failed to penetrate the growing dread.

They needed to find Thomas. With luck, whoever hired George would be able to help. He'd pound the information out of George if he didn't bring the man with him. He was tired of worrying that the joy he'd found would be snatched away. Crown secrets or not, they needed to work together.

As he strode down the hallway, Clara slipped out of Katy's door, a pile of laundry in her arms. The sight loosened the knot in his chest. She dipped a shy curtsy as she passed, a hesitant smile on her round face, then looked away. He liked Clara. She'd been horrified, according to Katy, at the bruises until Katy assured her he hadn't beaten her in anger.

Just as he reached the door, Clara turned back. "Excuse me, Your Grace, would you be knowing the time?"

Pulling his pocket watch out he glanced at the hands. "Quarter to two."

"Thank ye." She dipped again. This time, the clothes in her arm tumbled out, along with a neatly folded note. She snatched it all back up and hurried away, lip tucked under her teeth the same way Katy used to do.

Amused, he pushed open the door and crossed the cavernous room. The chill in the library wasn't quite as bad as in the foyer, but he bent down and lit the fire anyway. It spit, sparks flying as it caught, hissing angrily. When satisfied it wouldn't fizzle and die, he rose and wandered to the window and waited.

Outside, figures scurried through the unusual cold. Black clouds rolled overhead, threatening rain yet again, and the passing figures huddled into their cloaks. As he watched, a footman in familiar livery approached the front door. A deep green, with gold cording on the shoulders, it sent a stab of fear through him.

Within minutes, a knock shook the door and Stanley entered. With white gloves smudged with silver polish, he handed a note to Jeremy. "Alfred said you'd want this immediately." He quickly stuffed the smudged glove behind his back.

Jeremy stared down at the seal on the card; green wax embedded with the ivy branches of the Earl of Margate.

Thanking Stanley, he broke the seal, expecting the worst. His eyes scanned the words, tripping over the letters as they danced their irritating dance. Scratchy lines and words he didn't want to see forced him to read through it three times. Then he crumpled the note and swore. Tempted to toss it into the growing flames, he stopped, distracted by the sound of voices floating up from the first floor.

What was Emily doing here? Frowning, he crossed and listened from the doorway.

George's polite inquiry into Alfred's health drifted up, followed by Alfred's voice and another, one he didn't recognize. Deep, yet quiet, it resonated with an Irish lilt similar to Katy's. An ember of relief cut through the paralyzing dread the earl's note had fed, fanned by the distinctive sound of Miles' cutting wit telling George that if he didn't get upstairs he'd find himself unable to sit. Emily snapped back as she always did when someone attacked George, and a rumbling laugh followed. The Irishman probably. Hopefully, the mastermind who'd hired George.

More like an imbecile. Of all the people to recruit as a spy, George wouldn't have come to most people's mind.

Turning back to get a bracing drink before they

pummeled him with information, a flash of black caught his eye but disappeared before he could find it. Shrugging, he crossed the room, poured out two glasses of bourbon, and set out another three glasses. Miles would drink the bourbon. Emily might want Madeira or tea. George and the Irishman, he had no idea.

Stop it! Your wife's missing. No one cares what everyone's drinking.

He tossed back his drink and waited. Ned wouldn't lose her. He just had to wait for Tod to tell him where she was.

He'd never thought anything would be worse than waiting for Anna to give birth, listening to her shrill screams for eighteen hours before they weakened and finally stopped. But this was. Every second felt like a shrill scream slicing his soul.

Chapter Fifteen

Katy hustled down the street toward the St. Giles address, scanning the side alleys as she went. For a cold, rainy summer day, there were a lot of people about, huddled in their cloaks, rushing from one place to the next. Hired coaches passed by at rapid clips, splashing hems with the dirty puddles from the previous night, the coachmen cursing when someone stepped too close or a dog darted out.

She didn't like her plan, but at least it was a plan, instead of the hare-brained impulsiveness everyone expected. It hinged on her grandfather seeing through her lies and timing that was by no means predictable. She had to reach the address at the right time, or Jeremy would come to the rescue too early, or worse, too late.

At least her keepers were keeping pace. She'd known she couldn't lose them the way she could Gregory. Ned slipped into an alley, and the urchin who'd joined him at the tavern skipped down the street ahead of her, kicking a ball as he went. Every so often, he'd spin around, supposedly to recapture the wet rag ball, his pinched face peeking at her before running off again.

Someone else had been following her, too. She'd noticed them days ago. A pair similar to Ned and his sidekick, one in the guise of a packman and the other an older lad who begged or hawked goods, depending on the part of town. She might not have noticed them if not for her ability to remember faces and facts. She slipped into a doorway, glancing up at the sky, which had begun to plop down cold wet drops. Pulling out the black umbrella she'd borrowed from her grandfather, Katy scoured the faces behind her.

Sure enough, a man strode down the street until he noticed her, then bent forward and began to display ribbons to the passersby. Katy pursed her lips in annoyance. She didn't like unknowns. Was he friend or foe?

Lifting the umbrella, she flipped it open and stepped back into the street. There was nothing to be done about it. Just like her flimsy plan, it would play out one way or another.

With a shiver, she glanced at the pearled watch pinned to her bosom. Quarter to two. She'd told Henry two o'clock, and she had a few blocks to go. She pulled her cloak closer and hurried away.

The pace helped fight the chill but did nothing to calm her nerves. What would Henry do if she was late? Would he take it out on Thomas? She shook her head. *Don't think about it.*

Could she even do what she needed? Bile rose up, burning her throat. She had nothing to stop Henry. Just a rickety old umbrella, a long sharp hatpin, and her body.

Someone slammed into her, knocking her off balance. With a rushed apology, the woman kept running. Katy's umbrella went flying, carried off by a gust of wind. She stared in dismay as the ratty contraption tumbled back the way she'd come. The woman hurtled in the opposite direction after a toddler rushing for the spinning wheels of a barreling carriage.

Katy clutched at her chest. The toddler veered at the last moment. The woman scooped him up, her strident yells muffled by the now pouring rain. Ned's gaze met hers, and Katy's eyes widened. He was too close.

She turned and ran. He'd ruin it all if he caught her. Feet slipping in the mucky water, cloak billowing behind her, she sped past his compatriot. With a yell, he turned and chased her, but she was already in full flight. Breath straining, she pushed herself, slowly gaining distance. Flying around two corners, she paused to gaze up at the street signs. Mentally, she compared it to the map in her mind and flew around the next. She was close, but it was the wrong street. Slowing to a brisk walk, she peeked up the street bisecting the block. A deserted narrow alley, she slipped through the dark shadows, desperate to find the right one before her pursuers rounded the corner.

There!

Hesitating, she stared up at the house numbers, stomach twisting.

"Hey, Lady! You the Duchess?"

Katy jumped, a squeak lodging in her throat. A ragged-looking boy with shrunken cheeks and pock marks stepped out of the doorway. Big black eyes rimmed with red peered intently.

She nodded, glancing down the street, back the way she'd come. Ned rounded the corner, a lad and the packman close on his heels.

"This way." The boy bounced down the steps. She swallowed. Should she follow?

A yell from Ned decided her. She wouldn't get

another chance. She ran after the boy, following him around the corner, back into the mass of people and carriages she'd just left. He gestured frantically at the open door of a carriage, the same one that had just missed the toddler. With a final glance behind her and a silent prayer, she picked up her skirts and plunged into the already moving conveyance.

Scrambling up, she peered out the window and watched her last hope explode in a cloud of oranges. Ned went down, legs flailing in a sea of round orange globes. A moment later, his boy rushed toward her until the second young boy careened into him. Both went down, kicking and punching. The only one left standing was the packman, too far away and too slow to be much hope.

She was on her own. Again.

****

"Where's Katy?"

The voice boomed over him, and Jeremy's gaze snapped toward the sound. At least six-foot-three, the man had a pair of shoulders that rippled with muscles even his shirt couldn't hide. Giant steps chewed up the distance from the door, halting close enough that Jeremy could smell nutmeg and rum. Instead of eyes, blue topazes bored into Jeremy, demanding in their intensity. Something about the man looked familiar.

"Who the hell are you? You the bastard that masterminded this mess?"

"I'm your brother-in-law, you feckless bastard. Now, where is she?" The man's head swiveled about, as if he could make her materialize from the shadows. He turned away, his gaze taking in the room with a speed that impressed Jeremy. A reddish glint in the short blond curls tickling the giant's nape furnished the proof of his claim.

"I wish I knew." He tried to smooth the crumpled note, giving up and just handing it to him. "Jeremy." He stuck a hand out. "You must be Thomas."

Thomas glared at him a moment, then turned his attention to the wadded paper.

"Fuck!" The expletive burst out so fast Jeremy hated him. He'd had no trouble reading the snaking letters. Then the raging temper turned toward the door and pointed at Emily. "This is all your doing! And yours." He stabbed at George. "You told me she'd be safe, and now that sadistic bastard has her."

"Let's not jump to conclusions." Jeremy stepped between Thomas and his cousins, pushing the other filled glass at Thomas even while his own stomach clenched at the words. "I know your sister tends to go off without considering the consequences, but we have no reason to believe she's in danger."

Nothing but the gut-wrenching fear twisting through him.

Thomas spun. The glass flew through the air, crashing against the marble fireplace. Flames leapt, then fell back. "You don't get it," he said, growling. "He's already got her. He lured her in, just as he did my baby sister. And he's gonna rip her to shreds if we don't find her." His eyes burned into Jeremy, then he spun away. "Shit. You don't even care."

Dredging up the last bit of control he had, Jeremy fought the urge to lash out. The fear Thomas' words engendered, he stuffed into one of the little boxes he'd always used to rein in his own sadistic tendencies. "I care. More than you can imagine. But unlike you and your sister, I think before I act."

His eyes flicked over the three near the door. Miles stood against the doorjamb, arms crossed, a knowing smirk on his lips. Emily stared, hands wringing, while George's gaze flew back and forth between the two men.

He'd get back to them.

"What did you mean," he asked the circling blond bear grinding glass shards into his expensive carpet, "about your baby sister? Is that Caitlin or Nora?"

The names slowed Thomas. Rubbing his neck, he paused. "Caitlin. Nora's just a bairn." The crags in his face melted, and his eyes turned to water. "He uses them. He finds a sister, or a lover, or a cousin, and he courts them long enough to know what his target cares about. Then he uses it to get information. He leaves them alone as long as he gets what he wants. When he doesn't, he—" A shudder wracked his body. "You don't want to know."

"I've heard." Jeremy poured more bourbon, passing it around while he shoved that information into its own little prison. The power of it turned him cold. Katy would respond to a threat against anyone she loved no matter the consequences. Assuming she even considered the consequences. "What did he do to Caitlin?"

He saw the silent communication between Thomas and Emily, and Emily's nod before he got his answer. He filed that away, too.

"He whipped her. To shreds. He was about to rape her in the dirt when Katy ran in."

Finally, the nightmares made sense. And the fear of whips. "I can't imagine Katy took that well."

Thomas grinned, transforming his face. "She picked up his own bayonet and skewered him with it."

Jeremy blanched, his heart squeezing with anguish at the guilt she would have suffered. He could see her doing it though. He could see it more clearly than he could imagine Thomas as the quiet spy Miles had described.

Thomas' grin crumbled. "We thought he was dead. George and I dumped him on the battlefield so no one would know. Then a month or so later, the bodies started showing up again. That was when I connected the two; the leaks and the bodies."

"So, you know who it is?"

"It's Alysham."

Jeremy's gaze snapped toward Emily. "Alysham? How do you know?"

"I suspected it for a while. But when he saw her at Madame O's, it confirmed it. I'm sorry, Jeremy. We needed her to lure him out. If I'd been prepared, I would have had someone follow him from there, but I needed to get Katy home first. By the time I was able, he'd already vanished again."

The sick feeling in Jeremy's stomach threatened to turn explosive. Slowly, his gaze jumped from Emily to George to Thomas while the last pieces fell into place. When he turned his gaze on Miles, his friend was staring at Emily, wide-eyed with shocked comprehension.

"You're Wickham's specialist?" Miles' choked, a statement as much as a question. "Damn." Awe dripped from the word.

"Umm, I know I'm probably the least intelligent person here," George said sheepishly while his head swiveled from one person to the next, "and all this information is very interesting, but shouldn't we be saving Katy?"

Four pairs of eyes locked on George, and four sets of lips curled in varied states of amused scorn.

"Where do you suggest we start?" asked Jeremy in a sarcastic tone.

"Stop it, Jeremy." Emily's demeanor changed, going from the apologetic damsel in distress to the competent Domme Jeremy knew from Madame O's. "You know I didn't marry him for his brain." She glided to her husband and patted his shoulder. "George, honey, you need to trust me. We'll go save her as soon as we find out where she is." Emily's brows arched at Jeremy. "You have that fellow Ned following her, right?" Then her head rotated toward Miles. "And you have a couple people watching her, too?"

"You do?" Jeremy interrupted, glaring at Miles.

Miles shrugged. "You think I'm gonna let her slip away after I watched you mope for five years? I like you happy. If we have to chain her to your bed, you know I will." A wolfish grin appeared for an instant, then he sobered. "The whole situation made me nervous. Too many unknowns. I didn't trust her at first, then once I did, I knew how you felt. Besides"—he smirked again—"you're paying for them."

Suddenly, a shriek split the air. "Lemme go!"

Jeremy gaped as Thomas dragged a kicking, screaming Clara into the room. How had he crossed the room without anyone noticing? Last he'd seen, the man had been next to the fireplace.

"What are ye doing, *cailin*, skulking in the hall?"

"I ain't skulkin'. I be waitin'." Clara jerked her arm

out of Thomas' paw, an accomplishment Jeremy doubted she'd manage if Thomas didn't allow it. Her scowl was as fierce as an angry squirrel, her black eyes flashing with anger.

"Waitin' for what?" Already intimidating, Thomas' huge form moved closer, arms crossed in a manner that puffed up his already massive chest. His craggy face glared down at the diminutive girl.

Clara merely stared back, as if he were a little boy, then her gaze flitted toward Jeremy. Her lashes dropped, and she turned beet red. Her hand slipped into a pocket beneath her apron and pulled out the note he'd seen earlier.

"I be waitin' for two o'clock. Her Grace said I was to give this over then."

Thomas snatched it.

"Hey! The chimes ain't rung yet." Clara swiped, but Thomas lifted it higher. She jumped, barely reaching his elbow extended over his head.

"It's all right, Clara." Jeremy stomped over and grabbed the note. Smudged and torn, all it contained was an address in St. Giles Circus and a date— yesterday's date. He read it aloud, hope adding strength to his voice.

"It's an empty flat." Emily dashed the hopes before he'd fully formed them. "We've been following Clara, too." She peered at Clara coldly, then turned back to Jeremy. "She passed a note to a footman there. We only had one person following her, so we couldn't check it out immediately, but Thomas did it this morning. It's vacant."

"I didn't do nuthin' wrong. Her Grace made me do it." Tears sparkled in Clara's eyes now, pleading for forgiveness.

"It's fine, Clara." Jeremy squeezed the bridge of his nose and began pacing. Alysham would probably meet her there and take her somewhere else. But where? Ned would follow her, assuming he hadn't lost her already. Would it be soon enough for Tod to get here in time to help her? The panic he'd been shoving down began to choke him, rising up and lodging in his throat.

"Katy's smart," Thomas said in a gentle tone meant to be comforting, no doubt. "I'm not sure she's smart enough though."

A sudden rapid pounding turned all their gazes toward the door. Seconds later, two young boys tumbled into the room, tripping over their own feet, panting as they jostled each other.

Miles stepped up and grabbed one of them by the neck, dragging him backward. "Enough!"

Tod leaned over, sucking in deep breaths. The other struggled to escape Miles' clutches.

Miles jerked his collar, setting him on his feet. The boy scowled but stopped fighting. "I lost her, boss." He gulped in a couple breaths. "Pip's still looking." He glared at Tod.

Tod shook his head, sending Jeremy's stomach plummeting through the floor. "We lost her, too, Gov. In Bloomsbury Square." He sucked in another breath. "Some boy…stuck her in a hackney…then he plowed into…a fruit stand." He inhaled, then straightened, wiping the sweat from his forehead. "Ned tripped. I couldn't get to her." If his eyes were daggers, they would have sliced the other boy to shreds as he pointed at him. "He ran into me."

More shouts and accusations broke out, but Jeremy stopped listening. They'd lost her. He'd lost her. And he had no idea what to do.

****

Katy tried to get out. Even though the coach was moving at full speed, she considered jumping out. But when she pushed the door, it wouldn't budge. The latch and wood rattled, as loud as the blood pounding in her ears, but wouldn't open.

She beat on the door, fists thudding hollowly in the vain effort, not even loud enough to be heard over the sound of the wheels. The carriage rocked, wheels singing, jolting her off the seat every so often. Wet and cold, she slid on the seat despite the layer of grime coating it. All she could do was clutch the sides of the seat and hope the trip ended soon.

Damn Thomas. Her eyes pricked with tears. She wouldn't be in this predicament if not for him. But she couldn't abandon him, any more than she'd been able to stand by and watch Caitlin suffer. Momma had made her promise. *Be good and take care of your brother and the baby.* She could hear the words as clearly today as the day Momma died. She'd tried. She'd protected them both, even standing in front of them when Da had drunk too much and started using his fists. But until now, she'd never had anything to lose.

She'd kill Henry this time. She didn't know how, but she would. And when she finished, Thomas and Caitlin would have to take care of themselves. She had a life of her own now. One she wouldn't risk again.

She swiped a tear away. Jeremy would forgive her. She wasn't running away. She'd promised she wouldn't, and she'd meant it. She would never leave him willingly.

With a sobbing sigh, she settled back as best she could and attempted to calm herself. A glance at the confines of the carriage offered no encouragement. There was no weapon, no way out, just the cold blackness of a hired coach.

Turning her head, she cataloged the landmarks they passed. Largely unfamiliar with London, she nevertheless made mental notes in hopes she'd need them later to get home. They passed Grays Inn and shortly afterward the artillery grounds, then the landscape began to change. City buildings became fewer and farther between, and a beautiful church appeared. By the time the carriage slowed and pulled into an area of warehouses, she had gathered her wits and her breathing had slowed.

When they stopped, Katy peered out. Nondescript square buildings dotted the view. Still raining, the landscape looked as cold and dreary as she felt. No one moved except for a lone rider who galloped by so quickly she didn't even have time to react. Her eyes connected with a kindly face. Rain-drenched and moving at full speed, all she could do was register a slight nod as he passed.

With a sinking stomach, she watched her nightmare exit the building in front of her. Instead of the red tailcoat and white sash of a military man, he wore black and tan. Unlike the last time she'd seen him, his face was fully exposed. A handsome well-groomed man with a strong jaw and clear skin, evil still showed in the icy glint of his eyes and the cruel smirk on his red lips.

The click of the door lock releasing startled her,

and she shrank back. A bare hand reached in, a long scar running the length of his hand and down his ring finger.

"Welcome, Duchess. I was so pleased you accepted my invitation. Rest assured, I'll do my best to make your visit enjoyable."

"Where's my brother?"

His gray eyes flashed. "So that's how it's going to be?" His hand lashed out, fingers locking around her wrist without mercy. "Just as well, I suppose. I never did like the niceties of society."

He dragged her forward, fingers pinching and twisting, so tight that her gloves couldn't temper it. Gasping, Katy tumbled from the carriage, wet skirt tangling against her ankles. Unable to catch herself, she fell against him. He stepped forward, lifting her wrist until her toes were the only contact with the muddy ground. Even that threatened to slip away from her, forcing her to lean into the only stability available.

"Impatient, are we?" He smirked, his eyes going dark and ugly. His free hand snaked along her waist, then up her back. A quick rock of his hips revealed a burgeoning menace.

Revolted, Katy swallowed the bile burning her throat.

He chuckled, then released her.

Off-guard, she stumbled, then righted herself. The tight grip on her wrist remained, trapping her as effectively as a pillory. A quick glance convinced her she was on her own. The coachman sneered at her from his perch, and there was no footman.

"Come along, my dear." Henry, or Alysham, she supposed, jerked her forward, toward the gaping black hole leading into the warehouse. Even the half boots she wore didn't help. She slid through the mud as if it were oil. Nonetheless, she dug in her heels, forcing him to glare at her.

"Where's Thomas?" She schooled her voice this time. Demanding hadn't worked. Maybe asking nicely would.

He laughed, throwing his head back in the rain. "You really are an innocent, aren't you?" His mouth curved like a sickle, then hardened. "Thomas isn't here. Yet."

Wide-eyed, she stared in horror until he turned around and yanked her forward. "What do you mean?"

Sick, she followed, all too aware she had no choice. Inside, she scanned the dimly lit room. An empty shell, all she saw was a bag on the straw-covered floor. No other doors were visible, just blackened shelving and support posts.

"Thomas and I have been playing cat and mouse for years," Henry boasted. "He's very good. Took me a year and a half to get even an inkling of who was countering all my hard work. All those poor innocents I had to sacrifice, all for naught. Every bit of information I gleaned became useless almost as soon as I learned it."

Once inside, he released her wrist and shoved her forward. A thunk echoed behind her. When she gained her footing and turned around, she saw him squeeze the shackle of a padlock. The click sounded deafening.

"You ruined everything." He spun around and bore down on her, eyes hard with anger. She shrank back. Fingers bit into her jaw, forcing her against a wooden pole. His knee ground against her skirt, forcing its way between her legs. "Your sister was supposed to teach him a lesson. Now, I'll have to use you instead. It's too bad. I liked her. She tried so hard to please me."

Before her eyes, the anger vanished. The bite of his fingers softened, turning into a caress. His thumb stroked her bottom lip. "Do you like being whipped? I've heard rumors about your husband. We went to school together, you know? He always thought himself better than the rest of us. Him and that cousin of his, and Beccles. When I heard the rumors, I thought it couldn't be true. Not Jeremy Wyles, the perfect duke. He'd never do something so improper and depraved. But I had to try it." His eyes glazed, as if he'd transported himself into the memory. "It was so freeing. So empowering. Seeing the fear grow, the desire to do anything to make it stop. It was heavenly."

Too terrified to move, Katy stared, willing the waves of revulsion to stop. He was utterly mad. Snippets of conversations filtered through her mind, hushed recounts of people murdered in the vilest ways, reports of events too horrific to be shared openly, especially with women or children.

"You aren't paying attention!" Pain lashed her cheek. Her head slammed into the pole. An instant later, his hand slashed down, silver glinting. She gasped, tensing. Ice raced down her front, gliding between the mounds of her breasts. A wave of cold rushed over her skin. Her cloak dropped from her shoulders, held up only by the pole behind her. The thick wool of her dress flopped open, exposing bare skin. "I'm waiting for an answer!"

Heart pounding, Katy reviewed his words. What had he asked?

"I…I don't know," she stuttered. "He hasn't whipped me."

"No?" His gray eyes narrowed, his face leaning so close she could smell garlic on his breath. "That's hard to believe."

He eased back, the crazed look dwindling as his gaze traveled over her heaving breasts. Try as she might, she couldn't control the panicked rise and fall.

"Of course, he's probably like all the others." His lips curled in disdain. "Let's you decide. What does he do? Does he tie you up? Flog you?" His finger snaked down, creating shudders that chilled her to the core. Rough and scarred, the tip felt like tree bark scratching her skin. "Well?" he snapped. A tortuous twist of her nipple caused her legs to buckle, white-hot pain searing through her. "What does he do?"

"Yes!" she practically screamed as he pinched her again. "He ties me up. He flogs me."

Her back slid down the pole, the rough wood biting through the wool. She scrunched her eyes closed. It didn't help. The rain still drummed overhead, reminding her that no one would hear her scream.

"What else does he do?" Once more, the monster receded. A firm gentle grip grasped her forearm, and a length of linen slid over her wrist. Opening her eyes, she watched as he bound her hands together. "Does he lead you around on a leash? Make you service Beccles? Or does he take you in the ass?"

"No," she answered, instinctively. There was a connection between his bouts of rage and her non-compliance. Caitlin was the good girl of the family. He liked her. Because she tried to please him. And he'd fooled them all until she'd walked in on them that day.

He didn't like resistance. His guard went down when she gave him what he wanted and went up when she didn't.

"He…spanks me. With a paddle." She contorted her face, as if she hated it.

He grinned and cupped her jaw. "Does he leave marks?" His other hand grabbed the waist of her skirt. A hiss rent the air, and a wave of cold followed. Then he spun her around, pushing her neck until she bent at the waist. "Oh, that's pretty."

A light touch made her jump. She gritted her teeth as he passed his rough hands over the bruises Jeremy had left the previous night. It was a gentle touch, but her skin still crawled to get away.

His hand wandered lower but thankfully stopped before it reached her pussy. Instead, he clamped his hand on her arm and yanked her up to face him.

"Would you like me to spank you?" Heavy-lidded with lust, his eyes wandered over her face, a question in his eyes.

What answer did he want?

"No. Please." She did her best to cower and beg. He liked to hurt women, but he didn't want them to fight. She needed something for a weapon. A heavy paddle might be the best she'd get. He'd not tied her to anything, only bound her hands together. She could wield it two handed as long as she could grip it.

When he didn't move, she lifted her gaze. He considered her, head cocked, as if unsure.

"Please…" She added a silent prayer to heaven. She had to make him believe her. "I hate it."

"But you let him do it?"

She swallowed her sigh of thanks. "Sometimes. He

doesn't do it often. He prefers to let me decide. He's…weak. Not like you."

The first hope she'd felt since entering the carriage flared when his face beamed. She sucked in a breath for courage as he spun around and walked to the bag on the ground. A long, wicked whip appeared, then he put it aside. A cat-o'-nine-tails followed. Soon, he pulled a hefty round paddle from the bag and smacked it against his hand. The crack sounded like lightning, crisp and hollow. It would sting. Badly. Depending on how he hit her, it might be more than she could handle, but she'd suffer it. The longer she played along, the more his guard would drop.

What followed taught her exactly how much care Jeremy took. Henry made her kneel on the floor. Roughhewn wood stabbed her knees, the straw so old it smelled like rotted meat. Then he began to beat her. The first blow stung. The second felt like fire lancing her entire body, jerking her forward, slivers gouging her hands and arms. She tasted blood with the fourth and fifth while her mind went numb and tears pooled in her eyes. She began to sob uncontrollably on the sixth. Still, he continued, landing each blow with every ounce of his strength until she lost count.

It took her time to realize he'd stopped. Tears blinded her, and her lungs were on fire. She'd sucked in half-breaths between each cruel blow. Now, she couldn't take in air deeply enough between the sobs. Her tears hit the floor, splashing up, the salt hitting her open mouth. She'd never imagined pain like this.

She lifted her face, afraid to move. Henry stared back, arms on his thighs as he studied her. His eyes were blank pools of ice. He gave her just enough time to get her tears under control.

"Shall we continue? Or do you need a minute?"

What was the right answer? She needed more than a minute. More like a lifetime. He wouldn't want to give her what she asked for though.

"No." She sobbed, wishing she could wipe the tears from her face. But she'd not grovel in the dirt to do it. "Just get it over with."

He rocked back on his heels then leaned forward to tenderly wipe one cheek, then the other. The soft touch sent shudders through her. "So pretty. And so biddable. But you need time. I wouldn't want you to faint, after all."

In one move, he stood, his shiny brown boots inches from her face. The paddle thudded to the ground next to her. Close enough to grab. She ground her teeth in frustration. She'd never be able to use it as a weapon from this position.

"What shall we do next?" he asked as his feet pounded on the floor. She followed his movements with her head, calculating. He wandered back to the bag and bent to rifle through it. "Shall we use nipple clamps?" He lifted a nasty-looking piece of metal from the bag. "Or would you like to be whipped? Since the mighty duke hasn't bothered? He's probably afraid to disappoint you. It takes a lot of practice to hit just right."

He lifted the whip. A crack split the air near her head. She winced, glad she wasn't closer.

"Or I could use the clamps on your pussy. That's a rather exquisite pain." He continued to ramble on happily, discussing possibilities she couldn't imagine, until it dawned on her. He was trying to scare her. And it was working. The shudders of pain had morphed into shudders of fear. He'd done the same thing to Caitlin, telling her he was going to rape her in so much detail it had turned Katy cold.

She closed her ears and concentrated on making her body obey. He wasn't paying attention. All she needed to do was get to her feet.

She managed to push herself to her knees and grabbed the nearby post. Her knees screamed, and she saw blood on the floor as she moved closer to the discarded paddle. She could smell it, too, coppery and sweet.

"Ah, you're ready." His hand grabbed her hair. He snapped her head back until she felt as if her neck would break. He looked like a child who'd just received a gift, beaming with excitement. His eyes sparkled with glee.

She'd almost made it. Another minute and she would have been on her feet. Instead, her hands clutched the pole, her back arched, and she stared up at her tormentor.

"What did you decide? The whip or something else." He smiled and loosened his grip enough to relieve the strain on her neck. "What do you hate most?"

Released, her head fell forward, stopping in front of his crotch. Inches from her mouth, the weapon she needed pulsed, struggling for freedom. She shifted, forcing her knees to support her. Biting her lower lip, she closed her eyes.

Jeremy would never forgive her, but she had to do it. It was her only chance.

"Please." Her voice came out even more pleading

than she hoped. "Don't…don't make me say it."

"Say what? What does he make you do?"

She waited long enough for him to tug her hair.

"He…he makes me…" She made herself shudder and dropped her gaze. "Take him in my mouth," she whispered.

It was one of her favorite ways to please Jeremy. He resisted it as often as not, because he lost control. It stole his concentration and left him weak. With luck, it would do the same to Henry.

"Umm." Henry's hand rubbed his crotch. "That does sound fun." He paused, and Katy waited, afraid to breathe. "Can you do it with your hands tied? I like looking down at you like this, on your knees with your hands tied in front of you."

"Yes." She could do it either way, but if he untied her, it would be even easier.

This time, he disappointed her. "Good."

He unbuttoned his fall, the soft doeskin dropping to reveal exactly how much he liked the idea. Small and ugly, his cock pulsed purple. He spread his legs, steadying himself, but didn't move any closer. She'd have to crawl to him, a plus in his mind no doubt, but it would also allow her to shift her weight to maximum benefit.

Revulsion threatened to spill the contents of her stomach, but she swallowed it. She could do this. All she had to do was pretend he was Jeremy. She'd learned what worked best, what robbed him of his sanity.

"Well, get on with it. We only have…forever." He chuckled, amused at his own joke.

Katy inched forward, balancing so her weight was

on her legs and knees, freeing up her hands. As she neared, she lifted her arms so her hands could land properly, and crawled marginally closer.

She glanced up through her lashes. Henry stared at her, eyes heavy-lidded and dark. For effect, she licked her lips. His cock jumped, her stomach convulsing with it. With a deep breath, she grasped the base as best she could. Her forearms hit the soft flesh of his balls, giving her incentive. Her mouth opened, and she slid her mouth over the head.

Gagging, she held back her shudders and used what she'd learned. She used her tongue to wrap around the ridge and lave the front, pretending. The pretending was hard. He didn't taste like Jeremy. He was smaller, and he smelled like a bad mix of urine and garlic, but she ignored it. She took him deeper, using her bound fingers to coax him until he began to move his hips. It took longer, maybe because her heart wasn't in it, maybe because he had better control, but eventually, his breathing grew faster. She hated the feel of his hands in her hair, tugging at all the wrong moments, but it kept her focused.

Don't rush it. Wait until he's too far gone.

Tears pricked her eyelids as she gagged repeatedly, not because he hit the back of her throat, but because she hated what she was doing. It felt wrong. Not like it had with Jeremy. She hated the taste and smell of him, and she hated the way he pushed his cock at her with increasing determination.

When she could stand no more, when his breathing was so ragged she thought he'd collapse, she tensed her muscles. She slipped her lips up the shaft until he locked his hands on her head to force it back down, then she opened her mouth and dropped her hands.

She chomped and locked her jaw. A spurt of liquid gushed and dribbled over her chin. She slammed her arms up the way Thomas had taught her, levering and lifting with her legs until his balls gave way.

With a scream, he dropped, writhing in pain. Katy scrambled away. She grabbed the paddle and lifted it. Lunging, she slammed it on his ear. A horrendous pop exploded, and he shrieked. She lifted it again. It landed on his neck with a crunch. Then again, smacking his spine. Over and over, she hit him until her lungs and arms burned, until his body twitched, arms and legs jerking, and he stopped moving.

She backed away, paddle held before her as if to protect her. Knocking into the support beam, she stared, then sank to the floor. Her eyes darted at the shadows, waiting, afraid he'd move, afraid she'd have to hit him again.

Slowly, after an eon, the trickle of tears started. She wiped them, hands still bound, paddle knocking her in the forehead. She'd done all she could. She'd just wait now. Wait for him to wake up and kill her or for someone to come and rescue her.

"Please, Master," she whispered into the darkness. "Please let it be over. I can't take any more."

****

It took less than ten minutes to get to the warehouse, but it was easily the longest ten minutes Jeremy had ever experienced. Emily's man had pounded on their door forty-five minutes after Tod's pronouncement of failure, making it close to an hour of living hell. Four of them now stood before the line of warehouses that had cropped up to support the silk weavers. They all looked the same, ten or twelve square brick buildings. No distinguishing marks, no way to know for sure what each contained.

"Are you sure it's this one?" Jeremy wanted to pound the door in, but a small part of him feared what might happen if he did. Would she already be dead, or would the time needed to break through the door result in just that? How long did it take to kill a woman?

"I'm sure. I looked her right in the eyes as I passed. You can see the wheel ruts still." Emily's man, Adam, pointed at the ground. A pair of mud-filled ruts marred the sludge, wider in front of the building. A patch farther ahead was stomped flat, evidence of horses held in check.

"It's too quiet." Jeremy scanned the area. The rain had cleared twenty minutes before, and a calm lay over the buildings. Intimately familiar with the sounds of whips and other instruments of torture, the silence unnerved him. Either she was dead, or they were in the wrong place.

"Feck this." Thomas leapt into action. Bounding from his horse, he slammed into the door with his shoulder. The building shuddered, then, with a crash, the door burst open. Straw flew up, scattering dust into the clear air.

Jeremy followed as Miles and Adam dismounted. Jeremy and Thomas rushed in, the others in the rear.

The transition from daylight to the dim warehouse blinded him. He didn't need to see her though. He felt her. His heart jolted to life.

"Katy Button?" Thomas stopped dead in front of him, so Jeremy skirted around him. His feet knocked into something, but a quiet whimper redirected him. He headed for the sound, then hesitated.

Curled into a ball, a large wooden paddle lifted in front of her, Katy rocked in the straw. A puddle of blood crept toward her, the smell of piss and feces strong, but he fell to his knees anyway. "Katy?"

Wild-eyed, she stared at him, then sobbed, a wretched sound that tore him apart. The paddle fell with a dull thud. Her eyes darted over their faces, landing on each of his companions before settling on Thomas.

"Tommy?" Her hands flexed, straining at the bindings, then fell back in defeat. "Is that you?" Her gaze flitted back to Jeremy, and tears dripped from her eyes. "I'm sorry." Her entire body convulsed with gulping sobs. "I had to save him. I couldn't let him hurt him."

"Hush." Jeremy reached forward and unwound the linen from her wrists. The bastard hadn't even tied them correctly. Indentations bit her skin, and her fingers felt like ice.

"I didn't want to." She stared at her hands. The knuckles were raw, and she flinched as he rubbed them. Slivers tore at his skin. "I couldn't think. I had to." The anguish in her voice sent chills down his spine. "Please don't hate me," she whispered.

"Mother of Mary." Miles sounded far away. "The bastard's dead." A heavy thud and the rustling of clothing preceded an awe-filled, "She bit his cock half off."

Jeremy's eyes widened, and the blood on her chest and hands registered, as did the fact she was naked and shivering. She still hadn't moved, eyes still locked on his face, fear-laden.

Stripping off his cloak, he placed it over her

shoulders. A shudder rocked her as his fingers grazed her skin. Her eyes squeezed shut, and another sob ripped him to pieces.

She was afraid, afraid of him, afraid of what he'd do. Or not do.

He glanced at the lump of refuse Miles had rolled. Somehow, she'd killed him. He doubted it was blood loss but rather the nearly severed cock that had incapacitated him. And it meant she'd had to do something she promised never to do.

"Come here, sweetheart." He opened his arms.

For the instant it took for her to move, his heart stopped. Then she threw herself at him, and his soul shattered. His arms locked around her, pulling her close, but not close enough. He buried his face in her hair and neck, inhaling until he found the lemon and rosemary essence beneath the blood and fear. "I could never hate you. Never. You didn't do anything wrong. You did what you had to. I would never hate you for that."

"Are you sure?" She tried to curl closer, rubbing her cheek against his chest. "Because it felt wrong. It was horrible."

A torrent of sobs soaked his shirt with hot tears. He just held her, rocking on his heels, ignoring the knives of pain shooting up his calves, until she calmed.

"I…I think…" she told him between the lessening bouts of sobs. "Take me home. Please."

With one surge, he lifted them both, cradling her against his chest. "Don't worry, sweetheart. I'm never letting you out of the house again."

****

Two days later, Jeremy returned from the Home

Office. There would be no inquiry, no repercussions. Wickham's relief at termination of the mole who had chewed through their efforts meant Viscount Alysham's death would raise no eyebrows. They'd spread rumors of an illegal duel amongst the Ton. For a hefty fee, Miles volunteered to be the suspected opponent and Thomas his second. A lack of evidence would leave them free. Within a week, the new tidbit of gossip that Thomas was heir to the Margate earldom would distract the Ton's attention.

The knot in Jeremy's stomach loosened to the point he might be able to eat again.

"Where's the duchess?" he asked Stanley as he handed over his hat and cape.

"I believe she's still in her rooms, Your Grace."

Jeremy's gaze flitted toward the grandfather clock. Nearly three in the afternoon. "Has she eaten?"

"Clara took up a tray, but Her Grace never touched it." The footman's face remained placid, but his eyes mirrored Jeremy's worry. "Will you be needing anything further, Your Grace?"

"No, thank you, Stanley." Jeremy took a single step toward the library hallway, then pivoted. "Actually, give the rest of the staff the remainder of the day off." He couldn't tolerate it any longer. The last two days felt like the barren, soul-wrenching emptiness that had followed the loss of the baby. He couldn't live through that again. "If anyone arrives, we're not at home. We're not to be disturbed. For anyone. I don't care if Prinny knocks and demands to see us. Am I clear?"

"As clear as air." Stanley bowed, but a tiny sigh rustled the air, and when he straightened, his shoulders went back farther. "No one will get past me, Your

Grace."

Jeremy peered at the young man. He'd seen Stanley adopt that posture after the day Miles and he had ordered Katy off the ladder. He used it on Clara who went tongue-tied and blushed each time.

Was Stanley a Dom? That Clara was a sub, he could easily believe. But he'd never considered that his servants might harbor dominant tendencies or even have sex lives of their own.

"Tell me, Stanley, what do the servants say about me and their mistress?"

Stanley stared impassively at the wall. "We all enjoy serving here, Your Grace. You've a fair and even hand, and everyone knows what's expected."

"Even Gregory?"

A faint white appeared on the edges of Stanley's lips. "Gregory especially." His mouth opened, then snapped shut.

Jeremy's eyes narrowed. "You don't think I should have reinstated him?"

Their eyes met, then Stanley's shifted and glanced upstairs. "I wouldn't have, Your Grace. He..." With a deep breath, Stanley spit it out. "He endangered Her Grace. That's unforgivable."

"And if I told you Her Grace begged me to have mercy?"

"I'd tell you Her Grace doesn't always know what's best." He paused, then added, "But I'd understand. It's difficult to deny Her Grace anything."

He ought to fire him for his cheekiness. Instead, he asked, "And what do you think Her Grace needs right now?"

"I think you know exactly what she needs, Sir."

****

The emptiness was absolute as Katy stared into the darkness. Clara had left the drapes shut, darkening the emerald and walnut of Jeremy's bedroom to near black, and the air lay still. For two days, she'd done nothing, felt nothing, moving only when her bladder needed emptying. She couldn't cry, couldn't sleep, couldn't even find the energy to roll into a new position. Jeremy tiptoed around her and wrapped her in his arms each night, but still she felt nothing. It was as if she too had died with Henry, or Alysham, or whatever name the devil used.

She heard the steps outside the door, then the door opened and closed. A whiff of sandalwood penetrated the thick air, but still she didn't move. She might never move again. There was no reason. He'd said the words, told her she'd done nothing wrong, but it didn't feel like it. She didn't feel forgiven.

"Katy?"

She stared at the drapes. She wanted to move, wanted to answer, but she couldn't find the strength, as if she used it all up that day.

"Kathleen Brennan Lexham!" The names fractured the silence. She felt her lungs inflate. Jeremy's feet pounded through the stillness, then metal scratched against metal and the sun pierced the darkness.

Her eyes moved. Outlined by the light, his form loomed before the window, face shadowed.

The glimmer of hope died.

The air moved, and he inhaled. An instant later, his boots pounded toward the bed and pain exploded along her scalp. He wrenched her head up, leaned over, and snarled. "I've had enough, Kathleen. I know you heard me. Get on your feet. Now!"

Her heart beat once, then twice. Silver eyes bored into her, commanding her to respond.

"Jeremy?"

The eyes flashed. "It's Master." His hand fisted and pulled at her hair. The other slapped at his thigh. "Now get up."

Her sluggish blood started to move as she stared at his hand. Each smack against his black-clad thigh forced another beat of her heart. Without conscious effort, her legs moved, sliding beneath the down duvet, and her arms lifted her torso until she could sit. Cold air bit at her bare legs.

"I'm done watching you feel sorry for yourself," Jeremy said, his voice a low growl. "You put yourself in danger, Kathleen. Do you think I'd let that go? Do you think if you lay in bed long enough, I'll forget? That I won't punish you for it?"

The cold she hadn't noticed the last two days shunted through her veins. "No."

The single arched brow sent a sliver of warmth through the cold.

"No, Master," she corrected.

After a timid knock and a curt command, Clara entered with a silver platter. Curtseying repeatedly and darting glances at the duke, she deposited it on the desk. The top came off, but no smell rose from the food.

"You requested I bring the same platter as earlier, Your Grace?"

Jeremy strolled over and peered at the fare. Cold eggs, toast, and thick oatmeal that plopped from the spoon as he lifted it.

"Yes, Clara. You'll remain with the duchess. She's

to eat every morsel. When she's done, you'll give her a sponge bath and attend to any other needs you think necessary. She's not to speak, and you'll inform me if she disobeys in any way. I'll be back within the hour. I expect her to be ready for me by then."

Stunned and embarrassed, Kathleen's heart began to beat faster. She rose to protest, then sank back. Clara had seen bruises on her buttocks and lash marks on her back. Aside from a crimson flush, she'd never remarked on it.

Anyone else and Katy wouldn't be able to stand the embarrassment. But Jeremy knew that.

"Do you understand, Kathleen?"

"Yes…Master." Heat rolled over her, but Clara sent a shy smile her way.

His footsteps thudded toward the door. As he reached for the handle, he rotated. "You're not to prattle, Clara. I expect your mistress to use the time to think about what she's put me through, not listen to you."

Clara sank into an even deeper curtsey, but the door clicked before she rose. The fog began to clear from Katy's brain.

She deserved punishment. Wanted it even.

"You best eat quick, Your Grace. His Grace don't look too pleased with ye." The spoon clattered against the bowl as Clara thrust it at Katy. Katy took it and lifted a spoonful into her mouth.

Thick and pasty, it stuck to the roof of her mouth, but she swallowed it anyway. Clara rushed around the room, filling a basin with water, while Katy spooned another clump into her dry mouth. Clara turned toward the door, pitcher in hand, then set the pitcher back down and cast an apologetic look at Katy.

The water was cold, but she deserved it. She didn't deserve the warm, deep baths they normally brought. She didn't even deserve to bathe. Jeremy had lovingly stroked the blood from her when they returned, and she'd never thanked him. She'd just lain there and let him.

Another spoon of oatmeal gagged her. She didn't deserve to eat either. She'd broken her promise. Taken Henry in her mouth.

"Here, Mistress." A warm, fruity scent wafted beneath her nose. Madeira. "'Twill help wash the oatmeal down."

Obediently, she opened her mouth and let Clara pour. Sweet and cloying, it cut the thick paste but did little to remove the taste of revulsion that choked her every time she thought about what she'd done. Still, she swallowed. Jeremy had ordered her to eat every bit.

She shoveled in another mouthful. Then another and another until the spoon scraped the sides of the bowl clean. Then she placed it on the platter and proceeded to devour the eggs and toast. When she'd started, her stomach cramped and rebelled, but by the time she finished, the empty hole in her center no longer clawed at her. Guilt still beat at her though.

"Finish the wine." Clara snatched the egg plate away and replaced it with a large goblet of ruby red liquid. "You're already shivering. I hope His Grace isn't wantin' ye to catch the chills." She clamped her lips shut, then whirled to retrieve the basin of water.

Katy drank from the goblet. Heat slid down her throat and spread through her.

Resentment took hold as her limbs warmed, and

she lowered the glass. She didn't deserve heat or the numbing effects of alcohol. She'd already let Jeremy hold her at night, and she didn't deserve the warmth of his body against her. She'd betrayed him. He pretended it didn't matter, but she knew better.

"Please, Your Grace." Clara wrung her hands before her. "I don't want His Grace mad at me, too." Her eyes jumped to the clock. Forty minutes had passed.

Clara didn't deserve to be punished.

Katy drained the sweet liquid. The glass clinked, and she reached to strip off her nightgown. She stood up and held her arms out like the obedient child she'd never been.

The cold cloth slapped against her skin, washing the warmth from her. With a brisk rub, Clara scrubbed two days of salt from Katy's arms and torso. She turned pink as her nipples wrinkled at the sensation. When Clara started on her legs, working her way up from Katy's feet, she hesitated, but Katy squeezed her eyes shut and spread her legs.

"Why don't you do it yourself?" Clara pushed the cloth into Katy's hands.

Katy shook her head and wrapped Clara's fingers back over the washcloth. Jeremy had said Clara should do it, and she had no right to modesty.

She gasped as the cold hit her pussy. A flush of answering heat swirled between her legs, and she felt her face burn. Shame flooded her, but Clara gently swiped the folds, her own face bright red.

"There, Mistress. That should do." Water splashed, and Clara turned away.

Numbness gone, Katy took a deep breath and

turned toward the dungeon room door. Locked, the servants weren't allowed entrance. Jeremy always cleaned it himself.

Clara trudged toward it now, the key clutched in her hand.

"I'm sorry, Mum," Clara said as her hand trembled and struggled to slip the key into the lock. "He said I should unlock it, see you inside. I'll never breathe a word though. Ye've my pledge on that." Finally, the lock clicked, and Clara removed it. "You might want to use the chamber pot 'fore you go in."

Glad of the reminder, Katy took her advice, then hurried into the room. After a silent half-smile of encouragement, Clara set the padlock on a small table near the door and left.

Certain it might be the last time, Katy's gaze wandered the room as she lowered herself to her knees and waited. Her eyes paused on the blindfold, the one he'd refused to use on her after the night at the inn, because he wanted to see her reactions, wanted to know she wanted him. It had allowed her to see that he too needed her to want him.

Then her gaze moved toward the St. Andrews cross, and she thought of the time he'd refused to whip her and how he'd said he wanted to give her what she wanted and needed, not what he wanted.

As the memories replayed, the loneliness of the last few days dulled, replaced by overwhelming guilt. She didn't deserve love, never had. Jeremy had offered her everything, and she'd thrown it away. For a brother who'd neither requested nor wanted the sacrifice.

She didn't move when the far door opened and a rush of cool air slithered over her. She stayed as still as possible, spine straight and eyes ahead, as his boots dropped on the carpet and the pop of buttons snapped the air. Her breathing quickened, and her heart squeezed as his bare feet padded across the floor then stopped behind her.

Did he truly love her as he'd said? Or did he just love the fact she let him do this to her?

The questions hovered while he stood behind her for what seemed an eon.

"Do you remember, Kathleen, what I told you would happen if you ever put yourself in danger?"

"Yes." She'd not be able to sit. "Master." A trickle of moisture tickled her pussy, and his hand lifted her hair. It fell back and drifted along the top of her buttocks.

"Are you sure?" His finger traced her collarbone, threatening to create a shiver.

Her lips pursed, and her brow furrowed. There'd been something else. "No. Remind me, please, Master."

"Tell me what you remember."

As he circled around, Katy glimpsed his bare chest and dropped her gaze. Her fingers tightened against the urge to reach for him until she noticed there was no bulge in his breeches.

He didn't want her.

"I…I remember you said I'd not be able to sit down." As she said it, she heard his voice in her mind. "And that I'd not be allowed to come." She shouldn't be. She deserved to hurt and want and never reach a climax.

"Yet you did it anyway." He paced the room, hands clasped behind his back. She followed him with her eyes, peeking through her lashes while dread settled over her shoulders. The candlelight from the bedroom flickered over the planes of his chest, but the darkness of the room reminded her of a confessional, a fitting observation. "What else did you do that you shouldn't have?"

"I lied."

A hiss of sulfur shivered through the air, and a taper flared. With a touch, a candle blazed on the right.

"Lied about what?"

After three more steps, another light flared to life.

"He…he asked me what you do to me. And if I liked it."

"And you lied. Why?"

"To trick him." Why did Jeremy care? Why didn't he just punish her and finish it?

His feet padded near the cross, and two more lights cut the darkness, one on either side.

"Then you told him I spank you and flog you, and you said you don't like it? Because you wanted to trick him?" His voice hardened. "Or was it because you wanted *him* to do those things?"

"No!"

The taper died, snuffed as his hand closed over the flame. Then he stomped over and grabbed her arm. Fingers bit into her and dragged her to her feet. "How many lashes do you think a lie like that warrants? Compared to what he intended to do?"

"I don't know." *None, really.*

"Well, I do. None. But you'll get five, for not addressing me properly."

The certainty in his gaze ripped the guilt away, and Katy moistened her lips. She stumbled when his hand dropped, and he spun back toward the candles.

"What else did you do that requires penance?"

The taper reappeared, and another light blossomed.

"Please. Master." Her stomach revolted, the heavy oatmeal surging up her throat. "Don't make me say it."

"Sorry, my dear." The last light flared, and the scent of the taper dying burned away the sour taste. "You don't get to ask for anything. That's a privilege reserved for subs who obey. Now tell me."

Even though she closed her eyes, the vision had etched itself on her eyelids. "I...I...I took him in my mouth." She retched and hugged herself.

"I couldn't hear you. Tell me again."

She repeated the words and swiped at the tear that trickled over her cheek.

The whisper of his breeches told her he crossed and stopped before her, but she couldn't bear to see the revulsion in his eyes so she kept hers clenched tight.

A silken touch caressed her cheek. "Did you enjoy it?"

Her hair stung her breasts as she shook her head.

"I'll not pretend I'm happy about it, but given the circumstances, it's hardly a transgression. Though you've earned three more for forgetting our basic rules."

Before her eyes could open, she found her hands lashed together and stretched above her head. A slight tug unbalanced her until she fell against him. Despite his words, there was no mercy in his eyes, just that lust-kissed glimmer that made her innards weak.

"Anything else you feel deserves punishment?"

The thoughts that had beat at her while she prepared flitted through her mind, but one look at his face held her tongue. He'd only dismiss them as inconsequential. He'd already deemed the worst forgiven and would only punish her for thinking his opinion worthless. Indeed, much of her guilt seemed eased, now that she'd spoken it aloud. "No, Master. That's all."

"No guilt about killing him?"

Her chin lifted, although her lip trembled. "No. He deserved to die. I'm only sorry I had to be the one to do it."

"Good." His eyes flared, and Katy gasped as his cock hardened against her leg. "Because you've earned more than enough to make your ass sore for a week."

He dragged her to the spanking chair and pushed her onto it. A discarded paddle lay on the floor, but he reached for another, one with a rougher surface.

"Make yourself comfortable." He gave her mere seconds before the first blow landed.

"This one's for putting yourself in danger."

Already sore from Henry's paddle, the pain sank deep. Unlike then, this time the familiar softening in her core absorbed the sting, turning it to heat.

"One." She shouted the number in relief as life flooded back into her.

Four more landed in quick succession, too quick to count, each hard enough to make her gasp and clench her teeth. At the pause, she offered up the count, then hissed as he stroked her skin. Raw, even the gentle stroke streaked like agony through her nerves. But each sliver carried away a twinge of guilt.

"I need a number for pain, Katy."

"Six, Master." In fact, it felt more like eight.

"Liar." His bare hand smacked her right ass and tears pricked her eyes.

"Eight, Master." She shrank away hugging the solid wood beneath her.

A cat-o-nine struck her back, and she sobbed with relief.

"There will be five extra for lying just now and not expecting me to know."

A gush of need rushed over her, and her muscles collapsed. His arm slipped through the air, blow after blow, stoking the warmth she'd feared gone forever. There was none of the usual pussy fondling and professions of encouragement, just the freeing throbs of sensation flowing beneath her skin.

She lost count soon after, too focused on the throbbing in her cunt and the confident pronouncements that Jeremy offered up, indiscretions she'd felt but never understood enough to name.

"For involving Clara and your grandfather."

"For not letting me protect you."

"For not taking comfort from me."

"For doubting I'd always love you. No matter what you do."

As he mouthed the last, Katy felt a dam burst within her. The fear exploded, and the tears flowed until her whole body shuddered beneath the torrent. He'd told her he loved her, but she hadn't believed it. She needed to feel it.

"That's it, baby." Jeremy lifted her from the bench and hugged her to his chest. "Let it out." He strode to the bed and dropped to sit with her in his lap. The bindings on her wrist fell away, and his lips pressed moist full mouth kisses over her face. Her body shook, and she melted into his heat.

"I'll always give you what you need, Katy. I'm

sorry it took me so long." He pulled her onto the bed and thrust his cock into her. His mouth devoured her, tongue delving into the depths of her throat, erasing the memory of anyone but him. She opened and breathed him in, passion igniting a flame that burned away the doubt. She strained toward him, hands clawing until it felt as if he'd cleave her in two.

"Feel me, Katy. Feel how much I love you." His hips levered forward, and her head fell back. He pushed away the emptiness, filled her with love and sensation. "Let me love you." He pounded at her, urgent and demanding, sinking into her until she no longer knew where he ended and she began. "Let me take it all, darling." His chest labored, and the words were battered and raw. Her own lungs struggled, as if they'd explode. "Give me all the guilt. All the anger. All the fear. Give me everything."

Powerless against the demand, she arched. He grabbed her hips and ground against her until she gasped.

"Now, Katy." The need filled her. "Come for me."

Her wail filled the room. Every muscle in her body screamed, then splintered. The world went black, then burst into a million colors. All the hurt, all the loneliness, all the fear spiraled away.

"I love you, Katy." He mumbled the words against her throat and groaned. Body plastered to hers, his hips flexed one last time, and he shuddered. "I'll always love you. Never, ever doubt that."

Chapter Sixteen

As usual, Katy had made the right choice.

Jeremy's neck swiveled to examine the greenery decorating Lexham Estate. He'd always hated the dour Elizabethan prodigy house, and this room especially. The long hall ran the entire length of the upper story and looked out over the hundred acres of lush green landscape. Frequently banished to their room, he and George had spent much of their holiday vacations trapped here, cold and bored, staring out at the freedom below. Noise hadn't been allowed, and the fires had been miserly since they were *strong young boys* who could tolerate a bit of cold. It was here that most of the scolding and subsequent punishments had taken place as well. But Katy had declared it perfect for the Boxing Day celebration.

Now sprigs of holly brightened the space and George's children raced up and down the length of the house, shrieking with an abandon that hurt the ears. Two huge fires blazed at either end, and all the candles were lit, despite the bright sunshine streaming in the windows. Furniture that Katy had ordered to be moved up clustered before the fires. Comfortable sofas and chairs with small tables were strategically placed so that drinks and plates could be set down. Alfred sat in a huge wooden chair that resembled a medieval throne, his knobby hands held before the fire. Giles squirmed on a blanket before him, rolling and trying to crawl, and Alfred beamed down at him as if he were his own grandson.

"Uncle Jeremy!" As soon as they noticed him, small arms and legs hurtled toward him, pattering across the worn rug, and began leaping about. "Is it true? We're to have march pane and plum puddings? As much as we want?" Their excitement made it impossible to tell which one spoke.

"Well, I don't know," he said, grinning and sinking down to their level. "Who told you that?" Julia toddled up and wrapped her pudgy arms around his neck. He hugged her close, inhaling the baby smell of her. A sliver of residual disappointment made him squeeze harder. While he'd hoped he was wrong, after six months and almost losing Katy twice, he'd let go of the hope of a family like George's. Katy was his family now, and George and Emily. His worry that George would run the dukedom into the ground was gone too. After ensconcing George's family in the Dower house and firing his larcenous overseer, the estate had begun turning a profit that it hadn't seen since before his grandfather's death. George had seen to the cottage repairs and settled into the job.

"Aunt Katy told us." Alice scowled at Julia but hung back, too old in her own mind to cling anymore. As usual, her holiday dress had a tear along the hem, and she held a squirming puppy to her chest, proof that some things would never change.

"It must be true then. Your Aunt Katy makes the rules in this house, so I expect you will. Probably so much you will burst."

Emily's throat cleared, and she stepped forward,

George three steps behind. "You'll not get march pane if you don't behave. Let your uncle up and go fetch Lucifer before he pees on the rug."

"I'll get the puppies, Ma'am." Stanley stepped up, resplendent in his new butler livery. "Hand over Lilith, Miss Alice. It's time we take them out for a walk."

"But Aunt Katy will be down soon. I don't want to miss her surprise." Alice snuggled the puppy closer and backed away. Emily sighed and reached for the girl's hand, but Stanley stepped in before she spoke.

"You may stay here, Alice." Stanley dropped down and tugged the wiggling Dalmatian from her arms. Another of George's schemes to make money, this one actually had a chance of succeeding. He'd bought six, one for each of his children, with the intent of breeding them as coach dogs. "Gregory and I will take the dogs down. We'll be back before the surprise. I expect Her Grace will wait for her brother before springing it on us."

"What's taking her so long, Uncle Jeremy?" John skipped about, a wooden horse stick tapping on the floor as he circled the adults.

"I wish I knew. Clara wouldn't even let me in this morning, said it would spoil the surprise."

"What do you think it is?" Edward asked, eyes drawn toward the pile of boxes near the east window. Along with the usual Boxing Day gifts for the servants, there was one for each of the children, their names prominently displayed on gaily decorated gift tags. Every morning, Katy had disappeared into her sitting room with Clara and packages that arrived from London. Every afternoon, more boxes were stacked into the room. It wasn't just the children whose eyes were wide. The edges of the room were lined with the servants, all dressed in their finest, milling about nervously.

"If I know my sister, she's made us all new jackets." Thomas' voice boomed from behind him as he stepped into the room, a hand on the Earl of Margate's elbow. "Likely in some god-awful color like jonquil or Pomona green."

"Good God, I hope not." Miles slipped around Thomas and reached a hand out in greeting. "You've already made enough of an impression." His gaze scanned Thomas' frame, now clad in the latest light puce-colored waistcoat. The mauve-like shade enhanced the red in Thomas' locks, and with the ivory breeches and his size, he'd not lacked for feminine attention since joining the earl in London. His standing as the earl's long-lost heir didn't hurt, either. "The rest of us unattached men would appreciate it if you stood out a bit less."

Thomas grinned and shrugged, then gestured toward the far end of the room with his chin. John dropped the wooden horse and shouted, then a flurry of small legs and arms hurtled away, shouts of excitement bouncing in the evergreen scented air.

Jeremy turned and his heart skipped a beat. Every time he laid eyes on Katy, it struck him how much he loved her. She floated toward them, smiling and stopping to greet each of the room's occupants, gowned in a simple emerald green velvet that matched the sheen of the holly greens. The gauntness he'd seen the first time he'd met her was gone. Her rosy cheeks had filled out, and her smile reached into her mossy green eyes. With the sun behind her, she glowed so brightly it hurt his eyes.

When she looked up and saw him, the smile stretched wider.

His feet began to move unbidden until he reached out and clasped her hands.

Annoyance tickled his neck as she scanned the room instead of focusing on him. "Is everyone here?"

"Just about," Emily said. "We just need to wait for Stanley and Gregory to return. Shouldn't be long."

"Alfred, I know you've retired, but would you mind? Everyone should have a dram of whiskey for a toast."

Whiskey?

"Of course, Your Grace." Alfred rose as if he'd known about it and headed for a table sparkling with glasses. A number of the footmen hurried over and began passing the drinks about.

"Do I get one, too?" Edward asked as he sidled up beside his uncle, as serious looking as an eight-year-old boy could be. Hands behind his back, he stuck his chest out in a pose so reminiscent of George that Jeremy had to smile.

"No." Emily laughed. "You may have cider. Julia, love, don't be climbing up your aunt."

Katy swung the toddler up and cuddled her. "Julia may climb me any time she likes."

By the time everyone had their whiskey, Stanley had returned with the dogs and everyone's attention turned toward their hostess. Julia clung to her, her brown curls burrowed against Katy's neck, thumb popped in her mouth. With a sigh, Katy passed the little girl to Emily and took her own glass.

"Thank you all for coming today. As my first

holiday season as the duchess, I want you all to know how happy it makes me to be here." She raised the glass and swiveled slowly to include each member of the crowd. "You've all made me feel so very welcome and taken such good care of me, and I can never thank you enough for that." Finally, she turned toward him, and Jeremy felt his heart swell in his throat. "My husband, especially, I want to thank. He could have married anyone, but he chose me, an unworthy—" A murmur of disagreement made her lift her hand. "—Irish rebel who had nothing to recommend her. And more importantly, he not only wed me, he's let me love him."

"Yuck!" Alice's interruption created a stir of laughter, quickly hushed by George's hand whacking her bottom.

With a hint of a laugh, Katy continued, "As a result, I'm now in a position to share the benefits I've gained." She gestured at the pile of boxes. "But first, I have a special surprise for our duke."

Suddenly nervous, Jeremy looked around. It was supposed to be a surprise for everyone, not only him. But everyone else looked as clueless as him. Everyone but Alfred, who stood clutching his glass of amber liquid so tightly his knuckles gleamed white. And Emily, who smirked knowingly.

"Go ahead, Edward," Katy coaxed. "Give it to him."

Edward started, then pulled a small box from behind him, a flat box made from brown paper folded over and tied with a red ribbon. Jeremy couldn't even guess what it might be. With a courtly bow, Edward handed it over, brow furrowed as if it might fly away.

Jeremy took it and turned it over. Only as thick as a

pamphlet and about the same size, a wax seal shone as the light hit it, an oak tree, acorn, and bee etched in the wax.

With a glance at Katy, who now looked even more nervous than he, Jeremy slid a finger beneath the seal and broke it. When he lifted the flap, an ivory card peeked out.

He pulled out the card and began to read the elegant gold ink.

The Duke and Duchess of Lexham
Would like to formally announce the birth of

His gaze flew up and collided with Katy's. Tears shimmered in her eyes.

"The name and date will have to be filled in later," she said, "but it should be in about seven months."

Too stunned to move, Jeremy merely stared, fingers curling around the crisp vellum to make sure he was alive.

"What's it say?" Alice whispered in a voice loud enough that everyone heard.

"It says your Uncle Jeremy's to be a poppa soon. And your Aunt Katy's going to cry, so why don't you run over and grab a napkin for her?"

"Wohoo!" Edward and John began to dance around. The dogs started to yap, and voices penetrated the dreamlike fog. Noise rolled over them, a wave of joy so intense it threatened to overwhelm him.

"Truly?" Jeremy whispered as he enfolded Katy in his arms. Liquid spilled down his back, an apple scent permeating the air, but he clutched her tighter and buried his face in her neck just as Julia had done.

"Yes, my love." Katy's fingers slipped through his hair. A warm wetness slid down his cheek.

Giles began to scream, his infant wails filling the room.

"Are you sure you want a baby, Jeremy?" George asked as a grin split his face and laughter followed.

Unable to contain the happiness, Jeremy lifted Katy and whirled her around. "You know I do. As much as I want this woman."

About the Author

Terry Graham has been imagining love stories since she began playing with Barbie and Ken. In high school, she read Barbara Cartland along with Dickens, Austen, Asimov, and everything else she could get her hands on. After two careers, as a chemist and a computer programmer, she retired to try her hand at writing.

Terry lives in upstate New York with her cat Amber. She's divorced, with a grown son who makes it all worthwhile, and looking for a new Ken.

~*~

Visit Terry at

www.terrygrahamromance.com

~*~

To chat with Terry Graham and other Wild Rose Press authors of erotic romance, join us at

www.groups.yahoo.com/group/thewilderroses.

Also Available
from The Wild Rose Press, Inc.
and major retailers.

The Red Heart
The Red Heart Club Book One
By Kristal Dawn Harris

Julianna Lockland, the Earl of Lockland's illegitimate daughter, has one night to secure the heart of the famed Renauld Pirate. A masquerade presents the perfect opportunity to do just that. Her sister doesn't love him; she savors her role in high society and looks down her nose at Reynauld. Bent on seduction, Julianna dons her sister's mask and enters the private quarters of the roguish buccaneer.

The bastard son of a duke, Thomas Reynauld has come from the high seas to seal a contract with the Earl of Lockland. In exchange for exclusive shipping rights of the earl's liquor, Thomas must wed Lockland's daughter, Evelyn. He remembers her as cold, but the masked siren setting his sheets on fire proves him wrong…in the most delicious way.

Can one deceitful night of passion lead to love?

Also Available
from The Wild Rose Press, Inc.
and major retailers.

Heart of a Highlander
Real Men Wear Kilts
By Maxine Mansfield

Former Staff Sergeant Ian Mackay didn't care if he lived or died. He'd left what really mattered strewn across Afghanistan three years ago. All the self-help groups and doctors in the world couldn't assuage his guilt. But when an accident takes his life and Fate steps in with an offer to fix what was once unfixable, he jumps at the second chance to save his men. Now he's stuck in a strange land, in an even stranger time, and expected to bed his equally strange but desirable new bride.

Healer Aila Gordan of the Sutherland clan thought her betrothed dead, had even seen his lifeless body the night before their wedding. Why then is her sworn enemy, Ian Mackay, standing before the priest, waiting for her to repeat the vows that would make her his wife? The fairies must have possessed his body, a frightening notion, indeed. But marriage to the handsome laird, possessed or otherwise, couldn't be any worse than living in her brother's castle where, like all women in 1643 Scotland, she has no freedom. And if the kiss at the altar is any indication, she could just steal the heart of a highlander.

Thank you for purchasing
this publication of The Wild Rose Press, Inc.

For questions or more
information contact us at
info@thewildrosepress.com.

The Wild Rose Press, Inc.
www.thewildrosepress.com

To visit with authors of
The Wild Rose Press, Inc.
join our yahoo loop at
http://groups.yahoo.com/group/thewildrosepress/

www.ingramcontent.com/pod-product-compliance
Lightning Source LLC
Chambersburg PA
CBHW050035030726
47506CB00001B/283